Praise for *Pina*

Winner of the 2017 Eugène Dabit Prize

Winner of the 2019 French Voices Grand Prize

"There are novels which crack like gunshots. Those of Titaua Peu mark a revolution in the literature of the Pacific. With *Pina*, it is the other face of Tahiti that appears; that of a society ravaged by cultural uprooting, worn down by misery and colonialism."
—**Mediapart**

"Titaua Peu reappropriates words long monopolized by Europeans and returns them to their place in the 'natural' part of Polynesian heritage." —**Christine Chemeau,** *Le Monde Diplomatique*

"The novelist seizes the reader with her fiery prose, serving her whirlwind story about the crossing paths of many different characters." —*Télérama*

PINA

Pina

Titaua Peu

Translated from the French by
Jeffrey Zuckerman

Introduction by Rajiv Mohabir

RESTLESS BOOKS
Brooklyn, New York

Copyright © 2016 Titaua Peu
Translation copyright © 2022 Jeffrey Zuckerman
Introduction copyright © 2022 Rajiv Mohabir

First published as *Pina* by Au vent des îles, Pape'ete, Tahiti, 2016

First Restless Books paperback edition July 2022

Paperback ISBN: 9781632061553
Library of Congress Control Number: 2021948388

This work received the French Voices Award for excellence in publication and translation. French Voices is a program created and funded by the French Embassy in the United States and FACE (French American Cultural Exchange).

Cet ouvrage a bénéficié du soutien des Programmes d'aide à la publication de l'Institut français

This book is supported in part by an award from the National Endowment for the Arts.

This book is made possible by the New York State Council on the Arts with the support of Governor Kathy Hochul and the New York State Legislature.

Cover design by Keenan
Text design by Sarah Schneider
French Voices Logo designed by Serge Bloch

Printed in the United States of America

1 3 5 7 9 10 8 6 4 2

Restless Books, Inc.
232 3rd Street, Suite A101
Brooklyn, NY 11215

www.restlessbooks.org
publisher@restlessbooks.org

Contents

On Oceania, Representation, and Translation: An Introduction

Rajiv Mohabir

Oceania is vast, Oceania is expanding, Oceania is hospitable and gener-
ous, Oceania is humanity rising from the depths of brine and regions of
fire deeper still, Oceania is us. We are the sea, we are the ocean.
                    —Epeli Hau'ofa, *We Are the Ocean: Selected Works*

HAVING ROOTS IN THE CARIBBEAN, I have thought much about the
ways in which Western writers portray "paradise." Lands with beautiful shores, the sun to coax an amber glistening of the skin that will
engender a good-hearted envy from one's coworkers after returning
to the office from a paradisial vacation, curated for the Western gaze.
Never mind the complicated histories of plundering white genocidal
maniacs called "explorers" who devastated communities, instilling
Christianity like a misplaced lace doily on a lauhala mat. It is too easy
for these beautiful places to be portrayed from the outside, from the
inheritors of the wealth wrought by colonial destitution, to have the
social issues that plague the survivors of colonization and occupation
be conveyed as simple historical inevitabilities—the authors nostal-
gic for a time that never existed. What is this desire for the pristine
untouched but colonial longing?

The time I spent in Oceania, in the occupied nation of Hawai'i
Nei, a constitutional monarchy overthrown by the American government in 1893, expanded my consideration of what for Native peoples is a lived reality. The rhyming of such pathologized paradise (to
borrow the idea from Supriya Nair) of the Caribbean and Polynesia
are multifaceted and dazzling. Tahiti was forced to relinquish its sovereignty to France on June 29, 1880, when the King Pomare V ruled
after his late mother Queen Pomare's death in 1877.

What most people know of Tahiti is depicted by Western media,
removed from the lived experience of Pacific peoples, presented
through the flattening concept of the transpacific, as though the
connections of islands are stepping-stones for Western powers to
expand their control of the world, to test their atomic bombs as in
the case of the Bikini Atoll and the Moruroa Atoll. What remains are
the echoes of holidays captured in photographs by tourists: Tahitian
dances, cocktails, floral-print shirts. In Boston, paintings by Gauguin
hang in the Museum of Fine Arts. Gauguin himself was a contro-
versial character who attempted to render the Pacific through the
warped representations in his paintings, never revealing the power
dynamics of his whiteness that enabled his rape of local women. His
art shows the Western imperialist gaze at its most *thingifying*—as
Césaire laments, "*L'Europe est indéfendable*" (Europe is indefensible).

Bob Marley's lyrics to "Time Will Tell" remind the people of
the realities of postcolonial fallout—the psychic and material destitution that imperialism causes in the brown and Black world. He
says, "Think you're in heaven but you're living in hell." The heaven is
the world of the tourist, those who take our islands and treat them
as Disneyland when they are not. This heaven is illusory, postcolonial, and capitalist, controlled still by the French government. The
ignoring of the social concerns that the living Pacific Islanders face
feels tantamount to an account penned and painted by those who
have disappeared the Native or made them into noble objects—to

be rendered (in both meanings of the word) through representation. The ills that create this Marley-esque postcolonial hell can be traced to the colonization of Tahiti and of the Māʻohi people.

Pina, this novel written by the highly accomplished Māʻohi writer Titaua Peu, comes crashing to its readers as a testament to the endurance of the protagonist, Pina, and the complicated web of narratives that bind her to destitution as the reader watches her come of age. We encounter the family: Auguste, Ma, Pina, Moïra, Rosa, Auguste Junior, Pauro, and Hannah as they circle one another in the concentric orbits of love, hatred, destitution, and furtive acts to ensure survival as they crash past and into one another. Addiction, sexual abuse, neglect, racism, and despair work together to accomplish the colonial mandate of erasure, yet hope grows as a dandelion through cement as this narrative unfolds. The family's descent from Māʻohi warriors shows how the struggle for individual sovereignty has incarnated generation after generation of Māʻohi people as they interact with other characters from France, the Polynesian diaspora, China, and the Caribbean. *Pina* is a text necessary for understanding the postcolonial history and future of Polynesia—especially what is colonially known as *French* Polynesia. It is a representation from a Māʻohi person, a representation of life in Huahine, Papeete, and Tahiti as it is known today.

What then does it mean to relay these experiences of a Māʻohi family into prose, to write them in the French language, and then for another to translate the text into English to be published in North America? It requires an attitude toward translation that holds community in great regard. *Pina* is a Polynesian writer's wresting back the control of narrative, enlivening a non-English-, non-French-speaking world, and lays bare the Reo Māʻohi world indelibly marked with white scars—a heaven and hell coalesced into one. This translation, this new incarnation of Peu's work, shines lush and culturally responsive, with the precise and capacious translation of

Jeffrey Zuckerman. His labor achieves much in its striving toward an English that makes space for nuances of Pacific Islander linguistic and cultural identity. *Pina* is a path toward wholeness for us now in the English-speaking world to marvel at, to hold with delight and responsibility.

Rajiv Mohabir
Malden, Massachusetts
March 20, 2022

PINA

In memory of Patrice Aka
To all the Pinas of the world

Note on Pronunciation

FOR TAHITIAN WORDS, VOWELS ARE PRONOUNCED as in Spanish, and are each individually pronounced: the exclamation *'auē!* is pronounced ah-oo-eh, while *poe* (pearl) is pronounced po-eh. A macron (ˉ) over a vowel indicates a longer pronunciation: the *a* of *fare* (house or home) is pronounced like the vowel of *pot*, while the *ā*'s of *māmā* (mother, but also an elderly woman, such as a grandmother) are pronounced as in *palm*. Double vowels are generally separated by a glottal stop (the sound separating the syllables of *uh-oh*), indicated by an apostrophe that is sometimes omitted: the commune of Faa'a could also be spelled Fa'a'a and is pronounced Fah-ah-ah. Tahitian words do not take an *s* in the plural; rather, as with the English word *deer*, plural and singular are indicated by verb conjugations.

A small body sways. Spins, rather, this way and that. Calmly, a calm far too calm. A calm that means that was the last gasp, too late now.

Prologue

SOME QUARTIERS NOBODY EVER HEARS ABOUT. Tenaho's one. East of Papeete, just about buried in Pirae. The neighborhood isn't all that run-down or dangerous; families have been living there a good three or four generations now. Wedged into a valley, the quartier's split by a river that still flows fast. The river . . . Nobody who's left Tenaho has ever forgotten it. They still remember one of its big basins and that perfect diving board of a rocky outcrop on the right. The river. Its coldness. Its secrets. The way it somehow takes all the Tenaho kids' hurt and worry and soaks it up, just for a few hours. The water. Its flow, its willingness to wash away those wounds that came far too soon in their fresh new lives.

To this day, everybody in Tenaho still remembers the T family. The one with too many kids. They'd had their fair share of misery, no more or less than any other family, but fate hadn't spared them a single blow. It was beyond all expectation, and then some.

Nobody's ever forgotten the mother. Or her hollering. Everybody all around called her Tera Vahine. If she had a first name, they didn't know it, let alone use it. What she had was better than a first name. Tera Vahine. *That Woman*. Nothing cruel about those two words. Not when they're just words. Just a way to name the person they all steered clear of. And That Woman never stopped hollering. Never stopped making the second-to-last of her kids, a girl who wasn't even nine, a girl named Pina, do all the chores, while she let her other daughter, Rosa, the one who was fifteen now, get down and dirty with just about every single one of the neighborhood guys. And That Woman's younger daughter just called her Ma. Not māmā. Never mommy.

Still addled from the bite of the burns she'd just brought on herself, Pina looked at Ma sideways. Ma, in a badly worn-out bra. Her hair yanked back into a huge bun on top of her head that made her look just plain mean when it didn't make her look ugly.

In the kitchen, Ma was still hollering. It got her mad that nothing was ever right. Like this milk pan full of boiling water Pina had just gone and spilled on herself like an idiot. And now Pina standing there, gawking at Ma. Without a word.

In the little girl's eyes, after all the buts and becauses, through all the hollering, was something close to sadness or even pity. Love, maybe. Not much of a difference between pity and love, really, they're not so much kith as kin ... Whatever it was had to be what Pina felt for her father. Pity ... some way of feeling somebody else's feelings or troubles or secrets. Pity, then. Pina felt it whenever her father asked for her. Not every night. Just on occasion. When he'd gotten himself a bit drunk. He'd sneak into her tiny room with no door. Make himself as small as he could. Lie down. Start breathing a bit louder. It always smelled god-awful. Like booze. No, her father's breath couldn't be foul. Just a little bad. Only a wee bit. It was her father's breath, after all. And she had so much pity to give. So she'd let him do what he did. Pina never could make heads or tails of what he was doing by himself, faster and faster. And then he'd stop moving, wait a bit, and then let out a tiny yell right there and then. A little one nothing like Ma's hollering. As if he'd had trouble holding it back, this teensy grunt that got through his clenched teeth. A mighty strange thing for her to pity. She was making her father feel better, but then he'd get to crying. Pina couldn't make heads or tails of any of it. Every time, before he got back up, he'd promise to buy her something the next day. But she never got a single present from him. Pina reckoned he was crying on account of Ma. That woman didn't have one shred of pity in her. Really, all that hollering like a madwoman, it must have done her man's head in.

Dinner would be any minute now. On the table a huge pot full of pinkish soup had already been set down. It was what Pina hated eating most: corned beef stew. She said she wasn't hungry, and her older brother got up to walk her to her room. Pauro was all of sixteen years old and a fine-looking man, not an ounce of meanness in him. Plenty scarce, that sort of person, in a place like this.

She set her sights on her bedroom, but not before taking one last look at her mother. Pity. Yes, pity was what Pina was feeling. Pity for a heart that didn't always get so tight-fisted. Pity for a mother who knew how to give a proper hug once in a while, when she could spare the time. Not sweet hugs, but proper hugs all the same.

As Pina made her way up the small step to the living room and the bedrooms, Rosa came full tilt out the other room to wolf something down and leave. She just about knocked Pina over. She couldn't be bothered to look as she was spewing Tahitian. Pina didn't stop, didn't even trouble herself to call her older sister *bitch*. Not when she already called Rosa that, all the time, in secret.

Rosa's hair was light and her eyes even lighter, but a good sight lighter than both were her thoughts, which consisted mainly of finding ways to fuck as many guys as possible. Pina was different. Everyone called her ugly. Her hair was frizzy, kinks going every which way, and her skin was so dark, so black that people called her a dirty siki. And they were nasty enough to laugh out loud at those thick lips of hers that trembled so easily, at the drop of a hat.

The woman who's always carrying on, Ma. Yes, her, Ma. She loved Rosa to the bottom of her heart. She let that stupid girl do whatever she wanted. And what Rosa wanted was to do nothing. Eat, sleep, go out, and fuck. And since Ma loved that girl enough not to ask for a thing in return, Rosa was a rare sight at home.

Rosa wasn't one to go do the laundry either. Backs bent under heavy bags, hands full with washboards and Marseilles soap, walks without a word. Every morning, just when people were rubbing the sleep out of their eyes, Pina and Pauro set off up the damp back road, to the end of the valley where they always did the day's laundry. A washing machine at Pina's house—now that'd be asking for the moon! They say the stones are still white even today, down there where the water comes down hardest. Still white from so much scrubbing, from so much sweat and tears.

The Father and the Mother

EVERY STORY BEGINS WITH A FAMILY STORY. Every family has its people bound by blood, no question of that. Some families, though, their fates go every which way, barely any detail in common between them. Which means mishaps, missed chances, misunderstandings. That's just how things are. That's life.

And this story begins with Ma and Auguste, the man who ended up her husband. They had plenty of kids, that part's clear as day. First being Auguste Junior, who's now twenty-five, then Pauro and Rosa, sixteen and fifteen each. And after them comes Pina, and last of all, Moïra, a wise little soul. But there's also the "twins," Xavier and Gilles. They're a year apart, twenty-three and twenty-two, but exactly a year apart: they're twins because they were born on the same day. Ma sent them off to live with her parents on Huahine, that island a full night's boat trip from Tahiti. Every so often they come see their family, but never for long. Ma loves them plenty. They're a handsome sight, the two of them, with hair as light as Rosa's . . .

And after the twins there's Catherine, who's twenty-one. Some French couple adopted her and whisked her away when she was three days old. Out of sight, out of mind. So she's got no part to play in this story, let alone this family.

Which makes eight children of Ma's. Well, no: nine. It's plenty easy to forget that last one, the second-oldest child, because nobody sees her. Not here in Tenaho. She's as good as gone. Her name's Hannah and she's twenty-five years old just like Auguste Junior, only nine months between the two. She's all the way in France, just like Catherine; she's been there for years. They say she's the head of a company, or just about. That's what Ma always hollers when she's fed up with all the kids, when she's so mad she could just up and leave this unholy mess of a house. Pina doesn't remember Hannah one bit. Rosa says she was very pretty. Pretty and elegant and refined and on and on . . . smart too. But then again, it's anyone's guess whether or not Rosa's telling the truth.

Hannah went off to a boarding school in her teens, and the minute she was done with the bac, she went off to France. She was going to get some degree there, and that was the last anyone had heard from her.

Which makes Pina number eight. Her parents must have been especially keen on having an eighth kid, seeing as she came along a good seven years after Rosa was born. Almost too long. The day she had Pina, Ma was turning thirty-seven. Getting old, almost dangerously old. They'd been so keen because Rosa wasn't really little anymore. By the time kids get to be six or seven years, they're too old for hugs. They tried over and over, Ma went through three miscarriages, before number eight came along. Too many times she'd been up the whole night worrying. The first thing Ma had blamed was her husband's sperm. He'd been a wily old goat, shilly-shallying for so long that he'd brought that black mark on himself: *impotent*. It was a label she hadn't gotten out of her head ever since one of her friends had whispered it before declaring it a sin to believe things like that. Best for Ma to go see someone. Not a normal doctor who knew nothing about matters of that sort. No, Ma needed to see one of their people, a healer, a good one who'd know what had happened and how to put it all right.

One morning, Ma set off to meet an old woman in Paea whose house was as run-down and decrepit as she was. That day, when Ma went and stood at the yawning hole where the door was supposed to be, shivers ran up and down her back. Real shivers, not like some woman showing off or trying to get sympathy. No, that day, she was more scared than she'd ever been in her whole life. She wasn't scared of someone, she was scared of some*thing* that didn't exist, something she felt in her gut, troubling her, digging its claws deep. Something that had no explanation. Right then, she'd have given anything to not have come here. Precious few people went all the way south from Pirae to Paea, and even fewer by truck at the crack of dawn. She had reasons heaven knew nothing of. When the old woman suddenly showed herself, Ma would have shrunk down as small as possible if she were able. She couldn't see a thing at first, it was that dark, but there was a presence, an awful smell that was piss, half rotting dog, half jasmine perfume. Ma was about to throw up and bolt home when the old woman said something like "I know why you have come" before letting out a cackle through all her missing teeth. It was curiosity, no, pride actually—Ma was nothing if not proud—that set Ma's foot back on the step. She stayed stock-still, waiting for the next thing out of the old woman's mouth. And so Ma learned that her belly was dirty. Filthy. Because she'd had kid after kid after kid, because she hadn't drunk any brew after a single one of them, that belly of hers, where babies and earth grew, was rotting from the inside out. And then the old woman said there was a deeper, darker problem at the root of it: some evil thought, some hex someone had put on her. Ma's shivers only got worse, running from her lower back slowly all the way up to her neck. Words like that, visions like that weren't just old wives' tales.

The minute she was back home, Ma started gulping down a bitter, greenish potion. It took a good three days for it to do its work. Three days of going to the bathroom and swearing up and down that anything this foul had to make something happen. The old woman had told Ma, that day, right before she left, that the child who would come that year would be a boy and that he would be the handsomest of all. Ma couldn't be sure whether or not to believe her, but the idea that a new boy would show up put a smile on her face and a glimmer of hope in her mind. A boy—how could she not love a boy? And so, when at long last Pina came into the world, it was hate at first sight.

It all happened on Ma's birthday. The morning had been off to a nice start, a special morning. She'd never seen the house abuzz like this. They were going all out for Ma tonight. Birthdays didn't happen every day, and Ma's husband had just been paid his leaving wages. Tomorrow he'd have to scrounge around for new work, but today they'd live like kings. Auguste, Pauro, and even Rosa had scrubbed the place clean, set up chairs for them to get some sun, and Ma was just taking in the sight of her family, not thinking for once about her fingers swelled up or her belly sticking all the way out. The tiny radio was spitting out songs that any other time Ma couldn't have stood one bit. The Bee Gees were carrying on about fever, and the disco rhythm had Ma tapping her toes, rocking her body back and forth.

It had been ages since she'd smiled, hadn't it? Ever since the man who'd become her husband had laid on the charm for her, years and years ago, a good twenty years ago. When Ma was seventeen, she'd been pretty, the prettiest one of all in tiny Huahine. She didn't have a care in the world back then, all her dreams had been about simple old things. Finding a husband, one who wasn't from her island, so she could move to the big city, to Tahiti. She heard about it all the time. Wild nights at Quinn's, being happy and drunk and free. She'd been told water was flowing inside houses nowadays, coming out of pipes that could be turned on and off whenever you liked. That was magic, and maybe that could be her life. When Ma was seventeen, that was what her dreams were about, and every few days she made her way from her village to the Huahine harbor, where schooners came and moored, their bellies bursting with Tahitian dreams and smells. It was at that harbor that she met Auguste, the man who'd give her all these children.

"Back then . . ." The guys were fond of saying that: "Back then, I did this, he did that . . ." and in their eyes there was the gleam of something delicate and tender, something beautiful and sad. They'd say "back then," as if that could make up for everything . . .

When they met, Auguste was a handsome, handsome fellow. Jet-black hair that came down past his eyes and made him look something . . . like he was outside time. He looked every bit proud of the body he had at eighteen. Auguste was a hungry sort. He was unloading all manner of goods and then loading copra by the ton. Ma was peeking at him behind his back, and he already knew what he wanted was her, to lose himself in her. He'd already gotten a taste of a woman's body, nice and warm, a body that forgot itself, gave in. He'd already done the deed with his cousin, and they'd never said a word about it again ever. One afternoon, after the boat had been maneuvered in and moored, Auguste had jumped down onto the quay and told Ma that he wanted her. The next thing, he was talking marriage. Not two weeks since they'd first laid eyes on one another, Ma was headed off with him, and all Ma's mother had to say about it was that she'd never be happy in Tahiti, not with Auguste.

She was turning thirty-seven, which wasn't all that old. Her eyes were on Rosa who'd slipped on a flower-print pāreu and was sway-ing that small butt of hers to the pounding beat of a fifties tāmūrē. Ma had let out a guffaw at her daughter's hips moving this way and that. A guffaw that had her bent over laughing when all of a sudden she felt her baby kick hard, so hard it hurt. The kicks were at the bottom of her stomach, quick sharp ones. Ma hollered at Auguste and then it was all shrieks because she felt water running down her legs. The only thing to do was to get up, grab what they needed, and go to the hospital straightaway. The baby was only seven months along and Ma was sure she would die. Not a single one of her other pregnancies had ever given her so much pain. This thing thrashing around in her belly couldn't be a baby. It had to be a monster. She recollected the old woman's words. *A boy, the handsomest of all*, and she passed out.

When she finally came back to, she felt something like a gash down her stomach. Both sides held together by an enormous bandage, and Auguste saying that she'd been cut open. Ma was crying bloody murder and her child was brought in. A tiny, pitch-black baby. When the nurse announced that it was a pretty little girlie, Ma could have hit the ceiling. She knew not to holler the way she always did or it would have torn her right apart. She narrowed her eyes at the bundle of blankets and saw an ugly dark thing with tightly coiled hair. A boy? "The handsomest of all"? No. A girl who wasn't one bit pretty, who kept crying nonstop, even after she'd suckled ... Ma was as angry at the old woman from Paea as if she were God up in heaven and could have given her a boy or a girl upon request. For weeks, Ma didn't feel a shred of warmth for the baby. She could go and cry in her filthy, soaking diapers—and so she did.

It was years before Pina was told about all that. About the day Ma turned thirty-seven, about the rage she flew into. If she'd had any say in the matter, Pina would have chosen not to know about any of it, but people were monsters: family or not, they didn't worry themselves about the feelings of others, not even children. And when the facts only got laughter and leering out of all of them, she was left with sadness and nights that felt downright lonely ... So Pina dreamed up a world she'd survive in, dreamed up voices she could listen to, so as not to have to think about the world she was in.

Fact is, Pina's name actually isn't Pina. Ma and Auguste had been expecting a boy, and they'd picked out first names as such. When they saw the tiny little baby was a girl, they'd been caught unawares. So they saddled her with the name of Ma's aunt: Aeata. A Tahitian name and a beautiful one at that, an old one that'd fallen out of use and been forgotten. Some two years later, when the doctor told Pina's family that her left eardrum was misshapen and she might get some tari'a pinau, trouble with her ear, Rosa started calling her little sister Pinau. And after a while, it stuck: the only name anyone knew her by was Pina.

Most people don't have the faintest clue that at four or five years old children's heads are full to brimming with war dances and dreams of revenge and aspirations of fame. Even when she was little Pina was quick to think about death, especially for those who hurt her. Rosa, say. She often dreamed about Rosa getting hit by a huge truck. Rosa wouldn't die right away. Pina would finish her off with just a look, without even a word . . . She knew how to be cruel. She was no Cinderella. Or maybe she was, a little, when she was working her fingers to the bone, just about breaking her back under massive, old wooden furniture. There wasn't anything fairy-tale about her. This girl knew how to hate with all her being, all her little body. She had seen contempt in other people's eyes enough to know the way it tasted. Cruel thoughts were something she could catch, and that horrible itch to hurt people too.

Night had fallen. The neighborhood was asleep. Ma had to be snoring. Pina's belly was red, and the boiling water had raised huge, trembling, violent blotches all over her skin. She lay on her side in the bed, looking up through the window at the faint sky with no stars. She still hurt. It didn't have to be like this, she thought. Why had she grabbed the milk pan, why did she care so much about doing the right thing, why had she gotten punished twice over—the pain of that pitiless water, the hurt of her mother's heartless slap? She was always the one these things happened to. As if it wasn't enough that she already got laughed at every day.

When Pina stayed with her aunt all the way out in the district for a few days, she learned about going to church, about the Bible. She came to know about the Lord. He was merciful but he knew how to punish when he had to. Did she, ugly Pina, deserve God's anger? She must . . . everyone gets what they deserve. Ma always said so.

Her aunt out there was named Poe. Poe was Ma's sister and the oldest girl in a family of twenty children. Nobody knew how old Poe was, if years could be added up for her the way they were for everyone else. To Pina, she had only ever had graying temples and scraggly hair that she used a small, long-toothed comb on. Time and again Pina felt like she'd have been better off living with Poe, but she had as many children as there were at Sunday school. Pina wanted a proper existence, at least now and then, to not be just another kid who got fed by people who couldn't give her any more attention than that. All the same, going out to the backcountry was always better. Better than living there, in a tiny house that always smelled like mold and dirty diapers. Better than living here in a hovel made of wooden planks and sheet metal taken apart and put back together differently after every cyclone. Pina's shame was red-hot and if she could have destroyed the entire earth, she would have.

Once it was dark, the night's quiet and the river's sweet song steered her into those dreams she always had, even with her eyes open. Pictures, clear ones, pictures of people and places she'd never seen but already loved more than anything. A man, a woman, then her, only her, and a very big garden. In the middle of this garden, a house, a real one, big and white with a veranda where beautiful macramé plant holders would be swinging and where bright-green ferns would be swaying while a loving breeze whispered. Sweet sights, visions of a paradise that was only in the brochures that people sometimes tried to sell her. Pictures right out of the books that two blond men on bikes showed her mother every week and that she never had the money for. Pretty pictures that Pina kept in the back of her mind, that more often than not were erased, shoved aside, by other pictures, real ones, pictures she had actually lived. Like the one of a class headed for the cafeteria. Smiling, singing children two by two in a long line. Girls holding girls' hands, boys holding other boys' hands. And the line's going at a nice easy pace, and the schoolteacher's holding the hand of a little girl with light hair that's almost blonde. The schoolteacher smiles, and her teeth are so white they almost ding in the sunlight. The line is so pretty and touching. And at its end is a very dark-skinned girl who's straggling and feeling all alone. Slow on purpose because she wants to be forgotten, wants the other children to not keep looking back at her like that. Every day it's the same. If only she didn't have to eat at the cafeteria, didn't have to be behind them all. But children with no money can't eat at home. The little girl holding the teacher's hand cried when she realized that there was nobody else. That she'd have to hold the black girl's hand. The schoolteacher doesn't like to see little blonde girls crying . . .

Pina's welts stung so much, and she ran her outstretched fingers across her skin, making their way ever so gently between red blotches. That soothed her nice and good, and she shut her eyes. On her belly, a speck of warmth had just landed, drawing out small moans that could barely be heard. She let her fingers go and glide over those walloped spots; she let her fingers do the healing. She'd never felt this

before, had no words for it, and it was growing. Warmth spreading
all across her stomach, coming from down below. Her fingers didn't
belong to her anymore, they were digging into every corner deep
inside her body. Between her legs, she found a spot all but telling
her to go fast, give it everything she could, all the strength she had.
Her fingers didn't belong to her. Pina couldn't explain it, she just let
it happen. She saw the pretty pictures she'd dreamed up. Tall, handsome man, smaller woman who was so elegant. She let a thousand
little things whisper and a shiver as big as the ocean ran through her,
from head to toe, and died out in a spasm that had her all tensed up
and then freed. She clenched her legs tight as well as the two hands
caught between them. She opened her eyes again, she wouldn't say
a word to anyone about this. She'd never so much as whisper this
love she'd found, that she'd managed to make all by herself. It was
her secret and she already liked it. She thought of her father and
suddenly she got it. She'd never tell him, all she wondered was why
he didn't do that by himself, away from anyone's eyes, away from her
own eyes. Some things ought never, ever to be shared. She suddenly
felt ashamed, of him, of herself, but she didn't know how she'd ever
give up this happy feeling that was brand-new, that was hers and
hers alone.

Car Accident

WHEN SHE WOKE UP the next morning, it was already nine. She'd slept like never before, gotten all the sleep she could have wanted, and not one dream had whispered to her. She walked into the kitchen, stopped right in her tracks by the thought of her mother's wrath. Oh, so Ma had to go and do the laundry, did she? Wasn't there already enough on Ma's plate without having to do Pina's chores too? The silence had her flabbergasted. Never had she heard quiet like this, not here. She went through the bedrooms, found nobody. Not outside either. She ran straight to the valley bottom where she always washed the clothes . . . It was empty and hushed around the waterfall.

At the table she sat down again, all alone, and her mind tried to think up reasons: Her mother must have gone to the doctor or left to see her sister. That wasn't impossible. Ma did that often enough, when the mood struck. But what about Pauro and Moïra? Ma never could stand bringing them along. Pina's mind cast around for some clue, some hint that she hadn't thought twice about. Then she made herself some coffee and decided not to worry herself sick. She was a bit tired, her stomach was still a furnace, but her mind could have a moment's peace. She sat back down and took in the calm house. She felt so selfish. How nice it would be to catch hold of this silence that the river burbling right outside only made even bigger. She smiled and thought back to those moments of taboo happiness, in the dark of her room. She thought back to what her body was capable of, what brought it so much joy.

How long did she let herself enjoy this brand-new memory? She didn't have the faintest idea.

"Well now, Pina, what are you doing there, are you stupid or what?"

Mere, the girl next door, was standing in the doorway, slack-jawed, almost shocked. Pina started, blushing, as if Mere could read her thoughts, especially the ones reeking of sin.

Like always, Mere was sneering at Pina and that head of hers, which God had clearly forgotten to fill up when he was making it. Both her thin, nasal voice and the chest she seemed to be thrusting out made her look like an old know-it-all schoolmarm. It wasn't as if she had anything new to tell Pina; all she wanted was to make her jealous. That was what being grown-up was all about. Business, adult problems that Mere always knew something about while Pina, poor little Pina, was a backward little kid who'd never get her head around things like that. After a few minutes of looking sorry, she explained that, a few hours earlier, Ma had woken up Mere's parents. She had been in a tizzy, begging them to drive her to the hospital for Auguste. Mere didn't even try to act modest; she went on about just how big-hearted her father and, for that matter, the whole family was. Of course, all this being such a perfect soap opera tragedy, she couldn't just shut her mouth, and she let on that Auguste had drunk himself blind again. On his way home, he'd lost control and killed a woman driving in the opposite lane. Ma had been told that he was done for.

Pina didn't bat an eye. Right then, that felt too unreal, too far away. She hadn't seen any of it, she couldn't imagine even for a second that things could be as serious as that. She couldn't bring herself to worry, not when she couldn't hear her mother hollering. Reality was her mother and her fits of anger or sadness or a precious rare

bout of happiness ... then, and only then, did she get that something was real. Only then did Pina know what to say, what to do. The
least decision she made, the smallest action she took—unless she was
someplace else, school, say—was just her reacting, sometimes even
before the fact, to whatever Ma was thinking and then doing.

Pina walked for almost an hour. When she came to the hospital, she
saw Pauro and Moïra out front, under the shade of a huge flame tree.
It was nice outside and warm. Pina asked Pauro where their mother
was. What about the others? Rosa, their brother Auguste?

"Don't get your hopes up. Rosa's likely asleep somewhere in town.
And Auguste has to be out of it someplace else."

Pauro's words were weighed down, as if bone-tired, and Pina felt
for him. Weary, worn-out sentences; Moïra, the youngest of them
all, was fed up, bawling because she was so hungry and because that
diaper nobody'd changed must have given her a rash.

She took her sister's hand, walked her to the bathroom, and got
her smiling again. While she was calming Moïra down, the thought
came to her that not even for a second had they talked about their
father, or the accident ...

Lying in bed, just about buried under bandages, Auguste slept. Thin
tubes ran in and out of his big hairy arms. Pina felt so tiny. As her
eyes landed on the much bigger tube sticking out of her father's
throat, she couldn't help but feel something she knew was wrong,
downright bad. Disgust. That's what it was, disgust. She could just
faint, she knew it, but she held herself together, just a few steps away.
She almost wanted to stop breathing.

People were telling her about comas, trying to sound smart and
grown-up. Whispering knowingly. "Papa is in a coma. Do you know
what that means?" "He's sleeping, like he's dead, but he's still alive."
The nurse, a Caribbean lady, had a soft voice and an accent that

practically set the beds and white walls full of death dancing. The Black woman wasn't like the other nurses running around whom Pina always seemed to be in the way of. She was different, she wanted Pina to stay strong, to not cry, even though Pina had no intention of crying . . . The nurse was plump and her gelled-down hair had a funny smell that almost stung and reminded her of the thick, heavy Chinese goop her grandfather had rubbed on his head. She smiled at the nurse because she was falling all over herself tending to her and her family. Pina actually felt bad for the woman whenever she tried to get Ma talking. Even on her better days Ma had never been one to talk to strangers.

Auguste was only allowed one visitor at a time. When Pina was in the room on her own, she peered at her father wearing a weird mask that covered his nose and mouth. In there, cleanness had an off-putting smell that made her head spin. Pina finally got up and close to her father and that did scare her, a little, that body just lying there quiet. She didn't say a word, even though the Caribbean lady had been asking them all to talk so that Auguste wouldn't fall asleep for good. What was there to tell him? She felt stupid and useless. In her thoughts, she told him she'd pray for him to get through it because Ma was worried about money running out. As things were, there wasn't much left. Pina decided she ought to go to Auntie Poe for a few days because over there everybody prayed plenty and out loud. She'd have better luck being heard. She kept waiting for some sign from her father, fingers moving, or eyes opening, just a little, like in the movies. But nothing. He was well and truly asleep, and his skin was gray. Nearby, the machines with shaky green lines were a good sight more alive.

When Pina went to be with her mother, on the fourth-floor balcony, she wanted to hug her as tight as she could, like in the books, and tell her all sorts of things. Ma's eyes were all swelled up and bloodshot.

Ma wasn't looking terribly pretty, but in that moment she'd become a real woman again. Dignified, delicate, distraught, down to fight. Pina, of course, hadn't bounded over and wrapped her arms around Ma's neck. She just came up beside her and leaned over the railing. Her legs hurt so much they could give way any minute. She was looking off in the distance, over the old flame trees, and for the first time, her lips whispered "mommy," with so much quiet and pain. She thought hard about the word. *Mommy.* It was the prettiest word God had ever made up and that the wind had ever carried.

The night of the accident, Ma had felt terrible things deep down in her heart. She'd started sweating and her head had started pounding. When she'd slapped Pina's head, because that brainless git had knocked over the milk pan full of boiling water, Ma hadn't even realized what she was doing. It was pure instinct. She wanted the noise to stop, wanted to not think about whatever problem had just shown itself. And so she'd slapped her daughter and slapped away all her dark thoughts.

In the quiet of the sleeping house, Ma had been waiting for some sort of sign, for somebody to come bring news. She had no idea who about. Her children, her husband doing God-knows-what out there. Maybe Rosa bumped into some madman all worked up about those curves she sashayed around like a whore. Probably both Augustes were staggering around, drunk and high on whatever drug was wearing away at her son every day. They'd be getting fist-happy with other men, stronger ones this time, and end up flat on the ground, maybe for good. Her mind was filled with all those thoughts and then some. About what her mother had said when she'd left for Tahiti. About living off of absence. For the first time, she thought properly about death. Of her children, of her husband whom she suddenly didn't hate anymore. When an ambulance's spinning blue lights started running across the walls of her little room, Ma didn't move, and she almost felt relief. It was two in the morning, the wait was over at last, her worries were finally being heard. A young man started hammering at the door. When she saw his face, she was sure God had come to speak to her. A young man with a soft voice and a baby face—she had no idea such things were possible. In Auguste's car, they had found papers, their address. The ambulance was making a quick stop before picking up a sick grandmother downtown. Ma remembered Mere's parents and they'd all gone to the emergency room.

A small body sways. Spins, rather, this way and that.
Calmly, a calm far too calm. A calm that means
that was the last gasp, too late now.
A small body dangling from a rope tied
good and tight to an old ceiling.

The Hospital

THE LIGHTS THERE were so white they hurt her eyes. All around was commotion and glares and got-no-time-for-you-now. Ma sat there three long hours, not saying a word. A little one-year-old girl was crying bloody murder while her mother with bloodshot eyes and a face too young to be a mother's was pleading for anything, anyone ... for them not to be let down. She bounced the baby up and down, pacing, rocking back and forth, anything to calm her baby down.

A ways off, on the other side of some glass that had cracks in it from angry fists, a nurse barely blinked as she took in the hubbub of what could hardly be called a waiting room. She peered over her massive glasses at that mess of so many people scared sick. Every so often, Ma noticed ambulances dumping the cuts and bruises and gashes of a boozy weekend. Drunken, filthy, half-dead men who couldn't see straight, covered in wounds red with bad blood, red with the hurt of lands and women taken from under their noses ... Mere's parents had already gone back home. All Ma knew was that Auguste was getting operated on.

When Ma finally learned that Auguste had had a near miss with death and still wasn't in a proper state, she went out for a cigarette. The sun was coming up, orange in a still-black sky. She took a long drag, and harsh, angry whorls of blue burst out of her mouth. She let out a sigh, but maybe not for Auguste. She let out a sigh for that sobbing baby girl, for her mother, for the young ambulance guy whose eyes were sweeter than a baby's. Ma went back in to sit with Pauro and Moïra, both of them asleep on benches. These sorts of things only ever happened to poor people.

Some hours later, Ma had to deal with the police and their questions. Pointless questions like how many beers Auguste could drink. Ma reckoned it wasn't in terms of bottles these days, and besides she didn't keep track. Auguste didn't drink around her anymore; he reeked of booze, and that was all she needed to know. Sometimes he got unsteady and jabbered on about any old thing. He beat her up plenty often, but Ma didn't have time anymore. Didn't have time to whine and beg for help from up on high, or anywhere else. Didn't have love anymore, maybe. At home, it reeked. Yes, it stank every day, every minute. It reeked so much that it actually seemed normal.

"When did Auguste start drinking?"

When? Oh, since always. But did those policemen believe a thing she was saying? If she'd found out that Auguste had been born in a still, she wouldn't have blinked twice. One of them, she could tell, was fed up. Ma didn't look scared, not even bothered. Auguste had killed a woman because of the drink. Did she realize that? All Ma could think was that he'd already done in his own family, years before.

Once the cops were gone, Ma went and sat on the balcony. She lit another cigarette and saw her daughter Pina walk over. It hit her like a bolt of lightning: she hadn't thought even for a second about her children, about her family. When she saw the girl, Ma was shocked to find herself wondering who this weak little girl was, hardly pretty but nice enough. It was as if her girl had grown up overnight and what was now standing there, right beside her, was a stranger. They didn't trade a single word and she watched Pina's eyes looking far off, past the railing. The red of the flame trees was all atremble in a bit of wind. What future was there for her, for all her children? Then Aunt Poe turned up. That calmed them all down. Poe was their rock, the strong woman. Sweet voice, steel arms. Ma let her take charge. In Poe's massive bosom, Ma broke down sobbing under the weight of holding it all back. Under the weight of not knowing what was next. What came after this? Darkness, nothingness. Someone, Poe or someone else, would have to help her make sense of all that. Ma wasn't strong enough. She was cruel, sure, but she was weak.

Aunt Poe decided to take the kids with her, out to the backcountry. For Ma, that was a relief. Now she had time. All the time for Auguste.

Happenstance

THAT NIGHT, AS SHE SAT and watched her husband, she didn't think one bit. In and out of her head it was all a jumble. That's what weariness had to be. The machines kept going, letting out small shrill beeps, at moments it was almost a little tune. Auguste's face was full of peace now. Ma didn't say a word, didn't ask a thing. No prayers, just quiet. It hadn't really hit her. After a few hours, after thinking for half a second that she might end up as gone as Auguste, Ma left for some air.

She opened the door and came face-to-face with a man who looked so lonely it gave her goose bumps. The man stared at her, his eyes full of toughness and a little sadness too. Ma took a step back, wishing a nurse, any nurse would come. It was eleven at night. Nobody. The help she was hoping for wouldn't be coming. She knew deep down that she had no chance against this too-big, too-tall man. She kept quiet. She didn't want to get herself killed.

They stayed that way a long while, right by the door to the ICU. A long while during which she couldn't bring herself to smile or cry or yell. Then the man said that his wife had died, that morning, before sunup. In an accident. Dead, killed by a drunk driver. The man's words were helter-skelter, his thoughts too. A perfect picture of loss, of distance, of horrible luck. The man had no wish to see Auguste, he just needed to get his head around the worst. The hospital would make his pain feel real. His head was a mess, and his life would be no different. Everything had been taken from him. He needed other people to know that. He didn't hate Ma. All he wanted was for her to have a clear memory for years of this face wrecked by the nameless, harsh way the woman he loved had been taken.

They went down and sat on a bench, by a half-empty basin tinged green by water that had been standing for months. In the sky, the moon was very small. The man didn't talk, nor did Ma. It didn't seem to be worth it. Behind them was a room. Faint light made its way through a thick, grimy window of small panes. A yellowish, almost orange light. It didn't illuminate much. It wasn't any real comfort. But it was there, and because of it Ma could see the man. She didn't even know his name. He was Polynesian, but not like Auguste. In his face Ma saw a stranger, from Spain maybe. Huh. Strange . . . like this hunger she suddenly had. The hunger of a lost man. It was too hazy, and there was no rhyme or reason to it. She wanted to share this sadness, lose herself in her thoughts and in him, and maybe it was because deep down Ma had so much love, so much feeling. But she had nothing to give. Her body, her sex were nothing next to death. So little, but still maybe that could help this man. Around them were four buildings each three stories high, with lights from hospital rooms shining here and there. Maybe there was someone awake like them, walking around the garden . . . There was no rhyme or reason to it, a heart beats, nothing more. The man had on a jacket and the skin that showed was blunt and male. Ragged jeans were bunched around thick, ruddy thighs. He was hunched over slightly, and his hands clenched by his groin. He stank. He must not have washed, or even thought to. He smelled like a man, a sharp smell as strong as the sun. Ma brought her legs together, hiked up her long skirt. She slid her panties down with a shaky hand, and her head was pounding, booming. Everything in her belly, in her gut felt so flimsy. She could hardly breathe. It was wrong, but she'd never wanted anything so bad. Never ached so much. She could feel how wet she was, had no idea if the man was interested in her. He was there, not moving. Maybe he didn't see. She got up. Walked up to him and stood over him. He looked up. She didn't say anything. She leaned over and pressed her hands on his thighs. Her fingers moved up a bit. He was hard, so hard. Hot, too, purring, growing. The man spread his legs, a sound slipped out his throat, rough like sadness. He leaned his head back and Ma rubbed where he was swelling, gently, carefully. Her fingers had never been this light. He undid his jeans buttons one by one. Grabbed her. His long fingers slipped around Ma's butt. She could feel his huge, calloused hands spreading apart her cheeks, reaching where it was wet and deep within. It was violent, it was almost beautiful. His eyes sank into hers. Ma found herself kneeling on the bench, her legs bent and hurting. Her hands locked around the man's neck. With a thrust he had her sitting on him. It was hard, it was strange, it hurt, but all the same it was so good, terribly good. When this unfamiliar thing pushed in, she rose up, sure she would split in half. It was too new. They were swept up, drunk with pleasure, their eyes were shut as they were surrounded by the night and maybe even some strangers' gazes. They were alone in their pain, alone in feeling their way through what they had no words for. The man let out groans and thrust up hard, quick, and Ma moved too, coming down violently. He'd made a mess of Ma's hair. She felt like she was going insane. She was letting out whimpers too, quietly, they had to hurry, but somehow overdo these stolen, lawless moments of being selfish. He was hurting her. His hands, his body were dripping with loss. It was brutal, almost animal, but she savored it. They moved together, but not like two consenting adults. They were two weak, frightened creatures stinking of death. They were Eros and Thanatos, bound together for just a few more minutes. And yet, there was no kiss, never would be. She took this wrath to the hilt, this force, this hate, all the way. In this unknown woman's body he let loose all his strength, all his sadness, but their tongues never met, their lips never touched. It was horrible, but it was what saved them. When he finally came in her, he pulled hard on her hair. He couldn't control it. Ma's head was tilted up to the sky. He couldn't see that she was smiling.

Her crotch was burning. Her legs, her whole body, had gone slack. She felt wrung out, full to the brim—she'd have liked to hold on to those minutes for just a bit, just a bit longer. She didn't know his name. He didn't know anything about her, just that she belonged to his wife's killer. It was too muddled in his head for him to make sense of it. Ma got up and then collapsed on the bench beside him. Their breathing wasn't calm yet. He told her that they'd be burying his wife in the Papeete cemetery. He didn't say that he wanted her there. But she understood, at least she thought so. He left. Inside her was anger.

Anger at this life that could have such odd twists. This horrible accident, this woman dead, her husband just about a vegetable and now her: thoughtless, self-absorbed, whoring herself out, and happy.

The Funeral

TWO DAYS AFTER PA'S ACCIDENT, Ma came to get me at Aunt Poe's. It was almost six in the morning, she hadn't slept, again. As I was walking over to the latrine, down there, in the dark corner of the garden, I saw her coming. She climbed off the truck, her hair down, it stood out to me, and I couldn't stop thinking about how weird that was. It was so new to me. I almost thought Ma had gotten younger, even though the bags under her eyes were even heavier. Suddenly I didn't need to do my business anymore. I walked over to her, my heart was pounding because I was scared that Auguste was dead. It took Ma some time to open her mouth, that was how she always was. We went into Poe's kitchen and Ma made coffee. Black for her, no sugar either. I took my time shutting the door and shooing away the scrawny chickens always pecking at one another for something to eat. Then I came and sat across from Ma. I waited, jumpy because I was that scared. The night before, I hadn't slept a wink either. For the second time, I'd been thinking about death. The first time was when Māmā Aeata, my mother's aunt, had died. One day, coming home from school, Ma told us that she was gone. Then, when it was time for bed, I realized that *to go* meant to die. To go, and never come back. I hadn't said goodbye to Māmā Aeata so I was a bit sad. And then, when I'd gone to her deathbed where she'd closed her eyes so calmly, I'd sobbed. It was all so pretty. I saw people singing for her. It got me shuddering and pulled me a long way away. But this time was different. We still needed Auguste, Ma especially . . . at least, I think so. So he can't be going. Not now. I'd spent the whole night bawling, quiet at first and then out loud. That's how people know you care about someone. The more you cry, the more everyone knows you loved them. Aunt Poe came to cluck over me and Pauro said that I was doing it for attention. Maybe he's right, I do like it when my nose and mouth are up against Poe's breasts, especially in the space between those two big warm things.

Across from me, the fortysomething woman was staring at me weird. I knew Ma didn't like me much, but the way her face was just blank made me want to cry even more. So I had no idea what was happening when she came over and gave me a big kiss and wrapped her arms around me. There was no way I would ever understand grown-ups, women especially. They're crazy. We stayed that way for a few minutes, just her and me. Then she told me to go wash up because we were going to the cemetery. And when I heard that I let out the biggest howl of all because I thought Auguste was already buried, and it wasn't fair because I wanted to see people around his deathbed. Lots of people, a whole choir, with a few māmā wearing white hats and sobbing. I think I scared Ma. She pulled away and scolded me. But when I told her that I was really sad for Auguste, she figured it out. She reassured me, explained we were going to pay respects to the lady Pa had killed by accident. But that didn't really make me feel better because I didn't like knowing that he'd killed someone. I'd already been thinking about it, and it made me so scared that I felt like I'd pulled down a big black curtain as fast as I could so those thoughts would go away. I tried to tell Ma that I didn't want to go, but just like always she was having one of her moments, so I shut my mouth, looked down, and pulled on my cousin Fanny's white dress.

◈

I was alone with Ma, and next to us, in front of us, and across the big hole in the ground were lots of people. Lots and lots of them. Not Tahitians like us. Some halfs, and I think some "wholes" too, all-French people with pale skin, nice clothes. They were all sobbing and then I was too because I had to. Ma was crying as well, a little. I think because the very nice lady we could see in the brown coffin was there because of Auguste.

Ma didn't know anyone. Except maybe for the big strong man with black hair past his ears. When we came, they were all there and the coffin was right by the hole. I saw Ma looking over to the man. He nodded. He didn't smile or anything. It felt weird that he and Ma knew each other. The killer's wife, at the victim's funeral. It seemed sick. The man had really dark sunglasses and his children, who looked like they were about as old as me, were clutching his legs. A boy and a girl, each on a leg.

"Dear sisters, dear brothers. As we remember Nora . . ."

It was a Catholic funeral, with a priest, a real one, in a white robe. When he said that Nora, the woman, was gone too soon, but that even if it seemed unfair it was all God's will and we had to accept that, everyone had started crying into their hankies and sniffling, some of them were hysterical and some of them were quieter. I don't think anybody liked what the priest was saying . . . I didn't stop looking at the man. Someone must have forgotten to give him a hankie, because his tears were running down his face into the snot over his mouth. I would never have forgotten to do that. That's always the first thing I think about, the snot, I can never stand seeing my little sister's . . .

Then a woman yelled and cut off the priest reading from his Bible. In her big black dress she said she would kill whoever had taken her daughter from her. Thirty-six years old was too young. The lady seemed really angry, and I peeked over at Ma. She was looking down at the ground really hard and I was scared for us, for our lives and Auguste's. The man glanced at us. He scared me, but he didn't say a thing. Poor Ma, I don't know what was going on in her mind. I don't think I'll ever understand her. There was no reason for us to be there, but she couldn't help it.

At the end, they lowered the coffin, and each mourner threw some dirt over it, very slowly, as if they had to move as slow as the sun. Then it felt like the funeral needed to be just the family. Ma took my hand and we left and went down a nice tidy path. I stayed a bit behind her, full of tears and pain I hadn't been expecting. I tried to read the dates on the gravestones. I came across one that said 1870–1960. That was a long time ago. It shook me, it was almost prehistory and I couldn't imagine it. But Ma was walking fast and I was definitely making her upset. I stopped being a fool and ran to catch up.

Auguste was still sleeping; the machines were still working. He'd been there for two days, like a doll that wouldn't ever move. Nothing had changed, or maybe something had, Rosa and Auguste Junior were at the hospital when Ma and I came back sweaty and worn out because we hadn't taken the truck. Ma said she'd forgotten her wallet, but I knew she was lying. She was saving what little there was, or maybe it was worse than that, maybe there wasn't any at all. Rosa's head was on Papa's legs, she was crying, maybe for real, although this girl was such a good liar, a perfect actress. But when I peeked in Auguste's room, she was sobbing so wildly that she was shaking, pleading for him to wake up again.

"Aue ho'i e, papa! A ara papa. Eiaha 'oe e na reira ia matou . . ."

If she was yelling at him not to do that, not to abandon them, then that meant she was crying real tears. Hard enough that it made me uneasy. Then, after a moment, she turned to Ma and spat out that we should have tried to find her. And at those words, for the first time in her life, Ma gave her a slap, a big one that left her cheek red and that I can still hear. Rosa was more shocked than anything, then ashamed on top of that. Ma was shaking and getting hysterical too. She said in Tahitian that she had better things to do than go looking for her daughter in every old bar or on the street, because Auguste and the children and everything else was too much for her to deal with or just think about. The two of them looked right at each other for a few minutes. Their first fight had to be something they would remember forever. My sister said that she would go get her things at the house, and she thrust a big wad of money at my mother. Then Rosa walked out, and I went and gave that mother I couldn't stand the first hug I can remember giving her.

Out in the Backcountry

A WHOLE MONTH NOW, and Auguste was still in a coma. Hadn't moved one bit, not even when the nurses came in to wash him. If he'd had any idea, that'd have given him a real smile, I think, considering how he loved women, loved playing with them. Ma was thinner now and dressing different. Shorter skirts, hair combed nice and proper so it looked shiny. She was even using a little eyeliner to make her eyes pop, like pretty Tahitian women who knew a thing or two. French perfumes special ordered from catalogs thicker than the Bible. Ma had a look now, but whether it suited her, whether I liked it, I couldn't quite say. She was changing, the same way our own lives were.

Pauro, little Moïra, and I were all still with our aunt out in Tiarei on the east coast, living in an old house that was still plenty pretty. A house that people called colonial, with big rooms, a bit dark but only because of all the trees outside sure to fall on us. Like I said, the bathroom was still outside, some latrines at the end of a garden, a big one, under an avocado tree with lots of fruit that we never ate because we were convinced they grew out of our shit. Of course, we kids didn't want to go there at night. We crossed our legs and twisted around, our undies and sheets got soaked, but we stayed put until morning, until dawn, and even then our hearts were thumping because we could never be sure whether the nighttime ghosts were still hanging around for a bit. Those ghosts were in our lives a little, our whole family's lives. We were terrified of them, but really, wasn't everyone?

When the accident happened, it was right at the start of vacation, which meant two whole months of not having to get up for a long day at school where we listened to a woman with no more brains than us drive us mad saying, "Sit up straight," and "What have you learned?" and calling us and only us pō'iri ma and all sorts of other things. Two months without the hassle of school meals or single-file lines, just peace and quiet and worrying about nobody but ourselves.

I don't know if I already said that Aunt Poe had lots of kids. I must have done, being that's the first thing anyone thinks when they see her. Big, fat, quick on her feet all the same, boobs as big as those mountains by home that nobody ever climbed. That was Auntie's body. A body for having as many kids as possible, for soothing a toddler's boo-boos no matter how big or small. A body that her husband must have really liked, would go on liking until there was nothing left for the sun and the earth to remember. Until then, he'd love it, even though their lives wouldn't be lives anymore, even though there would have been thousands and thousands of moons, even though we would all be well and gone. Sometimes I do get carried away and think things like that, with my head in the clouds and up in the sky. I'm not saying I'm a poet, I'm just saying that I like playing with words and making pretty little songs out of them. No, I can't be a poet; I get bad grades in French class, worse grades than in my other classes. Come to think of it, that's weird . . .

I reckon they're still going at it even though they're old.

❖

One night, I heard Aunt Poe holler "'auē!" like she'd forgotten herself, a yell cut short by a muffled sound, a hand clapped to her mouth.
That was the secret part of their life and if Aunt Poe liked that then
good for her, what harm did it do for her to be happy every now and
then, when even the night was getting drowsy.

Auntie's husband was a man who could be called respectable, a
Protestant pastor, average height, dark skin like mine, and fake white
teeth. I figured they were fake because the jaw they were in seemed
awfully red. He started working when he was fifteen, on Moruroa
Atoll. Once France had decided it'd learned enough to be able to
stop its nuclear tests for good, Teanuanua retired. Thirty years on the
atoll and in top secret was plenty. And so he started working in the
fields upslope. He fished by night, didn't drink, didn't smoke, and
loved his wife and kids. He could still keep track of the moons, knew
the names of the nights, the best times for planting, how to find the
best fish. He knew the magic words that would open the doors of a
time that had been forgotten, a time that was good and dead now.
He knew the Bible and its words that could save a soul, believed in
his ancestors and felt that the religion of white men oughtn't to have
killed off that of his forefathers, even if, deep down, he knew full well
that there was no going back and that he himself would never go so
far as to follow the cult of our old deities. Where Poe was the rock,
he was the warden of dreams, of some little-known world nobody
dared dig deep into. He was a man of the earth too. Which is how he
was the last one to still know the original name of every plot of land
around him. His name was Teanuanua: rainbow, all the colors of a
plain and pretty life, all the colors of Aunt Poe's happiness. The man
whose hands were thick with callouses, whose nails were black from
so much work, whose dark veins stuck out as much as his nose did,
strong veins that commanded respect. Teanuanua had sired twenty
children by Poe. By the time I was old enough to keep track of who
was who, the oldest of my cousins had just had a grandson. Who

knew how many years there were between a father, a grandfather, a great-grandfather . . . who knew whether it even mattered. There was no rhyme or reason to it, not even any decency maybe. In my eyes, though, it was all touching, like a dream. Feeding that whole family wasn't a problem for them. Teanuanua said that was what the earth was for: bearing fruit, soothing hungry bellies. Men were born to work it, to sweat over it, to enjoy its bounty. I could never understand why Ma and Auguste didn't have half their glow, why they had eyes only for things, for dreams that would never come to be. At Ma's, there never was any money. At Poe's, there never had been any, but they took pride in never having to give their kids bone-dry biscuits wet in sweetish water.

For a month, I learned what it was like to live without being slapped or even scolded. In Tiarei, we ate different things: vegetables, fruits. Taro, fish, often, every day, at least once. Tiarei meant Poe's sweet voice, her sweet eyes that kept resting on Teanuanua. Down there, I barely ever thought about Auguste anymore; may he have mercy on me. I was still a bit sad for him, but I thought about him less and less often. Maybe, deep down, I was wishing him dead, they say that a body can foresee or foretell without even realizing it what will happen to them. Looking back on all that now, I can say that his end would have meant my freedom . . . but only now. Nobody can guess what the future will bring, after all, not perfectly. Ma was a rare sight too: at first she came by every Saturday, then every other weekend. And as we got to the end, not at all. It must have been because of the changes within her . . . That little baby who couldn't possibly understand, Moïra, missed Ma. She must have missed her on some nights considering that she woke up and let out wail after wail. So many that she had the whole household up, and then Poe's two youngest children, hardly any older than Moïra, started in as well. I took Moïra and held her tight and I could feel my heart hammering. I felt downright happy, I think, because this little thing actually needed me. I sang her a little lullaby that Ma had learned from her parents about a mother's kiss on a baby's cheek, about a breast that gave milk and life.

And Pauro was growing up. He was turning seventeen soon; he was turning gloomy already. Being a boy was hard, a boy with feelings even more so. He was falling in love, but I think it was the taboo kind.

Life all around was calm, and for me it was just about beautiful.

"Don't you tell anyone."

"But we have to! You could die. When it happened to Rosa she hurt so bad she fell in the toilet pit."

Fanny had just started going through those big-girl things. She'd called me over while I was doing the laundry. She'd been saying "Pina, Pina" so quiet I was half sure it was a voice in my head. But when I got up from my rickety stool, I saw Fanny hunkered down over the latrines. I just about jumped because I was certain the ghosts had come early. It was noon, there was no way they could have woken up yet. I didn't want her to see that I was shaking, so I walked fast and my cousin started bawling.

Once I was there, she showed me her undies. I was a bit scared and then I could see why women, other than Aunt Poe, sometimes hurt, and why this pain made them, Rosa and Ma especially, so mean. It wasn't right that we should have to suffer like that. Blood pours right out and people say that's just the way it is for all women! I stayed put for a few long seconds, not saying a word, just praying hard that it would happen to me as late as possible. Fanny was in a panic, maybe she'd been hoping I would help her, but I didn't know the first thing about any of it.

"I'm going to go find Poe."

I had no idea what I was saying. Before I even realized it I was over by my aunt. She was sitting on the doorstep, peeling taro. I just told her that Fanny wasn't doing okay. Poe was the kind of woman who wasn't flustered by a single thing.

She got up, slow and heavy, and went over to the latrines. I didn't want to know what they were talking about. I went back to my laundry, the water was slopping over the cracked sides of a huge worn-down blue basin, the clothes were floating, swirling this way and that like dead twigs that couldn't float away or reach land. I held my washboard, pounding with all the strength I had. Pounding, pounding so that it would all be white and clean and right. Pounding. I wasn't much younger than Fanny. She was growing up, and now she was a woman. I was so scared. Being a woman meant going through and doing things that I wasn't sure I wanted. I wasn't stupid, I knew the blood they tried to catch with huge napkins meant that it was time to have children. I was worried for my cousin, for her skinny body. I was worried for myself, so I started singing prayers to settle my heart.

I saw Aunt Poe smiling. Fanny had gone off to the washhouse. From where I was, I could see her feet under the shower.

A few hours later we were all at the table. Teanuanua had come back from his valley, his back bent under a heavy burlap bag full of coconut husks. Fifteen of us were sitting there, the men starving after having worked the land, Poe trying to feed the little ones as best as she could, and me busy with Moïra. And as the little ones shrieked and Teanuanua smiled wisely and Pauro stayed quiet, Fanny was glowing. Poe must have told her all sorts of wonderful things about who she was now. I was looking at her differently. She wasn't a little girl anymore, which had to mean we wouldn't be playing with each other anymore.

The next day and the one after, she didn't come take a bath with us, and when she left the house, sometimes, Fanny wrapped a head-cloth around her hair to protect it from the sun. Thirteen years old, menstruating, her breasts growing, some pubic hair . . . It had to be time.

Siki was taking an interest in her. He was fifteen. He'd started working with Teanuanua and the others. At noon every day, they sat across from each other at the table, silent, eyes full of want and shame. Aunt Poe started teasing them, Fanny blushing, while her suitor's face was glowing with triumph and the prospect of not spending nights alone anymore.

A small body sways. Spins, rather, this way and that.
Calmly, a calm far too calm. A calm that means
that was the last gasp, too late now.
A small body dangling from a rope tied
good and tight to an old ceiling. It ought
to have collapsed but hasn't, that shirker.

One-on-One

NOT LONG BEFORE a young nurse came to wash Auguste, Ma wondered whether there was any way to give this room some life. Flowers, brightly colored sheets. A bit of the life they'd been sharing not a month ago. Then she thought better of it, shooed away those silly ideas. A hospital room isn't made to be brightened up. The bare minimum. Emergencies, lives to be saved, the smell of ether, the snap of bandages being pulled on and off and making any old live body howl, while Auguste . . . Any old live body! What a thing to think, as if Auguste were dead! No, he was still alive. Barely, maybe, but his soul was there, Ma knew it. He would wake up any day now, why even think otherwise? Sure, it was taking a while . . . but what did time matter? Time didn't exist anymore. How long had Auguste been there now? She had stopped trying to keep track, she didn't count the days anymore, because they'd all gone under as well. Miserable, unforgivable time that gives life and takes it away. Filthy, grubby time that always forgets to give anything to those who have nothing. So time, in Ma's eyes, could go fuck off. She'd decided not to give it any more thought. What a pointless fight . . . her believing that she could ignore it was a victory, but an empty one.

❖

Then the blonde nurse came in, no smile to be found on her face, her movements odd and jerky like a cardiograph line from a decade ago, and then she went right back out, all ice and cold.

Ma had managed to make a friend, Candice, the Caribbean lady, with gelled-down hair and an accent that made her want to laugh, have a drink, and go dance. She felt good when she was with Candice because nobody could quite understand either of them—Ma because she didn't speak French well, Candice because Caribbean folks always had a strong accent . . . Candice didn't have a husband or any kids. She was free and Ma thought, deep down, that maybe they'd become close enough that Candice might come by her place when things were well. That they could tell each other all sorts of secrets. Ma had been overcome, ever since the night she'd cheated on her husband, by a horrible need to talk, to retell. Pleasure—she'd never experienced that before. Shudders, her body shaking whenever she remembered the smallest detail. To talk about how sometimes she wanted to drop it all and go beg him to love her. No, maybe not that . . . it wasn't love. She'd beg him to talk to her, bare all the wounds and nightmares, so that she could kiss them. She needed so badly to talk about so many other things. About how she was smiling for no good reason. How this memory was all she wanted to keep.

Today, she wouldn't see her friend. Candice had the day off. Today she would be alone . . . with Auguste.

A poor body lying flat and not moving. Straddling the line between life, which was one thing after another, and death, which would be freedom. Ma ran her eyes over every last bit of this skin that was no longer dark. Pale, almost drained dry. His breath was mechanical, strange. Poor husband, poor father.

A little flashback to all the horrible pains she knew well, to those few spots of happiness.

A little monologue. This little woman who'd been hurt so many times but still loved all the same. Who'd tried one day to give out some love in a life with not a scrap of happiness.

Auguste was there. Open. It was the first time. A body stronger than anything she'd known and now a life that could just stop forever, if she wanted. Ma thought . . . She thought: "Well, why not?" What if Auguste didn't exist anymore? All those tears she'd shed would be behind her, all those screams from her children scared that their Ma might not come out of it, not this time. All would be behind her. No more stench, no more sound of booze and trouble.

No more coppery taste of blood in Ma's mouth.

The green lines of the cardiograph kept on dancing alone. Tiny waves here and there caught Ma's eye. Green lines, Auguste's face to make sure he hadn't died for good . . . Green lines, face, face, green lines.

Like before. Wine bottles, beer bottles, harder stuff, and her heart, which started beating faster. Bottles, man's hands, too-big hands. Booze, Auguste, fear . . .

And making things worse. No talking, Ma. But talking always got the better of her. Coming up with excuses when that was the last thing she ought to have been doing. Making things worse. A word louder than the last. Her voice shaking. And making things worse. Flashes and darkness in eyes. Cowering. Scared of losing her sight. Losing her teeth that fell out anyway, those cowards. Swallowing the earth that was the floor of their kitchen. Praying. Not thinking of anything. And hollering all around. Promising herself that the next day she'd leave, her children in her arms. But never anything.

Poor life that she kept turning over and over in her mind. A hospital room now a courtroom. Her husband on trial and Ma the prosecutor. Nobody else. Her and him, one-on-one. Ma the strong one now, staring him down. She could go and, just like in those stories, those films, unplug the machines.

A few scenes of happiness. The wedding in Papeete. Her family who hadn't come from Huahine. Barely any money but it didn't matter. Auguste and Ma were young and full of hope. It was Poe's delicate, beautiful white dress that she'd borrowed, the one that looked like it was a noble lady's. A European dress that everyone oohed and aahed over. The promise to love forever. The friends, hers and Auguste's. Laughter. Everyone looking on and making Ma feel beautiful. Pampered for that one day. Auguste knew how to smile.

He'd left his job on the schooner. For Ma, he'd become a bricklayer and that worked out well enough. Building houses for others and dreaming off and on about their own. Soon, before long. Maybe a beautiful one. The old Auguste: of course Ma loved him. But then life in Tahiti had started to show its ugly side. Auguste stayed a bricklayer forever. Thankless work. Taking orders from strangers in hard hats spouting off about things he'd never heard of and whose hands were soft, too soft. Then life started to fill up with booze, grudges. The land: there wasn't much, but it'd sure be nice to own a bit of it. The pinnacle of modern life, land of one's own.

Then Auguste started in on beer and bad wine. Every Friday at first, then every weekend, then every night.

Ma wasn't even a full adult yet, and she was expecting Auguste Junior. Having a belly so big and a baby to carry made her proud. Being a woman, pure and simple. But Auguste was changing. The sun under which he worked was getting more and more pitiless. On weekends, on payday, there already wasn't enough money. Loans taken out and used up on nights of drinking. The money was definitely good and gone now. Ma got to whining; Auguste got to lying. He'd had to pay for their house, for them, still had to pay. But what kind of ideas was this little lady getting in her head? That life was going to be a bed of roses? Then he started beating her. At first it was slapping her and pulling Ma's hair just about to the ground. Then punching her face. Kicking her back and stomach. Auguste Junior nearly ended up stillborn. He was born earlier than he ought to have been, with a twisted leg. And that's why he limps now. That has to be why he doesn't seem to understand much, why he hasn't ever been much of a talker.

Yes, Ma could kill Auguste. Could, should. But she needed freedom for that. Freedom to take someone's life. She needed to be strong. And Ma wasn't. Not yet.

Meetings

ANOTHER NURSE CAME IN. Older than the one from the morning. Visiting hours were over. Hours gone in seconds. The thought shook Ma. Thousands of minutes, more or less, thinking about the past, about Auguste, about herself, without even thinking to get up.

"But time doesn't exist anymore, Ma. Don't forget that . . ."

She up and went into town, to eat, to think about anything else. Some old street, maybe the one where she'd find Rosa. Come to think of it, she hadn't seen Rosa since that day. Since the slap and the wad of money. A hundred thousand francs, that wasn't nothing. Rosa.

"No, Ma, don't you think about where she got all that money. Don't you think about it. Don't you think about being a failure of a mother. Rosa can live her own life."

To eat . . . Chinese, or something else. Just to eat, as Ma's stomach was starting to hurt.

That's when she saw him. From the other end of a greasy roulotte with no customers, a food truck among a dozen others on the Papeete quay. In it a Chinese woman was waving a flyswatter and wiping down her neck. She stopped there, just for a bit of peace. And she saw him. Him. The sadness. Him, and her body calling out. She was sure the earth would open right up. So many thoughts filled her head. She could just bolt. But then he saw her.

Ma felt ugly, far too ugly, not worth the least glance from him. He could have just kicked up a fuss and told her to go hide because he'd never seen a lady that ugly. He could have yelled that he hated her. She'd have understood that. She wanted to die. For all this. For his wife who was gone forever. He could have even killed Ma, and she wouldn't have been upset.

He got up and walked over to her.

A wisp of a woman. A tall man with eyes full of loss. A loss that drew her in.

Did they talk?

Yes, for hours and with plenty of silence in between. His name was John. Had a Tahitian mother. A British and Spanish father who'd left when he was two. John's children had been sent off to his in-laws. For a while, until things got better.

He didn't have the faintest idea how to be a father anymore. He was scared.

Ma said she was sorry. Sorry for his life without Nora. For his loss. Sorry.

John. Ma. John and Ma, two souls not from these parts, thrown into an odd world. Two lives corralled together in such an odd way.

They walked a ways off to the Papeete dike in the darkness. Walking made it easier not to talk, not too much. Made it easier to think about the sweat and tears and not the fact that they'd done a horrible thing. That they'd loved each other the way animals did: human beings that were worn down and broken.

The dike was empty on this weeknight. The wind was coming off the water, and Ma wished she could have held it off because it was just like the wind when she was little in Huahine, when her body and her heart hadn't been hurt yet. That wind had brought her dreams of other places.

She wanted him to tell her everything, from beginning to end. That he was hurting and that he would kill Auguste soon. But nothing doing. He held her hand and they sat down beside the sea. Their fingers locked together. Like there was love there. Ma didn't know what to think anymore. "Don't you think, Ma. Don't you dare."

Pins and needles up and down her legs, her back.

Still night. Still dark.

John told her about his childhood, about his mother dying when he was sixteen. Nora's parents who'd taken him in, people with the thoughts and habits of settlers. People with maids, maids who did too much, sometimes, or not enough, usually not enough. Men for the huge garden, men who were always drinking. But that was life in Tahiti. What use was there in trying to change them? Settlers who were refined, who always had distant, hifalutin smiles. John's mother was both cleaning lady and nanny. A sweet country girl who was irreplaceable, who never raised her voice. John's mother was the only one who lasted six months. Who stayed for months, years. Then she'd gotten weak, achy, sick, and died. And then, later, John's marriage to Nora, who could well have been his sister. But Nora loved him so much.

He told her about being a failure at school. Laughed. Nora had plenty of money.

At first, Ma had been listening, because it was hard for her to talk. Because of all the feelings she had, of course, and how scared she was that she might trip over her words, how hard it was to put together words in a language she didn't know well. John understood. He knew Tahitian. That was easier for Ma.

And there were silences too. Bigger ones, nicer ones. Better not to say too much, to protect herself, and because that made things more proper, more serious. Was there any hope John might ever accept being widowed, losing his wife? These were questions Ma didn't dare to ask out loud.

They took in the colors of Papeete twisting and turning in that sea that looked so flat. They turned their eyes away to hide something from each other. They must have smiled too, at where they'd landed themselves, at this little whisper of something that wasn't love, not exactly.

Then John drove Ma home. He saw, he knew the kind of place she was from. Neither she nor he asked if they would see each other again. They were grown-ups and they'd long since left their dreams for dead.

That night, I couldn't sleep. Outside, the moon was so big, it lit up so much of the garden and the road that it was like God had forgotten to turn the lights off. I shut my eyes and thought: "Sleep, Pina, sleep." I wanted a lullaby to rock me to sleep. I don't think anyone's ever done that for me. I tried counting sheep, but that just bothered me because I don't like numbers. The house was quiet, and the generator had been off for a bit already.

I was walking back and forth in my room, doing my best not to look out the window with no curtain. There could be ghosts out there and other things besides . . . I was scaring myself. Maybe I shouldn't. So I opened my eyes and stared at a coconut tree in the middle of the garden. I stayed right there for a few minutes telling myself that I was no scaredy-cat and that all these stories had to be made up. For half a second, I was sure I was winning because I'd been brave enough to make the ghosts go away for good . . . and then I saw him.

I reckon that when we're truly scared, scared for our life, we forget to make a sound. I saw a shadow move. Of course, in my mind, I was thinking of dead people's souls flying around. I couldn't move, I even forgot to shut my eyes.

And because I forgot and spent a minute just plain worrying, I saw Pauro. He was walking fast, with his T-shirt over his shoulder. That did calm me down. The next thing, not so much: a man headed for him. A man, no question about it. And a white man at that. His hair was light, and he wasn't very tall. When they were facing each other, I was half convinced God or even the ghosts were playing tricks on me. The man grabbed my brother by the waist and laid a kiss right on his lips. Pauro wasn't moving, not really. Then they went off to the beach, and I didn't see them again.

It was too much for me.

I didn't know that could happen. Pauro . . . My heart started shaking and I felt a funny sort of sadness and loneliness. I could already see all the problems in store for him. I couldn't tell anyone, as I loved my brother too much. But the Pauro I loved was no cross-dresser and no girly boy, and that was what I didn't get. He didn't wear girl's clothes, he didn't walk like a girl, and he didn't flap his hands all around like those half women. The Bible was very clear that a man should only love a woman to people the land. A man loving another man was an abomination. So if anybody found out, they wouldn't understand. Now that I'd seen him and the man, I got why Pauro had changed so much. But he didn't have to, he didn't need to hide this from me. My brother could talk to me, I'd have understood. I thought about him again, about us, and I went back to bed. Then I cried, very quietly. I was losing him, my god. Ma and Auguste couldn't ever find out. That would be the end of it all.

I thought about it over and over for what felt like hours. How would I ever tell him that I'd seen them, him and the other man? That older man who'd had such a wide, honest smile?

On the beach, they weren't so close together anymore. Pauro especially. He was distant at moments, quiet. The other one's name was François, and he was a métro. This guy all the way from France and

Pauro had only known each other a couple of weeks. Pauro hadn't ever put any of it into words. It was just an odd new state of being. He was aware that this was wrong, taboo. But then again there was this pleasure. The odd pleasure of being hugged by someone the same sex as himself. Flat stomach, strong arms, a body that was both manly and gentle. A man's thighs next to his own, their penises rubbing, touching.

And then the sex itself. Tradition had always called it shameful. That was a mighty queer pleasure, a man offering himself up when his eyes couldn't see, behind them, another man's face screwed up in pleasure. Queer. Feeling and holding someone else's manhood. Exactly the same yet different. That was their relationship, all things they'd known but there was still something unknown that scared them. Pauro had no idea how any of this had come to be. A bit like an accident, something that just happens, with no warning. It was at a dance in the backcountry. Pauro had come with some other guys: cousins, neighbors. Men. And the night was supposed to be top-notch, the booze was supposed to be flowing. In the massive fare amuira'a, couples were dancing, old people were having a grand old time watching and joking about kids these days, about how they didn't know the first thing about anything, girls, nature, respect. And Pauro had laughed, forgetting about Auguste who was sick and maybe dead. François was having a drink with his own friends. François had laid eyes on him and in that first glance love put down roots. Pauro was so young, and his face was charming, maybe too charming.

At home in the quartier by the city, they sometimes called him *the girl* because he wasn't like the others. He helped around the house, helped Pina. Did the laundry out of sheer kindness. And above all he liked to read, and nobody could make heads or tails of that.

When Pauro walked in, François could tell he was going to love this one for good. He was going to get attached because there was something about this awfully young man that just made time stop. And also something about him that ... But there was no need to put his finger on it; François could feel it and that was what mattered. He'd been in Tiarei for nearly five years now. He was an archaeologist and had landed on that backcountry district because it felt like old Tahiti. Not crowded and disappointing yet. He was catching a breath there, taking a step back from all his gallivanting across the oceans of the world. He'd decided to settle down a bit. When it came to sex, he'd done too much, been through far too much.

Waking up at the crack of dawn in the beds of strangers who suddenly looked ten times uglier in daylight, hopping into cabs, when he was in one country or another, running out because things had gotten dicey. So much stuff that could be called unnatural—back rooms, sickos, pervs obsessed with pain, bringing on and going through things that never got any more normal, any more human—and still François didn't ever feel off. He liked to think that being different was what made him hold tight, what kept him part of the group, the world. But then he decided: no, never again. He wanted to be happy. One day, he'd had to do a dig in one of the Tiarei mountains. And then he'd stayed.

As for women, he'd only been with one, and it hadn't taken him long to ask her to leave and never call him again. Even when he was little, he'd liked men's chests, especially the ones that looked like they'd been carefully drawn by hand. Two curves for two pecs. Two promises of strength that would protect him forever. But it didn't work out all too often, and never for long. Being gay felt just as natural for François as having two legs or a head of hair did for other folks, but for the men he slept with, it was a real bother.

Being that living in the countryside was no different from living on any island, everyone talked to one another, even if there was nothing new to be said, and so François walked right over to Pauro.

They'd gotten to talking, which had surprised Pauro, then, later, in the room that he was sharing with his cousin T., he found himself thinking back on that Frenchman. Never seen a farāni like that one, he whispered to himself as he recalled the foreigner's bright eyes. The next day, they saw each other again. And then every night after that. Pauro snuck out to find François when the house was asleep and they talked together, and for Pauro this was something new. It was one week since the dance and François was so sweet. Pauro's heart was hammering like never before. François had walked over and very gently set his hand on his friend's leg. Then their two bodies had pulled in close, their tongues went seeking out places that would have them bent over in pleasure. Their hands touched, grabbed tight. Pauro started wondering what the others would think. But right then, inside that pleasure, he wasn't going to bother with answers. François had been so sweet the first time. His kisses and his whole body were full of love. A funny sort of love, and still. Pauro came. He'd never reckoned that it might not be all that painful. Was that because of his feelings? Feelings could change all sorts of things.

That night when Pina spotted them, François hadn't been able to wait a second longer. He'd gone and waited for his lover to sneak out.

By the sea, Pauro wasn't saying a word. That moment, that exact moment, was something François had seen plenty of times. When it meant no more joking around with his "friends," because they wouldn't let themselves think they were homos, even though loving women felt so boring, didn't even come close to this. Meant they had to clam up for their families who'd never hold with such things. Disappointment was something François had seen plenty of times, and he'd learned to live with it.

"What are you thinking about?"

And the answer Pauro gave him was "nothing," of course, and François laughed. Pauro did too, a little. They got up and by François's house they let themselves talk a while longer about the love it would be such a terrible thing to lose.

Pauro said that he couldn't understand. Nothing in himself, nothing in his life had given any hint of this. Why him and nobody else, why? Why was it so easy for him to fall into all this and why was it that, right after, as soon as he'd come, he wanted to cry so bad?

It was the end of his being a child, it was his first step into a secret life full of lies or, if he wouldn't hold with lying, silence.

The moon that night was terrifying. It almost seemed to be trying to see everything, know everything. Goddamn it. This loneliness. It was too much. Pauro stared at the huge moon. François felt terrible.

First Fight

WHEN I WOKE UP, my mouth was dry. I thought it was funny. It was heavy, all around and deep inside me. Deep inside especially. Moïra was eating breakfast with Aunt Poe, it had to be seven in the morning. The first thing that came to mind was my brother. When he was being hugged and not moving. That was the part I couldn't believe. Around him, time and trees and everything had stopped.

I sat down by Aunt Poe. She had her early-morning smile. Just like every day. It was as if she never forgot to thank God and the world for having put her there, among us. And that was what set her apart from Ma and the others.

"Eat, it'll get cold."

Aunt Poe had cooked some fish. Small rainbow runners swimming in a puddle of oil with heaps of onions. She said that the onions killed any worms you had. Of course, Poe didn't have any tapeworms that could steal her breakfast and everything that she ate. I looked at the greasy little plate and shook my head no. I would never understand people who ate like that first thing in the morning. It would do me in.

"Well, that's why you're so thin!"

Then, in Tahitian, she mentioned that men weren't keen on scrawny weaklings. I told her they could just wait and see and Poe pulled my head in for a hug. Sometimes I think I'd have liked being her daughter because Aunt Poe was so nice. Always happy, always proud of all her brood. No regrets, none of that. In short, perfect, except maybe for the times she talked and talked and talked with her parish friends, trading gossip about people who weren't there. Having a laugh while running down their faults and every time telling those old ladies not to say a word to anyone else, even though she knew well and good that everyone repeated everything. That was her favorite way in the whole world to while away the time, sharing rumors and always adding a bit more on top. When she did that, Poe disgusted me a bit. But really, those little bits of news that nobody ever quite knew where they'd come from were never mean-spirited.

I was thinking about all that when Pauro came into the kitchen. My god, I could feel the tiled floor almost open right up. I had no idea how to act. My brother waved at Poe then gave me a big smile. And I looked down. I had no idea whether or not his smile was supposed to be a sly little wink, like he was saying, "Now we've got a little secret just between the two of us." Pauro had always been the nicest one to me, but that morning, it was something more than just niceness. Well, when you find out a secret like that, of course you'll look at people different. As he filled his plate, I wondered if maybe I was the one who was wrong. What if Pauro had never been who I'd wanted him to be? What if he'd always liked guys? I didn't say a word and Poe asked my brother not to forget to take out the copra. Pauro said no problem, while I kept on staring at my bowl.

"Pina, is there a lot of laundry to do this morning?"

I hadn't expected him to ask about that, so it took me a minute to answer, a minute for that question to make its way into my head. A minute for me to figure out why he was asking me.

"Did you hear my question?"

"Yes, okay! I'm not deaf. Yes, there's lots of laundry."

I'd spat that out and my brother realized that I wasn't all right.

"God, sometimes you're such an idiot. I was asking for a reason. Because I know a place where we can do laundry, in a machine. An actual machine, you know?"

Yes, I knew what that was, and where he'd have found one. In the house of someone with money enough for one. Money enough for restaurants and movies and all sorts of other things. Money and more money. My head hurt. It hit me that Pauro loved this man because of that money and more money we'd never have. And because of the nice things this farāni had to have, his trips, all these things that of course he had to know more about than we did, and all of this just pulled me further away from my brother. Maybe this white guy was actually nice, who knew. We'd see.

It was a fare with bamboos and the prettiest wooden floors. A home built out of dark wood, solid wood. It smelled nice too and it shone, a bit like a rich person's coffin. The wood of Ma's place was anything but sturdy, it creaked and groaned all the time whenever we walked on it. There was a little terrace and macramé plant holders swinging back and forth, just like in my dreams, with pretty ferns in them. I love ferns, they're so fragile even though they can grow anyplace they like. They carry little spores inside themselves that they drop everywhere to make more, to put out pretty little shoots. It all seems like magic. It was beautiful at François's place. Pauro had taken Moïra and me and our bundles of dirty laundry almost as heavy as Poe there.

When we finally got there, after a long slog, the house was empty but not locked.

I did my best to tread lightly. It all seemed so fragile. Beauty's a delicate thing that deserves to last as long as possible. Moïra was hopping around and trying to touch so many things: books, pens lying around . . . I reckon she'd never seen anything like that before, and she just couldn't hold back. It drove me crazy, it did. Running after her, yelling, trying not to leave any trace. And her snot was dripping all over the place because she was a bit sick from some-thing. She had gotten some in her mouth, on her finger, just like that, without anyone noticing. That morning, she was the most difficult child I'd ever dealt with. At one point, I was putting away one of those thick old books that Moïra had grabbed, and put my finger in a huge clump of snot, brand-new and stuck right on the cover. It made me gag and want to bend her over and spank her hard. But Pauro caught me, letting out a huge guffaw. And that was the straw that broke the camel's back. I was hopping mad because what had my brother laughing wasn't Moïra's tomfoolery but the fact that I had this filthy thing in my hands, that I'd touched it and was so grossed out by it. I'd never seen him laugh so hard, bent double as he guffawed. And this was what hurt so much. That was when it all happened, I yelled the loudest and meanest "fag!" that could have ever come out of my mouth and out of my heart. I really was think-ing that. For the first time in my life, my brother disgusted me. *Fag*: what a little word for such a big insult. The slap came right away, and then another one, and I thought I would keel over. Deep down, I was blazing, I hated him, and the sort of hate that a person can actually feel, even just for a second, the sort of hate that people can somehow feel for whomever they really, really love—there's no worse feeling in the world. It's better for people to hate someone they already can't stand. When people start wishing the worst, the absolute worst, on someone they'd never have wanted to lose before, that right there is the end of everything, of love, of what matters. I saw Moïra stare at me, addled, and then open her mouth and start bawling in terror. In my head, I already knew I'd never amount to anything anymore, and it felt like I was hearing echo on echo on echo on echo on echo. *Fag*: I promised myself I'd never say that word again. Never ever.

Pauro ran out of the house and my sister and I were sobbing for different reasons. Moïra because she didn't know and me because I knew too much and I couldn't bear it.

Moïra had worn herself out and I set her on a nice soft armchair to sleep. I found Pauro sitting on some steps leading up a hill. Some rich person's plaything. I didn't say anything at first. I just stood right in front of him. Pauro's eyes were red, and I said I was sorry. I told him everything about the night before. He said he wanted to die and he couldn't make himself change. At that moment, I think it was because of my love that I finally got it. My brother would always be my brother and the whole world and everyone in it with all the venom they had to spit could go and do whatever they liked. I understand it all, Pauro. I'm okay with it all. Nobody has any right to call the shots. Nobody has any right to say what's good and decide that means everything else is bad. Not to my brother. To me, maybe. He pulled me onto his lap and I thought that maybe life could be okay again, if only some things changed, not all of them, just some. I felt so small and his breath got quieter, little by little. Pauro had become a man, and more than that, something different from what anyone expected to see, but I was still his little sister. We'd been through so much together, Ma and Auguste, their slaps, for all that and for his own happiness, Pauro had the right. He had every right.

A few days went by. Even if, around us, the world didn't seem interested in getting its butt moving, Pauro and I were closer than ever before. He was gay and that was a secret to keep, and I felt thankful for that. Secrets were something I loved, they made me feel important.

Auguste wasn't getting better, and we had no news from Ma. Time was starting to get stretched out and heavy. It wasn't that we missed our house or even our neighborhood. It was something else. Answers, really. We needed answers, we needed to know that our father wasn't going to die, not yet. "Pas de nouvelles, bonne nouvelles," Aunt Poe said. It was so weird to hear her talking in French. She almost never did, and it sounded funny. Most of the time her French came out in fits and starts, unless she was spouting off lines like that one, and she probably knew plenty of them. "No news is good news" and "the cowl doesn't make the monk" and I don't know what else.

But there was lots of waiting, lots of quiet, and the same thing over and over. Wake-up, meals, work, bedtime, over and over and over . . . I met François, the same day I got to see how nice laundry machines are: waiting for the washer to finish doing its job. Now we're friends, I think. I like him a lot, enough anyhow to be sure that my brother will be happy with him. Maybe one day they'll move away, far away, together. That'd do Pauro good. A plane, some big cities, snow. It must be wonderful. François told me about being gay, I don't know why, he said I was old enough. Almost a woman, at nine years old. That made me feel all grown-up. People didn't say those sorts of things at home, not often. For him, being gay was something he had to talk about and wear on his shoulders, like clothes. Like something normal, I reckon. And what did it matter if guys didn't get it, either they were idiots or they refused to look with their own eyes. François talked carefully and rolled his *r*'s just like us. Come to think of it, that's what made me feel like I could trust him. François didn't stare off in the distance, didn't scrunch up his forehead, didn't shrug all the time like so many Frenchmen. He was funny too when he got to talking about himself in the third person, saying, "Well, this auntie here . . . !" At first I thought he was talking about Aunt Poe and I couldn't make heads or tails of it because she'd never talked about him, and God knows she talked plenty about others. It was only later that I finally got it.

A small body sways. Spins, rather, this way and that.
Calmly, a calm far too calm. A calm that means
that was the last gasp, too late now.
A small body dangling from a rope tied
good and tight to an old ceiling. It ought
to have collapsed but hasn't, that shirker.
That long frizzy hair's loose and free for once.
The only keening is a river not far off.

The Wake-Up

THERE'S MORE LIFE in an ice cube.

There are looks that chill your spine, that make you want to not be alive, to have never been there. Candice saw him first. In the ICU, she heard the machines making new noises. High-pitched ones calling out. She rushed over to make them stop. She didn't see Auguste right away. Then the music in her head cut off, an old Billie Holiday jazz thing that started, "This suspense is killing me . . ." The suspense of love is dead, just like that. In front of her was evil.

There's more love in a corpse.

He remembers that life wasn't so distant, wasn't so ugly. In Auguste's open eyes is loss, nothingness. Candice jolts. The gaze came from far too far off. From out there, where nothing exists anymore, meaning that he's forgotten what being human is.

Candice couldn't say a word or holler. Auguste was there and later on the nurse would say that there was something animal about his eyes. Something foul. "In my twenty years on the job, I've never seen such a sight. Not one bit happy to be alive again . . . Conscious, that much I can say. Not even shocked, just nothing. Conscious, like he'd never been a vegetable, like nobody ought to have ever stuck a tube in him, washed him, all that." Candice was a God-fearing Catholic. Back in Guadeloupe, where she was from, they were in the habit of praying to Mary and all the saints but also believing in wicked souls come up from hell. In that moment, she didn't know who or what she ought to pray to. She rushed out and called Laurent, the intern, to go and see what was happening in room twenty-two.

That day, Ma woke up around eight, like a young girl. It had been ages since she'd heard children hollering from sunup. In her bed, she could finally stretch her arms and legs out, relax, and smile. The day the house had gone quiet, it had been the start of a new ritual. Her days began with her waking up, then having her first cigarette, then her first coffee. The bathroom came after all that, and that was a real change, laziness was getting the better of Ma. The bathroom came last because, as Ma said, there wasn't anybody around for the smell to bother one bit. She always looked back one last time, at a house that wore her out, and then set off for the hospital, happy when Candice was there. Like this morning.

The Caribbean lady had spotted her from the balcony as a cigarette hung from her mouth. She was shook up, still shuddering. She went and met Ma at the elevator, and that was where they said what had to be said. Auguste was getting all sorts of tests, neurological ones mostly, and he'd been moved out of the room. There had been a hubbub, and they'd called for a professor who was in Tahiti for a short spell and who specialized in people waking up from comas and other miraculous things. Some time before, they'd suggested pulling the plug. Ma had said yes, a bit faster than she ought to have, or maybe a bit too late. This morning, it was too late.

As soon as Ma heard the latest, she knew nothing would be the same. Auguste was born again. That was the hope, of course. Of course everyone wanted him to wake up from the coma. Everyone. And so, she put on a smile, to look like a woman who was finally seeing her husband again. In front of Candice, she acted happy, as if all her prayers had been answered. But there was no fooling the other woman. She knew Ma and the whole story, her past and her shortcoming, her one shortcoming. Ma didn't have to act around her, that wasn't doing her any favors. The Caribbean woman warned her friend that Auguste might not be the same, that she had been downright scared. She told Ma that back in her country, people believed things well out of the ordinary, a bit like in Tahiti. Just a bit of advice, because the two of them were close: Ma had better pay close attention. The days were numbered.

The Announcement

WHEN MA CAME, the next day, as I've said already, nothing was the same. Teanuanua had warned us that it could be bad, and we'd feared the worst. The night before, I don't think anyone had slept a wink. And I think each of us cried, each of us thought matters over, prayed, begged. Poe washed her white dress, the one for mourning, dusted off her hat. She pulled out clothes for Auguste too. Dark pants, a starched white shirt for his final trip. Dressing the dead was something my aunt had done plenty of times because everyone knew she could be counted on. In rooms that would be closed off and kept quiet forever, she'd stayed beside people who couldn't be saved. Then she washed them, singing all the while, so the family could leave and cry.

Teanuanua had his Bible, the one dog-eared all over, open. On the dining room table, the words of the Gospel, translated into Tahitian, were singing about a more beautiful world, after life, and about courage, the unwavering courage of folks who stayed. The light of the kerosene made a circle dancing this way and that on the boring old ceiling. Nobody touched the food. Pauro was off with François and I was sure I was alone. It was so heavy in me . . .

❖

Loneliness.

I watched the grown-ups, their faces all looking so safe when they really weren't. I stayed in the room, alone, just thinking about what could happen when it's all over. We'd have slipped out of our bodies, floated up to look down from on high, smiled because now we knew for sure the people around us, if not all of them, really, really loved us. Our family, our friends would be there and crying. And tears can't be fake. We can only cry real tears, how can we pretend? Those things can't be done just because we feel like it.

Death.

Just not being anymore. I tried to get my head around nothingness, emptiness. François says that when we die, even our soul becomes dust, he says that's because it's material and because the body is an envelope that contains our soul. If our bodies die, then our minds, our memories, our souls, all of that, have to go up in smoke too. It's like the heart, when it stops beating, our eyes stop seeing. And that makes me shiver deep down, this thought that nothing exists any-more when our time is all used up. What about babies who die? Are things so horrible and cruel that those babies would never have any life of their own? It scares me just how final it has to be. François might be the most educated man in the whole galaxy, but sometimes he's so hard-bitten. No, death can't be that. It's leaving and looking at the earth from up on high, if we even get there, way up by God, or someone else, who knows. When we die, there have to be angels and a big white light. Then we'll be led to the door of what's called heaven, where all the children are brought together. We'll answer some questions and then we'll go into a place like a palace. And that's where we'd see our past go by, with all our mistakes and all the good things we could have done on earth. Then we'd say goodbye to life, for good. At that point infinity begins with songs and love. No more suffering, that's a rule. And that's death in my eyes, if that's a selfish vision to have, that's because it's we who are the happiest ones, when the time for our death comes like they say at church or in the Bible. And what seems sad is the emptiness that we leave behind, especially if we were someone good, known, and loved. I don't think I'll leave behind lots of unhappy people. I'm not the most spoiled one in the family, that much I know . . .

I didn't pay the crickets filling the night any mind. Teanuanua was shouting that those were his ancestors talking. That's how they came back for him, for us. If that isn't ghastly, I don't know what is. Then the singing stopped and all around there was nothing but Teanuanua and Poe deep in their thoughts, their memories, their fears. Auguste dead . . . They'd have to reckon with the prospect of adopting his children for good. Poe had cleaned the house, set out the mourning clothes, and then she'd sat down right next to me. I could smell her. Bitter and also tender, I remember. The smell of housework, of being a woman. A smell of weakness and self-satisfaction, a smell of forever . . . She asked me to be strong, but I wasn't going to tell her that was something too far away for me. I've hated plenty of times. Some days I've hated my father. Some nights I've wanted him dead.

A Whore's Life

FOR HER TRICKS, Rosa was using a studio belonging to Georges, an old métro. He had to be at least fifty, although it was anyone's guess how old he really was, let alone what he really was—a businessman, a bar owner, a pimp, a gay man at other times. He said he was Corsican, but the Corsicans in Papeete weren't so sure about that. What Georges *was* was a bright shiny car, hands waving all over the place, calling everyone here tu and never vous—apparently that was tradition. In other words, a big fat smug phony. And the studio where Rosa saw her johns was no different from Georges himself: tiny, moldy, stinky, dingy.

That morning, Rosa was asleep next to a military guy, probably an NCO. The night before they'd danced and practically started fucking right in the disco reeking of piss and soldiers. Rosa'd had too much Cutty Sark again, and something else, she couldn't recollect what. A wild mess that had her feeling horrified and wishing she could forget it all, say that wasn't her. The honking cut through the whir of the pathetic ceiling fan, and Rosa got up lickety-split, grabbed the money she was owed, and stuck it in her filthy bag. Two glances in the cracked bathroom mirror. Ugly, old, completely run-down—and she wasn't even all that old. A painful picture of another painful night. She kicked the addled man out and wiped off her makeup. She was

waiting for Alain, one of Georges's pals. Alain was supposed to be a
proper businessman, no ifs, ands, or buts about it. He'd made a fortune in pearls, like lots of other Chinese men. But what set him apart
from them was that Alain didn't speak a word of Tahitian, didn't even
know the names of the men he had working for him at a farm in
Tuamotu. But that hadn't kept him from getting filthy rich and the
locals had let him, had given away their little islands. They'd just let
him, not imagining for a second that giving away their land meant
giving away everything. Alain had been a Thursday-morning regular
of Rosa's for months now. Married, of course, but what difference
did that make, Alain and Rosa, that was the same old story. Maybe
there wasn't love in it, but there was tenderness. After their quickies,
Alain always started whimpering about his woes, about being in his
forties now. If this little girl who was so easy to sleep with, who was
so patient as she listened to him, if this little girl weren't Rosa, she
would have been such a sweet thing. But she was Rosa, and she didn't
have the least bit of heart even for her family, for Pina. Meaning she
wasn't sweet at all. A little girl who'd been filthy even before the first
pitch-black pubes showed on her crotch. A little girl who slipped out
at night to listen at her parents' bedroom. She liked hearing it all.
Her father's disgusting gasps. She loved it, spying on Auguste Junior
and watching when he was hidden away in an abandoned hut on the
hill. A filthy little girl who'd never been any different ... She tidied
up the room, opened the door for Alain, and pulled her clothes off
again, still drowsy, her pussy still full of the military man's sperm.
Poor girl, poor idiot who was just as fast as any man to say no to a
condom for a bit more pleasure.

Alain had a straight back and nice clothes, a scowl on his face and
a huge body. He was stronger than Rosa. Each time she started whining like a bitch. Then she started rasping her *r*'s, hiding her accent.
No more rolled *r*'s that dawdled in her mouth forever. What she
needed was to feel like someone else, to not be a girl from here. Alain

was the tom and she was just waiting for him. They didn't bother with the bed she'd just made. They went at it right on the floor.

At eight, Auguste had just opened his eyes. Rosa had a sinking feeling in her belly. Saw herself arching her back. It had nothing to do with the man's thrusting hips. Whore! She's just a whore. In some sort of half dream, as her lover started to come, her father was yelling that she was the biggest whore of all. Auguste had come to see her, to see this naked young body sloppy with all the filth of all these men who'd stopped by, all these horny travelers who'd gotten their rocks off. Auguste had seen those legs spread wide. Auguste . . . Rosa was hollering, bawling. And Alain thought he was doing a bang-up job. But the truth had her sobbing. Her screaming in pain. The pain of being nothing better than a whore . . .

A few minutes later, Rosa up and left. She saw Georges at the bottom of the stairs. Waiting there just like every Thursday morning. Just like always, she gave him his cut. Soon enough Georges would be dead, he'd meet a grisly end. That's what always happens to greedy pigs.

The Sentence

AUGUSTE THE FATHER. An all-powerful father. A boozer, cantankerous, rock of the family, pillar of the family. Auguste, stronger than all the others. Back from the land of the dead. Like Jesus, like God.

A man to fear, a man who'd always made people fearful. Did his children, his wife really think he'd go that easy? He was a warrior descended from warriors! Grandson of fighters, son of those who had sounded alarms, who had gone and warned everyone that their lands, their country would be stolen from them and who'd fought to the death for all that, while everyone else had just grinned like idiots, pleading with those white men from another time who'd worn those hats as they invaded colony after weak colony. Was he just going to pack his bags like that, like he was the biggest fool of all? His wife, his kids, his friends were all huddled around his bed. Not daring to touch him, not daring to say a thing. Auguste was a ghost. He'd seen death. The father and husband stared them all down. Ma had changed. She'd moved right on . . . Poe and Teanuanua had their doubts but they showed some respect. And the kids. Pauro had gotten bigger. He'd be a hero. He'd be a warrior. Junior wasn't there. Passed out on the streets, probably. Rosa was the brat, the pretty face. Rosa was sobbing because she knew. She'd seen her father and at first Auguste's eyes were full of sadness. Then anger. He was fit to be tied.

His daughter was selling her body . . . to the enemy. All that would have to be straightened out. He hadn't tasted death for nothing. And Pina last, looking so innocent. Pina who everyone thought was stupid. Pina last, half the time a wounded little girl. But in the end she was a sphinx.

Poe was the first to speak. "Auguste, how . . . ? Thanks be to God!" Teanuanua uttered a prayer and launched into the story of Lazarus, whom Jesus had brought back from the dead. Auguste-Lazarus, that had a nice ring to it. Auguste, wan. His eyes were yellowish. Everyone was standing ramrod straight in terror. Everyone, like so many men who'd just been sentenced. Sentenced to what? To feeling guilty for having looked away, at least once, while this man was dying. Guilty for taking just a little pleasure while this man was taking his final breaths. Sentenced to being just plain average. While this man had stayed honorable, his eyes were completely different now, almost like ice. What he really seemed like now was a judge, looking long and hard at his wife's face. Not because she was beautiful now but to lay accusations on her for it. A nightmare of a family reunion where Poe's words were limp things that couldn't cover up the quiet, the heavy weight that went past all words.

The doctors hadn't found anything special in this spook's brain. They just allowed that he would need lots more rest. That such wake-ups weren't such a rare thing. He wouldn't be talking right away, or walking. He needed time, lots of it. And rest too. They all left, letting out their breath. Outside, they almost said "whew." Whew! It was an outright relief to see Auguste out of danger. And to get out of that room where only the father seemed fine with knowing so little about what was to come in a changed life.

The Place of All Possibilities

HIS MOTHER PULLED HIM out of his sleep. It was still night, but day wasn't far off. No watch, no clock, he just knew, the way his parents before him did, and his grandparents too. He knew this moment well, when even animals were still asleep, the moment when his body was already ready for an hour or two's walk to get there, down in the valley, where they'd planted enough to feed the whole village. Before long he'd be living his life in town, but this moment was one he'd remember for always. First was the hand, his mother's hand. A woman's hand with stubby, bruised fingers, an old, calloused, well-worn palm with creases carved deep by sweat and pain and hard work. No words needed. He opened his eyes, first with some fight, until he remembered it was time. His mother had woken him up this way since he was seven, since he was old enough to put his strong arms to work. When even animals were still asleep, the smell of coffee beans, ground and filtered, filled the kitchen and almost got into his bed, his sheets. Then he got up, still bogged down by a dream that hadn't ended just yet. His older brothers were at the table already, and their father too. Four men and him, half a man, because he wasn't as big and tough as the others yet.

After eating, they all left the kitchen. All the sons, oldest to youngest, trailed after their hulking, hardy father not saying a word as his first dark-tobacco cigarette dangled between his lips. The smoke swirled, like always, and nipped at the boy's nose, or maybe it was him, the boy, nosing around for that sharp, sweet smell. Before they were off, they ground their machetes until they were sharp, washed off their shovels and spades. Then the cocks got to crowing, the air didn't seem so crisp, and the wind died down.

Dawn was breaking, they had to get going. Through the garden and up the paths. Away from the beach where the whole family lived and down the route to the fa'a'apu, the cropland. Then, on a slope to the right, as he started on another path, not a hundred meters from the plantation, Auguste glanced back, always did, at a huge stone and at the odds and ends of a cobbled-together village, one his great-grandfather, Matahi, had lived in for years and years. Auguste had to have known this name and this man's shade since even before he was born. An ancestor who'd brought honor or maybe shame on his family. As a kid and now as a teen, not a day, let alone a week, had gone by without Auguste's father saying something about that man who'd fought to the bitter end. It was in the 1880s, or a bit before. Tahiti's king had abdicated, and the island was annexed to France. But Raiatea, the island where Auguste and his ancestors were born, like some other islands, wanted nothing to do with France.

A simple enough story. War. Resistance. Matahi didn't go on and on about it. He just felt the weight of this land in his guts. His land. He resented his status, but he had no idea how it could be otherwise. He wanted to keep his stone gods because all that these men with rotting teeth were offering him was pain and terrible things before the mercy of some force that never showed its face. It wasn't just new, it was nonsense. A god could only bring good or bad on you here and now. Not some other time. Not some other place. Matahi and his fellow men were bent on hanging on to this ignorance the white man claimed they had. What they felt, really, was pride at being first, native, discoverers of this whole place. What they knew, really, was that their islands, the futures they were diving right into would be full of devilry from then on. Never any rest, any respite. Vaita, the first prophet, the visionary, had foretold: In one or two or three centuries the earth will be despoiled, the oceans emptied out, desecrated forever. And their children tormented and lost for having forgotten the very name of the moon that saw their birth. Shorn of their memory. Stupefied by abhorrent, foreign beliefs, they will wander, orphaned from the breast and the placenta that nourished them.

War would come no matter what. Matahi was the village chief then, a man who stood more than two meters tall, stout with a massive chest and shoulders nobody, not even his wife when she wanted to heap her love on him, ever managed to reach all the way around. Hands and arms were too fragile, too human to ever make a man like Matahi bend.

The behemoth had already gone nose to nose with the French and their interpreters again and again. He'd shaken his head no a hundred times, and each time the French came back on their boats, weapons in hand. One day, he finally saw that there was no holding France off for good. And so he met with the old enemies, the chiefs of the other villages. The white men had cannons while they had spears, their bodies, and their beliefs. They didn't blink twice at ultimatums. Thus began the war, a war that lasted years. It was from this mountaintop that Matahi and the others had kept on fighting. The blood had poured on both sides.

One day, Matahi and the sturdiest men had come down to the beach, where they came across those pale young soldiers, the sort who got sent off for every war without the faintest idea of why they'd been put there. Raiatea's men were bent on finishing them off, set on fighting like true warriors, in plain view, no cowardly ambushes tainting their victories. Matahi, standing two meters tall, held a spear. As he came down there was a silence as when one's time has come, when death is near and sure. The warriors from another era now faced off against soldiers who thought fighting against natives couldn't be hard work. But, long or short, remote or not, all wars spare no soul; all wars are the same; all wars are unfair because all wars end in suffering, tears, the gaping void of lives that ought to have gone on. A boy all of seventeen years old was in front of Matahi. He looked like a drawing, golden ringlets and a face as pink as a baby's. This boy had set foot on these shores thinking that this New Cythera had to be as pretty and sweet as in his dreams. He'd enlisted and set sail because he believed that down there, peace and love alone steered men's hearts. But that was a lie, even the farthest-off islands held fury and violence to protect what they held most dear. The young man was shivering. For a slice of paradise, he would die. Matahi looked every bit a god or maybe the devil, as if there were any difference. The boy was their best marksman. A single, quick, clean shot, then a second, then a third . . . Under the bullets, the behemoth kept walking, getting closer and closer. The soldier saw a Matahi driven by the wind, driven by a hellish halo. They were there, the two of them, their two gazes could have become one, their fears fused together, the one in the other. Under Matahi's hands, the young man's bones cracked, without any trouble, without any sound. He wasn't even twenty . . .

The French soldiers shot as one, but there was no stopping Matahi. Gunshots came by the dozen, by the hundred, but there was no felling Matahi. He walked on, the others pulled back, they wouldn't stop shooting and still there was no felling Matahi. His fellow men were dead. Matahi had killed dozens of soldiers. Bullets were nothing to him, nothing more than flyspecks . . . He walked on, stronger than ever. He'd never been so sure of his strength. The bullets were almost laughable. In his language, he cursed the whites, their world, their bloodlines for generations and generations. Then a bayonet went through his heart. Just a bayonet. Matahi fell, bringing down with him these strangers, these men with strange thoughts. Bringing down torrents of tears from mothers and widows at the other end of the world.

There's precious few scars of this war now. Where words were once hushed, silence has settled. Except in Auguste's family. Now a song tells of Matahi. A song the old men sometimes chant, like a dirge. A song of courage cut down in its prime. Setting a beat to the memory of a glorious past for posterity. And because France never spoke of it again, because schoolteachers wouldn't ever bring themselves to tell of it, this song of Matahi goes on. This song alone. This personal, painful song. This song and nothing more telling of the sadness of a scorched earth.

Auguste's father was all of four years old when Matahi died. He could remember every last bit of it. His famous grandfather borne back on the shoulders of twenty men. The courage that the French soldiers had paid their respects to by kneeling when it was time for the natives to surrender. He remembered the women's tears, their scarred-up faces. The broken looks on these men who'd never go to war again. In his head he could still see a time that wasn't so much lost as stolen . . . And Matahi's sons took French names, all of them, from then on. They let those whites, those civil servants, those morons do it. It was a small thing, so they let them do it. It meant so little. Easier to get things done that way, taking a French first name so they'd leave them alone, no matter how that broke their hearts.

When Auguste's father and his sons got to the plot of land at long last, they all sat down and the father took out some dark tobacco that the older sons were only to try well out of their mother's sight. Then they set to work. Clearing the ground, replanting, harvesting taro, fē'i bananas that had ripened. Sometimes the father left his sons to their work and headed for the old village, Matahi's corner. These days it was a hideaway of sorts where Auguste often got some fresh air . . . In the village, in the fields the days were all the same, hard going, a man's work, and only sometimes pleasant.

Life was simple back then. People worked to eat, not to have. Even coffee couldn't be bought, it just had to be made. Kids were meant to go to school, but Auguste had never been. It was only because of Protestants and educated pastors that he and his brothers could read or write a thing.

Life went by, of course. The boys grew up, the father and the mother got old. Then, one day, Auguste fell in love. He was just sixteen and just out of childhood. Of course, once he'd turned eleven, he'd been subincised, and with that rite he could now have sexual relations. But it wasn't until Auguste was sixteen that he met girls, or rather just one girl. Shyness, probably, was what kept him from going any farther than those daydreams of his, those lonely fantasies. Auguste wasn't like his brothers, he'd always been quiet, and girls . . . well, a railroad had to cross the island at long last for something to actually happen . . .

His first was Mata. His own cousin, the daughter of his mother's sister. Mata lived with her parents at the other end of the island. In the village, and even in Auguste's house, it wasn't quite clear what had kept the two families from seeing each other more often. Maybe it was a secret . . . It had to be a family secret. One of those things left unsaid that nobody was quite sure how or why so. He only had to see his mother with her sister to know that the two were uneasy together, that he'd get no straight answer as to why these sisters wouldn't ever be close. Between the two of them it was icy, downright frigid and it was a relief for so much distance to allow them to forget about it all.

One morning, Auguste, all of sixteen years old, went with his mother to the village where the family they scarcely ever saw, saw only at funerals, lived. For no clear reason that anyone could say, he was to go with his mother. The village wasn't big. A teensy harbor for the schooners just beginning to ferry goods from Tahiti. It was Auguste's first time, his first gander at another life, another sort of life. It was how he learned of businesses, people from China, men with narrow eyes. It was almost too much. That morning, after his father's canoe had set them down on a shaky wharf, Auguste saw how there was far too much time in between him and here. He didn't have the faintest idea of how intent his father was, how iron his will was when it came to protecting his sons from that place. And yet, what he learned there was nothing compared to Tahiti, which was starting to become *the* capital. On the quay, his mother was in a hurry, her head scrunched down by her shoulders. She was moving so fast that it looked as if she were in a desert where Satan had gathered together all the world's temptations. The depots that morning were all hustle and bustle. Every morning he got the copra ready for a man from the village to come pick up, and now he saw that this was where it ended up.

He also saw men with bare chests caked in black grease from the heavy jute bags they lugged to the outgoing ships. At the entrance to a hangar facing the sea, a white man with a fat gut and a filthy face was watching these men and spitting out what sounded like orders. It was nice out, the sun so fierce it just about cut.

It was there that Auguste came into the real world. A world that he could tell was unfair, where men, those of his race, of his land, were never to be masters again, not even of themselves. A world that heaped contempt and humiliation on them. Auguste had no idea that anyone's back could be bent this low, that anyone's head could bow this deep, that anyone could lie to themselves this much that they were just passing through, that the orders they were obeying weren't really orders after all. He'd never heard people talk this way. Even his father's words, when he caught one of his sons making a mistake, were words he could respect. Even his father's anger, when he was all fire and fury, still had some love in it. There was no calling that white man human, not when the other men were scared of him. When Auguste's father talked about those people, it was with white heat. And so scorn stirred in his son's heart right there and then, all the worse for having been lulled by so many years of sleep. Auguste walked up and the white man yelled that there was no more room, "No more room, you hear me?" And the younger man kept on walking, sure of himself, sure that he would be all right. He might as well not have heard him. The light and the heat stoked the fire and fury that had been lit almost a hundred years before, that had made Matahi act. In the name of his people, in the name of his land, Auguste's fist clenched and punched the man's face with all the strength he had. The white man crumpled, weak and quiet all of a sudden. The dockworkers all rushed up, eyes full of thanks and smiles stretching their faces. But the fury was still there. It wasn't just this stranger that had the young Auguste raving mad. It was an unthinkable thing, as unthinkable as a Jew turned anti-Semite. Hating his kind, his fellow men. There was so much against them, and here he was hating his own people . . . He talked in Tahitian as he aimed his fury at these men who were all skin and bones, starved of other places, other ways of living, soon to be starved of booze as well. They pulled back, growing even smaller, and let Auguste go off. He was grown-up now, maybe even a king. His mother was waiting for him off a ways, on the street, by a pathetic, filthy market. She didn't say a word.

They'd sat down at the only restaurant in town, by the water, and a short Chinese man served them food while hawking his wares. Some dresses hung from a light-green wall. Those dresses with floral patterns that got unthinkably narrow at the waist and they were meant to show the knees of those wearing them. Auguste's mother ran a eye over them, looking shocked then downright ill. She herself was wearing a big dark dress that came down to her ankles and covered her neck and arms. If she hadn't been so dark-skinned, she could have passed for the wife or daughter of one of those Southern

Baptist preachers. But she was dark-skinned, almost black, and this dress, which was like a heavy flag on her that she loved all the same, amounted to the last memory she had of her father who'd converted to Christianity when he was little.

For Auguste, there was something mysterious about this day. The shock of discovering another world, his fiery hand that still hurt, and now his mother so quiet it seemed on purpose . . . He wasn't sure what to think anymore, but he knew it was hot, stifling hot, and the clouds were a gray wall on the horizon.

Flies started flitting around them and one of them, the biggest one, landed on the rim of his yellowed bowl. He didn't bother to swat at it; it was almost a nice distraction. His head was hunched forward, his eyes caught two shadows getting close. Women. Thin ones, he could tell, maybe even agreeable ones. One of them seemed smaller but just as thin.

The taller one was his aunt Clara, the youngest of his mother's sisters. And the other was his cousin Mata. Auguste reckoned there was some hurry in his mother's voice, as if the introductions were dragging on, and they'd forgotten to get to the point. The mother and the daughter were each wearing one of those dresses hanging on the wall that had made his mother nearly furious. He had a vague recollection of his aunt now. She'd always looked elegant. And one day she'd come to their house along with a tall man with a thick red mustache that looked like sunburn. But weren't memories always shaky, shapeless things that could be colored and recolored by however matters stood now? So, yes, he recalled her and maybe it was this day and this heat and this weather turning stormy that had him thinking how he'd always found this woman to be pretty, even if that was questionable, even if her perfume was so sweet and so strong as to be a distraction. Of course his aunt was saying he'd grown so much, even if deep down she couldn't be sure she'd ever even known of him. She had lipstick on, and sea-green powder slathered on her eyelids . . .

Mata stood by Clara, acting all shy with her arms behind her. She had to be fifteen. No older. Her skin was coppered and her hair was a bit light. Anyone with eyes could see she was mixed. Auguste had never laid eyes on someone like her before, but the guys around him were always calling those "half-and-half" girls the most beautiful ones in the world. To them in the valleys, they were real, living myths. It was a rule that mixed women were the most beautiful ones. They were Hydras. Beings to be feared, beings that would swarm your nights. They weren't from elsewhere, from that strange world none of them would ever touch, but they weren't exactly from here either. Mata was Tahitian for eyes. He could almost feel her breath, her stare that showed that, actually, she knew what she was, she knew what secrets she'd never share. She smiled and that shook him. He couldn't put his finger on why.

Mata's mother told the two of them to go and let the women talk, and she handed her daughter a ten-franc bill.

They walked awhile and ended up in a building off one of the hangars. And that was where Auguste did the deed. The schooner bound for Tahiti and the entire quay were empty, stock-still. It was raining. The old building was where things the local government didn't need anymore went: documents, Bastille Day flags . . . Mata didn't bother to talk, let alone pretend, while she undressed him, got him hard, kissed him. Later on, with some years' distance, he wondered which of the two of them had had the idea first, or the desire.

She'd done this before. She knew what she was doing. She knew her own body, and his. She knew the noises, the wheezes, the words, what they meant. He let himself be led and the movements, the motion, suddenly became almost natural, like waves ebbing and flowing, like the sun's path through the sky. That day, Auguste's childhood died two times over. Auguste heard himself breathing, the girl gasping. He saw her closed eyes, her smiling lips. She was beautiful, she was there, this mixed-blood stranger, and he took her. For the rest of his life, he would remember his first time. The way everyone else did. But for long after this first time would have something taboo, something unfinished about it.

By the time they heard men's voices getting close to the building, too close, it was too late. Two city hall workers were talking about a woman from the next town over who'd left the island for Tahiti, just like that, for no reason, which meant her eight children were at their aunt's now and her husband had tried to hang himself. Auguste couldn't stop or do a thing. Pleasure had gotten the better of him, deep-rooted, fiery, bullheaded pleasure. The old door groaned and opened. Auguste wasn't able to do a thing. If he could have killed her, killed them all, he would have. The young man's bare body was hunched above Mata's sweaty belly. His arms outstretched, his hands flat on the ground, his torso bent, his buttocks clenched, and he felt their eyes, heard their quiet, sensed their shock, their disgust, maybe even their lust. For long after he would recall that afternoon and how humiliated he felt, Mata begging him to keep going. Him stock-still even as his penis swelled, getting closer and closer to the point of no return. And she was rolling her hips. Because she didn't know, or maybe she did, maybe she knew she was being watched and maybe she even liked it. Auguste would have almost bet she did. He hated her, she wasn't so beautiful anymore. With her eyes screwed shut, she wasn't any different from a dog. Vile: it was her fault, it was because of her. She had no right to look like that, gone and no longer there. It all happened so fast. He felt like he couldn't go all the way, that it wasn't worth even thinking about anymore. His first time wouldn't even end right. She was frozen in the harsh air of an outbuilding full of papers and useless things. Mata, the beautiful girl. Mata, who was a slut now. Auguste felt so small, so weak, so wronged. And maybe that was why, later, when he was with other women, Auguste never was able to take his time, the time he should have allowed for pleasure. Loving became a matter of hurrying up, just so he could come as quick as he could. He didn't care: it was his revenge for that first time that had saddled him with a sharp pain in his belly.

Of course, that afternoon, when his mother and he got back to their house, Auguste got the thrashing of his life. Once the young man's mouth was full of blood, once his eyes were so swollen they stayed shut without his trying, his father bound him for a full day and night to a coconut tree. The knots were so tight that there was no wriggling free. His mother and even his brothers actually felt sorry for him. But his father's fury had no end to it. For twenty-four hours, the father had watched over his son bound up there, his head dangling like a Christ on the cross. Nobody was to get close or bring him water or food, the midday sun bore down on him and yet the father remained there, unshakable. Auguste dreamed, hallucinated. He saw the valley's waterfalls, imagined himself drowning in them. He saw food, fish, pork, all prepared for feast days. His father smoked his tobacco, still as could be, showing no hate or warmth. Sometimes he sharpened his machete, mended his old fishing nets. Twenty-four hours of this face-off where the father didn't have to say a word to scold him for all of this, for his stupidity. Auguste was left to wonder whether his mistake had been sleeping with his cousin or rather daring to touch the body of a girl from the other shore. Both, probably. Or was it that the father couldn't accept his boys no longer being virgins, having known love or sex? That had to have him seething, this old man who'd gotten married at sixteen and who'd only ever known his wife.

And when his mother came up nice and quiet, when she started sobbing and pleading, the father slapped her. Auguste didn't see, he only let himself listen and maybe that was worse.

❖

From that day on, things were different. As if madness, idiocy, acts and deeds that had no rhyme or reason to them were a lead weight on Auguste's house now. Nobody talked much anymore and the sons wouldn't set foot in church anymore, to the father's great shame. And the mother wouldn't do a thing, or just about, anymore. She wouldn't cook or clean. It was as if she'd quit all on her own. Two of her children put to sea one morning without any warning, without a single word. Now there were only three boys living with two old people who barely talked anymore. Their father hollered about wimps, wusses, weaklings. As if the two older sons had up and gone with all the family's strength and muscles and more. It wouldn't be long before Auguste headed off as well, but he didn't dare to just yet, as if he were scared that so many men having gone might be the end of his mother. Of the men who'd stayed, one was the weakest. He'd come right before Auguste, and in his features, his whole body, there was something graceful, something fragile. When he was fourteen, people started saying that something was off about him. He cared how he looked, spent hours at the river and washed three times a day. Even in the fields, he never missed a chance to go over to a small waterway further down. Tongues were starting to wag. An odd duck, that one. He sought out girls, but never to sleep with them. Just to look at them for a long while and think. Sometimes the girls themselves straightened their backs when he said they ought to stand just so or put a flower in their hair. An odd one, him. At fifteen, people (again, because all any village has is people) noticed that he always had a hand on a hip and that this hip was tilted up just a little, which made it look like he was limping. But it was actually to show off how his butt moved when he started swaying it like a girl's. Their father stopped talking to him. When he wanted to talk to the boy, he said "you," but in Tahitian, he only used the plural *you*, as if the boy wasn't worth singling out. The graceful brother didn't make anything of it. He let his father's looks go and always went off to find the girls he was friends with or asked his mother what she wanted. Ever since the only woman in the house stopped doing any work, he was the one who'd tended to the house. Before long he decided to take over for her and that was a relief for the father who'd be spared this "thing" in the fields.

And Auguste's other brother didn't have it any better. He wasn't much of a talker because he had a lisp. But he was still strong, and he had both his arms. All the same, his troubles with words were enough for neighbors to make fun of him too.

Now and then, Auguste got to thinking about Mata and about the pain he'd felt in his belly. He was getting older. His work in the fields was digging cracks and grooves and worry lines into his face. There were only the two of them, and hectares on hectares . . . For some time now, the father had done nothing but watch them dig, turning the earth, and then he'd go and settle in Matahi's old refuge. One morning, Auguste saw the man talk to a stone statue, a thing from yore. Nobody had any idea where it had come from, who had lugged it there. He saw his own father another time making some sort of offering to the stone that was meant to be a stocky man's body. A queer sight for a man who was Protestant, who had no taste for icons, forbidden images. A queer sight for a man who'd prayed to God Almighty to offer flowers and food to an unmoving thing. One thing was sure: his family was losing all reason, all self-restraint, all who-knew-what.

The last picture he had in his head of his parents was one he'd never, never put words to. Not even to Ma, the woman he loved. None of his brothers had ever talked about it because they'd never laid eyes on one another ever again. It was a Monday at dusk. Just as night was falling. He only remembered it being a Monday because the next day he took the tiny boat to Papeete. There was just one boat, and it only came on Tuesdays. That dusk, when he and his brother had come back to the house, after a too-hot day in the mountains, it was far too dark. Neither the mother nor the father had thought to light the kerosene lamps. They didn't hear a single thing, didn't smell a single bit of food. Their brother who looked like a girl had left for a day to go to the next town over and help with the Protestant assembly that was starting on Sunday. They weren't worried until they got to the kitchen and noticed the buzz of swarming flies. There had to be hundreds, at least, because their sound was dizzying—or maybe it was the smell. Harsh and unearthly. A smell that made you think that it was the end. Which it was. The end. The older brother, maybe having mustered some courage or maybe just not thinking, finally went and lit a lamp. He groped his way through the dark house. And in that time, Auguste's eyes accustomed themselves to the dimness. Enough that after a minute he could make out, not far from his own bed, a body on the ground, huddled up like a ball. The flies' buzz came from there. Then, on his bed, sitting and rocking back and forth, was another shape. Little by little, he started to make out another song, a more human one that was like a funeral song. Mixed in with the insects' roar, a voice that wasn't really a voice, chanting words ever so quietly. Chanting words he couldn't understand. To Auguste's left the weak light grew. Auguste tried to say no, to say, "Don't come here. Stay where you are," but the thought stayed put inside his head, a thought he couldn't set free on his tongue. And the light got closer and young Auguste could feel his guts clench and twist and hurt. He could have run, fled, but he didn't. It wasn't time. Everything was rising up, the lunch he hadn't eaten, hot liquid bubbling in his stomach. Then his brother let out a scream and set the lamp on a table nearby. Right then, Auguste wondered what devilry had set the lamp down there just so. If his brother had let go of the light in shock, that would have been better. But the devil knew what he wanted, and it was for him to lay eyes on that. Then it all came rising up and out. For several minutes he vomited. Spewing out his meal, his whole body.

Their father had to have been dead since that morning, and it was starting to smell something awful. It was February, the hottest part of the year. And their mother was rocking like a madwoman. The old man was soaked in his blood and when Auguste's brother turned him over, his face full of tears, they saw a machete blade sunk into his throat, nice and deep. And right then, as their father's limp head bent farther back, the blade dug in with a horrid noise. A machete through the throat was something done only to pigs. Their mother had to have believed she'd married a pig. She was sobbing a bit, she'd clearly lost her mind. She was lost, or gone. She'd completely lost her head and now even as she carried on crying she was giggling. Only lunatics could be like that.

The whole town turned up. The stronger-stomached men and women cleaned everything. Auguste didn't take any of it in, he just watched people at a loss for words moving this way and that through a mist. He couldn't make any sense of it and that gave him some distance from the hurt, from this pain. The next day, he collected the few clothes he had while the village council ruled on the previous night. Just before he left the house, an old man told Auguste that everyone would keep the secret. And they would look after his mother and his two brothers. No police, no white-man justice. And they would be burning the house down too. Better that way. The old lady was still rocking back and forth. She was saying things nobody wanted to hear: "pig," "devil," "Satan worshipper." Auguste thought back on Matahi, on the ti'i stone carvings, on their old father and the new thoughts he'd gotten in his head. He was bone-tired. He went to the Raiatea harbor at the other end of the island. He was going to leave and put it all out of his head.

Months later he decided he was in love with the girl who'd become Ma. And there was one other thing about her. It was her eyes and head that made her look proud, never mind how young she'd looked the first time he saw her. Or maybe it was exactly that, her youth . . . Of course he'd lied to Ma about the whole thing. He'd told her that his mother had died two days after his father. It wasn't far from the truth, she was as good as dead, she'd lost her mind, and going crazy is one way of dying.

Home Again

WE HAD TO GO BACK HOME. He'd gotten better. School was starting again in a few days. Auguste still wasn't talking because they'd stuck iron rods in his mouth. He could walk now, but it wasn't easy. Still, the doctors felt that he'd been in the hospital for long enough. Maybe it was that it would have gotten to be too much if he'd stayed longer. I never let myself dwell on how much it had to cost but I figure when you're poor you don't pay for those things. That would be best . . . Rosa came back too. It was Ma who asked her to, one night when we were all together. It was just a week after Papa woke up. It was the first time we were together as a family and when Ma told us, the night before, that made it sound serious, important, mind-boggling. We'd all be sitting calmly around a table and Ma would be talking like a chairwoman, like a wise head of the family. So, the morning of the council, we left Tiarei. Poe and Teanuanua drove us because they'd be there too. When I walked into my old bedroom, I started to cry a little, just to myself. I missed them already. Shit. I said shit. It was too much. Of course nobody saw how sad I was. I just thought . . . I loved them so much now. Nobody should get attached like that because sooner or later they have to go, unless we're the ones to leave. Life is strange like that, but more than anything it's unfair.

❖

The car went down the coast like one of those old little boats, and my aunt gave me the saddest and strangest "keep safe" I'd ever heard. Feelings like that, sadnesses like that that don't say their name, loneliness and heaviness like this shouldn't ever exist.

So Papa was home now. He was in a wheelchair most of the time, except for when the physical therapist came to see him here. The two of them held hands for a few exercises. Not too hard at first because Auguste had to learn everything again, bit by bit. The physical therapist said that at the hospital, our father had been doing a good job. He'd outdone himself one morning, managed to go a short way with no help, but it had taken so much out of him that he'd collapsed. It had scared them all. Then, for the rest of the morning, he'd stayed put in bed, his head facing the ceiling and his eyes staring off. He didn't seem to hear a thing, none of the doctors' orders, none of nice nurses' requests. Not a thing. He'd gone limp and sometimes his eyes fixed on invisible things. His mind was somewhere else.

Strange Love

DOWN A WAYS, in the river, the children were playing. With this sun, he imagined how nice the water had to be. As he lay in bed, all Auguste could do was listen and imagine. In his head and his mouth was silence. No more words, no more speech. When Ma came in, it felt like she was intruding, just coming in so she could . . . he wasn't sure . . . spy on him, maybe. It bothered him. This woman he'd loved, wanted a hundred times over. This body that had heft to it, a mind of its own, that sometimes got hard when she wasn't interested . . . but never for long. This woman, this warmth that he felt and that ate at his guts, was a stranger now. Too pretty, and maybe too lost. Like Mata, maybe. Like all the women he'd never been able to go all the way with . . .

She'd just come in, clean laundry all folded and heaped up in her arms, a glimmer of a smile on her lips that had plenty of color to them. Well, what was she thinking about? The smile was a funny one, like she was happy all of a sudden. Whore. She was hurting him out of love. She, this pretty Ma, this mother, this wife, was slipping out of his hands. In her head she was already good as gone. She wasn't there anymore. She needed to stay here. Yes, Auguste still loved her, he loved her and that ate at him. She went to the armoire with its mirror cracked here and there. She opened it, got down, her rump

on display. There was something obscene, dishonest about her little
ass. Oh, Auguste! Look closer, she's different now. She's thrown out
those bras that were falling apart, gotten new ones padded with a
little lace. And her body looks stronger now. She's got a tiny dress on
with spaghetti straps, it fits her perfectly. It's got his head aching, got
him wanting to puke. And the purple dress swirls around. Dizzying.
"Auguste, remember this dress, it looks a bit like the other one, the
one that almost did your mother in that morning on the Raiatea
quay. Think about it, it does. Remember now?" But where did she get
the money for it? "Auguste, listen to that voice in yourself!"

Ma turned her back on him, pulled a few clothes off a sagging
shelf.

She was singing now. My god. "Auguste, listen to her. There's
something off about her voice. Too much happiness that you don't
know the first thing about. It's mad, it's too much, doesn't it remind
you of . . . Yes, that thing your mother was singing, yes, her again.
That night when you discovered that filth, that hell and when you
did your best to forget it all right away. But there's no forgetting that.
Memory is the strongest, the worst, the sneakiest, the most unfaith-
ful woman of all. It'll lie low for ten years, twenty years, and then one
day it shows its face again, it hollers, and everything comes crashing
down."

"No. Stop it, Ma. Stop all that music."

Auguste reached down deep for strength, there was this horrible
need to off her, to have her, because she was his, wasn't she? Yes, she
was Auguste's, and she would be his forever. No ifs, ands, or buts
about it. It was all he had. He pushed her against the mirror cracked
here and there. Boxed her in. Then he pushed himself in her, she
couldn't see, she had her back to him. A pain that was fire. Ma's dry
vagina. Painful for them both. My god. Auguste was strong, brutal,
fervent. Marriage meant accepting everything about the other. "You
have to obey, Ma. It's not going to kill you, not really. Move your

hips a bit, yes, like that, that's better for you, Ma. Take it and do
what's best for you. It's not the end of the world, it actually tastes
a bit bitter like a vagina that's gotten what it needs. Maybe that's
not true, but act like it is. That's what being a woman is. That's what
being Auguste's wife is." She heard his groaning, it reminded her of
so many bad things. How was it that the accident hadn't broken him,
broken that member that he was so proud of? That thing only knew
how to be hard, had no idea of how to be gentle or slow. He'd never
change. In ten years, twenty years, he'd be a bit tired, but he'd keep
thinking with it. His life, his body, his thoughts would still all sum to
his member, to the pain it inflicted, from his core to his piss slit, to
the very end of himself. A hard life softened only by sex and drink.

Ma was swishing the spoon in a pan full of sauce. Somehow she'd
saved a handful of beef from dinner the night before, and now she
was adding a bit of tomato to the ragout to take out the lumps. With
a nice bit of rice, that might do the trick. Yes: pour as much sauce as
you like over the rice. That'd tide them over. The kids were all over
the kitchen, little Moïra couldn't stay put and Pina was running after
her. What a racket. Moïra was whining, she was starving. The sickly
sweet bottles of Nestlé baby formula weren't enough for her. Ma had
been slaving for hours over this dish that wasn't really a dish. She
needed to cast her thoughts on something else. To stop thinking
about Auguste, about any of that. What if the kids had come back
from the river early? She'd been doing her best to be a better woman.
To stop hating her husband. To love Auguste because he'd come back
to life. She'd gone and given this man a smile even though he was
dead inside. Her eyes were stinging. It had nothing to do with the
heat from the old oven. Moïra was crying, she was just plain hungry. Pina and Pauro had set the table without a word. Ma looked at
them and felt some tenderness. They seemed so grown-up. Young
but thinking about grown-up things. They were so beautiful, the two

of them. She kept her eyes on them so as not to think. She'd worry later. Pauro went to check on his father. They'd been waiting for Rosa to come back from next door. Ma came in and looked Auguste over. Both the quiet and those eyes that never looked away had something cold, something steely about them. Not bad blood. That would be too easy. No, what that quiet and those eyes had about them was something downright inhuman. Ma said grace as Pina started feeding the baby. Auguste Junior had gotten home an hour ago and showered, which was a relief to his mother.

Hannah's Life

THIS STORY COULD ALSO go across the world, all the way to the
other end. Why not, really? It could go flying through the sky and
it could touch down there, in that land some people actually call the
motherland, in that land of books that not Ma nor Pina nor Auguste
nor the pastor, not a person in all Tenaho had ever heard talk of.
France, that big old fancy country? They don't give a fig about it.
They know Frenchmen, the métros who live here, but what do they
care about that land of light . . . All the same one of their own's been
squirreled away there for eight years now. Hannah T., the daughter
of Ma and Auguste. And those pigs there call her a completely different name, they write it their own way. Two *n*'s and two *h*'s, one at
the beginning and one at the end, if you please. Two *h*'s facing off,
holding off the masses. Only numbskulls would write "Ana"! Hannah. It was Ma who found this name, one day as she was walking
past Papeete's very first bookstore. Of course Ma didn't know the
first thing about Hannah Arendt. About the banality of evil, about
Eichmann, not a thing about the war. It was just that *The Origins of
Totalitarianism* had caught her eye. Beside the book standing all by
its lonesome in the display window was a photo of some German
woman with an oddly beautiful, sweet face. On that day, Ma was
waddling over to the Papeete market, her stomach full to bursting

and her feet feeling like heavy things. And neither she nor Auguste had picked out a name yet. So that worked out. She went into this store that was too bright, too clean, too European, and asked for a pen from the doddering woman at the register whose stare showed just how old and clueless she was. Ma copied down this first name that made her think of beauty and tenderness, on the palm of her hand, and thus begins the story of the name of Hannah T., a Tahitian girl who was the daughter of nothing at all.

Just another Friday night in one of Épinay-sur-Seine's grungy slums, not far from Enghien-les-Bains with its casino and its oh-so-pretty lake that nobody but her must be able to see was filthy and ugly brown. She looked through that window every bit as grubby and grimy as the building she lived in. She could clean it, pane by pane, but why bother? Four years she'd been living there, and the pigeons had kept on coming and doing their business on her balcony, the upstairs neighbors had kept on tossing out their leftovers that always landed on the windshield of her car down below or on the teensy porthole of her kitchen, for no good reason, just to be petty, a pain. Four years of this—she could clean and clean, it didn't matter. What mattered was not getting raped in the stairwell that, how nice, didn't have a single light bulb. What mattered was not getting killed or beaten up because she was a single woman. What mattered was staying alive . . . Just another Friday night, like a hundred others: her on her fifth screwdriver, listening to a LP of treacly-voiced Tahitian singers from the fifties, mawkish lyrics backed by a so-called orchestra of white-boy jazz. Whether or not that counted for "local," it was nice enough, it got her plenty teary, and she'd played it a thousand times. Just another weekend night with her drinking herself to death, thinking about her country, her island, her whole family that she couldn't stand. Just another night pouting at the clubs, the same old thing, just to land herself some big strong guy with no brain. That was the life she was living.

It was early September, it was nice out, she was back from seeing her Tahitian friend in Cap d'Agde. They'd met each other back in Paris the one time that Hannah had gone to the Foyer des étudiants polynésiens. They'd been thick as thieves ever since, until her friend moved down south with some sales rep. Her guy barely ever said a word but her friend was still calling him "my sweetheart"—ugh!— never mind that she cheated on him every chance she got. For Hannah, Cap d'Agde had just been days watching her friend's two little urchins and nights on the beach not far from some nudist camp. She'd seen orgies on the beach, hadn't let herself get pulled into what she figured had to be a mess, hadn't met any interesting guys, and in no time all she wanted was get back to her shitty old neighborhood, even if that meant all the beach she'd be seeing would be the packed Aquaboulevard water park by the Porte de Versailles.

There wasn't much to say about her vacation, and there was even less to say about her life. Twenty-five years old, a heart broken too many times already, a body hurting all over from too much love-making with no love in it, a future that she'd once figured would be shining, extraordinary, but now figured was just as numb and lifeless as the towers all around these parts. Those dreams of hers were a shambles worth less and less each day, just pathetic paychecks that her business degree hadn't helped much with. Her life and the capital weren't all that different. When she'd first come to Paris, she'd lived within the city itself. Months and years had gone by, and her income had pushed her out to the banlieue. The poorer you are, the farther out you go. And that was her to a T, even if she never dared think it to herself. Every so often she took a look at her life, felt an urge to give it all up and start over again somewhere else, but she always stopped herself, sometimes even before getting started. She couldn't stand those "professional evaluations," that good old "self-improvement." Only people with no memory or a real love of pain ever enjoyed those. It was horrific.

❖

A new track, the saddest one. Another love song. Her head was starting to spin: time to get up, get ready. Another shower to freshen up.
Her limbs felt light and powerful somehow. Of course she couldn't
see she was stumbling. If ever there was a day when she might be
floating on a cloud, like the little Heidi of her memories, she'd feel
exactly the way she did right now. Airy, free. She liked that about
alcohol, the bitter taste of vodka: sometimes it let her recall being
a child, recollect a stretch of time and how much nicer it was, let
her feel strong. No worries holding her back now; liquor let her feel
pretty. She wasn't about to go out looking for a guy, but she already
knew that she'd wake up the next morning in a man's bed.

Her hair was sopping wet, she didn't bother to dry it as she sat
down at her mirror. She wasn't ugly, she was all of twenty-five, but
she looked older. She'd always looked older. One night, an old man
just back from vacation in Tahiti had wanted to take her home
and bed her. They'd been at one of those tiki bars in Montmar-
tre. He'd gotten it into his head that it was a good idea to call her
features especially delicate for a Tahitian woman. He'd figured that
would make her smile, she'd jump into his lumpy arms and maybe
even offer him that hand that was covered in small brown freckles.
Didn't she have such delicate features, compared to all those lazy
vahine, really, there wasn't a single pretty skinny mother to be found
anywhere in Tahiti . . . With those words a mean little smirk came
over her and her eyes got narrow. She took her left hand, grabbed
that limp flabby ball sack of his, and squeezed hard. What business did he have yapping like that about women from the place she
called home? She didn't like the sound of that. He'd been doing
so well, charming her, and now he'd gone and disappointed her.
No, no, she told him, Tahiti is just like any other place. It's got its
share of ugly people, and beautiful people too. Maybe he shouldn't
wait around for mermaids to come and stroke his lecherous old

dick. She had her sixth drink in her hand, and her new black dress hugged her ass and her boobs just so. Now those really were some "delicate features"...

Mohamed gave her a little smile as he said good night. It was the same every time, this way he tried to be friendly. Yes, he was her favorite cab driver, she had his personal number, she had him come and pick her up in Épinay every Friday, but all the same Hannah liked some distance. He wasn't someone she'd get drinks with on the patio at Le Soleil in Ménilmontant. She wasn't racist or anything. She just didn't like the way he looked at her. Shameless. She let herself think about calling the Paris taxis next Friday. Always quiet, those drivers, they only glanced back through the rearview mirror, good and distant and professional and nothing more.

Sure enough, the bar was packed. All the regulars were back from vacation. The owner had spent two weeks in "Ta-hi-ti" and insisted they had been "ma-gni-fiques." Her face looked ghastly. She was too tan. Her skin was just about orange and her hair so blonde it made her look like one of those nipped and tucked Saint-Tropez hookers. All those ladies with fake tans and fake flowers stuck in their greased-up hair. What a joke. Maybe in an hour she'd get out and go on down into Ménilmontant. To Le Soleil or Lou Pascalou or maybe all the way out to Saint-Germain, who knew.

"Oh, sweetie, it's been ages!"

Two kisses, a *mwah* on each cheek.

"Now tell me what you've been up to all this summer!"

Always the same questions, always the same nonsense.

"Oh, I went down south, it was great." She rolled her eyes: only an idiot would think the south was great.

"Fabulous! And what can I get you?"

"The usual, vodka ..."

The owner had gotten a bit older. Among this little gaggle of Polynesians in Paris, rumor had it that she was going out with a musician, Polynesian of course, right in front of her old husband. She really was head over heels, but that new boyfriend of hers was a womanizer, going through ladies at all hours of the day and the night. The sort of guy who made your hair go gray overnight.

A little Paris-style tāmūre number came on. The dance floor was already plenty tiny, and now it was overrun. Hannah got closer to the door. The song was still playing in her head, she felt light, euphoric, good. Now she could cozy up to the bar and soon her umpteenth glass would be half empty. Damn it. A dozen euros for this round. That old hen running the place was going to be one happy bird. Twelve euros for a vodka, thirty for the cab, the drinks that she'd just end up ordering more of, or that would be sent her way, wouldn't that be nice. And then the bill would turn up, never a pretty sight. It wasn't that she was broke, it was that she had to keep her wits about her. And, honestly, couldn't the bartender have given her a drink on the house, a little welcome-back thing? Ha! They could cheek kiss all they liked but of course the two women didn't actually care about each other. It came down to some old argument they couldn't remember a thing about—at least that was what the older woman had decided. Anyone could see she'd noticed that her lover was drooling over Hannah. But she didn't get that he wasn't Hannah's type. So all the owner really wanted was for Hannah to call a cab.

Oh look, that Marquesan girl's turned up. Taia. She's a bit distant. "How are you?" Taia's answer has a giggle to it: "Same as always." She's always giggling like an idiot. Even when it's no laughing matter. Or maybe she's always getting tickled. Hannah has nothing to say back, she turns to her drink. She sure could use another one. She was just thinking about how she doesn't really have any friends, how other girls don't seem to like her much. That's just how it is. She

doesn't have friends to go to the movies with, not counting Anna-
belle, the one down south, and of course she doesn't count. Not when
they're so far apart. In front of her is a huge mirror and rows and
rows of bottles. Just like in every other bar, nothing special there. It's
all reeling a bit, the music's sucking her in. She peeks over at those
idiots writhing and wriggling. The ones just back from Tahiti, still
all hyped up, with big tattoos that mean something but they don't
know what, or they've forgotten. But in any case they're all thirty-
something nimwits who've taken a couple of trips to the South Seas
and now they're Oceania experts. Pfft. They're wasted and shaking
their asses like morons because they think Tahitian music is the kind
of thing you shake your ass for. And now she's got a proper smile on
her face, a big fat smirk that places her high above the crowd. Oh,
there's nothing original about those people. They're all so different, so
unique, and they're still set on being just like one another.

That's what Hannah is known for, for being there but not really
being there, for making you feel stupid. That's probably why she
doesn't see many people, why she doesn't get involved in Tahitian
activities that are all about "getting to know my country." She doesn't
care that Tahitians in France are idiots, she cares that they're hyp-
ocrites. What good does it do to revive a country, a so-called culture that they left behind back there, at the other end of the world?
Hannah left that place to forget her life, and it keeps on coming
back anyway, doing its best to get its claws back into her. Some days,
though, she'd kill to see her country again. They've been there for
ten years, twenty years, and they talk like they're in exile, don't have
any home anymore. But not one of them's actually been exiled. They
have apartments bursting with vines and vines of fake flowers, pareos
hung up for curtains, CDs from home. Maybe it's easier to lie and say
that Polynesia is the most beautiful paradise of all. Maybe it's easier to call yourself Tahitian when you're not there. As for the young
students, she doesn't think they're any better with their getups, their

looks that make everyone look too much. Flower-print shirts, actual flowers in their ears. How silly. Well, she's not going to say no to this pathetic excuse for a Polynesian bar, but being nothing like her "compatriots" is probably her biggest problem, maybe even her biggest mistake.

She goes on watching Taia swing her hips, her shoulders. Her hair is long, and she wants to get everyone's attention, as if to say, "see, I can dance." Taiai's got to be in her forties, her boobs are huge and pushed up. Her husband's waiting back home for her and a young guy is starting to spin her around. Perfect, that's just what she was hoping for.

She hadn't seen him right off, of course, she was lost in thought about being a bitter, lonely girl. Oh, now nice, her drink's been refilled. At the other end of the bar, a man is looking her over. He's not all that handsome, he's badly shaven and his hair is going gray. She figures the drink was sent over by him and the owner gives her a little wink. He has a way of looking at her that bothers her. She fawns like a coy little thing. Maybe she's gone all ruddy. He's staring at her, he's not smiling like the other guys. There's something off. Or maybe something missing. His eyes are narrowed, maybe because of the smoke. It's not just that. Hannah falls in love so easily. Maybe it isn't the right moment. She's just gone through a breakup that took two or three months. "I like you, but that's all," the ups and downs that drove her berserk, out of her mind. Sleepless nights, and then it was all over, she'd done everything she could. She smiles just to be polite, to thank him for the drink.

And then she sees how stupid she was. He acts like he didn't see, turns his head to Taia. He seems like he's chuckling. A little gleam in his eyes as he looks the dancer's haunches up and down. Hannah's eyes land on her ass . . . it's a sight. She's stunned, broken, embarrassed, at a loss. He shouldn't have. She wants to get in his face, send him packing. She thinks about her Tahitian friend Teariki—she could have just said a single word and the guy would have crumbled to bits. And of course he's doing nothing of the sort. She stares at the mirror again, throws back her vodka in a single gulp. She's pretty, so pretty. "That's the only real thing." She thinks about a Boehringer poem, so she doesn't have to think about other things. She whispers, "I gotta quit ya, alcohol . . ." And Paris rises up in her mind: "It's so pretty, this city at night." It's so pretty, Paris at night. She reads the weirdest things. Sure, she likes Boehringer. He's not a writer, at least that's not what he's known for. But what does she know, she just wanted to read him. She likes his mouth. She thinks about him so she doesn't have to think about how gone she is. She gets out, while the others start hooting as they get into another up-tempo tāmūre. That was the best thing for her to do. The air outside's a shock: cold, dry, almost biting. It would be nicer further down in "Ménilmuch." She could walk too, she's not scared. She's never been scared of Paris proper. Maybe she hasn't entirely lost her Tahitian joy, her belief in some sort of force that's there and protecting her. A sort of cross between God and her ancestors, the ghosts. Or maybe it's just that she believes that she's strong enough, has the balls, if that's possible.

But who is she, Hannah? Most of the time she says she's Tahitian and proud of it. And most of the time she feels like that's not really it. She doesn't want to be like everyone else. Sometimes being Tahitian suits her, makes her feel important. She knows it, she's seen it in the eyes of other people. In their eyes, and in their gasps. Tahitian, Tahiti, she's hit the jackpot. What a wonderful little trick. What's so Tahitian about her? Her eyes, her hair? How blunt she is? She's in Paris, and she's stuck thinking about her island. That's a funny way to love her country: almost hating it. She's always thinking about it, it's the first thing she thinks about every morning. Usually, after letting her thoughts sit, she decides that being Tahitian, being Hannah the Tahitian, simply means being from there, but that's only the half of it. God, she doesn't know what else she can come up with to rack her

brain over. She knows she's not out of this whole mess, that sooner or
later she'll have to go back there. That's just how it is, it's not all said
and done and dusted yet. When she left, it was like she was running
away, she'd only told Ma a week before she went. Of course all there
was to say hadn't been said yet. She had her back to the Basilica now,
and all of Paris was straight ahead. Down there was life and death
and success and failure. She didn't feel all that different from that
Balzac character at times. Rastignac. All his social climbing hadn't
ended well for him though. Well, it was just a novel . . . Rastignac
was a heck of a role model for a Tahitian woman. She'd had too much
to drink, no question of that now. A few couples were in each other's
arms and watching all that. They were talking, giggling. Ugh. All this
happiness made her want to puke. She started making her way down
the steep stairs. It wouldn't be easy. A happy girl piped up and asked
if she was okay. Hannah wanted to tell her to watch her own ass.
She didn't need anybody's help. The steps were swaying under her
feet. The other girl chirped again: "Well, pay attention in any case."
And the man with her snickered. Hannah shot back: "Go fuck yourself," and a "Likewise!" came through the air as the couple walked
off, muttering something or other. Sigh. There was no way she'd get
the rest of the way down without some help, not right now. She sat
down. She had to catch her breath for a second. And then there
was no going back. The booze made her want to cry, went and put
all sorts of dangerous thoughts in her mind. Yes, she needed a good
cry, needed to think about something sad. Like when you're about to
puke, when the right thing's to stick a finger down your throat and
let it all out, get to the bottom of it all. And it's no different here,
she's thinking about what's missing. The love she's never been able to
hold on to, the mother always pitying her. No, she's not going to turn
out like her. She'd rather stay alone forever. If she has to cry, better to
do it for herself, because of herself. Hannah knows how to be selfish,
but tonight really is something else. It's because of that man at the

bar. She doesn't want to think so but she knows it's because of him. So she starts singing an old thing, an old song from her country. She hasn't forgotten it, she's kept it in the back of her head, in a corner of her suitcase. "Motu one," the lost island, covered by the sea. One big wave, and everything gone. One disaster, and it's wiped off the map. If only humans and all their weaknesses could be wiped out too. She's rambling now, poor old thing, she's had far too much. A man sits down beside her, all quiet. She's got her head in her hands, hidden between her knees. She doesn't hear a thing, just smells tobacco and cold sweat. She looks sideways and sees two legs beside hers. She doesn't move. She starts to feel scared. She knows that there's other couples sitting nearby, hopefully they'll come if she needs help. She's not so sure of herself. She can talk a big game and the alcohol does help her pack a punch though. She stands up. The man watching her is there. He smiles a bit. She's going to crack. She's never felt love at first sight like that. She's going to crack, she loves him already. She's so oversensitive right now. She needs love that badly.

A fancy apartment in the seventh arrondissement, on the rue Fabert. The ceiling has to be fifteen meters up. The parquet floor is waxed so perfectly, it almost reflects the colors of the old masters paintings hung on a long stretch of wall. It's beautiful, it's glitzy, it's too much. Indecent, worse than indecent. Her head is still full of fog. Their meeting really was something else, they were off to a great start. Hannah's feeling everything right now: out of sorts, tiny, intimidated. The man's eyes are a light chestnut. Even right now what really stands out is his hair going gray. She can't guess his age. It's because between his body and his face, and his hair, nothing's clear. It's all sorts. His features are old and young, but his hair should mean he's old. She hasn't dared to ask him how old he is, that wouldn't be right. On the steps of La Butte, they'd just kept smiling at each other without too much talking. They hadn't been much for introductions:

"I'm Hannah," "And I'm Bertrand." Nothing groundbreaking there, nothing mind-blowing, as far as first names went, but it could have been worse. Hannah figured he could have been named Blaise or Jacques-Antoine. That would have been worse, so much worse.

Her eyes run up and down the room for her clothes, her undies. A lipstick tube. On his off-white couch, she notices some hair, maybe blond. She can't tell. Bertrand looks like the kind of man who goes for blondes. But Hannah's dark-haired. Any darker, and she'd be dead. What does that mean anyway? All of this right out of a movie? So he just wants to change things up. He probably heard that brunettes are hornier. Okay, just for the night. Tomorrow's another story. Bertrand comes back with two glasses of red wine. That's all he has left, they'll make do. It's no time for whining. He's swept her off her feet already. Him and his black turtleneck, his pale skin, his gray hair, gold, silver, ruby, all splendid colors. There's a whole life in his face, a whole lifetime of love and sadness and even money. She looks him over, she's twenty-five years old and she doesn't feel like she amounts to much.

"Do you go to that bar often?"

"No, never, but I . . . I could tell you're a regular."

Bertrand takes his time with that "I could tell." Hannah doesn't want to let herself think on it. Up to now, Hannah's never been one to tiptoe around her lovers. But now she's downright scared of hurting this man without meaning to. Just one word, just one line she says without thinking twice—that could bring it all crashing down. Bertrand would go up in smoke like some fairy, like a sign of good luck she meant to hang on to . . .

"Oh, I wouldn't go that far," she says back.

And she takes a big gulp of pinot noir to cover her embarrassment. This Bertrand isn't a man of many words. He hasn't even tried to touch her. Most of the time, at this point in the night, she's already naked and nothing's a secret anymore. But she hasn't even said no yet tonight. He's just looking at her. And she's staring at Les Invalides through the large windows. Her thoughts are all over the place as she starts imagining what success ought to look like. Huge windows overlooking the promenade right in front of her. Him sitting at his white Pleyel piano. Her sipping a fancy drink. His eyes shut as his fingers start playing a Bach tune, like he'd done it a hundred times. The cab has to be coming any minute now. That's the end of her fantasies. She doesn't belong in this world. She's in for a rude awakening. They'd never see each other again. There'd never be any love. She's sure of it. They stay where they are for some time, not bothering with words. He doesn't even ask her where she's from, doesn't even try to stir up any feelings, any dreams of exotic places.

Archaeological Gathering

WITH HIS TINY BRUSH in his hand, François looked every bit a painter or a mad scientist, as he whispered God-only-knew-what. At least, that was what people told him. His hair went in all directions, his glasses were teetering at the end of his nose, his back was bent over a tiny thing he'd just found; in that moment, what Pauro felt was all-powerful and weak and, well, just plain in love with François. They'd broken taboo after taboo. The farther apart the two of them got, the less the younger one felt like he could breathe or even think. Pauro still wasn't sure whether this was love; all he could feel was a wild rush deep down, a bit like a sudden climb up from way down below without any stop, without anything other than a need to go through it all again as soon as he could.

François was looking at the object up close. They were in one of Tahiti's backcountry districts. Pauro came along when he could, after classes, or on Saturdays, like today. It all looked like a big construction site, the minister had sent the archaeologist and a whole team to this spot in a low-lying valley without any sort of paved path. Some guy hunting wild boar thought he'd sighted what might have been ruins. They would see for themselves, come to whatever conclusions they could while they were on-site. They walked two hours straight through the underbrush. Pauro liked the dry riverbed stones more than the muddy path.

They came to a flat stretch, where an old settlement looked likely, possible. Around them, François had put down markers, strips of cloth on tree branches, small posts in the earth. Now there was a proper grid all around the researcher. The four men on the team were off a ways, taking a breather. They'd stayed back and kept quiet from the outset, seeing as it was their first expedition. They looked a bit embarrassed. Pauro could feel them staring, befuddled. That would pass, it had to. François was digging at random. This time a small square by a large stone. Who knew why here and not somewhere else. François was always walking wherever he liked and it usually worked out. Pauro watched his lover. Suddenly he felt jealous. A little thing had reached through the centuries and caught the scientist's attention, called him here. François had his head up in the clouds, he was talking to himself. As if he'd forgotten that his young lover was there, not a few centimeters off. Did he even feel Pauro's breath on his neck? Pauro who'd wanted to love, to be loved, to put down roots with this man . . .

The earth was falling away little by little, the brush's bristles brushing it away. François's movements were all instinct. The thing was plenty heavy.

"It could be a shard. Maybe an adze. The river's not far off, after all."

The earth was falling away, and history was coming to the fore, making the small life that Pauro led feel smaller and smaller and smaller. The boy was shaking. It felt like a moment beyond words, something almost magical. Years, hundreds and maybe even thousands of years were just crumbling away. Like fragile things. François went down to the bedrock of the past, and he'd brought this thing up into the present. Pauro felt almost ready to cry, right there, deep down. Magical! But no, it was all a sham, just lies. The earth had fallen away, and what was in François's hands was a broken Walkman, not even two years old. He and Pauro burst out laughing. The other men were like stone.

"Well, if this isn't the right spot, it can't be far off."

What Pauro liked about François was this wild belief he had in himself. Always so sure ... But that belief had never steered the Frenchman wrong, he was pretty much never wrong, and he never thought he might be.

Night would be along in an hour, maybe sooner. They unloaded their things; they'd be setting up there. The tents went up fast enough. The three men did have a way with their hands. They were Tahitian, and as fast as lightning when they wanted to be. François let them have at it, and he lay back. What he was good at was knowing things. Maybe that wasn't much, but here that was more than enough. Even so, he felt small and stupid compared to his teammates. They'd brought jars, some beers too, and two bottles of whiskey. The three men were hunters who'd changed jobs: Teuira, Marama, and Gérard. Of course there was some tension there. They wouldn't off the two faggots ... or would they? It was an easy guess that Pauro wasn't one of the Frenchman's nephews, or even a student of his. Later, after sundown, they'd all be in a better mood, once their Cutty Sark had set their spirits straight; they'd allow for a difference or ten—there wasn't any shortage of those, after all. The Cutty Sark was calling out to them; they'd been dreaming about it since they'd entered the valley. Maybe it wasn't the best whiskey out there, but it was plenty easy to lay hands on.

It was time for a bit of a drink. They built a fire in case they wanted to eat later ... around these parts, after all, dinner was just an afterthought, while drinking was required, a rite, François liked to say ... Teuira was the oldest one, and Pauro was of the mind that he didn't look all that different from Teanuanua. He didn't talk much, being that he only spoke Tahitian. It was his little brother who'd told them about the spot a few months before. But that brother had died two weeks ago, after a long bout of illness. So his thoughts weren't all in the right place. He wanted to focus on here and now. Make sure there wasn't anything special to take into mind. For now, he kept mum, didn't want to get ahead of himself. He just had various inklings, foggy ones, that didn't amount to much. Now they all had a proper glass, the dry wood was a-crackle, singing. It did them good to unwind. Pauro was the youngest. He was thinking back on things too. About the fire when he was little. The noise, yellow and blue twirling and rising up, coming down, steadied him. He recollected those fires on Huahine, at his grandparents' house. The water that was boiled for when it got chilly. His parents who'd always insisted that being from Tahiti meant progress and convenience and all that. They were ashamed of their oven outdoors, the scrubland they used as toilets, the water that only ran now and then. And so Pauro had never dared let on that shameful fact that he lived in a shack. Sometimes the right thing is to let people believe, to give them some hope . . .

François gave the Tahitians all the answers they wanted, but his face looked red and shy. Yes he'd been to schools, yes he liked this country, these people, yes, he was rolling his *r*'s these days, but he wasn't set on becoming one of them. All he wanted was to try his best to get a sense of their past, not to claim that he understood these people. A cheap thing to say, that—there was no hope of ever truly understanding these people. Better that way. If things were just laid all out, plain and simple, that would just leave them a frozen picture. François felt some bit of contempt, a rare thing for folks from far-off places with convictions, not just ideas they'd gotten into their heads but convictions that they really thought they could hold on to after a few months, after a trip or three to the fish stall at the market, after a "rustic" meal or two with some friendly neighbor . . .

François looked down. Right then and only then, he'd gone and said out loud just how close he felt to this foreign land welcoming him in. The men looked him over with a smile. A few minutes earlier, they'd been mocking him, calling him taioro, calling him "coconut sauce" because he'd never had one of those ritual subincisions. But not anymore now. There was real respect on their faces. They moved on. Got to talking about hunting wild pigs, and that left Pauro thinking about how, maybe, just maybe, he might introduce François to his family . . .

A Woman from Here

"I'LL PAY IT BACK when things are better," Ma said. Her voice was slow and shaky, she'd just about whispered those words. As if the money she'd just been given might go up in flames if she didn't take care.

Candice told her there was no rush. Goodness! Asking for money from folks she wasn't close with, not really, not anywhere near close enough. Ma suddenly found herself saying there was a truck she needed to go and catch right away, there was housework, she couldn't let that sit. Not an hour before, she'd made the trip out to the hospital. She'd gone past that half-empty basin. Her body was all shivers and recollection after recollection had been piling up in her head. And some shame, just a little, on top of it all. John. She hadn't thought about him so much lately, but there was no forgetting him. How could anyone? That pleasure had been so pure, so real. Actual pleasure, for once. An act that was just for its own sake. The sex had been just for its own sake. Ma had rushed right on down. She'd called Candice from a phone booth to say could she please see her, it was urgent, yes, really. Candice's voice had been full of sunshine and zouk music, all lazy and lush as she'd said, "Oh, darling, come on over, let's eat together."

And then a restaurant that was really a greasy snack bar across the street from the hospital. There had been so many people, so many white scrubs. It made Ma feel so stupid, so small among these accents that made her think of other corners of the world, France, of money too, and brains . . .

"You don't look okay, Ma."

"No, not really."

"What's wrong?"

"I don't like it here, I don't like it at all."

And Candice said not to worry because not a soul was even looking at the two of them. "So what if you don't feel like you're one of them, what does it matter?" Candice added that the others all "shit and pissed and fucked just like us." Did that calm Ma any? No, not at all. It was almost worse actually. Well, Candice was one to know, that she was. She saw the world just like that. Don't you worry about anyone but yourself, yourself alone, and if you want to stay human then don't get to worrying about what everyone else is looking at. It had to be a matter of education . . . Ma wasn't one bit educated. Her kids might be in rags, but she wanted, knew she had, to look respectable. Her head might be full of all sorts of worries, but she wanted to look poised. But in that restaurant she just couldn't.

"Okay, let's go somewhere else," Candice said.

They got sandwiches and found some shade in the hospital garden. After they were finally on one of the benches, Ma whispered her request, full of shame and guilt. "I need to borrow some money. If that's okay. I'm having trouble making ends meet." Candice gave her a smile because that was no surprise to her, and that felt like the worst of insults to Ma. Oh, money, of course. We all borrow some at one point or another. We all swallow our pride. It's normal. Ma felt like she had to explain herself. Auguste wouldn't be going back to the job he'd had before. He was going to be charged with a crime. Any day now there would be policemen, then prison. He was just starting to get better, to walk, to talk. Fuck. Ma started crying. She couldn't hold it in any longer. It was impossible. It was all a weight on her. She was tired of being careful, of using every last grain of rice, of begging for some fish from her sister in Tiarei. And Rosa was gone again. She hadn't seen Rosa in two weeks, so she just had to hope that the girl would be bringing back whatever money she'd scrounged up. She needed to get herself a part-time job in Papeete, that would help. Ma's words, with a heavy sob here and there, seemed meant for the horrible life she was set to live, that was a real burden, that was stifling them all. Only once her sobbing had died down some did she aim her thoughts at God, angry, mean-hearted God. God who only heard the prayers of good people, of people who had money and then some.

Candice gave her a smile. "Just you wait and see, Ma. It won't be long before things get better." And that did make the crying woman feel a bit better. Candice mentioned John, said she ought to talk to him again. Candice said that she believed in peace and happiness at home, and if that meant a threesome, well, she didn't see anything wrong there. The two women had themselves a giggle, and then Ma actually, yes, really had to go and catch a bus. Before she left, Candice gave her the address of a perfume shop that would be opening and that needed an assistant. Candice had suspected that Ma would be needing some help with money. And so right after Ma's call, she'd phoned up her friend, a métro who'd just come to Papeete, who liked perfume, makeup, all sorts of nice things, and who'd been saying that a career here in Tahiti wouldn't be a bad thing. Well, of course Ma wouldn't be rich anytime soon, but it was a step closer to happiness. Maybe it was a step closer to freedom.

Love Scene

ON HER WAY BACK, she stopped at the Chinese man's to pay off her debts. Not all of them, of course, she did have to save for later. Ma really did like this one, he wasn't like the others. He got what it was like not to have a thing. He'd gone through that when he was little. Nobody really knew his name. Everyone had to have a name, though, so the folks around these parts just called him Tinitō. It was just the Tahitian word for Chinese, but being clever didn't count for much in Tenaho.

School had begun again. Before she'd left for the hospital, Ma had set the baby down by Auguste. That was why she'd been in a hurry: she was scared. Did Auguste still know how to look after a kid, a little one? He didn't seem to have done too bad of a job. When she walked in, Moïra was napping and Auguste was out in the sun, reading the Bible in his wheelchair. Well, that's new, Ma thought. Something good has to come out of those accidents once in a while.

They'd never talked again about the rape. Ever since that day, Auguste hadn't tried to lay hands on her again. And Ma had seen that. She couldn't help worrying that he'd get the urge again. She knew her husband too well. There was no telling how much worse it might be the next time. She went and stood in front of him, and told him that she'd managed to buy some fish on the roadside. Auguste looked up. Yes, fish would be nice. The light was shining through her flower-print skirt. Auguste saw and could just imagine that spot between her legs, a spot that was like the curve of a circle.

To break the quiet, Ma added that she was looking forward to him getting better. He had to miss fishing, and getting back to it would only help. Auguste looked down. Behind all Ma's words he could hear what she wasn't saying. Yes, he'd get better, faster than she'd hoped or even dared imagine. He'd get to back work, back to fishing. He'd even go back to Poe's, down in the backcountry, to reacquaint himself with the fields. But he only thought that, he didn't say any of it. "Just you wait, Ma. Soon you'll be in love with me again." His wife was already in the kitchen, cutting the fish open. He stood behind her, grabbed her by the waist. Gently, ever so gently. When he was younger, gestures like that had been a rare thing for him, but even so he'd never forgotten any of them. If only he'd been cruel, nothing more than that. If only that had been the worst of his sins, it would have been so much easier. Ma let go of her paring knife, rested her head back on her husband's shoulder. All was forgotten. Suffering and betrayal and hateful words—all forgotten. They took this moment and carved it into their bodies, their hearts, their memories. Despite it all they loved each other. They tried to. The two bodies swayed slightly and one of them recalled some old song. "Remember that?" "How could anyone forget?" Their desire was coming back up to the surface. Desire for skin they'd known so well one time, that had been apart for so long. Skin they'd now brought back together.

They had sex in the afternoon light. They discovered each other again, smiled at each other. When it was over, Ma was curled up against her husband's body. Her back was curved, and her butt was up against his penis, soft at last. She was smoking and her heart was still hammering. They got to talking. Auguste said one day he'd tell her what he'd been through, what she'd always wanted to know. One day. He also said he wanted to save Rosa. Ma got tense. Save her

from what? And Auguste just told Ma she needed to open her eyes,
see the facts for herself. She knew what her daughter was up to, didn't
she? He'd practically had to keep his eyes peeled for her. Rosa was his
duty. He'd get her off the street, out of *that* world. Shit . . . What had
he been doing, or not doing, all the while? She'd grown like an unruly
vine that needed a stake. But the stake had been broken all along, had
been too weak. They came around to talking about their other kids
too and it was such a new thing for Ma, such a lovely thing. They'd
all grown up, she couldn't believe it. As if Auguste had gone overseas
and was coming back years and years later. Maybe all this emotion
was making her soft. They ran through the kids. Pauro, Pina, even
"Taverio" who'd been sent off to Huahine, and even Hannah. Even
Hannah. And there they got quiet again. They didn't know what to
say now. They'd never gone there. Ma would have to write her a letter,
better Ma than him.

That night, the table was set differently. Ma had pulled out a table-
cloth, a white one, and the plates that they never used. The ones for
holidays, and since holidays were a rare thing, most of them had
forgotten that those were there.

When they got home, at four in the afternoon, Pauro and Pina
saw that things were different. Not just little things. No, lots of
new things had changed, and the place and everyone was different.
Auguste was grating coconut and humming. Ma was making des-
sert. A butter cake. And there was some red mullet ready to cook.
As for Moïra, she was playing beside her father. A father just like
in books or movies, smiling. It was too much for Pina and Pauro.
They stared at each other, all shocked, and they were wary. When Ma
finally saw them, she gave them a wide smile they couldn't fathom. It
shook them. So many thoughts were going through the kids' heads:
she's gone mad, she's won the lottery, she's seen the Holy Virgin, or
maybe even God himself . . .

Auguste waved his son over. "Show me what you can do, what I've taught you. One day I won't be here and you'll be glad to know how to do this. One day." And those words came out of his mouth in Tahitian, because French wasn't something Auguste really knew. Pauro went and sat on a very low stool of sorts with a notched steel plate. The coconut covering the steel moved up and down and up and down. Pauro's strokes were long, a bit delicate. Auguste was saying that would make the pulp thinner and that would be better. All a matter of taste. Yes, the strokes were always the same. Nothing had ever changed. Pauro looked at his father sitting not far off and this new warmth almost hurt. Happiness, gestures, encouragement, head and eyes nodding.

Oh, Pa, if you had any idea, if only you had any idea, Pauro wouldn't be your son anymore.

Pina was in charge of stirring the cake batter. She didn't know what to think either. She watched her father, then her mother. She caught their two smiles as they met. Odd, that. The little girl had never seen that before and she couldn't believe it. Dinner was just the four of them. Auguste said grace and asked God to watch over the children not under his roof. And because Pina's mind was always going a mile a minute, she began thinking about her sister in a bed, and she shooed those cruel thoughts out of her little head as soon as she thought them.

Dinner almost felt like a family meal; it didn't feel real. They almost forgot they were poor. That night, Auguste wouldn't be tired out. He talked about his childhood, his father, even his mother. All sorts of new images coming into the house, into their minds. Ma listened. It was a holiday, they'd even found a bottle of wine hidden in Rosa's belongings. Auguste didn't have a drink and Ma knew that for this she had to thank the Lord. For once, she wouldn't have to curse this God she was sure had to be deaf. She poured Pauro a glass. Here you are, my boy, you're old enough. Auguste had Pina talking too, asking her what she liked at school, what she wanted to do later, silly little things like that. Things that people who don't know you would ask. She thought she might say, with a gleam in her eyes, that one day she would go away and visit lots and lots of countries. Then, when she was told that going away wasn't a job, she clammed up. The grown-ups had themselves a laugh, then looked at Pauro. He said "archaeologist." Auguste wanted to know what a French word like that meant. Once he had his answer, he looked down and grinned. Why not. A historian of this place, that didn't sound so bad. After all, it had been a long while since anyone had told our story, the story of Matahi. Why not indeed, Pauro replied. There are so many stories like that, it's part of our country, our people. The whole dinner was full of pride, a shy, quiet sort of pride. And Ma told him to keep on paying attention. All these stories about statues being moved and bringing bad luck, these ghosts who didn't like being disturbed, none of that was a joking matter. Little Pina felt like she'd been given a mission, to go and help her brother. And so she said that because Pauro was Tahitian those ghosts wouldn't dare to hurt him. It's true, they wouldn't dare lay a hand on one of their descendants, that simply wasn't done. Absolutely not.

Pauro wondered again what had changed. Why all these silences were just falling away. He couldn't make out any answer, unless it was love, pure and simple. After all, Ma and Auguste were married. Which meant they had to love each other. But that didn't make these sorts of changes any less of a surprise.

It was well into the night at this point. They'd all ended up in the little garden, on a mat, and Pauro had been asked to play the guitar because Auguste couldn't, not just yet. And the alcohol hadn't made things worse, it had made Ma a woman all wrapped up in happiness. She smiled, holding her glass close. She began singing, rocking Pina, for the first time. Of course, in the little girl's head, it was all muddled, everything was a mess. She felt embarrassed and shy and happy and calm. So many feelings at once couldn't possibly be allowed.

It had to be late, far too late. It was still a school night. Pauro said he just wanted to stay a bit longer on his own. He knew François would come get him, the way he did every night. The Frenchman had gotten himself a studio in town not two weeks ago, it was more practical that way.

Pauro was sure everyone was asleep, all the lights were out. Auguste stayed in the shadows, by the front door. Outside, on the lit street, he saw a car stop. A car he knew only white men had, and in the driver's seat there was indeed a white man. And Pauro got in, hurrying and clearly happy.

He didn't know what was going on, but Auguste already didn't like the looks of it.

Junior's Life

ALL THE WHILE, not a few kilometers away, Auguste Junior was holding up the walls of a pharmacy in Papeete. The street was empty, it was dark, too dark, nobody'd switched on the streetlights. Or nobody'd figured they'd be of any use . . . In that neighborhood, after five, it was better to be back home. Better to have a family that loves you, a roof to sleep under. Better not to know about life around these parts. About life on this street that everyone steers clear of.

Auguste Junior was punch-drunk. The buildings around him were swaying. It wasn't a migraine, that would have been drilling just into his head. It was more dangerous. It started with his feeling uneasy and then crushing his soul, his body, even his guts. And he was locked in, there was no getting out of this. Everything kept on sliding around. Auguste Junior could smell the booze on his own breath, and the drugs too. He reeked. Auguste Junior stank. He wanted to take a shower, but he didn't have the strength to. Where would he shower anyway? He could go home. He didn't feel at home there though. Ever since he was little, living at home had felt like being in a hotel, he'd grown up around strangers who only had first names, funny features. One of them was the father, and his characteristic was that he was the father. Same for the proprietress. And the others were just shadows that did whatever they liked. Auguste Junior was flat against the pharmacy wall, one of his arms behind him, one of his legs pulled up behind him. Auguste Junior was twenty-six, he was a hombo. Sure, but . . . It was always the same old story, people around you used the words that suited them and locked you in, just because that was easy for them. The tourists said hobo, and that was that. The locals said hombo, and that was that. But Auguste Junior didn't feel like he was one of those hombo. Hombo—not all of them, but plenty of them—attracted women. Outsiders, losers—that got women all teary. They're really something, hombo, an animal in bed, and what woman doesn't want that? And that was how he knew he wasn't a hombo. No woman looked twice at him. Junior wasn't even ugly. Sure, he'd let himself go a bit: a wild beard, camouflage pants and fatigues worn so thin that some of his skin, some of his ass showed . . . He'd only bedded a few women, but none of them had been keen on more than a couple of hours together.

In other places, he'd have been called homeless. But what did it matter, this was no time to go through all the dictionaries in the world. What it was time for was to watch a young man suffering without any words. Look close, there's blood trickling down his mouth, an ugly blotch on his forehead. And blood there too. His wrists . . . that wasn't a pretty sight. Not five minutes ago, he'd rammed his whole body against the wall. Without any help, like a big guy. If he could have, he'd have busted open his veins. But for once there wasn't even a bottle shard to be found. Life was a bitch, after all. A selfish bitch, so selfish it wouldn't help him die. Poor guy. Poor life, poor mess.

Just a couple of hours earlier, he'd left some older guy for dead in a vacant lot. Some wino, some guy who'd had his wife cheating on him, some drug addict, some guy up to his neck in debt.

Auguste Junior had been sitting at the edge of the filthy, dark Papeete quay, his feet swinging back and forth above the water that was every bit as filthy and dark. He hadn't asked anyone for anything, as usual. He was just a bit hungry, but he wasn't at all keen on going back to that family hotel. He'd gone through all his weed, and he didn't have a thing left to sell, let alone smoke. The sun was beginning to make its way down. The sky was red. His stomach was starting to whine.

A man had chatted him up. A guy from around here. He'd been talking in Tahitian. He seemed nice, looked honest and wise. After an hour, they'd had dinner together. Not some fancy restaurant, just a meal from one of the roulottes nearby. Auguste Junior had gotten to talking a bit about himself, he didn't really know why. Then they'd driven around a little. There was a bottle of whiskey that the man had been swigging from easily enough. And that was when things started to get heated. As he drove, the man had laid a hand on Junior's headrest. It had gotten quiet. Junior had trouble breathing. He'd never been through such a thing, but he was no idiot. Why that gesture, those smiles, those words getting whispered all of a sudden? And these funny hints about being odd, about this man's life? Auguste Junior's legs were hurting and he could feel his hands clenching on his thighs. The other guy looked all calm, not one bit bothered as he kept on talking. Junior thought he heard the man saying that he lived alone, really liked young fellows. He did lots for them, he went to some trouble to keep them busy. Sports, cultural activities, mountaineering. Junior didn't believe him, this guy was fat, had a beer belly that probably hung over his balls. The image had just popped right into Auguste Junior's head.

Then the car had stopped on some empty stretch. In the glove compartment, he'd pulled out a small matchbox with some cannabis flower inside. To get Junior's attention. Sure, Junior wanted some, he always did. They'd packed a bowl, but it hadn't made things any less awkward. They'd smoked, then smiled at each other, Junior not so willingly. That was when things came to a head. The man slid a hand up the boy's leg, his other hand still on the headrest. Junior felt the man's sweetish breath. Breath that came in fits and starts. Heavy.

Long silences. Breath that was foul. Words that made him want to puke. "If you want, only if you want, some goodies like that, I can give you plenty. And money too. But only if you want. You hear me? Just ask." And the hand had started working its way between Junior's legs. The breathing started getting faster. The drugs were going to the boy's head. His head felt so heavy, trapped. And he saw the other man's hand, felt that breath getting close. Too close. Auguste Junior couldn't stand any of it but somehow he had a hard-on. Even though he hated all this, which only made it worse. His stomach was in knots. The man was pulling at his zipper. Junior could see his hand about to do something he couldn't put into words or even thought. All around them was dark. Auguste Junior felt so alone. More alone than ever before in his life. He saw his father again. His mother too. He cried out for them, got to sobbing. He needed them. A cry that could just about break anyone's heart, a cry that could just about break anyone. "Come get me, save me." But nobody came. And then Junior saw that there was no getting out of all this without using his fists, without going for death. An elbow to the head of the man now bent over his crotch. Then a punch, then his whole body going berserk. He was going to kill this man. Now out of the car, Junior was aiming kick after kick at a face he already didn't recognize anymore. Junior was fighting back. Yelling that he wasn't "like that," would never be "like that." He'd never sell himself like that. And the other man kept yelling. Yelling for mercy, begging, pleading. Die, die!

He's leaning against the wall, the green neon pharmacy light shines on the young man's face, a promise of help that leaves him disgusted because of course it won't help him. Tears and blood. His face wrecked. And right then, his father, Auguste, sits in his wheelchair, thinking of him, his eldest son. Remembers him, and as he thinks on him images punch through his thoughts. He saw the man on the ground. He saw his son in the darkness. His heart's pounding, the father's crying too. He's hurting. Auguste saw it, his mother told it to him. Her gray hair was fluttering in the air, she was smiling as she told him a story never to be told again.

Auguste Junior lifts his head up, oh, that doesn't hurt so much. His breath's calmer now, relaxed. Not far off, Papeete's lights are a glimmer. Out there is life. A small white car goes past. Inside it, Pauro is smiling, a smile meant for the road ahead of him, the future ahead of him. Junior sees him and wonders who the man beside Pauro is. He's scared for his brother, but he can't move. No, Pauro looks happy, and that can't be a mistake.

And Junior can't take it anymore. Who's fucked all this up? Whose fault is this whole thing that doesn't deserve to be called life?

Gay Men

"LISTEN. LISTEN CAREFULLY. THERE. Yes, right there. Keep listening, she's moaning right now."

"Oh, you idiot. Why do you even care?"

"I don't, I just think it's funny."

"Sure you do."

François and his lover were on a small fake-leather armchair with cracked arms. As there wasn't enough room, François had to hold the other guy. This other guy stretched out across his lover's body. This other guy acting a bit like a baby, like that, begging for hugs. François had been talking about the girl next door who had men over all the time, who started moaning a bit loudly every so often, maybe she didn't even realize it. When François was alone, when it was the crack of dawn, he could hear whispers, laughter, and sometimes their fucking too. Even the thumping and so on. François didn't get bothered by those sorts of things, he wasn't that sort. At times it even turned him on. He'd told Pauro about it. He'd been living there two weeks now, and this woman had become part of his life. Despite herself, despite him. These groans had annoyed him at first, but he'd stopped caring, until one night when she wasn't back in her studio. That night, the quiet had been cavernous, a downright void. He almost knew the rhythms, the beat, the way her voice went up and

down, by heart. And now he was thinking about how this voice was
a friend at this point, almost a little sister. A little sister, yes, because
it was the voice of a girl. Sometimes she sang. He didn't care about
seeing her face. Or meeting her. He didn't judge her. How could he
anyhow? It didn't get him down. François had always figured that
women whored themselves out because they liked it. Not because
they had to. Nobody ever has to do anything. As in, they could
just as soon go cleaning houses or begging on the street. The way
François saw it, best to stop sobbing over all these prostitutes and
stop hollering that things had to change. All these people hollered
about women's dignity because there was no way they could imagine
that it wasn't a matter of buying and selling, but about making a gift
of oneself. What was "politically correct" and "feminist" was to say
that prostitution was the last resort of a "formerly" irreproachable
woman. But François figured that a whore had to be stronger and
more respectable and more able to love than all these women going
on and on about morality.

What if it was their choice to walk the street?

What if these "fallen" women's pussies could save the world in
their own way, by saving men from being miserable when it came to
sex? In this place that was meant to be a paradise for sex?

François felt like there was a relationship of sorts now between
him and the whore, through that welcome, through her saying yes to
the pleasure that sex was. Nothing obscene there. Letting go, letting
herself be weak was actually beautiful. A girl, a woman who lets go,
who forgets all the walls she's put up of her body that all of a sudden
can sink into total love. When they're doing it, even when there's
no love to it, this woman gets so close to something that has no
words to it. Not just pleasure. Another level, a place that's everything.
She reaches all the nos, all the voids. Not just that nothing can *be*
there, but when she's there she can see that feelings and truths are
there, close enough to touch, even if they still get away from her.

And so she keeps on doing what she's doing, now and always. Those words that finally mean something are out there, beyond life, in the moments when she forgets herself. François is convinced that normal life, her life when she isn't doing this, is flat, almost doesn't have any voice to it.

So she'll go and do this as much as her body allows. She goes and tries to reach for what's still missing from her body, this hole that needs to be filled. She tries to explain what can't be explained here. Nobody, nobody ought to ever judge her for that.

"Oh, that's such a pretty way of putting it. But you're talking too much. I can't always keep up with you," Pauro said.

The young man took François's hand and kissed it. There were so many things that he didn't understand, that he just felt. He decided that François wasn't like anyone else, that he was so unlike himself, so old, that maybe it couldn't ever work. His worries swallowed him up. Better to think on other things, good things, rather than things that might be impossible.

Every so often voices came from the dark street. Car headlights swept across the sleepy room. The bed could hardly be seen. Stripped, maybe because there was no hope. There was the smell of semen and sweat. A smell that was gross, sour . . .

In his mind Pauro walked out of this room, walked away from his lover and went over to his sister, Rosa, on the other side of that wall. It was her, he knew. He knew that laugh. He could have picked it out in a crowd: honest, not bothered by anyone, by any time of day or night. High, sharp, with clear *ha ha*s that dragged out.

There's few things so terrible as hurting for someone who doesn't know they're lost.

School and Pina

I'M TURNING TEN in a few months, it's my last year before collège where all the teens go. So far I haven't flunked any grades. I figure I'm lucky because I'm not all that smart. I just do what I have to do. Maybe I could do a bit more, if I wanted to, but I don't. I just do what I'm asked do, that's all. Our teacher's Chinese. At school they say he's strict with everyone. He doesn't play favorites. But on the first day of school, he told us all where to sit, and the classroom looks like this: in front are the students with blond hair. In the middle are the ones with black hair, but they're little Chinese kids. And at the back, there's us, the kids from here. Well, everyone's from this neighborhood. It's just that we're not Chinese, and we don't have light hair. Our hair is very, very dark brown. The class is a bit mixed, it's colorful, some at the top and some at the bottom. Maybe that's mean but that's honest.

Being at the back doesn't really bother me. I can hide a little. Another thing that's weird: the students up by the teacher's desk, just under the blackboard, raise their hands more. Those kids know so much already. The girls have nice pens too, in different colors, with hearts or Snow White or Cinderella on them. On Wednesday afternoons they go from their ballet class to the bookstore right by the market, they're still wearing their tutus and that's where you can find all the most important things in the world. The bookstore is called Quartier Latin. Pauro said that's the name of a place in Paris. And the store window is so pretty. Just like the door, made of wood that makes a nice sound when it opens, and then it's quiet. I only went there one time, but it really made me feel ashamed. All those girls in tutus and then this saleslady who kept following me. I think she was afraid I would fall and hurt myself. Actually, no. I'm no fool. I know I look like I'm a thief, it's the first thing anyone thinks. No surprise that I was only there for a minute, as soon as I was back out the saleslady let out a sigh. In my dreams, in my fantasies, I can see a very elegant woman holding out a nice big Pacific franc bill so I can go and buy a few treats at the lovely Quartier Latin. And then when I have to pay, I give the woman the prettiest bill she's ever seen. Her eyes go wide, then she says over and over how sorry she is. In another dream I walk in with a very pretty lady and she pays for it all using dollars. American dollars, to show off that she's not from here. But I know it's all just a dream.

The Quartier Latin . . . maybe someday I'll actually go to the real one. The Papeete store, and the actual place in Paris. Pauro who knows all sorts of things says that in that corner of Paris there are so many bookstores like that one, artists with a cigarette in their hand and their eyes on the ground or up in the air, they've got a pen in their other hand. It must be so nice. Any time I think about it I can see those writers, and then I see horse-drawn carriages too, with majestic horses. But I know I'm just dreaming about those horses, I know I'm getting parts of history mixed up. But who cares, in my mind I can think whatever I like. That's what's so nice about minds; we can dream up different things, different stories for each of us. My sister Hannah who lives in France probably goes to the Quartier Latin every day. I'd be so happy if she told me about it, but I don't know if she remembers me.

Yesterday, before Pauro and I went to see Ma at the perfume shop—she works there now—we walked past the bookstore. It was back-to-school season and there were so many people there. The girls weren't in tutus, because Ching's dance school hadn't started yet. But so what, that's just details. You probably figured out my brother and I couldn't go inside without any money. But we didn't care. We had just enough to buy one ice cream for us both, so we got that.

I like to walk like that with my brother. He's so handsome. It makes me look good. While we walk, I ask him to tell me about François because I haven't seen him since we stayed with Aunt Poe in Tiarei. He's fine. Things are going even better with them. They really love each other, and they say it to each other all the time. What I also like is watching my brother's eyes when he talks about him. There's so much light and warmth in them when he's doing that, it makes me smile to see that life, yes, life can sometimes be just beautiful. I've been staying closer and closer to Pauro. Maybe I'm holding on to him because things aren't great back home. You probably remember that one day not so long ago. Ma and Auguste were so happy that my brother and I couldn't believe it. But none of the days after that were like that. Ma and Auguste aren't fighting, not yet. But Ma is making all the money, and she still has to cook for us too. Auguste is the one who seems off. Sometimes he looks like he's in a trance, he's looking off in the distance for something that's not there. And he's talking very quietly too. And other times it feels like he's going to jump down your throat because of something you shouldn't have done, not ever. Just for a second, and in that second he's forgotten what he wanted to say. He reads the Bible like it's a dirty secret and he doesn't move around much. He's worse with Pauro. Auguste looks at him weird. Like he doesn't trust him. My brother doesn't explain himself. Our father keeps asking what Pauro's doing all day, wants to know where he's going, even if it's just going for a dip in the river. He's acting like some old woman who's afraid she'll die alone. So I pipe up and start talking about my new class, ask my brother to help me. Then Auguste calms down, he likes to see us talking about school.

I don't want Pauro to get hurt, I'm afraid for him and I don't know why.

Auguste isn't the same anymore. He's not the father we had before the accident. That man didn't care very much about us. I mean, he didn't have time for us, the only things he had time for were his drinks and his friends. Sometimes when I'm alone with my father, I feel a little bit of fear rising up in me. It feels like I'm standing in front of some god. You know, the sort that looks down on you and sees every one of your mistakes to remind you of them later. I hope things get better, that this is one of those things that goes away. Or that it's just me getting ideas, thinking up all sorts of things.

Anyway, back at school, the teacher had me share a desk with Roméo. He's a gang leader. Everyone's scared as hell of him, even the teachers—except for ours. And that's why nobody dared to expel him. They just told him, there you go, you'll be in Monsieur's class. He doesn't really bother me, but I do feel a bit worried anyway. I'm sitting right next to him. I don't talk at all so he won't have any reason to give me trouble after class. He's already loaned me a pen. That was nice of him, I only had one. In the schoolyard, there are all sorts of rumors about him. They said he'd already beaten up a guy two grades ahead at the collège next door. A big one, much bigger than him. And some of the others said he lives with his grandmother and he doesn't know who his parents are. His grandmother is the only person who'll protect him. She moved heaven and earth to keep him at that school. He's already been held back four years and he's starting to grow some hair under his nose. I don't know how things are going to go between him and me, I don't want to even think about it.

At school they call me by my real name: Aeata. It's so different, it always takes me a second to answer. So the other students think I'm completely deaf, and the teacher too. I don't dare to tell them that my name is Pina, it's not a first name a lot of people have. When I met François, he told me about some other Pina, a German dancer.

It made me feel better to know that I'm not the only Pina. And that's not all, apparently the German Pina is very talented, and she travels all the time because everyone wants to see her. I don't say out loud that I'd like to be a dancer because I think tutus look silly. I just say that I hope that having the name Pina is good luck.

Right now, as I talk to you, we're in math class. The numbers on the blackboard look so funny. Not pretty at all. It's not like words that can be put together in all sorts of ways. Singular, plural, with prefixes or suffixes. Words can be made longer however you'd like. And they change when they're put next to other words, or they mean different things. Sometimes they don't mean anything, they exist in some other way, for no reason, but they can still be pretty, while numbers are too serious to be beautiful. But maybe there's someone who thinks different. Roméo's just woken up from a nap. I gave him a teensy kick because the teacher was looking at us. I don't know what came over me, it was just instinct. Whew! Roméo gives me a smile, almost like he's thankful.

Cleansing

THEY WERE CUTTING a ribbon for some little street being closed off to cars. If we'd been in some other city, an actual capital, that wouldn't have been anything to sneeze at. But here? Kick up a fuss over any little thing, and we'll go and sneeze at it. Really, though, this was too much, this was just making matters worse. This car-free street was in the wrong place altogether, it made no sense here with these filthy old buildings that were downright nauseating. Sure, buildings can stink, but maybe it's really the gutters. Only here would people whine and mutter about a car-free street being opened. Maybe someone should have thought of tearing down those stinking buildings ... Really, all this ruckus has to be because the stones, the cobblestones used to pave the street and show that it's a car-free zone, are from abroad. From Italy! Before the opening there'd been petitions, lawsuits, grumbling, you name it. A car-free street, what's so bad about that? Well, it's that it keeps cars from going through. It's a main street, and it's the shortest way through for a lot of drivers. They'd have to prove it, though, and that's easier said than done in Papeete. It's jam-packed with so many cars everywhere, honestly it's shocking that worse things haven't happened already. Oh, bless those drivers. One day they'll finally get together, and they'll move mountains. It's really something just how all of a sudden this city became selfish.

Really unbelievable how they get so greedy. "No to car-free zones, yes to my big fat gas-spewing car. No to walking, yes to driving." That's about as logical as workers yelling, "Off with the unemployed!" No, of course it's more hush-hush than all that. Only a little more, mind. It's a car-free street people aren't so quick to walk down when they've got pale skin. They'll only go down that way by day.

On this car-free street, people can think the sea isn't far off, think it or rather know it because everyone knows it is. But there's no smell, no hint of the sea. It's a tiny street where Georges, who's just as filthy and old and downright nauseating as the buildings, has a little bar called Le Lido. There are some folks who've got everything and even they get all misty-eyed about it.

Auguste's on the sidewalk, across from the big heavy pitch-black door nobody ever notices, with a little window and huge gold-plated locks. It's not even two in the afternoon, and it's already loud in there, music is blaring: half techno, half rock, all stupid.

Auguste's taken up smoking again, which has his wife in a huff. He's got to have been there for at least four hours. At his feet spit-soaked cigarette butts are almost making a circle. There aren't many people in the street yet. A few drunk hombo are hanging around, looking depressed and a bit blank. Time's taking its time. At one point, he saw Rosa walk down a porch by the bar. He imagines that she came from somewhere upstairs and looks up at the old building. Tries to pick out an apartment, a balcony that would be his daughter's.

He's afraid she'll see him. But nothing happens. She's wearing a dress that's almost too red. She looks vulgar. The scars on her legs haven't faded. No shame. Auguste smiles, just a little. He remembers her being little and embarrassed by those scars. She goes on down to the harbor. He doesn't see her come back.

It's night now, and things are picking up. A few cross-dressers make their way over. Awfully young girls stand not far off from Auguste. This is their spot. He doesn't want to know what they're

up to. He does know, but he just doesn't want to accept it. Next
to them, Rosa's old enough to retire. He's afraid to look their way,
but he can't help himself. They don't even really have boobs yet, but
plenty of lipstick smeared on. They're braying. Auguste can't take it.
He shouldn't be here, it's none of his business. A man comes up to
one of them. She giggles so she doesn't have to talk, then she goes
with him. Auguste's sure that just yesterday such a thing would have
been unthinkable. In the bar across the street, the music's gone up a
few notches. It's all techno now. Lights are twinkling now, so many
colors. A māmā goes by, holding a few flowers tied into crowns, she
holds one up to Auguste but he shakes his head no and looks awkward. Night's in full swing, blackout drunk guys are stumbling into
Le Lido. It's a riot. Conscripts, whites, dark-skinned guys, everyone.
Patience is a virtue Auguste's picked up lately. He recollects seeing
Georges in a half dream not long before he opened his eyes at the
hospital. He recalls wanting to yank him right out of there, out of
this country, out of Rosa's life. He waits, going about it isn't all that
clear to him. Killing wouldn't be very hard, after all. But if he wants
to kill then he's got to have a superhero's strength, the heart and
mind of one. Enough that nobody'd ever stop him. Two guys are
thrown out of another grubby bar, thrown out like old rags. Maybe
that's what they really are, deep down. It's so loud it could shatter
glass. Just look at all this misery. Auguste hears someone nearby saying that it's because they were getting handsy with a waitress who
didn't like them. Misery, misery.

Another cigarette to roll, he's lost count. His throat is a bit dry,
his lips too, he really has to pee, but there's no chance he'll leave this
place. The bar's owner comes out of his den at long last. Auguste jolts.
He oughtn't, the two of them don't know each other, not yet. Georges
walks over to the group of little girls and gives them a loud "La ora
na!" That too-wide smile of his shows his brownish teeth. The pack
of girls giggles. Their cheek kisses can be heard all the way down the

street and Georges, that lover of the Tahitian language, asks them all, "Eatchiuru?" He's clumsy with his words, overdoes them. Well, that sorry excuse for a man won't be long for this earth. Auguste can't hear what they're saying anymore, but he's sure it's more or less "give me my cut, here's yours." After five minutes, Georges leaves. On the back of his floral-print shirt there's a huge circle, it's got to be sweat.

The night's going to be a long one. Auguste's sitting now. Still watching the street and the people going up and down it. Some hang around, others don't. Some boys are standing in a passageway just ahead. He can tell things are getting tense. A glance here, another there, all of them dead quiet, ready to land a punch. An old Tahitian man comes out of nowhere, a big cross hanging off his neck. He seems to know the place and the teens. He talks to them, he talks to the tops of their heads. His voice goes up and up, like a church song. Going by that cross of his, Auguste figures he's a Catholic. The teens go off. Maybe the man's a judge? He goes to the hombo. They leave too. Then things turn into a mess. The old man sits over by Auguste and just asks him what he's doing there. Auguste says, "I'm waiting," as if that's enough. He's screwed. The man goes off, saying things he can't believe. None of the sorry things on this street should be that way. Auguste nods, can't argue with that. Then the group of girls packs up and goes. Why? The old guy's ranting about the homeless shelter he runs. A smart idea, that. But he's rambling and all of a sudden Auguste sees that man's got no love for his fellow men, he's just in it for himself. He's jabbering on about how "I was the only one to take them in, to get them off the street. I alone, not the politicians, not the other religious denominations." It sets Auguste on edge when the other man gets to saying Auguste's got no reason to be there. The street's no way to live, in case Auguste didn't know that already. Then the old man starts in on how homeless people have no manners. They come in here and there for food and then they leave again, they don't even pray for a bit. Yes, prayer is what those people who haven't a thing to their name but their feet and their bodies are missing. Prayer to ask for what, to thank whom? Thank you O Lord for what you've let me become. Only an idiot would say things like that. And the other man keeps jabbering on, acting as if his heart is full to bursting for the human race. Auguste suddenly gets it in his head, he's not proud of it, and so he keeps that thought to himself, that "it's all well and good to feel some impulse for charity, but it shouldn't be a job. Pull two people together, but with no money or business or love or sex in it—that's a recipe for disaster. You get saved, you'll owe a debt to your saviors, but how do you get to repaying it when it can't be boiled down to numbers? That just leaves you with eternal debt and when you can't put it in francs, then it's just obligation. And submission. Volunteers without even the least bit of self-lessness are always going to look down at the downtrodden: 'Look how I'm saving you. You owe me everything, you owe me your life.' That makes volunteers masters, that makes the other person a slave. Where's the redemption in that?" Auguste figures it would be better for that sort of work, helping people, to be paid. Make it professional and there won't be masters and slaves. When there's money involved, things go smoothly, nobody's sneering at anyone else. All that was in Auguste's head. And he remembers that his job was to get his girl off the streets. But that's not the same at all, this is his daughter, his obligation. And it was God who gave him that command, yes, God himself. His mother comes and talks to him all the time, it doesn't scare him any longer. She guides him, she knows what God wants, and what God wants can't wait.

That man with a big cross around his neck? He looks plenty vain. He's talking about people on the street like they're barely human. What's compassionate about that? The way he talks about "them" just sets Auguste on edge.

The man can tell Auguste doesn't think he's a messiah. He says something about a long night ahead and moves on to the harbor. Auguste waves without a word.

It's almost two in the morning, Auguste would do anything to lie down, get some rest, but it's not time for that yet. He's still got to kill the other man, that's why he's here after all. This plan of his, the one he's got good reason for, feels like it means more than that. As if doing this would be pulling out the biggest thorn of all from this street—from this island, even. In the hours he's been waiting, he's warped Georges into the soul of absolute evil. Lucifer in flesh and blood. If he kills Lucifer, Auguste will save these little girls, he'll save his own girl, he'll save his country from debauchery. Auguste came back from the land of the dead, and not for nothing. The savior's here, he's looking on Sodom and Gomorrah, his face twisted into a smile, his eyes see into the far distance, far beyond this street. He's almost not there anymore, he's dreaming that the world's just waiting for him. Now he's talking quietly and smiling. His mother is there, right by him, almost beside him. She says she'll protect him, he mustn't be afraid. She strokes his hair, says she's sorry for not doing that more often when she was alive, so happy, or almost, on that other island. Finally she says words Auguste can't make heads or tails of. She says "forgive me, my son," and, like she always does, disappears, and all that's left is a warmth around him. It always does Auguste good to feel that warmth, it helps him remember that all those moments aren't just daydreams. He doesn't have to worry that he might be mad. That all these meetings aren't just figments of this boozer's, this boozer-no-more's, in any case a madman's imagination.

The bar's going to close down any minute now, the customers are stumbling out one by one, happy or not quite, alone or arms around whomever they're taking home . . . They're going to bed, back to their real lives.

And right then, Auguste sees his son Pauro walking with a white man, a short one who's skin and bones. They've come from the waterfront, and they disappear onto the porch where ruddy Rosa had showed up not a few hours ago.

Now's not the time to think about Pauro, but in Auguste's head thoughts and words are coming together already: if that isn't what masculinity and religion and morality all say is taboo, then he doesn't know what it is. Something terrible, something vile. It's almost shouting what it is. Homosexuality.

The street empties out, little by little. The bouncer at Georges's bar says one last "see you tomorrow" and goes off to his car in a parking lot down the way. It's time. The black door with gold-plated locks is half open, or half closed, depending, just like that old saw about glasses half full or half empty, not that it matters. Auguste can't guess whether he'll find Georges alone inside. But, deep down, he doesn't care. Whether it's one or two or three people he'll have to kill doesn't really matter, not now. He's waited too long for this, he's starting to feel tired all the way through. He goes in.

Georges has his back to him. He hears the man come in, says: "Is that you?"

Auguste could just chuckle, he says no. Georges turns around, the picture of shock. He asks, "What's Papa want now?" Auguste doesn't say a word. He sees the place is empty. Georges is tired, bone-tired, he's got a hand on his leg and is saying he's worn out, that the bar's closed, that he really wants to just go home now. He says, "What do you want, if it's money I don't have any, just go now, this isn't the unemployment office, Pops. You should go talk to that other nutcase who's always coming up this way at night." Georges is frustrated and that only makes his face look uglier as he keeps on talking: "This is my place, get out of here."

Auguste figures he's a good sight younger than this bastard. Bigger and stronger too. That's usually how it works out. As bodies go, he's got most other men beat. He doesn't like the sound of "This is my place," the snark of it. That's the last straw, he shouldn't have said that, not now, not here. Whose place is it ever, anyhow? The Tahitian man notices the room's still full of smoke, the gray ball's still spinning all by its lonesome over the dance floor. It's throwing off tiny silvery rays every which way; they disappear into the carpeted walls. Georges asks him to leave again. Auguste takes a seat at the bar, calm as can be, says: "I want my girl." That's no real answer. Got no place here. Inappropriate. Then Auguste says her name: Rosa. And he's slow and sure as he tells Georges the way he sees it, how he feels, what he'd like to happen. There are actual tears in his eyes. He's been waiting out on the street for hours. Hours where he'd pieced together these words, easy enough. "It's so simple, don't you see?" Then Auguste keeps on talking about when his girl was little. A little girl who loved to dance, to outdo herself, yes, she wanted to be a woman right away. She mistook making love for actual love. She didn't know any better. She was innocent. She could have been someone else, the mother of a proper family, a happy one even. But she met you. She became a whore. She put herself in your hands and you ate her right up.

What Auguste is angry at this moron for is for getting rich off his girl's ass. For making a nice bit of money off her being young and pretty. For turning a profit from all those young little girls he saw outside. Suddenly Georges is ashamed. Yes, he'd like to know whose place this really is and who's intruding. Which of them ought to be pushed out. He steps back. Between the two of them there has to be ten meters now. The father is suddenly making Georges feel scared, he's no homeless guy. He doesn't seem to have come in peace. The Frenchman starts giving him mumbo jumbo about how "she and the other girls came and found me." As if this street belonged to him. But yes, he'd asked the girls if they were of age and if they really were consenting. Of course they'd said yes. He has all sorts of old lines, saying "sorry, but . . ." over and over. And he caps it all off with how it's because of him that the girls are spending time with proper gentlemen. That he knows his men and that soon Rosa is going to be getting married. Probably to Alain, a rich pearl farmer everyone around here knows. She's a lucky one, that Rosa . . . Auguste keeps on staring at the gray ball. He doesn't want to hear another word. Georges keeps on going, his voice getting shaky, and finally he suggests that the two of them go into business together. Money wouldn't be a problem.

Auguste seems to be thinking. He's calmer now. He asks for a drink and the other man rushes to pour him one. A bourbon, here, it's the best kind we've got. Let's toast to it. Auguste looks down. Why not.

Things look like they're working out now. Georges is certain that money can solve all his problems, especially with other men. Every single problem. Even the police, even them, he'd been able to buy them off, now they act like the streetwalkers don't exist. No country bumpkin out of his mind with voodoo talk is going to change that. Money makes the world go round.

The bourbon goes down easy. Auguste feels better, refreshed. He smiles and the gray ball finally stops. Georges takes one step, then two, and then he's facing the Tahitian man. All that stands between them is a worn old counter. The barkeep leans on his elbows, looking at peace. He seems to be waiting, ready to hear the sad father's sob story. Of course he hasn't understood. Auguste opens his mouth, he explains in scraps and bits of French that it's not about money, but that's all right. There's nothing to explain. Death will take care of it all, the way it and nothing else can. He talks about bad apples. Nothing to them, you just get rid of them so they don't spoil the whole barrel, so everything stays good. In Auguste's jeans is a kitchen knife that's been waiting for hours, nearly forgotten. The blade's almost one with his thigh. It's stayed there, ever so quiet, all this while. It has a soul, this blade, it won't be erased that easy.

And suddenly Georges sees. He takes a step back, and in one last lonely outburst, begs for him to be reasonable, uses gentle words. After money, he tries pity. "Have pity on me, if you will, I'll go for good." But the Frenchman still doesn't get Auguste's mission, much less that it's his whole life. He's seeing to the world, to humanity as a whole. "You can go somewhere else, and you can start all over . . . You've really gone too far for this little slice of paradise, Georges. You could have been so happy here in this Tahitian hell, the way the rest of us are already. But no, you had to look down on us all. You had to try to make it a paradise of sex and money. And now you're done."

Auguste stands up, reaches right over to the other man so easy. A yank has the Frenchman's head crashing down on the countertop. Shattering. Like waves forced to crash against rocks. One, two, three blows . . . Until he's lost count. The head keeps coming up and then going back down between the bar and some spot in the air. Up and back down . . . and there's the sound of bones cracking, or maybe it's the wood. The nose is sunken in, his forehead busted open. His face is a completely different shape now, stained red. The cries come, but at this hour nobody's keen to hear a thing. And it goes on. Then comes the knife. Glittering in the last bit of silver light. Right to left, through a shaky neck—it cuts through the man's gasp. The blood makes a pool. A huge black puddle on the counter, a gaudy golden chain floating in it.

Auguste's eyes rolled back like a man possessed, dispossessed even. The smile on his face is a madman's. Driven mad by having carried out his mission.

The day after the next, all the papers have headlines about a "cowardly murder." As if they had any idea about the particulars behind the murder. It was a murder, no question. But "cowardly" was just assuming, an idea the journalists hadn't been able to stop thinking.

Really, who other than the murderer or the victim could say that it was cowardly? Of course rumors were flying. They had to have been settling scores. A journalist was spotted going up that cursed street in the morning, in the evening. Over time his articles turned into accusations. He claimed there was a prostitution ring that'd had enough of that greedy Corsican. There was some truth in that, plenty of folks would have been happy to see him dead, but the editor had no idea that it wasn't their fault, that the "network" was Georges and nobody but Georges. In short, Papeete after dark was a different mood now. The bar closed down, the whores had to lay low for a while, and it wasn't a good idea to get to talking with that local tabloid reporter with a big Marquesan tattoo of a furious ti'i on his right calf. No, it was never wise to make small talk with him. His grin was as wide as Jesus's own even while he was twisting the words of some poor nameless woman, say, the bar manager, into a cry of distress and misfortune. "Poor Georges who saved us from the worst." Sure, she'd said that, more tired than anything, seeing as now she'd have to go find another job. But that turned Georges from being a bastard, a lowly piece of shit, to a martyr. In terms of the investigation, there wasn't much progress, at least according to the police. It seemed to have come to a standstill. It was all a big fat nothing that the papers kept playing up and trying to make something about. They made mountain after mountain out of this molehill and dug up this whole story about this respectable social worker left for dead in a vacant lot. In Papeete, everyone was on edge. All the papers took the same tack, a poor victim killed, slashers running amok. And they had to keep feeding the story. So they fixated on those cross-dressers who sometimes beat people up. And then they cooked up Georges's past. He was made out to be a charity worker who went and helped girls and boys on the street. What a lovely thing journalism can be, cooking up a whole life, drawing a picture that ends up becoming your legacy, making up their own news.

Sure, all this hubbub around "l'affaire Georges" wasn't at all what Auguste had expected. After enough time, thankfully, everyone moved on.

Insanity

ROSA SHOWED UP at her parents' again the day after the murder. She was wound up, out of sorts. She'd quit alcohol and tobacco and weed, quit them all cold turkey. She lay in bed and only ever got out to go to the bathroom. Ma started telling people that her daughter was sick. She mollycoddled her now more than she ever had. And Auguste looked after her too. She was like a hurt little bird being tended to by two lovesick wolves. They moved an armchair into the girl's room for Auguste who still wasn't working and instead spent his days reading the Bible to her. He kept talking about the story of Mary Magdalene, the whore Jesus saved. Some reading, that, and some monologue too coming from a father whose body, whose mind had clearly changed too much. There was practically no recognizing him now. His beard had grown out, and his hair too. His eyes wide-open, bloodshot, bulging. At moments he seemed like some sort of visionary or prophet. He ranted about purity while his daughter sobbed silently. He was also saying that evil came from outside, from overseas, specifically from Frenchmen. He started telling Rosa, who had beans for brains, the whole story of Matahi. Auguste had been babbling about mystical matters but now he was slipping little by little into babbling about expelling folks, and it hardly sounded any different. Babbling about expelling the Other, which wasn't just some colonizer, some gravedigger of the past, some thief of history, but some Other that in his view was absolute scum, evil incarnate. What with the culture he'd imposed, the habits he'd trucked in, the Frenchman was no better than a tumor, a cancer, eating at a life that used to be so healthy. Those fenced-in days between his daughter and him shook with hatred he felt ought to be there. Auguste kept thinking on the day of his murder. He was sure that he'd done right and that this was only a start. In his head, it was so clear-cut. After all, why shouldn't he have? Yes, from a heartless, mathematical perspective, it was thinkable. Call it natural selection, maybe, or choosing Polynesians over all other peoples. From a strictly rational perspective, it was thinkable, it was understandable. The most barbaric scenes of history were all a question of pure, clean math.

Thoughts with no pity, no give to them. All about expulsion. In the face of that, of her father's ravings, Rosa's heart gave in. Yes, deep down Rosa had a heart, a stupid one, but even so she did know how to suffer. No, she didn't have beans for brains. She looked at her father heading for points of no return, points that didn't even exist. For days on end she lay in bed, trying all by herself to stave off the ravings of a mind that had lost all its bearings. By herself, she fought as best as she could against his pride and insanity. How, why had she come back into the family? That morning, right after killing the Corsican guy, Auguste had set off to find his daughter. Or rather, he'd set off to find her at her place. He said later that his mother had guided him, like always. He'd knocked at the door of a studio. When Rosa opened it, she screamed. It wasn't her father. It wasn't him anymore. Those piercing eyes were horrifying, sent chills down her spine. Insanity had a face, insanity was a thing she recognized even though she'd never laid eyes on it before. It might not have any heft to it, but she could point her finger at insanity.

❖

For Pauro, things were starting to fall apart. There was no sneaking away anymore. He had to be back home at four, no later. Auguste was insisting that his son sleep in the living room. That way, so long as the door was open, he could keep an eye on the teen from the bed he shared with his wife. There hadn't been any words between the two. The father hadn't seen fit to give him any reasons for all these new rules. The son had some inkling. So François and he only saw each other between noon and two, but that didn't stop them. Often the archaeologist rushed down his valleys with fear in his heart because he'd nearly forgotten their meeting. And he'd find his young lover furious because class was starting in half an hour. They'd race back to the studio and have sex like roosters, as fast as they could. In those moments love had little to do with pleasure. Each time felt like the last. The last chance to feel each other's bodies, because the next day it might not be possible at all. More than anything these moments were frustrating: their lives weren't about them, but about other people and their scowls. It wasn't enough that gay love had to be a secret; now it was dangerous, it could be the death of them. Auguste started hanging around the school at lunchtime. When he did, there was no chance of Pauro slipping out. The teen would have loved to poke his father's eyes out. His father there meant the whole day up in smoke. And François just a picture he'd forgotten to slip into his backpack, into his wallet. And because there was no picture, Pauro was terrified of forgetting his face. They were scared of it all slipping away. François was like a loss Pauro was suddenly feeling. And because there's no feeling loss until the lost person is needed, that meant it was too late. For him, if he didn't find his lover again, he'd have as good as lost his life.

Hannah and Michel

THE TREES UP AND DOWN the esplanade are scraggly and bare. A few kids all bundled up are playing on a grayish stretch, with their au pair watching them. Plenty of Black girls in the mix. Hannah's alone, like always. The greenish bench she's sitting on is a bit wet, like it was raining earlier. The sky is just about looming: low, shot through here and there with white. It's autumn, and a bit sad. Maybe too sad. It makes you want to give up everything. The day before, Hannah got a letter from her mother. Hannah looks at a man in a sailor outfit getting his picture taken in front of Les Invalides. He's giving his girlfriend a big grin. She's got to be his girlfriend, or maybe his wife. Her hair is brown and she's wearing a huge fur hat that's the same color. Maybe it's fake fur, Hannah thinks. Maybe. Or maybe not. She's had enough of that. Why does she have to spend time thinking about these animals who were killed? There are plenty of organizations she can pay to do that thinking for her.

The couple heads off down the rue de Varenne. The man looks back one last time at the gold railing. The woman's gone and buried her face in the man's shoulder. The wind is like ice, cutting through, wettish, and it works its way through Hannah's dark skin. She can take it. She's been sitting here for two hours, reading her mother's letter over and over. A letter full of pain. All this pain, Hannah can tell, boils down to one thing: Auguste, a father made a stranger by booze. Can she even remember a single day of him sober, warm? She's pretty sure not, but deep down, she can't bring herself to care. Her father not being there is a simple fact that she's never let herself think on, she'd figured there was no point in it. The letter's badly written, of course, full of pleading in not so many words, full of love she's not sure she believes, full of "but how are you?" over and over as if hinting that without her things weren't all right. Scolding her, really, so her mother won't be the only one to feel alone, even if she wouldn't dare to say it out loud. Hannah's learned about Auguste's accident, and his being born again. And his new quirks on top of how distant he'd always been. The letter talks about religion. Ma says that it was good at first, this return to God, but now it's all too much. And at that point Hannah wrinkles her brow. When has her mother ever, just once, had things under control? Not at home, that's for sure, not while they didn't have money. Ma says she's trying to keep up appearances, to make everyone believe that the family is now back together, even without Hannah. The children have grown up. Pauro's going to take the baccalaureate soon, he's a man now, after all, a proper man. Ma goes on and on about Rosa, Rosa who's got her worried, who's been lost and now found again. Right now Rosa's going through a hard time, but she's on the up-and-up. And the mother mentions Pina very briefly.

The letter is full of requests that aren't requests, she's pleading for help but not saying it. Come out with it, Ma, what is it you want? Hannah feels uncomfortable, she's reading things she has to guess at. What is it her mother actually wants? Can't you just say it straight out, Ma? What is it you need from me? For me to come and save you? I've just barely got my head above water! In her letter, Ma asks if Hannah's business is going well. Yes, she actually thinks Hannah is running a company. She's completely mental. Hannah's having trouble breathing. She undoes the knot of her scarf. That helps a little.

Running a company. God, if only! No, she's not running a company. For just a bit over a month, she's been helping with a business for her lover and boss. Bertrand. He's not really her guy, there's no way Bertrand is her guy, much less a husband in the making. No, it's far too early for all that. They haven't said "I love you" yet, haven't even dared to let on that they're in a relationship.

But for a few weeks now, she's been working at an art gallery that's a bit different from the others. One where art isn't out of reach. Prints of Klein have been selling like hotcakes lately. The store is called Art Popu and its walls are blotchy with rectangles of black and red and every other color. And that's all that can be seen, rectangles that make no sense to Hannah, but it doesn't matter, she's not there to understand them. She just has to sell them, set up small exhibitions, order more Pollocks (prints, of course) that always sell well, she has to deal with pimply teenagers, tall and talented art history students, and on Saturdays there are grown-ups in sneakers or on trendy in-line skates that have to cost a pretty penny. And she has to deal with people who know plenty of things too, who are well-read unlike Hannah herself, the poor thing, who has to learn on the job from Bertrand in between business trips. But, thankfully, the customers don't know about that. Just like they don't know that Bertrand is a gallery owner and a publisher, that he has five real galleries in France (plus this fake one that Hannah's managing), another in New York, and two in Italy, plus a huge publishing house here in Paris. Bertrand must have been a failed painter, he's so good at picking out the imperfections of the most famous ones: Gauguin, Picasso, and so on. He must have been a second-rate artist, he loves art so much that he almost forgets about real life. Of course Hannah keeps those thoughts to herself. Two days ago, Bertrand went off to Milan. He has to set up the exhibition for a young Italian guy he says is talented and still unknown. At ten in the morning, Hannah left the boutique on the quai Branly. She doesn't want to deal with anything. She gave the keys to the salesgirl and walked over to Les Invalides. She has a meeting with Michel, a friend, a computer engineer at the place she was working at just before this. He'll be right on time.

There's a few more people on the esplanade now, even in this crappy weather. She thinks about Ma again and whispers, look, Ma, look at where I am now. I'm almost a businesswoman just like you've always hoped. Her eyes run over the crumpled letter again. After so long, a badly written letter, a letter that makes this girl want to come back, to see for herself how much she remembers of that place, those few nice things. A letter that reminds her that she's too far away from everything too. She tries to recall the faces of her family and stops on Pina's. Pina with a look that always struck her as wise, not gloomy, but not happy either, just very clear for a four-year-old. And that's the last photo she has of her little sister: when she was just four. Thin face, frizzy hair. She almost looked like a little African girl, but without such dark skin. All that is so far away. What's she become, is she hurting too? Then Hannah remembers that the only child who never got a slap across the face was Rosa. But Hannah doesn't hold that against her. That's just how things are. Hannah always felt that children had to put up with parents who didn't do right by them, put up with those beings who played favorites and don't do a good job of hiding it. Put up with them because there's no other way to move on. She put up with it, until she left.

What's wrong, Ma? I'll send you some money, don't worry. Maybe I'll come back for a few weeks ... to see if things are okay, to see if there's any patching things up, mending bridges. Sometimes I half think it's all been a mistake. Yes, being here. Ma, did you really think I turned my back on you? Do you really think that being so far away wipes away those things we never said out loud? I'm at the other end of the world and I've been crying all the while, I'm still crying. We never really grow up, not really. Michel wrote such a beautiful poem, I still remember a few words of it, at least I think these were the words: "I'm ruined myself, like a ghost, by the dead streetlights of Paris." Michel's a real poet, he's all full of wounds. I'll call you later, that's the best I can do. It's a bit late to get into it all, but I'll call you.

Hannah's been sitting for a couple of minutes on the bench facing the métro entrance. She can see the top of the head she knows all too well, reddish-brown, starting to get thin, and then the lips come into view, always curling down. The sky's getting a bit darker. Michel gets to the top of the escalator, carried up while all the others in anoraks run up, even on Saturdays. Michel's eyes are looking down, like always. And what's under his feet is ground, gravel. He raises his chin ever so slowly. He's always got an annoyed look, but he's not being snobby; he's shy. Because he feels so small, never mind how tall and stocky his body is. His forehead's broad, almost like a scientist with brains so big they have to fill this stretch from his brows to his hairline. His forehead has to be ten centimeters. Today his hair's combed, he's wearing a shirt under a gray sweater, and he's also got a windbreaker on. He's dressed up nicer than usual, but as clumsy as always. Hannah's never stopped thinking that, that Michel's unusually clumsy, that his body's nothing like his personality. Energetic, alert, above average—well above. It won't be long before he's a famous writer. She knows it, she just knows it. That's just how it'll be, otherwise life wouldn't make sense. The two of them are so fond of each other. He sees her at last and smiles. At some point Michel let on that every so often he'd smile, just because he'd been reminded that smiles are the least ugly thing that people all have. So sometimes he smiles only so he won't be too unattractive. Being cynical's all fine and dandy, but not being unattractive. They give each other a proper hug. Michel likes hugging Hannah this way. She's so small! She barely comes up to his waist. It's always awkward for Michel when they talk, he has to hunch down and something in his spine starts hurting.

"It's always nice to see you, Michel."

"Oh really?"

"Yes!"

"It had to be nice for you to get out of the office too."

"Oh, you!"

"Don't tell me I'm wrong."

"Okay, okay, yes, I did leave, but you'd have done the same if you were a lowly secretary too."

"Well, duh."

"Where are we going?"

"How about Le Divellec? It's right there."

Hannah burst out laughing. Of course. He always got those silly ideas in his head.

"Michel, if you want to eat at Le Divellec, your last name better be Mitterrand or Delon."

"How about Lacan? Or—" He let out a little whistle. "Come on, let's go."

Hannah stopped smiling.

"Michel, no. I'm not going there."

"Why not?"

"It's not my kind of place."

"Oh, come on!"

"I'm putting my foot down. I'd feel out of place, and you know it. I don't like those sorts of spots."

"You're wrong. You're gorgeous."

"It's nothing to do with beauty. It's not about being pretty or smart, it's about having a nice chunk of money. And you and I don't have it."

"You're a looker, Hannah."

"Yes, you've said that. That's not the point."

Sometimes Michel really didn't make any sense. He hated crowds and gatherings, but he loved packed restaurants, hot ones most of all.

"Okay, fine, Hannah. Come on. We'll go somewhere else."

"Thank you."

They found a French spot with Basque specialties on the rue Saint-Dominique. The restaurant was next to Ed the corner grocer. It was odd to see the prices listed outside, right next to a filthy spot selling bric-a-brac. The restaurant was what Hannah wanted: affordable, not too trendy. Almost unknown. No chance of sighting any news anchors or other bigwigs.

Once they'd sat down, Michel got back up to buy some magazines. Hannah waited a few minutes and then started worrying. Michel always caught her off guard. He might have just gone and gotten back on the métro because he'd forgotten too many things. But Hannah did her best to keep her cool. She waited, she sipped a guignolet. It was sweet and even relaxing. Her legs were already starting to loosen. She liked this feeling. And then, finally, Michel turned up again. She could have wrung his neck.

"Don't do that again, Michel."

"Just you watch and see, sweetie."

"But why?"

"It's because you picked Bertrand. Such an artist, such a gentleman, such a dickhead."

"Oh, stop it. It wasn't some choice between the two of you. I like you, Michel, but as a friend."

"As a friend, my ass."

Hannah gave him a look.

"Okay, fine, I'll stop."

"What did you end up buying?"

"*Marie Claire*, *Féminin*, *Actuel*, and . . . *Penthouse*."

Hannah smiled again. She was thinking about how Michel was like an endangered species. Everyone loves them, but really, that's not the only thing people could do about them. Still, it's not like they live right there. Michel doesn't have a TV, he doesn't listen to the radio, he doesn't buy *Libé* or *Le Monde*. It's not that he doesn't care about the news, about the world around him, because that's what he gets his ideas from, but he doesn't want to hear it all, or read all these rundowns from journalists who always have and always will have ego issues. So he reads the letters to the editor. That way he knows what's going on: rants and sob stories from these "common women" sharing them with him.

Michel orders a whiskey on the rocks, has a smoke. They order almost without thinking. Get some confit of duck and then some foie gras with port-wine sauce. What they do care about, a little, is wine, the best kind, or so Michel says. Hannah's never heard the name of this one, but she lets him pick. They talk, she asks Michel to lay it all out. What's he really fixing to do? Any news about the manuscript he sent out? What's happening with those executives who don't know their heads from their asses? Michel says that he's waiting for them to call him or write him. It'll work out, Michel, just be patient. He's working on something else now. Already? About what? Michel says, "It's about you, Hannah," and of course she doesn't believe him.

"You know, Hannah, if you keep on not believing, not believing in people and not believing what they say, you'll end up like Bernier, you know, that woman in accounting. Just like her: old, ugly, all alone."

"That's not very nice, Michel. All I was saying was that I didn't believe you. Because I don't know. I don't get it. Out of the ordinary is what you are, you're so different, it's not possible. And then you go and say I don't believe in anything. Look at yourself! You cross out everything you write. When we finish reading you, we cry because we think there's nothing better we could spend our time reading. And then you destroy it all. That makes you the worst of us all, Michel. You're worse than I am!"

"You're wrong, Hannah. I cross it all out because we need more, because we have to believe in more things, in life if nothing else. You know it. Be fair. I'm telling you that I'm writing about you. And I think that's the best proof of all."

Michel didn't say "of my love." There are moments when there's no going any further in your thoughts. It's a dead end, or an impasse, or, here, pure modesty.

An old lady to their left looks at them warmly. It looks like they're having themselves a little squabble. It's sweet to watch.

The food comes. The two of them dig in, quiet, embarrassed. Michel went too far. It's like he confessed his undying love. I didn't think about Bertrand today, she realizes. She smiles.

"And how are things with Bertrand?"

"Funny you should ask, I was just realizing that I haven't thought about him today."

There's almost a gleam in Michel's eyes.

"Oh, I shouldn't have brought him up then! You're killing me, Hannah. He's no monster, but he doesn't love you the way he ought to."

"What would you know about it?"

"I just know, okay! What time is it where he is? Has he ever taken you on a trip, even once? You know what he's doing with you? He's using you to make himself look good here and there. You're just his exotic little arm candy on Fridays that he shows off at exhibition openings for cool Black artists. He gave you his store, and honestly 'give' isn't the right word. The store isn't anything special for him. He's got plenty of actual galleries, doesn't he? Ones he actually deals with? And there are stuck-up bitches at every one."

"You're quite the know-it-all, Michel."

"What, you think I'm just going to let you be fooled?"

"You're jealous, that's all."

"Oh, jealous, jealous, jealous. Open your eyes, Hannah. You said no to Divellec because you were scared. What if we'd gone? Boom!"

"Michel. Stop it, will you?"

Hannah isn't hungry anymore. She pours herself some more wine.

"That's low of you, Michel. I've never seen anyone go this low with me."

She could have yelled. Maybe it's the alcohol, maybe it's the stress. Ever since she started working by the quai Branly, she's only been getting four hours of sleep a night, sometimes less. She's doing everything she can to make Bertrand happy. To blow his socks off.

Michel's just blinking. That'll teach him. Everyone else in the restaurant is staring at them.

"I'm sorry, Hannah. I'm sorry."

She's ready to give him a piece of her mind.

"I'm so sick. Sick of not being happy. Sick of not having anyone to love. Bertrand is sixty. Is that so hard to believe? And I'm twenty-five. He's had three wives already. They're all classy women. They've all been to art school, and finishing school before that, they've all got huge stuck-up-bitch eyes. And all I've done is go to business school and not even a fancy one. I was on scholarship! Come on. Yesterday I got a letter from my mother. I have a mother, you know, and a father too. And a shitload of brothers and sisters. I've never seen the youngest one, not even in pictures. Her name is Moïra, but what do you care. I'm just putting that out there. Anyway, my mother. I got a letter from her last night. For the first time she actually wrote to me, and I felt like, back there, things are actually worse, and my whole night's been a mess. I wasn't much better this morning. Sure, we all have problems with our mothers. I've had my share too. When I was a kid, I couldn't see why she didn't dump my dad who was a big old drunk. I didn't get it at all. And then while I was waiting for you, it all clicked. She never left him because she'd sacrificed herself, forever, for a man, for her children. She really was sure it was the right thing, that it was what she was supposed to do. And I realized that I love her, I love that woman. I still do. She's never had a hug to spare for me. I was the one who helped with everything around the house because she had to deal with rug rat after rug rat like flies in the soup. But she didn't know that I had to take care of my father too. I had to deal with him. You listen here. I had to do things nobody should ever have to do.

Horrible things. I hated myself for years, I hated that man. I had to handle him on his nights, like a trained woman who's learned everything about her man down to the last little thing. Who knows what it means when he slows down, when he's tired. Who figured out how to get those horrible moments, those disgusting moments that were somehow freeing too over with as quickly as possible for him and me. That I had to make sure he stayed happy so he didn't feel lonely because Ma was getting pregnant over and over and over. I was eight! While I was waiting for you, I was rereading her letter and then I thought: You asshole, where were you when I needed you? Where? Where did you want me to be? Where did you want to find a woman like that? She had so many kids, she had so many bruises after every single weekend, some worse than others, she had black eyes, cracked ribs . . ." Hannah took a breath.

"Booze did all that, tore apart that family. Destroyed me. You know, deep down, what you want Bertrand to be like for me. He can't reach me, nobody can reach me anymore, Michel, it's all over. Are you scared for me? It's too late for that, I died a long time ago. It doesn't matter if it's Bertrand or you or someone else, that doesn't change a thing . . . Anyway, the letter. I finally got it when I remembered that my father did things to me that would break any girl, I got it when I thought I might be clinging to Bertrand, I think about clinging to people a lot, so I can forget. Even booze doesn't help. It's wrong to say that people drink to forget. Booze forces you to think about yourself. To look at your life like it's a rotting belly button. It's disgusting, but there's nothing you can do about it. It's almost nice to look at death and every day you have a drink you think about it again. Every single day. So you can find the one big hole in your existence, so you can daydream a bit too. I drink, but I can't forget. And there you have your answer about Bertrand and the store. They're how I deal with it. Fine, Bertrand's just a lover. We have sex every day, every night, all the time, whenever we can. That's how I manage to forget a little, and I actually do forget, yes, I forget somehow.

"I hated my mother. Sometimes I was sure she knew it. I was mad at her for squeezing out kid after kid. I hated it when she was pregnant. I still hate her, but I know she needs me right now. And it can't be easy for my little sisters. You're giving me all this hassle about Bertrand and about yourself, dropping hints about liking me. Thank you so much, Michel, but do you really think that's going to make things all better for me? And then you accuse me of not believing in anything. You're wrong. I believe in redemption, some kind of redemption. Not the Christian kind, for the whole human race. The kind that's just a single person who'll come and pull us, my family and myself, out of this. I'm waiting for that pure soul. I'm waiting for redemption for myself. My mother and father too. Yes, for them too."

She takes a breath and says it again: she hates pregnancies. Then she breaks into nervous laughter, a little hysterical laugh.

Michel's crying too. It really does a number on Hannah, seeing a man cry so quietly, no disgrace or hatred or fuss to it.

"You're the only one who knows all this, Michel. It's a lot."

And then a gulp of wine, still a bit bitter.

It's already five in the afternoon. Michel hasn't noticed that the restaurant's empty, Hannah either. The owner is silent, at the far end of the room, not even moving. Michel leaves him a fat tip and says thanks for not trying to kick them out. The hulking figure says a few nice words, with that Basque accent of his. "Hope to see you again soon," he says, and he watches as they walk out and leave.

It's almost night. The rue Saint-Dominique's empty, the metal shutters covered in graffiti are pulled down over the Clef des Marques storefront, leaflets are fluttering over the sidewalk. Hannah's tottering. They stop at the corner store for some Marlboros. Across the street is a wine shop. They get four bottles of chardonnay, Hannah's favorite.

"I don't want to go back home, Michel."

"I know. And I don't want to see you go. Not ever."

Clumsy Michel's holding her by the waist. He's really too tall.

They call a cab to take them to the rue de la Convention in the fifteenth, where Michel has a two-bedroom. The main room's huge, stark: just a couch and a bookcase.

He flicks on the kitchen light and leaves the door open. A rectangle of light between two worlds—one full of darkness, one full of light. They pick darkness.

"I'm forty, Hannah. Not sixty. I'm not some highfalutin aesthete. I don't travel much. I'm a bit claustrophobic. I don't measure up against your Bertrand. But I'll keep talking about it. Because I'm jealous, after all. I saw you that day when you started working at Mister Timid's, looking so uncomfortable. You were so pretty and I was already head over heels for you. Then you walked over to me."

"That's true, I did. I was the one who said hello. How funny. You know I'm not much for small talk. But it was different with you. It's always different with you. It's never like with the others."

Hannah has her feet up on the coffee table; she's already pulled off her ankle boots, her turtleneck. He's turned up the heat. She's still got her tight T-shirt on.

"I've never gone out with friends. Isn't that weird?"

The wine's there in glasses that he'd just washed a minute ago and then set by their feet.

"Do you ever tidy up, Michel?"

"I'm a guy."

"Look, stop talking about Bertrand like that. Things can change in just an hour. Sometimes all it takes is a word, a thought, that meant everything yesterday but nothing today. Or the other way around."

He's put on some music. A jazz compilation. Duke Ellington, Billie Holiday, a few others.

"Do you like jazz, Michel?"

"Not really. It's just to set the mood. To give me a bit of a personality when I have girls over."

"Gee, thanks."

"No problem whatsoever."

They have a bit of a laugh. It's almost ridiculous. It's lighthearted.

"Tell me more about you, will you?"

"Sure," Hannah says, and there's no dwelling on why he's asked, how wise or unwise any of this might be. Right now, she's feeling relaxed, not so weighed down. Maybe this was all the right thing for her to do, who knows.

"In a few minutes, Michel, we'll have sex. Then you'll have gotten your fill of me. My body, my past. Maybe tomorrow you'll kick me out. It's no big deal. Those things happen. I'll give this a try. I'm sleeping over tonight. In the morning, if you suddenly feel like you're all out of sorts, if I see that you're looking at me different, then you're just as stupid as all the others. But don't worry, don't feel guilty, just remember, I died a long time ago."

The minutes go right by. They look each other over. He rests a hand on her neck and pulls her close. She smells his sweat. Under his shirt, she feels some hair. Kisses, sucks on his skin. Reaches for his fingers and palms. He shuts his eyes, all of a sudden he's small, weak, at this girl's mercy. He sit down on the floor, takes in the naked body lying on the sofa. She's let down her hair and she's practically begging him. He strokes her, holds his breath over her crotch and her lips. Slips in slowly, differently. His tongue's forgotten all these things he thought mattered. So has the rest of his body. His tongue's got something new to do, it's nothing to do with pleasure, it's about marking his territory, nothing selfish to it, just wanting to do her good, needing to give her back some life.

She could have yelled. When he takes her, inside it's not just hot and soft. He's thinking that, of all the women he thought he'd loved, none of them had such a perfect body. The way she's squeezing him, pulling his penis in—there's something delicious, needy, hungry to it.

Men aren't something that's been missing from her life, but still, even with Bertrand, she's never felt pain like this, never felt fulfilled like this. Pain. There are too many things holding the two of them together. They didn't bother with condoms. Love, true love, means they'd be willing to die by or with each other.

Michel always figured he was a second-rate lover, that he had nothing on those porn stars men like him living all alone measured themselves against. He didn't have a body like theirs, muscles like theirs, he didn't reckon he could come anywhere near them. But Hannah lets herself go with him, like no other woman ever had. And she doesn't seem to be faking it.

Now he's on his balcony. Completely naked. He's smoking, he's freezing, but he barely feels it. It's November 25. In a month it'll be Christmas. He dreams that he'll finally have someone to give a nice present to, someone to wish happy holidays to. He goes back into the bedroom. Hannah's asleep in his huge bed that he always thought was too chilly. A peaceful face. He sits down and touches her ass, those rounded dunes. She's like a princess. My princess, he thinks, my island princess. With his tongue, he wakes her up. It's so good. Hannah feels her body shaking. Inside her there's a huge hole, the kind happiness leaves behind sometimes, a bitter happiness because it's so hard to believe. She lets go. She lets herself moan.

More Meetings

"NO, I DON'T WANT to."

"Come on."

John could just slap that son of his. It'd been more than a month now since he'd seen his kids last and he missed them, pure and simple. And this son was kicking and screaming at the thought of leaving his grandparents'. This ate at John. The grandparents' silence too, even more so. What was there for these kids to like about these two old fogies who hadn't smiled once since Nora's death? He could see with his own eyes how much the couple hated him. John had his limits. Last time, at a Sunday lunch at Nora's childhood home, his older kid, Steve, and his younger one, Maeva, just about threw the Nintendo console across the living room. Because they were tired of it, because . . . no good reason to it, they were just unhappy. John had had it with them. His kids had never been such spoiled brats, the most spoiled brats ever. He'd gotten up from that table where the hole of an empty seat, a chair none of them could stop glancing at, Nora's, was almost too much. The moment he'd walked out of the dining room to see what had the little snots squabbling, his fist clenched, his mother-in-law had hollered. She'd never been so different, or maybe she'd never been so *her*. About time he scrammed, he'd never even kept that wife of his under control. The night she'd died, she'd been headed home from another night on the town, another one without her husband.

She must have been wasted, but nobody in the house even so much as thought those words. They had to keep up appearances. They needed Nora to die a victim, even if this wasn't all the fault of the other drunkard, the reckless driver. Nora the pretty one, Nora the life of every party in Tahiti—they needed her to die at someone else's hand. For her own sake, for the kids, for the whole family, someone else had to take the blame. Everyone needed to think she was innocent. That mattered. So everyone did. Apart, maybe, from the police, those idiots who'd found far more alcohol in her blood than in the other bonehead and who'd dropped the whole matter there and then.

So where *was* he that night, John? Who did he think he was, insisting on keeping the kids when the whole marriage had been a sham? Nora drank like a woman never ought, like a whore. Nora had gone through lovers while John had kept a poker face, stayed mum, not reacted. John had never felt jealous. "That poor idiot," said the old lady who owned the place and sometimes ran it. "Poor idiot" of a son-in-law who only ever liked Nora in public, who only loved her because it never occurred to him to have other feelings.

Ever since that Sunday, of course, things had gone pear-shaped. There was a whole wall up now between their life before and their life now. John called and his kids only picked up sometimes. Because he had to play dad, he called his son. Because he really was a dad, he talked to his daughter. And then he got to feeling lonely, actually lonely, and he made up his mind.

The old woman was standing on the veranda, a small shawl around her shoulders. She told John to give them a bit more time. The kids weren't living with strangers now, were they?

John's son was actually crying; he wasn't faking it. Maeva kept her thumb in her mouth, he couldn't believe she wasn't bothered, she just looked annoyed. The old woman kept on watching them all, John in particular. There was something crowing in the woman's eyes, something crowing, so proud of itself.

And there were also the facts, as the man saw them. He was Polynesian, strong, good-looking, a bit of an artist, even if everyone was, a little. An artist who'd always wanted to stand out, even if he overdid it some, made it all pointless. He wrote plays and put them on, but not everyone was a fan. And there wasn't much money in it either. He made ends meet by working as a mason at Papeete's biggest building sites, that was what he'd been doing today.

Those were the facts. His wife was gone, his kids were living another life, without him.

He took off, had himself a chuckle at the thought of all that gravel flying off every silly which way.

He could have been leaving for good. Huh. Now that was reassuring. The place was huge, the coconut trees all over every bit as stiff as their owners.

Then he thought, he thought about the last time he'd had sex, with that woman, the other man's wife. A woman from here, not a light-skinned girl, not a highfalutin one. He also thought about how he'd enjoyed it, how he didn't regret any of it. Nora's body wasn't even cold, but it wasn't the adultery that shook him, it was this woman's gesture. A grand gesture, a gift of herself that couldn't be measured, that nobody could ever understand apart maybe from the two of them and the two of them alone. He didn't care to explain it away, he didn't see why he ought to. That was just how it was. Life's too odd, too unpredictable to warrant explanations. You do things, and sometimes that's all you can do. In the house that he'd shared with his wife, he'd cleared the place out. Sold off the furniture, given away his wife's clothes like a whole heap of broken toys just taking up space. All he used now was the kitchen, the guest bedroom, sometimes the living room. He'd locked the other rooms. One morning he realized that suited him. This new setup, this new layout, suited him. Another morning after that, he reckoned it was perfect, it did the job, it was perfect for him and only him.

A traffic jam—he ought to have expected this, being that it was a weekday and rush hour. He listened to the old government-sanctioned mumbo jumbo about the history and specialties of this country. And now it was time for listeners to dedicate songs to people. "This is for so-and-so who'll recognize this. I hope you're doing well . . . May I have a bit?" John always snickered when he heard someone saying "I hope you're doing well." It was the dawn of the third millennium, most everybody knew about Facebook, but phones were a scarce thing at times. So people begged for news from their friends through the radio. They got worried enough about those friends that they had to take the edge off with a song. John felt like he'd been born listening to this pabulum. Not a thing had changed but the songs themselves. John had a flashback to his teens. Nora had done it to him too here and there. "To my darling John, from you-know-who." "From you-know-who": it wasn't mean, or rude, it was just stupid. And of course Nora only picked out songs she liked, put John through Mike Brant and Hervé Vilard and even that old seventies singer Dave.

The cars were finally moving again. But John kept on replaying these moments of youth, and he suspected that if his teeth weren't clenched so tight, his laughter would have been the loudest thing around.

By the Papeete post office, some woman was walking down a brand-new, almost golden-brown sidewalk. He took one look at her back and recognized her. It was the way she arched her back and swayed her hips and shoulders, almost out of pride. It's her, yes it is. John started to get worried, he wanted to go faster, to pass her and see her up close, wave at her. Just wave at her. Maybe she'd be happy to see him. He sure was . . . yes, he really was happy. The traffic finally picked up. The truck revved, John nearly stalled. His car was so finicky that just the lightest tap on the gas got it all wound up. And everyone could hear it. Ma suddenly turned around, as if the noise that seemed to be too close were a bother.

Their eyes met, their lips smiled, shy and awkward. Behind him, the cars were honking. John didn't notice that the road was clear for a hundred meters ahead. He waved. She seemed to panic, wavered, dashed off. In his rearview mirror he saw her go into a perfume shop across from the post office. He'd circle around, of course, he had a feeling she worked there, she was carrying boxes. He smiled and suddenly those little radio lines "to my darling" didn't seem the least bit ridiculous. There was even a Céline Dion cover of a Jacques Brel song. The words were lovely. It was about love and all that. John was happy, at last . . . he thought.

Ma's arms were stiff, blotchy. The phone rang. "Can you get that?" Of course Ma could. The same way, of course, she could go two hundred meters every day from a car to the store with arms full of heavy boxes. Of course, she could pick up the phone. The boss was with a customer, and customers should never be left waiting.

"Hello."

"Hello, Ma?"

It all came back. Old images, just as sepia-toned and hazy as photos. She never forgot voices, no matter how long it'd been, how far away they were. "Yes, Hannah." Without a pause, without any surprise. "Yes, it's me." Ma turned to the owner and almost waved sorry. There was some static, like the two corners of the world weren't quite touching. It was so queer, their voices kept on catching. Time had done that terrible work of pulling the two of them apart. "What time is it there?" "Almost five in the morning. It's so cold right now. I couldn't get any sleep." Ma could feel a lump coming up, almost from her core. A fiery lump that rose up and came back down. Of all her kids, Hannah was the one who'd never gone to sleep easy. "I got your letter, Ma. I have so much to tell you." The lump grew, it was made of joy and pain and worry, it was almost fighting to make itself felt, almost ready to just burst. And it would, very soon. A lump that wanted nothing more than to say, "Sweetie, come home. My sweetie . . ." But the lump didn't have any words, didn't know any, didn't connect to the real world, the one around her. "How are you feeling, Hannah?" "I'm okay, I'm feeling all right. It's the family that's scaring me. Your letter, Ma! Your letter . . ." The boss was done with her customer, she looked shocked, wrinkled her brow. Ma turned away so she wouldn't see her glare. "Hannah . . . It's so good to hear from you. Don't worry, everything is all right here, we're all doing good." Empty words, horrible words in a conversation that couldn't, mustn't have any. "I must be interrupting you, are you at work?" "Yes." "All right, I'll let you go. Talk soon, Ma." "Sweetie . . ." and she heard the receiver come down, go quiet, and then here were beeps breaking off what felt like a dream. She heard the beeps. There's no explaining how firm those beeps were, how heavy that silence they marked off was. Ma turned to her boss and said sorry for not having a phone at home. And said sorry, she needed to leave early today. She didn't wait for an answer, she didn't care, she just walked out of the store. The lump rising up had found a word. "Sweetie," it could just shriek. My little sweetie, Hannah. Now she could let go, the people on the street stared, all befuddled. All this came from deep in her guts, from a placenta that had come out and that meant that there was only a hole now. And all this came from how she couldn't accept such a horrible distance, such a horrible gap between a woman who didn't know how to be the mother she needed to be and a daughter who didn't want to put up with her.

John circled the downtown three times. A filthy town where nobody could breathe. Not a single spot to park, how could there be so many people and how could they spend so long here? Then he got so fed up he parked on a sidewalk. He didn't care, what was another ticket to him anyway? Whatever. John the Daredevil only had one thing on his mind. He walked fast, scared he'd miss her. He was so happy, looked so silly for smiling to himself like that. He thought about what he could say to her, some old thing like "I just saw you, and I just had to give you a present from this perfume shop." But he didn't have to think any further. She was right there, in front of him, her eyes wet, she thought she was holding it together. But it wasn't just tears, it was like two dams breaking. It made John think of the stars he looked at when he was little. They'd besotted him because they were so far out of reach, they'd besotted him because they were full of mystery; they weren't important the way the sun was, they were almost too beautiful, but they needed to be there. This woman, this Ma was like those stars. He couldn't put it into words, she had no use in his life, not really. But he'd come to need her all the same.

He hugged her. Don't cry, it's over. He had no idea, of course, what had happened. He didn't know about all these unsaid things. Lost loves, meetings that were traps now.

They just walked. It was Friday night, there was music, tipsy men. Teens laughing. There was this one life, this whole world, in the market. As cities go, Papeete isn't the cleanest, but it's worth spending time in anyhow. The bluefin tuna were falling out of a rundown delivery van that looked sorry to be belching fumes. People were yelling. A few women slowly got out of their chairs, in no hurry to serve their customers. They were taking their time, yes they were. A māmā was running her fan over a skipjack filet. She might have been thinking about something else. She might be a bit annoyed too. Ten meters off, an Asian man was trying to get rid of his last heap of cucumbers. There was talking, voices rising, smiles. All these lives crammed together was a pretty sight; they weren't always happy, but they called for her respect. Ma broke down in tears. She was smiling. She decided she wouldn't be leaving. Where would she live? How would she make ends meet? She couldn't, that would be turning her back on them all. She remembered that not too far off, down that way,

some kids were bathing in the harbor. Twenty years ago, the water
had been clear. There hadn't been any skippers, any ships. She finally
looked up at John. There, she was doing better. John smiled. He led
her up the stairs. There was a bar of sorts. They ordered half-pints.
Ma had gotten to drinking beer lately, and wine as well. It was a new
thing for her, but she felt like she needed it.

It's never easy to talk to someone who isn't part of your life, not
really. They knew each other, well, they knew each other's bodies. But
that was a far cry from being able to share secrets, and Ma wasn't
ready to take that leap. Then the beer went down, doing her good
and not just slaking her thirst. It felt like something Ma had been
waiting all day for. Beside her, John had his arms crossed over his
belly, his legs spread out. Their thighs touched. As if the two of them
had been hoping to brush against each other, by accident, and neither had even thought it. They were on pins and needles, the two of
them. Ma recalled the feel of his jeans. Harsh . . . but she went for
it anyhow. She stroked the thigh, clutched the denim. And then she
felt urges, so many of them. Here they couldn't move any further.
There was just John sighing, his eyes half shut. And then he said it
was plain as day. They couldn't not see each other again. They got to
talking properly, no hang-ups. They laughed, a bit loudly. They were
on their second round. She told him everything, everything. Her life
with Auguste, their kids, the problems that were even worse now,
with her husband's recovery not helping matters any. She said that
he was starting to scare her. Then she added that for a month now
she'd been drinking on the sly. Oh, not a lot, just a beer or two here
and there. John listened, but it was odd. He couldn't focus when she
mentioned Auguste's name. It was odd, there was a twinge in his
heart. As if the two of them were old classmates who'd been secretly
in love. And then time had gone by, and they'd found each other
again, now changed, now different. It hurt. It was because he was full
of himself, just a little. He'd always known that women were crazy

about him. That if some sort of sickness only women caught could be dreamed up here, that it would be called Johnitis. Pure and simple. And so when Ma talked about a life without him, the famous artist around these parts, that put him in his place. Famous was a bit much. He shouldn't go so far as to say that, given that Ma didn't seem aware of that. This woman really must have fallen out of the sky.

But it was late, too late for them to reconnect. Ma got up, she needed to go home. She didn't want to get a beating. Auguste had to be waiting up, and the kids too. John asked her: When? When can we see each other again, make love again? He saw no shame in those words, but they were almost too much for her. Soon, she said, soon. And she felt warm inside, her legs were trembling, she wavered, she was sure she would fall. He caught her arm, tried to say something. She didn't have any more time. John didn't like that but he could live with it, he let go of the woman. She said, Tomorrow, same time. Okay, that wasn't a bad answer. Tomorrow. John couldn't wait. He was aching for it, his jeans were tight.

Another Night of Violence

FOUGÈRE. FERN. THE FRENCH WORD comes from the Latin word *filicaria*. It's a vascular plant with no flowers or seeds—on the underside of its leave there are spore-bearing organs called sporangia. Latin names are so far away and when you know them that makes you more important. Pina's sitting outside the shack. She's thinking about ferns, about the macramé plant holders in that white house of her dreams. Her arms are folded. *Fougère*. Ferns, she thinks, they can grow anywhere they like. Her favorite kind is the nahe, with its really big leaves and its nice smell. She's got her hands flat against her ears. She doesn't want to hear. It's too loud, too painful. Auguste is yelling like he's never yelled before. Filicaria is the Latin name. Latin's a dead language for the rich. Only rich people can learn it. This morning, Pina didn't go out at break time. She stayed in the classroom and opened the Petit Larousse dictionary. She wanted to know where ferns came from. Looking at the Petit Larousse calmed her down. She often thought that words were the only things people could take without hurting anyone else, without stealing something from anyone else. She was in the habit of learning words from the dictionary by heart. And looking up their etymology so she could feel like she was close with them. Knowing the meanings of the words was something anyone in the world could do, but knowing where they'd come from made you a bit important. And Pina figured that those weird languages, Latin and Greek, made you a bit stronger. Even if she didn't know those languages, maybe one day she could surprise someone. She still had her hands over her ears, so she didn't have to think. Her back was hurting. Ten minutes ago, Auguste had kicked her. It'd taken the wind out of her. It'd sent her flying against the pea-green wall of Rosa's room. Auguste was still yelling. Ma wasn't home yet.

Pina was supposed to clean Rosa's room. When she went in, Rosa had given her the stink eye. Worse than before. Rosa was lying on her bed, wiped out. Then she saw the little girl, yelled, "You dirty bitch, you dirty bastard." It was like she had that sickness from *The Exorcist*. And she wasn't joking. So Pina, who was no Cinderella, had shot back, "dirty slut." She shouldn't have. Rosa had punched her in the mouth. She was still bleeding. Rosa had shouted, started sobbing. She really was insane. And then Auguste had lost it, aimed his foot at Pina's butt. He'd yelled that Rosa was no slut, not anymore. Then Pauro had come in. And it all took a turn for the worse. Auguste was standing there, looking even more hellish than ever before. Pauro had been frozen, just centimeters away, looking his father up and down. Auguste spat out in Tahitian that he would deal with him later, that he just had to wait, but it wouldn't be long at all. Then he added that this son of his was a disgrace to him. A sissy. He'd been counting on Pauro becoming Matahi in flesh and blood. But that was a lost cause. All his hopes had been lost.

Pina had run to grab onto her brother's leg. Come on, outside, quick, don't tempt the devil, don't do it, don't listen to what Daddy's saying. They'd come to their senses. They'd always come to their senses. Before leaving, she'd grabbed a pile of dirty clothes from a corner of the bedroom, so she could wash it the next day. Rosa had let out an ugly laugh.

❖

"Ferns can grow anywhere they like." Pauro says: "What's the point?"
He's holding his little sister's hand, holding a small ice cube to her
swelled-up mouth. It's too late for ice, that won't bring down the
swelling. If a bit of ice had been all it took, things would have been
so much easier. Pauro strokes his sister's forehead. He's right here,
next to her. He says: "We have to leave." Pina shoots back: "Where?
You've got François but I've got nobody." "Don't worry about that,
let's just leave."

Ma's just back home. She goes to Rosa's bedside, like always after
work. They can hear Auguste asking her where she'd come from.
She must have lied because her husband doesn't believe her. Ma's
voice sounds so worn down, goes quiet. Then she finally hollers that
she'd had a drink, just one drink. Total silence. Auguste has to be too
shocked to even open his mouth. Or maybe he doesn't need to open
his mouth. Or say a word. What they do hear, in the end, they could
see coming. Punches against the wall, a few hollers from Ma. The
hollering of a body getting thrown against furniture. Rosa's sobbing
is just about hair-raising.

Pina's small body is rocking back and forth, her legs pressed to
her chest. Her hands aren't strong enough to block it all out. Pauro's
fists are clenched, his legs are quivering. Moïra's asleep in his lap. She
didn't hear a thing. It's got to be nice to not be able to hear all that.

In the kitchen, Ma's turning on the water. She wants to rinse off,
wash away the blood running almost everywhere. From the corner
of her mouth, from her left eyebrow, from her nose. Wash it all away,
to look a bit more like someone. How long's it been since the last
punch, since her husband's fists landed on her? Big, mannish, animal,
stinky, angry fists. There's no use thinking on it. When things are
quiet, when it's all peaceful at home, it almost feels like that sadness
and his fury never existed. But there's none of that tonight. The blows
were back, just as cruel as ever, just as much shock as ever, her eyes

are full of tears, just about overflowing. Somewhere, in some corner
of her brain, Ma's thinking it was all nothing. Just details. None of it
matters. All her thoughts, all her body are full with John's smile, that
excitement in his face, and she's also got her thoughts on Hannah:
her name, her voice, that shakiness Ma feels too. Hannah's a young
woman now. Maybe a mother already, maybe she, Ma, is a grandmother now. In the sink, the blood's coloring the water. A just barely
bright blood. The water keeps running and the red keeps dripping.

Pauro tiptoes over. He's going to tell Ma, "We have to go." But
he stops. All quiet, feeling so stupid, so small. He sees Ma's face, her
black eye, her cheeks with their bruises already starting to show, the
small scabs drying out in the gashes over her eyes. He looks down,
shakes his head, thinks: "He's got to die." And then: "I'm going to
kill him." Ma looks so ugly all of a sudden. She's still shaking, she has
to be cold. Ma looks so beautiful in this moment. Bigger than the
world, unshaken by life. But Pauro doesn't say anything out loud, out
of respect, so he won't have to show that she made him feel sad and
then scared for her. So he won't have to make her feel like he doesn't
want to see her anymore, not for now. Ma lets out small groans,
small sniffles, then starts whispering that it wasn't so bad, it wasn't
the first time. And then says it again, to herself, that it's okay now,
that it's nothing to fuss about. She's talking to herself because nothing, for the moment, could convince Pauro. All he's got in his head
are things that might make sense, feelings he can't pin down or push
away either. Horror, horror at this life, of you, Ma, too strong for this,
unbreakable, unreachable, too much so. He dreams that this woman
doesn't belong to their world anymore, his and Pina's. She can't even
hear them. Pina's crying quietly outside, he can tell. He's crying too,
but only on the inside. But Ma isn't, not her, not this woman who
hadn't gotten them out of there. Not this big woman who says "it's
not so bad." It wasn't so bad for her because she was selfish, she wasn't
scared of dying. Maybe that's all she was asking for, for death, or

maybe . . . maybe she's already dead. Pauro steps away from the sink, he can tell Ma's turning her face to him. He has a feeling she's going to open her mouth. He prays for her not to. She wavers. He thanks the quiet that's still there. Ma's already gone, somehow, but Pauro has no idea what this love is that's already carried her off.

He doesn't want to think anymore. He just wants to shut his eyes. He goes to find his two little sisters, asleep, carries them to their bedroom, lies down too. He hears his mother going into her bedroom, his father's in there, and it just breaks his heart. He wants to dream about nothing, about absence, about darkness, about the void, about meaninglessness, about pain not existing anymore. He closes his eyes. Close your eyes, Pauro. He cries. Go on, cry. What else can he do? The love he feels for François, for Pina, these loves, they can't ever snap under the weight, the horrors of what he's seeing every day. He falls asleep. If only he could dream of nothing.

Absolute Love

CAN ORDINARY PEOPLE, people not getting torn apart every day by screams and violence, imagine that the days after the worst are full of forgetting? It's odd, it's terrible, but it's true: last night the man hit you, the man seemed like utter scum, but this morning, the man is someone you'd almost want to forgive. He acts so small, says sorry from the bottom of his heart, comes up with excuse after excuse, really wants to know that you're okay. For Pauro and Pina it's a tale as old as time. No surprises there. Auguste's sad face is just like all those other old acquaintances they see around dinner tables. Not all that pleasant, but not all that disagreeable either. It's a déjà vu feeling, like classmates you'd forgotten about but suddenly can't get rid of, narrow grocery store aisles put you face-to-face with them. Yes, that Saturday morning, life starts over again. A terrible film they've seen a hundred times before. The husband serves Ma's breakfast on a fancy plate. She has to stay in bed. The father gives Pina a hug and then he's sobbing on her tiny shoulder. Pina stays calm, calmer than a dead body. Her back still hurts. Auguste tries to hold a warm hand out to Pauro, but the son gets up and walks right out of the kitchen. He shouts to his sister and the two of them head for the bottom of the valley, holding the heap of dirty laundry, the block of soap, and the washboard. Pina's going slower than normal, she almost seems to be broken. Pauro holds back, still red-hot with rage and scorn.

In a basin of the river, the laundry soaks. Blood-soaked sheets, stained by pain. Pina can't help but shudder. She can't take so much blood. The stains have gotten dark, stiff. How can anyone scrub that away? Pauro stands up. Serious, thinking. "Let's wait," he says. "Yes, the water can do its work." Pina's face is stony as she starts scrubbing Moïra's baby clothes and Rosa's underwear. In the water, white bubbles float up along with the smell of Marseilles soap, sharp and reassuring. She scrubs, scrubs. So it'll turn white, so she'll forget. She gives it her all, every last bit. Pauro watches her work and work, her distress and her thoughts fading away. His job is to rinse the clothes, to soak them again in fresh water, and to wring them dry. He can see that she's losing herself in the work, like Ma the night before, but that she's Pina all the way down. He picks up a handful of white foam, sets it on her head to make her laugh. It catches her off guard, and then she giggles, that's all she can bring herself to do. Some Marseilles foam, a few light bubbles, some laughter— their laughter—fill the valley, where a small waterfall is flowing, where nobody ever dares to go, apart from the poor. They get their hands on each other, trying to push each other into the cold water. They've almost forgotten everything, and Pina feels love . . . absolute love. Because she's being held by her brother, the one she worships, because his skin that's both hard and soft, the muscles of his arms, his veins are reaching out to her. Because she loves his man's breath on her neck. Because a fire is growing with each smile. Love, plain old love. How horrible this feeling is to say yes to death because you've reached your limit. She's felt it, and now it can all stop. Pina decides she'll stop there.

She sees her brother's hair sticking to his shoulders. They're lying in the sun, a few midges nipping here and there. The sheets full of water have lost their stains. Soon the washing will be done. The sun's high in the sky. Soon they'll have to head back.

"I miss Poe, and Teanuanua . . ."

"Me too."

They stop there before they start thinking about the memories they know will hurt.

In her bed, Ma thinks that it's nice like this, the calm, the dark of her eyes that won't open. She doesn't hear Moïra or Rosa anymore. The baby's with Auguste in the kitchen. Rosa must still be asleep. Sometimes the girl's sleepless, sometimes sleepy. Everyone prefers her asleep. Ma's body hurts, her arms and eyes especially. They ache, they've lost all their will. Her body has to weigh at least six tons, if she so much as shifts her wrist she wants to scream. He really did a number on her, that husband of hers. Again. In the middle of the night, he'd curled up against her. He'd cried, or pretended to. Like an idiot, a coward, he'd asked her to forgive him. Ma didn't reply, her lips were too swollen. She only thought about her hate, her worry. Only called out to John. Oddly, she felt stronger. She couldn't be sure, but she really thought John's arms would come, one day or another, to save her from all this. She didn't let herself think about consequences, her husband, her children. John would come and save her, nothing more, nothing less.

It has to be eleven in the morning, a van full of goods and junk drives by. It's beeping, telling everyone in the area it's here. Ma smiles a little, in her mind she sees Pauro, Rosa, and Pina a few years earlier, running to buy snow cones. Red for Pina and Pauro, green for Rosa. She remembers how those kids pleaded and begged every day for a few coins. That was the hardest part, but they always managed somehow. Who knew how poor people scrounged up so many coins. Clever, clever.

The children were grown-up, they didn't eat snow cones any-more, didn't ask for money anymore, they knew that there wasn't any. They're there, not far off. Pauro and Pina take care of everything around the house now. She can hear them hanging up the laundry outside. But she doesn't have any strength left, she wants to leave, all she can think about is John. Auguste calls the children in, he's made lunch. He seems to have forgotten everything. Unbelievable. He says out loud that the next day they're all going to church, with Rosa too, she needs it. So they have to pull out their Sunday best. A big dress for Ma that will cover her arms. And the huge hat, and the sunglasses . . . to hide her eyes. A breeze goes through the house, slams a few doors shut, like it's answering Auguste's commands, like it's laughing at them.

Rebirth

AT EIGHT, JOHN FIGURED it was best to head home. He'd been waiting on Ma since four, down in the market. He was alone and all the bar owner wanted was for him to go. He walked around the place for two long hours, 120 minutes, hoping, praying for her to come. But she didn't. He wasn't really sad. Just a bit worried. Suddenly he felt scared, of having been foolish, having believed in something impossible. She's married, after all.

At eight thirty, he was opening his refrigerator for a cold beer. The day hadn't started off well. Even when he woke up things had felt off. There had been a hole, deep down. He couldn't move. Locked in place by some sort of fear at the bottom of his gut. It had him shivering, sweating. Loneliness. Lying there, he'd gotten to thinking about his past. Being an antinuclear, anti-colonialist activist. How beautiful that time had been, when dreams had been all he'd run on. This morning, images had punched through his soul, his body. He saw himself again, walking around town, with his friend who was now gone. A friend now an image, an icon of an entire generation. The two of them and a few others making their way up the streets, going from car to car yelling, "Wake up, your earth's slipping away!" But nobody, or practically nobody, was heeding them. People had just gone on by, unbothered, almost laughing at them. There'd been the bomb they were yelling about, then the bomb was gone. All that remained was independence, taking back their country, but the people here were only afraid of one thing, being free. So things went on. Afraid, wary, scared stiff . . . of a future without France. As if that promised hardship. And then time had gone by, his friend had died. He'd had to work, get back on the straight and narrow, to make Nora happy. For everything, for nothing. This morning, when he was panicking in his bed, when he was thinking again about those nights they'd spent writing poems, plays, he'd wanted to sob, he'd been so sure it was all gone, shaky, up in the air. Now he had no ideas and no fight left in him. There are artists who only know how to dance, who only know how to put on a stupid smile for grants. Who only know how to write about themselves, talk about themselves, with no shame. A few years had gone by since those Parisian plays—the ones that made the French folks who'd come to live here so happy—had filled those small auditoriums that had once seen their brilliance, their talent, their passion, their fury right front and center . . . This fucking country didn't have any fighters, any writers, any filmmakers. Just fucking silence. Lives that didn't fucking matter. People who just did what they fucking had to. But truth be told, that sword of Damocles had hung over so many heads. This shaky thing that had no name to it—this suffocating government choking you and telling you that without it you wouldn't have anything, this government here hand in hand with that state some twenty thousand kilometers away that you'd never asked for, hovering over you, its tentacles reaching everywhere, but still powerless somehow.

Yes, this morning it was unbearably depressing. And even if Ma wasn't far from his thoughts, the world and the ground under his feet still seemed gray, just gray. Nothing seemed right. Things didn't make sense anymore, nothing seemed to have any point anymore. There was just this pointless feeling he had for this woman who was married with kids. This woman who was so quick to laugh, so quick to

cry. After all, wasn't that life? It began with dreams, fights, and con-
tinued into marriage, family. Bad luck sometimes came in droves but
maybe, at long last, there was belief, faith. You dared to let yourself
believe in matters of the heart and the body. And when it happens,
believing again, best not to let things slip away again. Yes, this father,
John, really was worn out.

He turned on the TV, heard the same old bullshit again. Things
that had nothing to do with here. Some faggot screeching about
knowing all the facts on one channel, and on the other was Mireille
Dumas—ah, maybe it'd be a nice evening after all. He wanted to
chuck it all out the window. He got up, but it was he who ended up
outside. The night was a pretty sight. He looked at the stars, the ones
from his childhood. They were beautiful, but it was odd: something
was missing, someone was missing.

Pyromaniac

LA DUCHESSE DU BARRY is on fire. The carved-wood storefront that cost a pretty penny, the fake vines hanging from a waxed ceiling, the champagne bottles, the priceless foie gras—all of it gone up in smoke. It's three in the morning, the sirens are starting to blare. La Duchesse du Barry is ablaze. The owners are on the street, a few meters off, waiting, still half asleep, not worked up yet, just shocked and sobbing. Farther off, firefighters are in a rush, shouting commands, carrying out orders, improvising. Thinking on their feet is important. The flames are already scarily high. Lucky that there are no apartments above. Just high-tech offices with large glass panels almost ashamed to reflect the mess on the street.

Auguste Junior sits on the sidewalk opposite. He's unhappy, maybe at peace. La Duchesse is all ashes now, it's too late. There's no saving it now. His arms are tight around his knees; the fire aside, it's cold out. Junior had such big plans to destroy that picture of indecency. The fancy shop had only opened two months ago. He'd gone to the ribbon cutting, its christening, and he'd wanted to tear that world down, kill all those stuck-up, suntanned bitches with flat white hair trying to be as flashy as the sun. He'd wanted to root out all these socialites who only knew how to flit around with flutes full of bubbly and lies.

That afternoon, staring at all that glitz, he'd gotten to thinking . . . yes. Like a cow left behind in some sad excuse for pasture, like a dog in heat but with no bitches around. Like some gimp stuck on his missing hand, his missing leg, stuck on how that hole is so heavy with what's lost. So he decided to get all that out. Some folks who get hurt or chopped up or skinned alive by life have reasons to stay here—art, sports, charity. Reasons to pretend. He'd landed on this, fire, in other words doing evil, with no shame in it, because that was easier, and also because he wasn't the only broke Tahitian who'd gladly have done so. Which meant, deep down, he felt a bit heroic.

He smiles; there's so much light on his face. There's the yellow of the fire that the huge jets of water haven't tamed just yet. His features have become magnificent. Majestic. He's like a matador. He's brought the animal down and his legs are still clenched. He's hard and it feels good. He's just set this fire, he's just set his demons, his hatred, his despair on fire. And here's the best of all the pyros. He's actually been looking human ever since throwing in the towel some weeks ago. Came back to the family home. And tonight he went and did this because there's no need to show off your wealth like this. It's as simple as a math equation. As tried and true as a proof.

What he or most of the people like him with no life or purpose in this stupid society can make in a month by keeping their mouths shut while their bosses (doesn't matter whether they're blue, white, black, yellow, or whatever) sneer at them, what they'd make in a month is something those higher-ups can't be bothered to spend two seconds thinking about during their Cellu M6 spa treatments. The cards are stacked against them. And they're all sick of it. So Junior's got plenty of good reasons to do what he's done.

An hour's enough for him to get bored. He packs a bong, lights up, and starts smoking. The first hit of the night. It's always a special one, like a good high just after a win. It tastes like the cigarette you dream of during an especially long trip, that you finally get to hold

between your finger and your thumb. The one you huff on like a
madman. Wild. Manic. Bitter. Watery. The one you catch and hold
on to, that stings, too much, and that you love. Then he lets things
fill his brain. Images of hell, of heaven, as if they're all that different.
He can see people, lots of people running after him. A bit like guilt
swallowing you up, or trying to. But as hallucinations go it isn't the
best one. So he gets up. He remembers that the next day he has to
show up at the employment office. Such a nice name for a place
that's supposed to find you something to do, no matter how badly
paid. They say it's better than nothing. They have you believing that,
thanks to this office, you owe something to the government and even
to the secretary offering you the job, they say you'll always owe them
everything. Nonsense. Junior knows perfectly well where he'll be setting foot and what they'll be doing to him. A cheek kiss just as he's
getting scammed. Forty-two hours of thankless work every week,
half minimum wage and so much shame in his guts. And that's why
he has to crawl in tomorrow, why he has to let himself get swindled
ever so nicely.

What a great future, huh? Junior's almost jealous of the stray dog
a few meters off. Scrawny, mangy, you name it, but heroic all the
same because in the eyes of all those city dwellers starved of safety
and cleanness that stray dog was a plague. And he was jealous of that
mutt, a disaster that couldn't be held off.

And Junior thought: What's the point in being like everyone? In
fitting in? These people here were lost souls left behind by the mad
rush of history paralyzing this so-called country. He kept returning
to the question of why he should bother settling down. Respect? If
it had half the weight of that dog there, it could easily be hidden. He
didn't need respect, would never need it. The most likely thing was
that he'd end up like his father someday. Hard pass. He didn't feel
like sweating it out under the sun, wrecking his liver out of sheer
rage. Junior didn't see the point of playing by the rules of a world that

always shit on dropouts, poor folks, idiots ... the scum of society. He was at the point where he had to decide, and he'd just done so. He'd eat them all alive for not just leaving him alone!

He wasn't going to bend over anymore; he wasn't going to listen to one more word of bureaucratese that he couldn't stand. The employment office could wait until tomorrow. Maybe he'd go there one night, maybe that very same night, and set it on fire.

Fresh Start

SHE TURNS AROUND, looking shy. It's never easy to leave someone. Even when that someone never really liked you. She can't say she's upset. She can't say she's not moved either. She'd rather have a breakup with punches, shrieks, tears, all of that. She turns around, looking shy. One thing still sticks out just as it did at the start of their relationship. That hair, silver, ruby red, a color that stands out. It's spring, women seem happier these days. She misses running her fingers through that shaggy hair. He's drunk most of his beer. It's spring, men always seem so happy in spring. But her heart's pounding, she's starting to hate it. It's not that she's having regrets. It's just how she is, she dwells on her decisions because she doesn't really know deep down what she wants. But this time she does. This time she wants to be done with it. She likes Michel now. She's seeing him, Bertrand, one last time. The sunlight comes in low, turns his hair gold. His hair. She can still feel it under her fingers. He didn't kick up a fuss when she said "I'm leaving." He just seemed bothered, disappointed, only a little. He'd still tried to hold her back and even let out a "but I loved you." But, in the thick of things, she couldn't see what that had to do with it. She'd said, "Yes, but." *But*, meaning "even if you didn't realize it, I liked you." It's a struggle for her to keep going. A struggle to leave the neighborhood. She loves it, Ménilmontant.

The patio of Le Soleil. The girls are so pretty. He's so handsome. So elegant. So himself. But in the end, for her, it has to be all or nothing.

She's headed for the métro. Turns around one last time. He's going the other way, to Père-Lachaise Cemetery. His hair in the sun. His shoulders a bit hunched. His hands bunched up in his pockets. She can still feel it under her fingers. She wants to cry, to let out a scream. She thinks, "I liked you, but."

Tomorrow she and Michel are flying out to Tahiti. Her mother's waiting for them. So excited it scares her. But she knows everything's going to have to be done from the ground up.

Pina and Roméo

ROMÉO WANTS TO DROP OUT. He told me yesterday. It's too much for him. Learning these things from other countries isn't his thing because he's Tahitian, not French. He says he doesn't give a fuck about their language, their grammar, their numbers, forget Louis and Antoinette and all of them. He keeps on saying that his grandmother's stories, those stories about the old times and the stories from the Bible, are all any Tahitian person needs to know. I let him have his rants. I don't have any feelings about that. I just know I don't really want to end up like so many folks here, cleaning rich people's toilets. And I'm pretty sure that there are poor people somewhere who have managed to get themselves out of this shit.

Roméo gives me so much hassle. I know he's not going to turn out well, just like my big brother Junior. It's too much, all of them just like one another. All these lives exactly like one another. Like it's fate. Always cursed. Boys who end up a mess with so much beer and weed. Boys who're already dads or in prison by the time they're old enough for high school. It's too much. The same life over and over, like some fate you just go along with for lack of any better option. They get arrested and they all end up in the one prison on the island. It's too much, all these things no different from one another. I want to do something to help Roméo. But I think it's too late already.

It's recess. He gave me half of his snack. Roméo's a liar. He told me that he'd gone out and bought it. But I know he sneaks out and steals it every single recess from a little Chinese boy two grades down. It's a shakedown, a robbery. Roméo isn't scared to use his muscles. I lick the ham sandwich dripping with mayonnaise. I'm too hungry. Of course I can see that little boy in my mind. I can imagine him hollering. But honestly it's not like I'm the one who stole it.

Roméo's my only friend. I think he's a real friend too. He'd protect me. Ever since he became my friend, nobody, just about nobody's dared to say anything about me or whatever. But I'm trying not to take advantage of that.

I get to the end of my sandwich. It really did me good. It's true that dinners aren't really dinners anymore. Ma isn't doing anything at home anymore. It's really late when she gets back from work. Junior tries his best to make meals for us. But that's not really it. Auguste's just getting weirder and weirder. He goes on rants. He makes me think of those people we sometimes see in the city who hide their faces. They say those men are on mushrooms. I don't think Auguste is actually like that. But his rants are getting worse. He's been saying that we're the people that God will soon free from the whites, that money dirties everything. Rosa's doing worse too. But nobody dares to take her out of the house. Well, Junior tried but he got kicked out by our father. I'm starting to get really worried about her. And Pauro, my Pauro . . .

François's in the hospital and Pauro is very scared. François got in a fight at his place. He was in really bad shape. Two months in a cast, three ribs cracked. He had to have a lot of operations on his face. They've been saying it was a hate crime. François doesn't talk about it. He doesn't want to, that's what he said. And besides, he doesn't remember any of it.

The other night, I was thinking about friendship. It's such a weird thing, friendship. It lets you tell someone who isn't family everything.

Roméo knows everything. But his life means he can't do much about it. One day he walked me almost all the way home. He said that this way he can come back if he's worried that I've got problems. I think that with the tear Auguste's been on, Roméo might have to come and stay with me.

The Slap

IT'S SIX AT NIGHT. Ma's back from who-knows-where, from some hotel room. Some empty room with nothing but faded sheets, a dark nightstand. She's back from there, from that place where bodies let go, where they hear the moans of those who can't do the deed at home. Ma. She's still dripping. She couldn't, wouldn't, clean up a little. Her crotch is wet. John's in her. His hands, his tongue, his fingers have all plowed her soil. Left their mark, their scent, their taste. His hands. John. He's stuck on her, dripping off her, oozing from her. She stinks, but she doesn't care. She wants to keep it all. She even wants everyone to know. Her hair's let down, her dress is rumpled. She's not there anymore. She sees Pina working away in the kitchen. Pina doesn't say a word, she's cooking a pot of rice. The chicken's cooking.

All Ma can bring herself to do is see, not even look. Her mind's only on one thing: John. She's such an idiot. Pauro's opening up some tomato sauce. He's whistling a bit. He's almost doing it on purpose. Auguste Junior is there, almost proper. Ever since Hannah got back from France, he's changed. He's always been devoted to her. They've gone and joined an independence group together. The only one in the country. They talk about it nonstop. Liberty. Hannah's peeling carrots, and right beside her is Michel who's watching. He seems so meek, so timid, so shocked. Michel's never spent time with such a loud family. He's only lived with his parents on and off.

Apparently Auguste is still on duty. It's been days, nights that he hasn't left Rosa's bedside except to do his business. Hannah and her brothers have decided that if this goes on for another twenty-four hours they're going straight to the cops.

Ma's only been there for five minutes. Pauro lets on that the kids have decided to talk to the police. She doesn't care. They can do whatever the heck they'd like, she doesn't care at all. Auguste Junior puts out the dishes. He's in a hurry. Any faster and the glasses would have broken in his hands. The others all look where even the shadow of Ma can't be seen.

"Moïra, come here."

Pina's playing mommy. How nice, Ma thinks. One less thing for her to worry about. "Good girl, Pina. Aren't you all nice and grown up now?" Moïra hasn't heard Pina, she's running around, she wants to dash out. The chicken's still cooking, it smells so nice. What a woman Pina's become. But Moïra's like an earthworm, there's no stopping her. She's running, too fast, slips out of the house, and ends up in the middle of street. Pina's just two steps behind. The boys, Hannah, and Michel have all gotten up, a bit too slow, and so has Ma, because everyone else has.

"Moïra, stop!"

The car's brakes screech. The little girl only a centimeter away from its bumper. The two touch. The pit in Pina's stomach could swallow everything up. A terror that sweeps away every other thought. Pina saw her sister's death flash before her eyes, she just about lost it. It's too much for her, she's not even ten yet. She can't bear all this. But it's too late, the feelings and thoughts and fury of a matriarch, of a woman who wants to protect her baby's life, all come over her. The car honks, the woman at the wheel, terrified, her hands are shaking. And what's inside Pina is stronger than Pina herself. Stronger than her small body. She hits Moïra, keeps hitting her, remembering what they did to her. Pauro stops her. Auguste Junior gawks. Ma. That idiot. Her head's still full of nothing but John's words and his little groans. She didn't take any of it in. She just looked. Then maybe it finally sunk in. Maybe the haze in her head finally let through some clear thought. Who knows. She suddenly comes to. She starts hitting. Nobody has any idea what good that might do, what train of thought she's following. While her children walk back into the house in shock, she takes Pina aside, grabs her hair, and starts wailing on her bent-over back. That's what being a mother is to Ma. Making people respect her this way. Pina should have been watching more carefully, it's all her fault. Pauro can feel his arms and legs tensing up. He's going to yell, or jump, leap. But he's half a second too late. Junior's the one who acts. That was all he'd been waiting for. He starts laying into her: "What's wrong with you? Leave her alone!" The slap lands on the cheek that only an hour earlier Ma's lover had been kissing. Ma's at a loss for words. It hurts. Pina gets up and runs off to hide by the waterfall. Pauro's rocking Moïra in tears. Junior isn't done staring down his mother, his eyes full of disgust. At long last he says: "Go wash yourself." The worst insult of all. It's too much of a shame for her to be told that. She looks down, suddenly feels dirtier than dirt. She doesn't know what she's done, doesn't realize it. Hannah's forgotten about her carrots. She and Michel left the shack to go look for Pina. Hannah only met her sister a few weeks ago. With every passing day she's seen more and more of this little soul. Has done her best to make herself lovable. Now and then Pina's still quiet, but they're actually talking. Hannah doesn't want any more of this. She can't do it anymore. She can tell that Pina isn't as strong as she, Hannah, was at that age. She feels so many things, this girl sometimes gets lost in her thoughts. One day Hannah found a line from Balzac in a little notebook of her sister's: "Suicide is a poem sublime in its melancholy." It isn't right to like those sorts of words at such a young age. It isn't right to think of such things as such romantic clichés. Hannah had been horrified. And not just that. She'd gotten so angry, so close to slapping her sister. But she'd caught herself. She'd been gone for too long, after all. She was hardly in any place to be teaching lessons herself.

As she makes her way down, she grabs Michel's hand and says: "That was my life. That's still my life. I don't know if I can put you through that." Michel's got a snarky answer: "At this point, the only thing you still haven't put me through is the soft, tender bite of leather straps . . ." Hannah can't help but crack a smile at that reminder of their first and only trip to a BDSM club. It'd been as vanilla as they come, but it still hadn't been one bit up her alley.

What Hannah and Pina could have said to each other nobody will ever know. Michel's dived into what they all call "little queen's basin." He loves how fresh the water is, what a shock it is. As he thinks about love being strong and clear, just like this water, Hannah and Pina talk. They smile. They go quiet. Look a bit rascally at the Frenchman enjoying that new pleasure. That day, they become sisters.

François

"SO SHE'S DEAD?"

"Yes. It was a pretty funeral. A pretty vigil. Everyone was there. Aunt Poe and Teanuanua. There were people I didn't know. I had no idea she had so many friends. Ma was strong, like they say. Almost no tears. We all expected it though. That she'd die. The police were asking questions. Auguste spent two nights at the station. They let him go free. They said he'd be summoned later. They'll summon him once they have proof that he killed her. In the police's eyes, Rosa let herself die. Maybe drugs had something to do with it too."

Nobody's going to hear her laughter from the other side of the apartment wall anymore.

Nobody.

Pauro's next thought was that they wouldn't go back to the studio ever again.

François had lost at least fifteen kilos. For two months now he'd been at a place that they were calling a convalescent center. It was really a place to go die.

Deep down, you know, it's better that way. For Rosa. If she hadn't died that way, someone would have killed her. She wasn't made for living on the streets. But she never had any idea where she ought to be.

All the while François was thinking about how she just wasn't made to live. To live the life she'd been put through.

Through the bay window in François's room, they could see the sea. Blue. Peaceful. A few white specks of breaking waves offered some distraction. But other than that, pure blue. Deep blue. Like the sky. It actually seemed like the wind outside, the one bending the leaves of a dwarf coconut tree, it seemed like that wind was just as blue. So many things around François looked as deep as his feelings.

Pauro stepped out for a few minutes. He wanted a smoke. He'd only ever tried a cigarette or two with his brother Junior. And weed too. Luckily, he didn't take to either. For the young Tahitian man, they were like booze. Both smoking and drinking made him think about himself. And ever since he'd figured out that he was gay, Pauro couldn't stand thinking about his decisions. Taking a hard look at himself was something he didn't know how to do, didn't want to know how to do.

François had his head against one side of the bay window. He'd been feeling good. Calm. And then Pauro had come to see him. And then Pauro had said that this time he'd make his getaway with him. That he didn't have to worry anymore.

Now he felt much better. A bit foggy from all the pills they fed him morning, noon, and night. But compared to how he'd been when they brought him in, there was no question he was better.

The blue down there reminded him of the Mediterranean. The Aeolian Islands where he'd lived for two years, where he'd first dug his shovel into the earth after snagging a doctorate in archaeology. Blue, he thought, wasn't like men. Blue was universal.

He felt good for a few minutes, very good even. But ever since he'd come here, to the center, it'd always been the same. In the morning, mostly, he was happy. And then things changed. He got moody. Depressed. It had to be the pills. He didn't want to think about his feelings, so he made himself think about the past. College, his coming out at a bar in the place Monge in Paris as he sat across from a few school friends. All of them tipsy, of course, while he acted goofy. But the girls in the group knew it had nothing to do with the booze. They were actually a bit disappointed. François was almost gorgeous. He had a glow to him.

He recalled how he'd wound up here in Tahiti. Sheer accident, that. It was always sheer accident in these cases. It had to be in the mid-1990s on the boulevard Saint-Germain. He recalled the bitterly cold winter air. He was going to see one of his friends at a small bistro. He couldn't remember the name of the place anymore, let alone the party there, or the other guys who'd shown up. He just remembered Mata, the Tahitian girl. At first, when he saw her beside his friend, he'd figured that she was his mother, or some other relation of his. But nobody actually knew her. She'd just decided to go there for no reason at all. She worked next door at the French Polynesian delegation, some sort of cross between embassy and Polynesian tourism office. She had flowers in her hair. Fake flowers. Because finding fresh flowers in the middle of the winter was impossible. Mata had ended up there, already drunk. She had to be in her fifties at least. She was one of those ladies who'd already seen it all. Or just about all. She was beautiful. That was what the young man immediately thought. And obviously they hit it off. Mata carried herself the way mixed women from her country all did. Like a queen, and arrogant too. She'd been living in Paris for twenty years now, and she'd never gone back to her country. She could talk about anything and everything: her bouts of sadness, how much she missed her country, her practically forced marriage to a métropolitain general. The long journey by ocean liner to France. Her children, the two she'd had. A boy and a girl. The boy wasn't her husband's son. He was full-on Tahitian. But she hadn't really said a thing at all about her daughter.

He couldn't be sure why, but the moment he'd laid eyes on Mata, she'd drawn him in. Ever since that night, they'd been inseparable. Good friends first, then thick as thieves, then bound almost by blood.

They spent whole nights talking about Tahiti, or rather about Raiatea, Mata's island. Even before he ever set foot there, he could already run down the whole family tree of that island's people. Their history. Their past as warriors. Their future as defeated people. Even before he landed there, he took care not to hang on to those necklaces of flowers or shells that Mata offered him. The old postcards, the old photos of paradise stayed tucked away in an old school folder. He knew that he'd go and live there . . . and die. It lasted almost five years. That friendship. There was something unshakable there, like all true friendships. Mata even came to live with him. She'd left her family. Her husband kept her children from so much as walking up to them, her and the other guy, the fag. Mata drank like a fish. Everyone knew that. But only François could watch her lose herself without losing his own head. Maybe it was out of love. He never played along that this drink, the umpteenth one, was just one for celebrating, one just between friends. He never raised a brow when she peed herself. After all, there was nothing romantic about booze. She spent the last three months of her life in a hospital. Her family had abandoned her. Her husband had met another Tahitian woman. But she didn't give a flying fuck. Near the end, she told François about her childhood. Her teens. The sex she'd had far too early. The red mustache of her father, an administrator, tickling her all over. The pleasure she'd learned about with boys in the town, country bumpkin lovers. Because of course her blood made them all look at her like she was a princess. She didn't really remember her first time, she whispered. She just knew that she'd only ever loved one man. It was a story that had marked her little family out straightaway and forever. She was fifteen, no older, and she'd slept with her cousin. A boy she'd only just met. They fell for each other in an old building on the Raiatea quay.

A few days later, she was shipped off to a Catholic boarding school in Tahiti. But she never forgot that boy. All these years later, all these thousands of kilometers away, he'd stayed imprinted on her mind. That day, in that hovel, she could have died a happy woman in his arms. She'd never had that kind of love that before, and she hadn't since. Never. He was a virgin, but he had a strength, he had wits about him that she saw and respected. She went on and on about those hands, that body, that chest. For years, she'd made love like she had that time, with all the fire she could muster, but she never did manage to find the weight of his body again. For years, she'd undergone therapy, all for naught. Therapy didn't work on people of her ilk. Yapping on and on for ten thousand francs a half hour, no thank you, she'd already spent enough. She knew quite well the reason for her sadness and her boozing too. It was him, this cousin who'd gone for another woman. A poor girl from Huahine who was only good for squeezing out babies. Mata had never been able to take it. Nobody, nobody before then had ever turned their back on her like that. She'd never held with the notion that, simply because they were related, their love was doomed. Because they'd seen each other again, in town. She knew he was working. Mata had done everything she could so their eyes would land on each other again. Auguste was going to become a father for the first time and his very young wife was waiting for him at home and she, Mata, snuck out two or three times a week, set on spending time with him again at the Métropole, in a crappy motel room just above an even crappier bar.

She was seventeen. She said that she'd loved him. That she'd only ever loved him. That it hurt to live without his body, his roughness, his awkwardness when he talked in French. Before dying in the hospital, she said his name, in one last rant that was hard for François to take. Auguste had dug her grave the moment he'd first laid hands on her, and he had no idea. Their relationship hadn't been more than a few months. It drove Mata mad to know that he was taken. When she'd gotten pregnant, she hadn't thought twice. For this child he would never have loved, she agreed to marry this other man, a military man, that her parents picked out for her.

In the nights and days and family get-togethers and snowy Christmases of Mata's dreams, her drunken flights of fancy, her moments of clarity, Auguste had been dancing. He'd been dancing these dances of death, branding his selfish victories on her body, all the thirty years she'd spent after him.

Mata. Dead all those years ago. In a way this was how François had ended up here, like this. When he'd been face-to-face with the elder Auguste, he'd seen it all of a sudden. This evil man had been the death of his friend. And so he'd told him about Mata and dug up the old envelope she'd put Auguste's address on and put the letter she'd written to August inside. The envelope she'd never sent but had left in François's hands for this day. For Mata, François was meant to meet him sooner or later. That was just how it was. Your fate, te utu'a, it'll always catch up to you. Oddly, Auguste hadn't looked one bit surprised. As if he'd known that that afternoon of sex, his very first time, would define the rest of his life, lead him down paths he'd never backtrack on. He knew, but maybe he'd been told that when he was little, that what goes around comes around. Soon. Too soon, never too late.

But Auguste wasn't a man to be swayed by nostalgia. He was there to punish François. To punish him and Pauro for getting up to things that the Bible called an abomination. For their love. And besides, the past couldn't return. Never could. So these blows had been bloodier than he'd ever meant them to be. Who knew just how little an archaeologist got. What he did get in the end was that he had no right to dig up ghosts, remains, like that. No right to take those things Auguste had put years behind him ever so slow and careful, had buried under what was left of love and hate and booze and life itself, and throw it back in his face. François was nothing next to that. He didn't have a chance. It was only Auguste who stopped raining blows down on him. None of the neighbors so much as moved. Pauro was at school, trying his best to learn philosophy.

They're all down there. You can see them if you stand up. On the radio they're saying ten to fifteen thousand protestors, and just on this side of the island. On the other side, they say it's worse. In two or three hours both groups are meeting in the city. It's going to be huge. Nobody's seen anything like it.

I can see the flags from here. They're blue, like the sky. Blue, white, and blue.

Yes. Blue . . . that's your color, François.

Because there's nothing more universal.

Hmm, Pauro replied.

You should go. They're waiting for you. It'll be your first protest.

Will you be okay? When I'm not here?

Go. I can't keep you from going, after all.

No, he couldn't keep his lover from going. And no, there was nothing more universal than blue. Or maybe there was: solitude. Solitude for two people who know, deep down, that life isn't like what so many people want you to think. Love doesn't conquer all. You just get a lucky break every so often. Otherwise, happiness is impossible.

Revelations

SOMETIMES IT'S CALLED A CARROT. When the bright orange end of a cigarette makes the shape and color of a carrot. A carrot cigarette is how you know the one smoking it is worried. Worried: that was what Maui Thomas, all of twenty-five years old, standing in his garden high up in Tahiti, felt. Soon it'd be midnight, the country was making its way slowly into the next day, a new day. A strange day: July 24, 2016. Maui took a drag on his cigarette with so much worry that it was starting to hurt his cheeks. Every so often he looked up at the sky with no stars. Every so often his eyes landed on the pool. Every so often he looked at the bugs, the flies sputtering in the chlorine of the water. He'd never thought that could be such a sight, a drowning fly making circles of waves. There was nothing to do. It was silly, but that was just how things were and he thought that sometimes men were like those flies dying in his pretty pool, they didn't have a chance of being saved. Ditto for those people murdered a few months ago, all of them dropping like, well, yes, flies. That wasn't a pretty sight, but nobody seemed keen on stopping it. There'd been Georges, Alain, Yves. François too, badly hurt, he said he hadn't seen his attacker.

It was Maui's first big case, and he didn't have the least hint of a suspect. Every crime scene was filthy, bloody, horrible. Like nothing he'd ever seen around these parts. For Georges and Alain, their cocks had been cut off and shoved in their mouths, which were crudely sewn shut. Almost a signature. Butchery. But these executions clearly had been carried out carefully, patiently. Yves had been a homosexual. When they'd found him, his genitals had been resting at the entrance of his anus.

The young inspector would have given anything for an easier case to start his new assignment. It'd have been nice for his career in Tahiti to slowly build up to the seamier stuff. The way things were going though, it was like he'd been thrown to the wolves, like he didn't already understand perfectly well that nobody transfers here by choice. Like the point was that this man who'd just been promoted to inspector didn't already know that a career in the national police never starts off nice and easy, especially not in paradise.

The night before, Maui had called his best friend, Kamel, who'd started in Noisy-le-Grand with its easy jobs of thugs, ghettos with their petty thieves. Kamel had teased him about that paradise turning into hell, then he'd said that things weren't all that easy for him either. Not one bit. It was actually worse than he'd thought because of what everyone claimed. Nine-tenths of the depositions started with "Actually, sir, I'd like to speak to your supervisor, after all, it's not easy for me to say this to someone like . . ." and Kamel had to say: "Like me, you mean?" And Kamel had to go and take the victims to one of his colleagues. No, it wasn't easy and especially not when it had to do with immigrants, or children of immigrants. He could see in their eyes, their smiles, their wide looks that he, Kamel, had crossed over to the other side and now he wasn't one of them anymore, wasn't part of either that community or the new one.

Maui took another long drag. Right then he got what Kamel was going through. It was about belonging. Being from one place, understanding it, but knowing that soon he'd have to take a step forward, and choose the other side. There had to be something connecting these murder cases, all signs pointed to it. And there'd been this heavy feeling over the whole town. Even before he'd shown up, a fancy shop had been lit on fire, men had been attacked, like the gay social worker, like François the archaeologist who Maui was sure was hiding something. Maui felt trapped like Kamel. He'd been born in Paris, but he was Tahitian and he didn't want to face the facts. It was a matter of honor, of pride. But the facts were there, right at his feet, plain and clear: these were hate crimes. Those cut-off genitals could mean a woman getting her revenge—Georges and Alain had bedded hundreds of women—but Maui could tell the crimes were all about strength, manliness, bullheadedness. And on top of that, the three dead men all had the same background and had the same life: once on welfare, now making millions five years after washing up here, all "kings of the night" and investors who lured in young girls and boys with promises of permanent residency permits. So the young inspector had a sneaking feeling this was a sort of moral avenger, out to cleanse and purify. And the chauvinist in him was certain that women could do everything but straighten out souls . . .

This time it was a wasp that got caught in the blue water. What a funny way to spend the night! He could have done the wise thing and gone to sleep beside his wife's dozing body, he could have given her a nice slow fuck, but he was standing there and thinking about this whole matter and contemplating this bizarre thing that had come about: none of the forecasts had predicted this country's fate. It had been a close race, a very close one. The opposition had garnered exactly 274 more votes.

Which was why Maui had given his wife a downer three hours ago, after he saw that there was no calming her down. What a day. That morning, he and Mareva had had brunch with the in-laws right after voting. His father-in-law, a councillor at the Territorial Assembly, had on his nicest shirt in orange, the loser's color. He'd been saying all along that it was in the bag. He was so arrogant. Maui had always hated him. As for his mother-in-law, she kept folding her napkin and playing with it, fretting because she hadn't been able to get one of her bungalows down the way rented out.

As he cast one last glance at the struggling wasp, Maui smiled and took a slow drag on the cigarette. Fact was, seeing the party in power go down was pretty nice. Maui'd voted for the independence collective. It was more a movement than a traditional party, and they'd caught all the experts off guard. They were outsiders and Maui liked that. It was Mareva he felt worried about. She had light skin thanks to her mother, born to a British missionary, and that pretty thing worked at the presidential palace and was friends with young businessmen who'd all voted for the party that'd lost tonight. She could be out of a job.

After brunch, there'd been two hours of cleaning the pool. Normally Andres did it, but he hadn't come the night before, and Maui's mother-in-law was expecting guests that afternoon, so the father-in-law had pitched in. Sure enough, guests had come and, sure enough, they'd put out cold beers and crates of champagne. Everyone had been there. The energetic businessmen with deep pockets and big plans, who'd been students he'd met in Paris during his school years ... and who he'd hated pretty much right away, along with their Paris apartments that Mommy and Daddy had come and bought even before their kids could settle in. Mareva had been one of those sorts.

As usual, Maui said he had urgent business at the headquarters, then up and left. But this afternoon, he didn't head out to a bar, he went to the committee room of the people Mareva called "filthy separatists."

The crowd in there was buzzing, young and not-so-young folks were gathering information about the polling sites, loading cars with manifestos and T-shirts the colors of the movement. It was the third time he'd gone. The first two he'd had to sneak in because the state had to keep an eye on "splinter groups," especially independence-leaning or fascist ones. But things were different now.

He found the gang there and felt a bit ashamed when his heart started going fast at the sight of Hannah. She had her friend Michel with her. Maui was very happy to see Auguste Junior too and his brother Pauro and John, who wasn't just a mentor or a committee chair but an artist everyone in Tahiti knew and a friend of Junior. John had brought them all to the party. Maui knocked back two or three beers with them, even took a drag on the joint Junior passed his way. He'd waited with them, patient and excited. With them, he knew something was going to happen, knew they were this close to winning. They knew it. And that was a real sight, all of them, with their hopes and dreams so bright in their eyes . . . after twenty years of the same old rulers, they needed a change, it was outright cleansing.

"Well, what are you waiting for? Why are you wasting your life with a woman you can't stand?"

Hannah had come out and said that after Maui's explanations, it was so plain that for half a second the young man thought: Yes, it really could be that simple. Yes, you could make a decision just like that, in the time it took to say the words. It was easy, a breeze. Such a breeze if you just pulled your head out of the sand. And on this evening, before he headed back home, Pauro confessed his secrets to him on the balcony of that place: that he was gay, that his sister had died not a month ago, that his friend François was on the mend after a horrible attack, that his father had gone mad and thirsty for blood. Pauro made it sound like his father had been the one behind the

attack. He also whispered that any day now they'd be escaping with
Pina, his favorite little sister. Any day now.

Before he went back to his car, Maui promised the others that
he'd find them the next day and they'd have themselves a nice bottle
of wine. Then, as the others went inside, he called Pauro and asked
him for his father's name.

He didn't remember much of what came after. Or anything about
the route he took. He just had that name rattling around in his head.
He just knew that he was sobbing. He remembered thinking that it
was useless, but still . . . He felt like he was crying his heart out. He
also knew that he was thinking more than ever about his mother
who'd died five years ago, just after writing to him from her hospital room to tell him out-and-out about "the truth" that he'd already
known, deep down, since he was a kid. He wasn't the son of Martial
Thomas, the now-retired general. In this letter, Mata gave him the
first and last name, the age, told him how they'd met, how they'd kept
getting together. The name made its way back up in his thoughts
today, all these years later, like a boomerang fate itself had thrown.
Pauro's description matched up to Mata's on every single point.

He knew he was yelling out his mother's name, his fingernails
scratching at the white denim. He knew he remembered her warm
body when she told him to come sleep in her bed. He knew he could
call up the smell of her pillow, that bit of perfume between her
breasts . . . He thought back on the wooden carousel in the Jardin
des Tuileries. The horse went up and down and up and down. The
other kids laughed and yelled. All he wanted was for the carousel
to stop. All he wanted was to wipe away the tears flowing behind
his mother's tinted glasses. And to tell her: No, Mommy, don't cry.
Not here. Not on this bench, the other parents are looking at you.
Just to tell her that he was there. At this age it's so easy to think
all grown-ups are strong. And now Maui wanted to find a detail or

two to kill this bad dream dead. A detail or two to prove he wasn't
Auguste's son. But nothing doing, and every fact just made it worse.
Maui had the same square jaw and the same small, deep cleft as
Junior and Pauro. He had the same huge thighs and slightly bowed
legs as his brothers. He had the same deep black pupils that made
him look like such a devastatingly charming man.

He felt his phone vibrate in his jeans pocket. On the screen he made
out his home phone number. Mareva. He let it ring. It was curtains
for her, for the two of them. In a few minutes he would get up, go
and tidy up the living room that she'd wrecked before he came. Then
he'd go to the bedroom, fall asleep. The next day he'd pack his bags
and ask straight-out for a divorce. He didn't love Mareva anymore.
He had important things to deal with, a past to piece back together,
maybe a whole family to meet ... He didn't care about leaving this
gold-plated life, those empty conversations with his wife, her friends,
her parents. He'd say goodbye to that house in Christchurch, that
wedding gift, and he'd move into the studio that he'd gone and
rented on the sly, not far from the police station.

All that was easy enough. But that ugly string of murders wasn't, it
ate at him more than the shock of finding out that his real father was
alive, alive and well, and not far from here. What was really doing
him in right then was his gut instinct telling him: "See, nothing's
ever an accident. Your father never tried that hard to find you, but
here he is, he's slipped into your life anyway. No, it's no accident,
the man you've spent two months hunting down, the man everyone's calling the Butcher of Papeete, of course it's him, the dad who
abandoned you. It's no accident. That's how the world is. It's so clear,
so straightforward: children have to wipe their father's slates clean."
Maui still didn't have any proof of what he was thinking. All he had
was his instinct.

The Grave

THE WHITE SAND CAME from his island, Raiatea. A weird, pointless little detail that almost calmed him down. It cost almost nothing for this Raiatea sand to make the grave look perfect. And that made him happy, made him calm. Right in the middle was a huge bouquet of red flowers, some 'ōpuhi that still had their huge dark green leaves. There were zigzag patterns drawn by rake teeth. The sun was at its peak. Auguste sat in a mango tree's shadow. He went and opened a tin of pilchards in tomato sauce and peeled two bananas. He and Pina had come three hours before. He'd sent his daughter off to find water at the entrance to the Protestant cemetery. She wouldn't be back for another ten minutes. Auguste closed his eyes as a nice breeze blew over him. This time of day, a breeze was always welcome, and he leaned against the fat trunk full of dried-up sap.

Auguste was bone-weary. Like anyone would be after being an avenger, after killing three men, three white men. After beating up a son's lover. After finding out about a new child, born from a secret relationship three decades back. It would break the heart of any man, even the worst son of a bitch, to have to let a child die, the way Auguste did with Rosa. Seeing a life snatched away leaves a man empty. Did he feel bad? Sorry? Scared he hadn't seen the worst yet?

It was just that his mission got harder, shadowier with each day. That this mission, which his mother who'd died nearly thirty years ago was making him carry out, was one he understood less and less. He was feeling smaller than ever before. The fire he'd had early on had him thinking that he, Auguste T., a farmer, a sailor, a mason, could somehow empty out the sea with nothing but a whiskey glass. And, as time wore on, reason filled him up with something else: the truth. The sad truth: the land, his land in particular, was big enough, wide enough, for all the idiots in the world or just about. Meaning tomorrow wouldn't be the day he made his mother happy.

His mother. A tough lady in a long, dark dress. The daughter of the village chief who'd converted to Christianity not long before dying. His mother, Haumanava—a name that meant "welcome peace"— had been the queen of his family, in her husband's shadow. When she was little, she'd seen her own father convert. If she could have, she would have become a pastor herself. She'd have sailed the seven seas to spread the word to all and sundry that God was merciless. That one had to atone for one's faults, the way she herself did. That one had to live waiting for Christ's return, not to hold us by the hand and lead us to some sky-blue heaven that would open wide upon our arrival, but to judge us. Only a few elect would get Christ's pardon. And when she was old, when she was waiting calmly for the Messiah to come, when she happened upon her husband practicing old rites at an altar built out of crude stones, there hadn't been much choice. She'd killed him. Stabbed him with a whetted machete. Her husband had been . . . possessed. He hadn't wanted to believe in Jesus anymore. He'd made it clear that she was the one who had it all wrong. That morning, before he'd died, his eyes had been funny, his smile smarmy, like a devil's; he'd said that one day she would see how this imported religion would never raise them up. Not them, not their children, not their children's children. This religion was a religion that shut people out. Only believing in one God meant erasing every other hope humanity had of making their way up to godliness and getting close to being perfect. With Christianity, man would always be doomed to be nothing more than man. Imperfect forever, unhappy forever, scared forever. Those missionaries with their rotting teeth and pale skin brought us that, and we used to be a brave people, but we gave up our rights in life for the hopes of some in the hereafter. Smoke and mirrors, shutting folks out, that's what the British brought on us one day. That's what they filled our heads and bellies with, with more and more of that big fat holy book.

The mother didn't blink twice. She grabbed the machete. She, her parents, and her family had all been rid of those old ways of thinking. They all truly believed that they'd found truth in this new religion. Even he, the stupid husband, a sire who'd given her hardy children who'd serve the Lord one day, could be a sacrifice on the altar of official, true, modern beliefs. He meant nothing . . .

Haumanava had fought against the past and all its stupid, silly superstitions. She'd fought against pleasure because it got you farther away from the opening of heaven. And now it was her son who had taken on the mantle and the fight; nothing much was different. Auguste had an enemy, the way his mother did in her time. His enemy was money and the power that came of it. Economic power, political power. Sexual dominance. When you have the women, you have the land. Auguste had to stop them, at all costs, from taking the land and its women.

Auguste could have passed for a member of a peace organization, if he'd just finished up his courses. It was a bit sad to say, but that was the truth, he didn't have the perspective needed for that. All he had was strength. And his bullheadedness. But deep down, maybe he'd realized, unlike all those idiots slaving away to protect native peoples between two international congresses, unlike all those folks who came and talked about the environment with a joint in their pocket, he, Auguste, might have understood that it wasn't time for "peace and love" slogans but for action. He understood that. He could see which way history was going.

And this little bit of feeling bone-weary wasn't holding him back. Really. That was nothing at all. Not even worth an idle thought. Not compared to the work he had ahead of him. Not compared to the gratitude he'd see in the eyes of his family, in the eyes of every member of his race. Nothing at all . . . but still, this feeling was odd. A bit heavy. Everything was slowing down. Like in the movies. He tried his best, but nothing came. He shouted at himself, screwed up his strength, clenched his guts. He tried to pick up one leg then the other, but nothing. Nothing was happening. He could feel his heart pounding in his temples. Right in between. Almost stabbing, tearing into his brain. The wind rose, but he couldn't enjoy it. Sweat was pouring down his forehead. He couldn't move, not his legs, not his hands. He opened his mouth, but no sound came. He wanted to shout for Pina. Pina ought to be back any minute now, right beside him. He didn't understand anything anymore. His head was throbbing. Both his eyelids were sealed by the mango tree's sap. Sticky, thick, sweet-smelling sap. The earth under him was starting to swallow him up. Then a cold wind ran over his face, his back, his bare chest, like a shiver. Suddenly his eyes opened, and he let out screams with no sound to them.

The sun was still at its peak. Time hadn't moved. Some meters off, on the tomb's perfect sand, was Rosa. She had her little red dress on, her shoes with red heels, her horrid red lipstick. She was smiling, standing, alive and well. Then she must have made a filthy gesture. "Must have," because he didn't see it clearly. She kicked up a bit of that sand he'd been so proud of and vanished with one of her sharp laughs he'd recognize anywhere.

He didn't have time to catch his breath, on the white sand, still beneath a heavy sun, was his wife on her back, naked. She parted her legs. Auguste could see that slit he knew so well, loved inside and out, deep in there. Wet, shining, calling to him. She looked hungry. She was twisting around on the sand under her back. In a lover's dance she was calling him over, maybe him, to come and take her. Fast, hard, harder. He couldn't move, but Auguste could feel his penis getting hard, getting big. Then hurting. She had her left hand over her breast, and the other going down nice and slow to her crotch, then on down to between her legs. Ma's eyes were shut. She was smiling, happy. She started moaning, the pleasure was coming, yes . . . she knew he was right there. At her door. He took his time, licked her very, very slowly, his fingers playing the tune he knew so well. And then, at long last, he entered. He wasn't gentle. At some point she turned over, pushed her rump up like a dog. The moaning grew. The movements got more desperate. Their bodies were gleaming, sun-kissed, coarse . . . like lovers. And at last Auguste screamed, at last he could hear himself saying that he'd kill them all soon, her, this slut and this moron she couldn't stop calling John while he took her. God, no! She was open to him. She loved him. She came once, then again, just as he came. No, no, no, no! And he shut his eyes like he already knew. They were shameless, moving like he wasn't there, like he didn't exist. They didn't even see him crying, all sad and lonely. Not out of hate. He was crying like a baby left on some roadside. They wouldn't know that Auguste had been crying like that; nobody would ever see big old Auguste crying.

Suddenly he felt his limbs free. Ma and the man were all tangled up on his daughter's grave. Auguste found the anger he needed, jumped up. The lovers went up in smoke, all he heard was a quiet chuckle. Auguste was dripping with sweat, his legs all wobbly. He could look up. He saw Pina, her eyes downcast, her face like a woman's smiling at him, maybe telling him those sorts of things just happened and she understood. She understood that he wanted to kill his wife.

He didn't know why that made him cry even harder. Like he'd been pulled so far off any path back to peace. Like everything else, absolutely everything was setting just so and now his family's lives would be full of chaos and blood.

Some voices got through to him, quiet like they were coming from a box, a crate. They sounded excited. It was hard to tell what they were on about. Then the voices got clearer. They were radio presenters.

Auguste saw what was happening and finally opened his eyes. It was just a dream, an ugly, dirty dream. He stared at the wet spots on the yellow ceiling. He knew them well. Then he recognized the curtains, the furniture in his bedroom. Their bedroom, his and his wife's. He pushed himself up, raised his chest slowly while his legs dangled off the bed. He was a bit foggy-headed. Upright now, he turned his head to the door. Pina was standing there, her hair combed nice and proper. She seemed so sweet. She had those sad eyes, that way of looking like a woman who knows everything, sees everything. Auguste startled. No, it was just a dream. He had to tell her that, the same way he had to tell himself that. It was all just a bad, bad dream. Don't worry . . . but Pina seemed to be staring at something else, his shorts or his body.

He looked down, and panic came over him. His shorts, his hands, his arms were all wet. In the middle of the bed was a huge, dark stain. Sweat and blood and . . . come.

Auguste looked like he was begging Pina. But he had no idea what to do. He got up but it was too late to act shocked. He didn't say a word. Tried to recollect what he might have been doing. He just prayed to God that if he, Auguste, had killed anyone, he prayed that it wasn't Ma. Not her, in any case not before he got all the facts.

◈

While he was standing up, Pina told him that the others had been gone for nearly two days now. She was starting to get scared, Moïra was almost out of milk.

For just a second, Auguste wanted to stroke her hair. Maybe pull her into his arms. She looked so businesslike and so pretty, with those pink-tipped breasts pushing through her old T-shirt. She was so . . . sultry. Auguste was still hard.

A small body sways. Spins, rather, this way and that.
Calmly, a calm far too calm. A calm that means
that was the last gasp, too late now.
A small body dangling from a rope tied
good and tight to an old ceiling. It ought
to have collapsed but hasn't, that shirker.
That long frizzy hair's loose and free for once.
The only keening is a river not far off.
A body that's a tender sacrifice on the altar of squalor.
The neck's going purple, the face deathly pale.

Lonelinesses

FOR THE REST OF her life she'd remember the sound of keys in locks. The connection was there in her head. The meaning, really. A heavy ring of keys wasn't half as easygoing or nervy when it was a young officer swinging it, not when it was a career policeman about to hang up his boots. There was no squeak that meant so much freedom as that of an old key turning in a lock. No hum from any city far off could ever soothe her like right then. For long after she'd remember those rangers' footsteps. Sneering, heavy. Going back and forth outside the iron door of her vile cell, never stopping. Smug, scolding her, looking down on her. She'd feel that stiff, cold concrete bunk on the side until the day she died. No skylight. Just this speck of light slipping through a few sweet millimeters of space under the door.

For the rest of her life she would curse those drunk people's yells. For the rest of her life, she knew she'd think of them as less than human because they'd let alcohol get the better of them. Right then they were banging at a door that didn't deserve it. Any second now they'd calm down, get a grip on themselves all of a sudden. Or maybe they'd just wear themselves out. She was worn out, but she was set on staying alert. Not like them. Not ever. Not knowing the time. Let alone the day. She had to think, to get the whole picture. To curse that baby-faced cop who'd gotten hamburger sauce all over his

white uniform. To starve like never before. And to push aside those
thoughts she'd been so sure of. To do her best to forget that she was
guilty. She was sitting on the berth. Her back hurt. Her shoulders
ached, and her eyes were swelled up. She pulled her knees up to her
chin. Like a baby, to try to breathe through her jeans, to sniff up that
last bit of air that the denim had caught while she was free. Hannah
was wrung dry, she twisted a lock of hair around her gnarled, shaky
fingers. Soon the only thing she'd care about would be getting away
from the stench of shit and piss from the squat toilet without running water. The smell of strangers, and herself too, was filling up the
small cell. This was nastiness, she decided. This was true punishment.
This was what being nothing but shit amounted to: doing everything
she could to get the least bit of oxygen in a sea of shit and filth. Physical shit, mental shit: dark green walls, peeling, first and last names
and dates and scrawled insults hinting at all the fears and nightmares
and doomed fates of people who'd been human until they did the
deed, lived through the accident.

The pain seemed like it could last forever and ever. She'd been
wrestling with her thoughts, her own noes and mistakes, and Hannah felt new tears coming, never mind that she'd spent hours already
crying nonstop. Shame had to win. Even when she thought she
couldn't last a second longer, even when she was sure there wasn't a
single neuron to make just one of her eyes close, there was still some
strength somewhere, some sort of reflex, to squeeze out one more
tear, just one. Then another, now and forever, because that was all she
had left.

Patrice M.'s shoulders were hunched as he walked, hefting that heavy
key ring. He was more tired than ever. He headed for the first cell
overlooking the wide street. Just twenty minutes, Patrice thought,
and I can go home. The night had been a hard one. There were nights
like this when he finally got the whole picture on a case, and he was

at his wits' end. It was a rare thing. It was only the third time he'd
had a case like that. He'd been with the national police twenty-five
years now, but there was no getting used to it. He got to thinking.
Childhoods and entire lives cut short and then omertà covering it all
up because justice had no power to fix things . . . If people decided
that only victims had any right to judge, to hand down sentences,
to get revenge, that meant not school nor the church nor the "new"
society were doing their job. How could anyone be proud to have
worked in the national police for decades? The police didn't understand a thing about this country that they were supposed to protect.
In a few months, Patrice would be retiring and settling down with
his wife who'd already gone over to Fakarava. They'd fallen in love
with the atoll and built a few fish traps. That'd come in handy later
on. For now, of course, nobody was sitting easy. Everything in the air,
all these invisible specks landing on the smallest bit of exposed skin
reminded him that a cop was above all a man. And a Tahitian cop
was above all Tahitian. Brotherhood and camaraderie were something he knew. All those years on the job, all the drama, the slights,
the boozy haze of weekends hadn't eaten away at what bound him
to this land: camaraderie. He was up to his eyes in it right this minute. There was no controlling it, reasoning with it, being professional
about it, it was almost violent. There was nothing fair about it, after
all. Or right. Because God, Te Atua, being world-weary, had to have
lost track of this family hurt so bad that they'd forgotten how to pray
for help. God had to have lost sight of these children with lives so
broken that only prison could save them. Patrice finally turned the
key in the lock. The pain in his belly stabbed at him. He'd have given
anything to turn back time. He could see that smile of the young
inspector. That self-assured look. That knack he had for explaining
all the methods he'd learned at the National Police Academy without
ever making you feel bad for not having gone there yourself. No, it
wasn't fair. Oh, Lord, why? If only, if only it was possible to start it all

over again. It was clear that, with the connections he'd made, Patrice could have kept this smart, nice, promising inspector from coming and getting tangled up here, in his homeland that had, in the space of a night, turned into the road to his own death.

Ma was on the ground. Flat on her belly, mouth open, breathing in the air from under the door. Then she got back up and went to kneel on the berth. There was no point crying. It'd been twenty years since she'd last cried. That was enough. These filthy, ugly walls of loneliness wouldn't keep her from feeling free for once. The mother of Pina, Hannah, Pauro, and others was calm as the grave as she put her hands together. She looked up. A smile filled her face. Never mind this new ordeal, this ultimate ordeal—she'd be thanking the Lord. Her life, and those of her children, would never be the same again. In a sweet whisper, she prayed for God to protect her, her daughter, every member of her tribe. "Forgive me, O Lord, for the time I wasted, for the courage and faith I lacked, forgive me for my deafness and my egotism. Free them, O Lord. I have lived my life in full." Then, just as she'd hoped, there was a moment in which her heart warmed all over again. A moment where everything was silence and light. Where everything could fall apart, like none of it mattered now that the facts were there: God up in heaven had already forgiven her, always had. She put her hand out and touched what had to be called fulfillment. She felt strong, strong with godly love. Strong with camaraderie. And she knew: it would all work out because love always, always won out. Stronger than anything else, it sewed all the soul's wounds shut. Love alone could fill her children's lives up to the top.

Then the hinges on the heavy door squeaked and she saw a tall, bald, pale man. On his face Ma saw mercy. It reminded her of the ambulance driver's face more than a year ago when he'd come and told her that Auguste had been in an accident. All this humanity had her thinking of the Lord again. It was him. She never should have doubted. She ought to have kept faith.

It wasn't easy for Patrice to keep a straight face. It wasn't easy for him to look self-assured right that minute. The shaky woman he saw in there, kneeling on her berth, was nothing like the monster he'd expected. This woman had the scars of those folks who just suffer in their soul; how could anyone believe that she'd had the muscle to . . . Patrice smiled at her at long last. She looked as queenly as those women of yore. She had the spine and the glare of those women who would have been clan leaders in other times. But the times were different now, and the land too.

Ma's legs were wobbly as she followed Patrice. In slow motion. It was so nice to taste the almost-pure air of the hallway, but she was still worried. Were they set free? As if he'd heard Ma's fears, he said that, thanks to her account, Hannah and Maui had left prison an hour ago. They had to see the investigating judge once again. But for now, only Ma was under a detention warrant. With those words, Patrice's heart felt like mush again and he looked down. She smiled. Didn't say a word. It would all work out. The undercover police car's motor turned over. Three officers were waiting for Ma. Patrice didn't have the heart to cuff her hands so she was led to the back seat, flanked by the two youngest sergeants. The flashing lights were turned on. They were headed for the county jail not ten minutes away on the west coast. Just ten minutes. Right then, a sinking feeling that she might never move on came over her. It wasn't something she saw or knew or thought. It was just a feeling in her guts. Like some sort of need to empty herself out. Not move on. Done. Finished. Life hadn't been easy on her. A little sunlight left streaks on the sky of her small, simple, plain Tahitian existence, yes. But apart from that, no, there hadn't been any happiness. At almost forty-seven, Ma knew that she would never be the pleasantly plump woman saved from ruin and meant for a glorious future, would never be the woman she'd dreamed of being

not so long ago. Nothing like those sappy Latin American telenove-
las that blathered on during the Tahitian afternoons was in the cards
for her. Like so many other women, she'd been sold lies, smoke and
mirrors that had kept her from seeing her fate. She'd just barely saved
a sliver of her soul. Barely kept some of that motherly instinct after
that one second's whim had gotten the better of it. A whim of sex
and fantasy. The worst part was that she'd believed a man from the
new world loved her. Anyone with a life like hers had no hope for
that kind of love.

The unmarked Clio turned onto the alley down to the avenue
du Commandant Destremeau. The day was winding down. Hannah
and Maui were standing there, on the roadside. For half a second,
the young woman had a vision of holding a gun. Had a vision of
shooting at the Clio. She had a vision of pulling her mother out.
Smuggling her off the way people sometimes did in those movies
where an innocent person had been arrested. She'd never held a gun,
though, not in her life. She felt a lump rising up. A lump made by
loss. Love she'd never put words to. A lump of absence. A lump of
anger because the life they'd had wasn't made only of tears, suffering,
and misery. It'd been made out of shame too.

Maui pulled at the glass doors of his studio. It was nearly two in the
afternoon. The place smelled rank, with the stench of the rotting
sashimi he'd left by the sink a week ago. It was a good ten minutes
before he could breathe properly. Another ten to see more clearly and
ten after that to realize that there was no way he was ever waking up
from this nightmare. Outside, the branches of the old albizzias on
the seafront were swaying, shy over the smog-stained trunks. Soon
the wind would pick up. It came from the channel to the west. The
refrigerator's solemn hum only made the lonely, naked feeling that
was coming up from the "boulevard" on this gray Sunday worse.

Inside, things weren't much better. The buzzing was as loud as his old fridge. He felt outside of himself in some odd way. Like he was dying slowly, even before the sentence had been declared. Death was pounding away, with metallic bangs and blows, almost hammering away. It filled the gaps of a bitter liqueur. It was heavy like vomit stuck in his throat while he was trying to throw up. What Maui took for his loud pulse was a rat-a-tat of regrets, of not enough time, of too many memories. He'd have given everything to be back in the hushed apartment on the rue de Varenne where he hadn't so much grown up as shot up and where the smell of his mother's glass of booze mixed with the odor of the waxed wood floors. He actually felt a soft spot for the Portuguese doorman who'd seen "three generations of Thomases" living there and who'd never been able to stand Mata, that "negress."

Only after he'd had a shower did he get his thoughts in order. He'd looked down and watched the strong, hot water running down his chest, his flat belly, his member. Funny, he thought. After everything the past two weeks, he hadn't bothered with getting off. He got to reminiscing about Mareva, or that Danish girl he'd met in the Marais some years back. Girls had always had crushes on him. He had washboard abs, a rugby player butt, a swagger like Benicio Del Toro. And he was an inspector, although maybe not anymore, or maybe only for a while longer, who knew . . . All of that made him the perfect heartbreaker. Maybe only at first glance, maybe, seeing as how all those women always ended up scaring him off and leaving him depressed. Just like his mother . . . But at that hour, after two days in the clink, what a nice thing it was to be alone at last!

He sat up, scared. For a second he'd thought he was in his cell, then was shocked to see himself naked, lying on the couch. His belly was dripping with come. His hand and neck hurt. He felt ashamed all of a sudden, wiped his brow. His head was pounding so much he wished he could blow it apart. He wished his heart would just stop, right there, just like that. Then he glanced outside. The street was dark. In the east were the Vaiete food trucks lighting up everything there was to light up: Chinese lanterns, multicolored blinking Christmas lights, ti'i torches, hurricane lamps, and of course ovens and barbecue grills . . . By his watch it was seven at night. He had to think through everything that had happened. He also had to go back to Tenaho at some point.

This living room, in fact, was where it had all begun. The day after the elections he'd moved in, just like he'd promised himself. He'd put a few of his belongings in a dingy closet. He'd made sure to say goodbye to Mareva by text, like a jerk; it was the cheap way to go. He was happy about it, a good nine and a half out of ten. It was a relief. It was all a jumble. The happiness of the independence party winning. The three letters of *oui* that meant so many good and new things to come. They'd gotten the upper hand on those sneaky politicians. This was a reset. And now he was part of a family, a clan. A clan that had no idea he was one of them. But a clan that would welcome him with open arms. He was scared too. Deep in his guts because—he'd have to deal with this soon enough—he was the son of a murderer.

Once they were all there, he'd come back down to earth. Yes, they'd won. Yes, it was great. But everyone had gotten carried away. Now all Tahiti's bigwigs were shaking in their boots. Ideology had won out over cynicism. But no. No, France wouldn't just go along. Soon they'd have to negotiate, maybe even fight. The race had been tight. There hadn't been any, well, mistakes, had there? Maybe in some small municipality squirreled away on one of the 170 islets of Tuamotu, some little chairman had messed up the numbers. Gotten them mixed up⋅∴. Yes, some results would need to be overturned. They'd have to bring out the big guns. Declare something or other. What exactly didn't matter, just that people had been misled. Back to the actual question. Put it another way. Turn it around. Make it a referendum: "For or against keeping Polynesia within the French Republic?" ought to be taken out and replaced with "For or against the development of Polynesia?" This place's growth needed to be at the front and center of talks, of everyone's hopes and fears. Polynesia needed to realize that it was still a baby. And the motherland was there for it. No mother ever lets her child go, not ever. Soon it would have to play Jocasta. A lover, a mother of the old kind. Offering her breast to assuage needs and impulses. But she'd been broken up with. Abandoned. The child and the lover had to suffer no matter what.

When they saw the riot police vans going down the avenue, they knew their days were numbered. A war nobody'd asked for was coming. Dreams nobody'd dared to dream were starting to be dreamed. Songs of glory that were to be forgotten on the spot were coming to mind. All these young people who thought they were so strong were about to look so silly. They were against the system, they wanted to think freely. They were angry and they wanted the world's eyes on them. And all of a sudden they had no power. Weren't so sure they'd made the best choice. Almost ready to go back because the motherland was strongest of all. Because who wanted to get pumped full of lead? They'd never had to do that. Tahiti was no Algeria.

Hannah was wearing low-cut skinny jeans and a tight black V-neck. It always made her look sexy. With one hand she twisted a lock of hair that she then pulled down to the corner of her mouth. She looked out through the bay window. Just like Maui not a few hours ago.

Michel

HAPPY IS HE who has never felt the pain of being at a loss for words. A loss for words to say or, worse, to write. The pain of nothingness. At his computer screen. At his wide- or narrow-ruled notebook dotted only with a few scribbles, some amateur drawings. Happy is he who can write, put himself into words, and cry out. Who can take satisfaction in those words set down a few hours every day or night and, the next day, start anew, with even more ease than the day before. Happy are those skilled typists who never have to hit the backspace key like madmen because the words that come and are typed are perfect. Because inspiration, oh, that fickle inspiration is there and has chosen you as its medium. Inspiration. Like the physical process of breathing: inspiring, expiring. Inspire, inhale a story. Expire, exhale it with all the delicacy or sharpness you can. Happy are those successful writers who crank out two tomes a year with that unmistakable new-book smell. Oh, that smell of paper. You could pick it out anywhere, absolutely anywhere at all. Like a madeleine. The smell of paper. "It's funny," Hannah said to me one day, "you always smell like paper." We were at the back of a bus, on the quai Saint-Michel. At that moment, I don't think that really pleased me. We were stopped at an intersection. To the right was a book stall. I think she said that because she noticed the bookseller

freezing his butt off. She was looking at the stall. A few carica-
tures framing an old pocket edition of *Promise at Dawn*. I smell like
paper. Not much of a compliment there. I must smell like my book-
shelf: Old. Silent. Like a library. I smell like paper. "So that means I
stink," I said. She shook her head no. I thought to myself: yes, that
has to mean I stink. All my reading has gotten into my clothes,
my hair, my early-spring jacket. It's funny. Suddenly I'm afraid. I've
read so much, worn out my eyes by the wan light of a cheap lamp
bought at a nearby flea market, dog-eared so many used books that
I smell like paper. And that scares me. As if the paper had swallowed me up. All those years of solitude have remade me, almost
transformed me into something inevitably old, inevitably solitary.
I'm suddenly scared of being as welcoming as those weathered
pages. I'm scared of becoming scary.

A moment of bookish ranting. Bits of paper fused with my skin.
Bits of man fused with other people's writing. Famous or unknown,
big or small. Magnificent or insignificant. I replay this scene and
Hannah's smile as she realizes that I've been dumbfounded.

I replay this scene, inhale this smell exuding from the books
bought in Tahiti a few months ago now that I still haven't opened.
I've been there for two hours now. Scribbling things. Sipping a beer.
Waiting for the love of my life. Who will never come back.

She stayed back there. She can't leave again. It's been six months
now. She said, when you figure out the words, the words that I don't
know, that can help me. Then we can see each other again, maybe.

Sometimes I feel hoodwinked. I have that sinking feeling that
she's toyed with my life, really, with my heart. A heart I'd walled off
the better to live. It really does upset me at times. But I love her too
much to ... No, I love *me* too much to tell myself that she's been
jerking me around.

I've never really had faith in life. What happened to us, to Hannah and me, that's taken the wind out of my sails altogether.

I replay the reel, like an old song. A happy film. Emotional scenes. I'm papering it all over with generalizations. Words that try to say everything but are just like all the others. All the other stories. Even more than the smell of paper and the silence that seems to surround it, this story that, I sometimes worry, won't charm anyone . . . Well, at some point I just have to stop caring. Let it bore some readers. It'll still have won out. It's a simple story. About simple, average people. Average for their corners of the world. Barbarians here. Obscurantists here and merely mystics back there. All the keys to understanding them are lost. Here clearly isn't in any way there.

And that's the problem in the end. There is indeed a problem. Of this "here," this "there." Not saying what comes from there, believing that it can't be said and then written here, would never interest those people there. Those who think: Who cares about your stories about "back there," about a world that'll always be foreign to us? An average Frenchman, you come and talk about us without even understanding us . . . And my takeaway from all of that, from those people, is that nobody is ever a gateway.

And they'd have every right to blow a fuse, to beat the shit out of some of those people stopping over on a land they're so convinced is theirs. They'd have every right to be prideful and choose not to reveal themselves. Ever. They'd have every right to set the sole international airport on their island on fire. Their sole connection between here and there. Because everything that comes from here can defile their there. Because everything that comes from here is nothing more than a heap of little vanity-scented and whim-scented things. "I came here as a friend to consume, to live well, to give you life. And to fuck your wife and your sister, to screw your brother with pitiful wages and buy more of your land that's gone back to the state." That's their there. Unimaginable. This is our here. A here that we presume only belongs to a few. The truth is that we're all that way. Suckling at the breast of māmā exoticism. And I haven't even gotten started on those nerds high on monoi, coconut oil, high on all those fancy historical-legalistic-paternalistic speeches. Total idiots who got riled up over an American flag on some old Tahitian shack. Total idiots who'd landed one day, eager and hungry. Declared themselves the scribes of a people without a pen of their own. They yelled and spewed words in shitty, sorry excuses for daily papers. They really did think they were God's gift to Tahiti. They huddled together all over the place, anywhere it was shiny and gleaming. Painfully lonely, always fleeing, seeking out some people that would actually want them. Seeking out some fame that nobody in the West would grant them and down there, it's more rain than shine. Hannah had every right to tell them to go right back home. Tahitians had every right to stay superficial. To be all parties and ukuleles. They had every right not to dredge up their deep aversion beneath their smiles to those with savior complexes. They had every right to hate these men who, on pretext of having themselves a woman, want to have themselves the Tahitian soul.

They have every right. And I smile, I laugh. Tahiti, locus of all incomprehension. Island of differences that separate.

Apparently the sun makes some people forget all sense of right and wrong. When you see what you want to see, you can't help but think about one thing. One thing that reverberates like an ad, a pitch-perfect tagline: "Tahiti, playground for idiots looking for something exotic."

For months now I've been lugging around this story, I don't think I'll make a book out of it. I know I don't have the right to. At most I'll keep the material, in case . . . for someone. For you, Hannah . . . Tahiti hasn't been a haven for me. I did expect that, though, a little. I didn't want it to be a haven. I wanted it to be a place to discover. But it wasn't. Probably for the best.

❖

So it's for her that I'm doing all of this. Hannah. A young woman who could have written books, who could have become the Toni Morrison of her godforsaken island. That was her dream. She said it to me one day once we'd had a bit to drink. Hannah who was getting more and more tired with each passing day. Of her country being overtaken. Of their particular, very particular accent being wiped out. Tired of these traffic jams. These hypermarkets exactly the same as the ones in Bondy or Pierrelatte back in France. Hannah, my darling, the one I won't outlive, or hope I don't outlive.

She'd changed, of course. But I found her again all the same. And that's how I wanted it. She'd become a warrior woman. Not one bit frail anymore. Not one bit like the woman I'd once thought I was protecting. And I only loved her even more. And yet. It's clear from our get-togethers, our debauched afternoon naps, our silences that she's growing distant. It's clear that coming back to her family has stolen away that libido I'd been bowled over by.

It's clear. I'm perfectly aware. I know that love, to some degree, makes your eyes all that much sharper, that all the doubts are gone. I understand that. The doubt has become love. Despite all this moral and physical distance. Even despite the death of desire in one's heart. What's been woven by bodies and souls now lingers beyond absence. Physical. Moral. Still, I'm crazy about her.

I've already said that she wasn't at my side. And yet I do believe, I the atheist, the impious, the expert in cynicism. A nihilist when I'm sober. A killer of humanity when I'm trashed. I believe she's watching us, observing us. Me and my half-pint, set on an old coaster . . . And yet I believe that her unwaveringly black eyes are resting, however briefly, on my notebook. I miss her . . .

I've picked up the pen. A Bic. I've put away my Mac for a bit. Details. My glass is dripping. All I have eyes for is her. And some images. Scenes. That the sun in Tahiti, harsher than the sun in Tijuana, hits with practically all its force. I remember her editorials in a small local paper that was every bit as pretentious as any small local paper, and the notoriety that inevitably came from an easily recognizable style. I remember her indignation. Her shrieks, her rants, her paranoia. Like that time. At the preview for a local artist's exhibition. A pretentious artist whose independence leanings verged on ridiculousness, who had distant Jewish forebears and supported DSK and the Zionists . . . Hannah hadn't let the contradiction in terms go unnoticed: all for independence and still a Zionist . . . We'd gotten kicked out of the viewing. I still don't understand why we'd bothered to go. But at this hour, at this point in our story, what is there to understand, anyway?

Oh, women! Mine is one to be proud of. Yes. Very much so. She was a poet, that Hannah. An underground poet, a working-class poet. A poet beyond all class. Her words still dance in my head. We were shoved out of that gallery. There really isn't any freedom in Tahiti. You can sleep with anyone you want, anyone you can. But it seems like, I'd say, good manners, paired with religious propriety (or as a result of it), has stiffened necks and, of course, words. Good manners. Proper thoughts. Not modesty.

Hypocrisy.

Soon Hannah would be known for the editorials she kept on writing every chance she got. On behalf of an association she chaired, she was called a troublemaker because she wouldn't let other people think that everything was just fine and dandy. That was Hannah's extremist side. She couldn't stand mediocrity in intellectual conversation, in thought. Fighting against ethnocentrism and her people's cultural world where they had no idea that their guilty silence covered up a bankrupt soul.

Now that I'm nearly fifty, I'm coming to think that I won't outlive her. She's shown me the depths of existence. Some people might say it's too much. But I don't care about those people. It's something I'd never have hoped for at my age. I'll always be grateful to her.

But where was I? I mean, apart from being on the patio of this café?

Oh, the idea that I'm trying, out of love, to reconstruct a story, the stories of people. I don't really know it all that well myself but it's so singular, and its wounds are too—doesn't one come from the other?—seems important to say aloud. If only to set particular things in a proper context, if only to tell you that in some faraway corner of France, deep in the South Seas to be exact—this thought seems both so crazy and so sad—there are people who are like you and me, still united under the Republic and whose lives, whose thoughts, whose behavior are wholly at odds with how we live and think and behave here. Who for so many people are just images. In Tahiti douche or Bounty TV ads.

"When we all talk about this people, I don't actually know who we're talking about. I feel like we're talking warmly about, say, Etruscans, you know, peoples who are only found in books now. *People*. This people. It's actually getting hard for me to say this word, to think it. What could I say about this people? Do we only have the right to try to describe them? For me there's still something unknown because they're so fragmented. Because they're absolutely, wonderfully fragmented. And will stay so for a long time, unknown . . ."

I confess she's scared me shitless. She got politically involved in the independence referendum. I'd be lying if I said I didn't care. That would be wrong. I wanted to keep her to myself. The fact that she would stay in France would allow me to keep our futures, our lives connected . . . I really was a lot more stupid back then. That didn't matter at all. Yes, of course she was right. I was a colonizer, and in her eyes I would always be a colonizer or the son of a colonizer. I'd have to pay for the others. I loved her to the ends of the earth. She didn't feel the same way. I came to hate her because she was unmoved by my weak arguments for voting yes. To shut me up, she pulled out all the stops. For her, there was "nothing more dangerous than letting people think you'll make room for them forever. And nothing more condescending than saying: without me you wouldn't even be able to eat. The longer things drag on, the more I think that someday we're going to have to leave each other. Not just separate, *leave* . . . But there mustn't be any violence, even if I don't really believe that's possible." I do know those words she wrote were meant specifically for me. I tried my best to hold on to her or rather to force her to keep me close. But her whole body, from her head to her toes, cried out for freedom. There wasn't a place for me in the revolution she wanted to begin. In this battle that she with her clear eyes wanted to fight . . .

Toward the end of our relationship, she turned back into the professional colleague I'd once known, although a slightly more self-assured one. One night she told me about this feeling of coldness she'd felt upon our arrival. These rifts, these separations between two, or even three or four ethnic groups. This apartheid that was never called that. These mutual suspicions. Of course it was a bit like that before she'd left for France. But this time she felt it in her bones. There would be an actual, bloody break. France, in her eyes, had let too many things happen, had let too many people do as they liked. Impunity. Contempt. She knew what those were. She'd seen it in the stores, in the restaurants, above all in the hotels. And what horrified her the most was that these people, the ones she'd lived with, grown up with, saw all of that at best as unimportant, at worst as almost normal. As if inevitable. But inevitability, fittingly, only lasts so long.

Of course, she told me this was no Russian or Central American prison. Their president was no Pol Pot—not yet. But there was still this keen feeling that you owed these people, both the government and also these strangers, the right, the mere right to breathe.

Of course, this was no Auschwitz. But there were these silences that
drowned out all other sound. This muted indignation that was rum-
bling, wasn't coming from far off at all. From a time that had made
their women, because they weren't too dark-skinned, the salvation of
all these men who'd washed up there. Apparently the idea that the
colonial period was firmly in the past was completely wrong. Even
framing what happened now as neocolonialism was wrong. Colonialism, and I've seen it with my own eyes, is limited to no era, to
no age. It's simply there. It's simply always been there. It's changed
a bit over time, but fundamentally it's all the same. The soldiers are
gone, replaced by golden boys straight out of France's fanciest business school. These golden boys, almost all of them Parisian, were at
the head of the big local businesses, here and there they had key roles
in the administration. They're pale white or sunburned, depending
on how heavy their workload is. They're part of a new generation,
the one of big heads who talk too much. Big heads that wouldn't
fuck a Tahitian girl, wouldn't even go on dates with them. Half them
are gay men who touched down with their partner in tow. And the
other half meet French girls who just arrived. And those women
are executives too. They all end up buddy-buddy with other young
couples with similar career paths, always fondly reminiscing about
Parisian spots where it was nice to see and be seen. All those couples were too busy, went to the same restaurants once a week, the
same clubs once a week, read the same books because they all loaned
them out to one another. They all tried to fit in: for example, they
got Polynesian tattoos on their ankles and on their lower backs,
sometimes even full-body ones. For them it was proof of their "good
intentions." The only Tahitians they actually associated with were
the night watchmen who patrolled their residences, or the gardeners
they saw briefly as they headed out to the office. Sometimes they'd
rub shoulders with a few Tahitians who were in the upper middle
class, in nice clean gyms they always joined as a couple, around seven

in the evening. They had knowing smiles of those who'd "succeeded" and now had some insights about everything: religion, politics, above all politics . . . "They're all idiots—except for me!" They could work up a sweat just like everyone else, after an intensive hour of "body combat" or "body attack," but they'd always remain certain that their social status afforded them some sort of intangible legitimacy. The worst was that the Frenchman who'd been there for more than five years always sneered down at the one who'd just arrived . . . Unless the latter had a more "desirable" position . . . "We almost feel bad for those soldiers over in Moruroa," Auguste Junior had said one day. He wasn't wrong.

Oh! Tahiti, playground for idiots looking for something exotic . . . If only it was just that. But wait, there's more . . . The era of governors might be over, but the era of their children is only just getting started. Those mixed-race kids who learned to shun their "darker" side. The side they'd inherited by blood from the world that their father had come to save years earlier. No, not a thing had changed. Not a single mentality, in any case. I felt so bad for Hannah and her family. All those perfectly white smiles were of my ilk.

It's ten at night now. But it's still bright out on the rue Saint-Honoré. Tomorrow's the longest day of the year. The worst one for me. Concerts, screams from every end of every street to celebrate music and so much boredom, thousands of liters of alcohol are going to quench the thirst of those who love to celebrate music—but only in Paris. I'll definitely be going to my mother's out in the banlieue for a bit of quiet. There's a high risk that on the way over I'll check Skype or Facebook and see her. I'll ask her for the latest news, share what I can about Pauro and François, whom I had dinner with the other night out by Versailles, and I'll take care, like I do every time, not to tell her that I miss her. Or I'll stream France 24 and try to keep up with that teensy strip of text running across the bottom of the screen providing the info that nobody but me cares about. That teensy strip connecting me to her. Sometimes they still talk about it but honestly it's awkward again these days. We're waiting for the decision from above. On one side, just as on the other, nothing is certain.

A small body sways. Spins, rather, this way and that.
Calmly, a calm far too calm. A calm that means
that was the last gasp, too late now.
A small body dangling from a rope tied
good and tight to an old ceiling. It ought
to have collapsed but hasn't, that shirker.
That long frizzy hair's loose and free for once.
The only keening is a river not far off.
A body that's a tender sacrifice on the altar of squalor.
The neck's going purple, the face deathly pale.
There's that small smile on those dead lips.

Rainbow

PACIFIC RISING POST. A fancy-schmancy title for a half-baked news site ripping off older sites. Padded out with official dispatches trotted out over and over again and never updated so that over the course of hours they just became vague mumbo jumbo. At the top they'd posted a picture of Hannah. The title was practically poison: "Paradise at war!" It was shared a million times across social networks. Hannah was setting off a buzz. All the uproar around the Middle East was quickly forgotten; everyone decided that the biggest news was now out of the Pacific. In French Polynesia. Everyone said their piece, there were hours of exclusive coverage, feature segments on news shows, droves of experts, all of them dumbfounded, offering up wildly diverging explanations, sometimes they even cursed one another out on air. But they all agreed on one thing: "This result was a catastrophe for the working class . . ." A referendum nobody'd seen coming with consequences nobody, *nobody* saw coming. Paradise, it was clear, was lost. Ma had managed to snag a color photo of this "front page." Her probation officer had agreed to print it out for her so she put the A4 sheet on the wall facing her bed, so she could see it before closing her eyes at night, upon opening her eyes in the morning. The cell she shared with Suzanne, a hardened thief and now a murderer, had little by way of decoration. She might look like an openly lesbian truck driver, but under that Suzanne had a bit of a seamstress side and liked to knit. Pink and orange and blue blankets covered their beds. A close-up of Hannah, her hair wavy with auburn streaks around a proud face. Her eyes dark with a few creases, her favorite Ray-Bans on her head. She could have been a South American revolutionary or a Palestinian student. Ma wondered if maybe she really was one. Nobody would have guessed she was proud of her. In fact, the shrinks said, later on, that she had to be afraid of her. The young woman in the photo had scared her shitless, but within a clan those sorts of things aren't said. They aren't even thought.

Sure enough, in the visiting room not a few hours earlier, they hadn't traded many words. Ma had been busy with Moïra who was almost two now. A chubby toddler starting to get fussy in this musty room full of couples with hormones seeping out of their pores. The other prisoners only had eyes for Hannah. And there was nothing the folks around her could do about it. But that was often how it was. There was something magnetic, hypnotic about Hannah for everyone who thought with their dick. It'd only gotten worse ever since making the headlines . . .

"You eating all right here, Ma?" The woman asking her that had put together two meals at the most in the past week. "Don't you worry," Ma replied. Not worrying was what mattered. It was almost a mantra. Don't worry, not even when everything's falling apart, for Ma there's never any reason to worry.

"What about you, Hannah, how are you doing?" It was a normal question but with Ma those sorts of questions always had her feeling like it was impossible to share more, unthinkable to get down to what mattered. All the same, Ma looking away, just about praying for Hannah not to say anything, to zip it and move on. But ever since she'd been set free, the young woman had been thinking over and over and over about what had gone down. "Why'd you sacrifice yourself, Ma?" She wasn't really asking, she was sobbing. For the first time, real words. Raw ones. Sacrifice? Sacrifice . . . yes, indeed, why? And, for the first time in Ma's life, there wasn't a simple answer. The tiled floor, as cold as all the other visiting rooms in all the other prisons in the world, with holes here and there like prisoners and visitors had gotten it into their heads to bury themselves alive there, was actually reeling. The prison itself wasn't solid anymore, was shaking off every-thing clear about it. Even here she wasn't safe. Let alone a heroine. Hannah had always had that habit of hers, Ma couldn't stand it, that habit of accusing you with no fuss about it. Why? "Are you asking me why, Hannah?" "Yes, Ma, why? Wouldn't it have been easier to let the boys end up in the clink? What am I supposed to do now that I've got my hands full with this girl?" Moïra was a colicky baby; she was already bawling and neither her baby bottle nor Hannah's pacing back and forth with her in her arms calmed her down any. Ma had never really taken in the facts but now she was shocked, gobsmacked by how strange everything was all of a sudden. Even her daughters, especially her daughters. In the older one's eyes she'd seen a keenness that caught her off guard. Sacrifice, yes . . . but that girl had no idea what she was talking about. Her heart was all torn up too.

"If I had let your brothers confess, where would you be now? Not strutting around like a peacock in front of the journalists, I'll tell you that! And you know it . . . Your brothers did what they had to. You're wondering why I sacrificed myself. So you could live, so you could move on. If your sister's that much trouble, give her to social services then, get someone to adopt her. I'll tell you this. My parents always said to me: E tahe tō 'oe vai mata, te utu'a. Go and cry a river, you had it coming to you. My baby, do what you think is best for your-self or even for your people . . . Well, whatever you call 'your people,' that's something you learned at school. Where's your people now? Did anyone lift a finger for you? No, they don't give a shit about you, they used you . . . like all those men in the party you joined. E tahe tō 'oe vai mata, Hannah. You knew this would happen, and now you're complaining? We've all been watching you as you dug yourself deeper and deeper into this hole. Putting up barricades like that! We did what we could so you could have your fifteen minutes of fame. And I sacrificed myself for my girl, for her above all, and I don't regret it. She'll go far and you don't know the half of it. Could you be any more self-absorbed? Do you really think you deserve to be a star? A face for this country but not for your brothers? Who do you think you are to decide who goes into the clink and who gets to stay outside? You really thought that I loved my other children any less? They've got plenty of problems, sure, but my sons have always been there, right by me. We're not going to get into Pina, but . . . not you! So, yes, I sacrificed myself, and what you've had to deal with is the easiest thing in the world to deal with."

Even as the Tenaho clan's spat had everyone present riveted, even as the baby's cries drove them all up the walls, Ma got up and waved to the warden that the visit was over.

Taramo 120

AT THE BACK of the nice and snug SUV, Hannah had Moïra's head between her thighs, so she could sleep stretched out. Her iPhone was vibrating, buzzing for attention. She knew the number, of course. It was the party. Those henchmen, those "strangers" she'd gotten fond of, were trying to reach her. It was the sixth time this morning. Hannah was the sort of girl they couldn't stand, but they wanted her for her "connections," her expertise . . . six times that morning even though she knew well and good that they hated her.

The roads snaking down the east coast, the ones she'd spent her teens going up and down, narrow and dangerous, the ones where you had to honk to warn oncoming cars, were nothing under the SUV. Thick, untamed, proud nature cast shadows over the asphalt. To her left was the stormy ocean without a single barrier reef. The seaside 'aito were barely shaking under an unrelenting wind. Suicide bay: that's what she'd called it when she was little. She'd been through so much on her own, dealt with so much in her family and on the island, but it was her mother's words that ate at her. Few people, not even the insanity all around, had ever made her doubt herself like this, had somehow slipped these drops of poison into her veins, a sort of sharp, piercing, painful guilt . . . She looked away from the ocean, turned her phone off, and let her eyes rest on the strong neck of the driver. She'd have loved to stroke this neck and the hair making a *V* on it, and so much more . . . She wanted him, she wasn't shy about it, and she'd made sure he knew it. Right then, the driver tilted his rearview mirror and suddenly his eyes met the woman's. It was nice out, especially so for July. Usually the ocean was churned up on this coast, but now it was flat and shiny with wavelets. He'd been keen on her too, up until the moment he'd realized that they had the same father. And then he'd felt lonelier than ever, sadder than ever . . . full of dark thoughts, screams he held back, like part of his soul was cut away. His heart hadn't asked anything of anyone, but now it was in pieces, and in his thoughts, he piled curse upon curse on his mother, his father . . . At some point the two of them saw reason at last. It was impossible, it was a taboo that was there for the sake of survival. He smiled. It was so nice out. She too looked so nice. But only when he looked at each little part of her body. Under her warrior woman persona she was full of fears, needs, nightmares. She'd died so long ago.

Five minutes earlier, they'd left Aunt Poe's house, shaken. Everything was unfair. Down to the too-high, too-white sun. It couldn't warm their hearts again. Unfair: Teanuanua's cancer. Unfair that France made so many lofty promises but was so stubborn, so set on not acknowledging the damn consequences of thirty years working on Moruroa.

It wasn't fair to have such thoughts, such love for a land, a people so far away. Wasn't fair for their lives to be stolen away. Wasn't fair that this Ma had somehow stopped Hannah's words and even thoughts in their tracks. The more she thought, the more she felt like her mother had no right to judge her. She'd spent years trying to forget or at least sand down the sharpest edges of images that came back to mind anyway. If Ma really had sacrificed herself, she wouldn't have let Auguste steal Hannah's first dreams. She wouldn't have let him dirty her like that, robbing her of being able to feel pleasure for years after. So many men, so many nights, so many hurts, so many wants cut short. So many stories broken off. And always, always, this unhappiness. At the bottom of her throat was dryness and at the bottom of her heart was the cold of fear, of loneliness. Only Michel had distracted her long enough to maybe be more than just "maybe." They'd become a couple, but not for long. Just enough to miss each other and then someone, something had hit the off switch on that magic. Once they had to face life in Tahiti, it had all stopped cold. Hannah was all alone again, like coming back to Tenaho meant coming back to life as a big sister, meant only getting to feel whatever was a problem right then, whatever was happening right that day, why she needed to escape, get them all out ... There wasn't any space for life as a couple. All those songs about eternal love were just lies told to little girls. Responsibility was the only truth. But who had come up with such balderdash?

In just five minutes they'd be at the bridge that crossed the Papenoo Valley.

It's gorgeous here, I love this side. It's my favorite.

Hannah just nodded, she didn't care whether or not Maui had seen her. The green mountains to her left had such proud crowns of clouds. Not threatening. Not dark. This green that was so far away, so close by. Those mountains. Unchangeable ... She could make out the peak of Mont Orohena ... And suddenly she remembered that psalm she'd learned as a child. That loneliness had been terrible. That hopefulness had been incredible too, and part of her nights at Tenaho. It was back there, in the bedroom she'd shared with all her little sisters, that Hannah had secretly learned those words that she thought would save her. The only Bible in the house, a gift from Teanuanua, had held all her screams, her pain, her hate. She tried to take refuge in it. Knowing that miracles were meant for other people. Good people, as she called them. All the same, deep down, maybe out of superstition, she'd held onto it like a shipwreck victim clutching a branch. E hi'o ānei tō'u mata i te mou'a 'āivi ... "I will lift up mine eyes unto the hills, from whence cometh my help. My help cometh from the Lord, which made heaven and earth . . ." But from whence would cometh *their* help? From Teanuanua, that wise man with the secrets of olden times. Teanuanua who wasn't long for this world. They'd said he had two months at the most. His cancer had spread. He'd refused all treatment. No chemo, no painkillers. He'd been clear: he wouldn't stand for dying in the hospital. This wise man of few words but much love, would be gone in a matter of days and the small commune of Tiarei was digging their pastor's burial plot already. When she was little, Hannah was convinced that Teanuanua had come right out of a legend. Rua-Taata. The father who'd sacrificed himself during a great famine, who'd been so desperate that he'd died and turned into a giving tree: the breadfruit tree. Teanuanua's body had only helped: it had all the strength of men who spent their lives slogging away, sweating away . . . men who never found time to laugh, to celebrate. "Do you really think that's a good idea?"

We don't have the choice, Hannah. We don't have the choice anymore.

Yes, you're right and besides Teanuanua won't be going to hell, that's for sure . . . if anyone is, it'll be us!

What's hell got to do with this? Maui was atheist. We're men with the gift of consciousness, we're totally free. When we die, we—our consciousness and ourselves—we just disappear. The only afterlife we get is living on through our kids, and their kids, and so on. But the genes we give them get watered down by other genes, get washed away, get to pop up again sometimes . . . Otherwise, no, there's nothing. No soul in heaven. Atoms decay and cells die. There's dust, then time, then forgetting. Maui didn't think that Mata, his mother, was somehow alive in some other realm, some other dimension. She was dead. She was gone. She'd never counted on anything when she was alive. Why would she count on anything when she was dead? For the people who are still alive after, what stings the most is the memories.

The wounds. The words they never said. The crazy love he'd had for her. Really, that he didn't have, it was like a long moan. A low, sharp sound. It wasn't reassuring, not really. Mostly it was too heavy.

You think Junior did a good job of explaining it to him? Giving him all the details? Teanuanua's sick . . . I don't think he's really got it into his head. Maybe he understands the words, but not what they really mean.

Maui didn't reply. He thought about those "things." Of course Teanuanua got it all. He was the one who'd begged the clan to leave him be. Poe hadn't been happy about it. But she felt enough of a duty to Teanuanua, to this man whom nobody had ever seen all riled up like this, that she just bit her tongue.

Ironic, all the same. I get into a fight with Ma and then we go to Auntie Poe and there it all becomes clear, it all changes . . . I wouldn't say that I'm happy. Just that I'm a bit less scared.

Did you see Junior? The others? The respect they all have for this man . . . It's just . . . Well, if I believed in miracles, I'd say it was one.

It almost was, Hannah shot back.

Almost, because in those sorts of places, it's never calm for long and miracles are only in books, or bad movies, never the real world.

The next day, Junior was supposed to take Teanuanua to the public safety agency. Maui had given them the name of the inspector who was taking over the case. They'd ask him questions and then Teanuanua would give them his deposition. He'd say that he'd killed Auguste. That he'd reeled him in and then finished him off two months ago. He'd say that Ma had nothing to do with it, even though she'd signed an official statement, sworn that her words were true. He'd tell them everything he had to because that was how it had to be. He had nothing to lose. And if they asked him too many questions, or if the inspector or the investigating judge laughed in his face, if they were dead set on sentencing Ma, then Teanuanua would tell them she'd done that to protect her kids because she was

convinced *they* were the ones who'd done it. But now the actual murderer was feeling guilty through and through, was confessing to them
now. It might work, Maui said, even if deep down he wasn't sure of
anything. As for motive, everyone in the clan agreed. It was actually
the only detail that was true: Auguste had gone insane. He'd beaten
up his kids, Pauro and Pina. He might have actually raped her. Teanuanua couldn't take any more of the violence they'd all witnessed,
and so he'd gone and offed him. The final straw had been Pina hanging. Teanuanua had gotten a bad feeling, so he'd left his valley right
away and gone straight to Tenaho. And he'd untied the rope from the
child's body. Then he lost control of himself. Yelled to the neighbors
to call for help, and then nothing . . . That had been that.

A week later, while there were political protests and mass upheaval
all over the country, he'd decided that Auguste's time was up. While
the police and the protestors were facing off, he'd lured Auguste away
from the crowd and suggested that they meet up with his family in
an alley farther off. It was night, Teanuanua pretended to be sick.
While Auguste was going to the trouble to lean down and help him,
the man pulled out a kitchen knife and slit his throat like a pig. Then
he'd beaten him up to make it look like a real back-alley attack.

During their long talk in Tiarei where Junior did the interpreting,
Maui went through every last detail of the murder. Calm and professional because that was his only way through. Of course, the young
inspector felt ashamed, so ashamed. To make himself feel better he
reminded himself that there was no other way out. They all had to do
this to protect Pina.

Revenge

HE KNEW THESE SHADOWS. He'd stood in them for years, now they were dancing in his head. The shadows of the pūrau trunk and branches along the beach, facing the house. He liked watching it at night from a distance. A sea hibiscus barely moving under a wind that never stopped. The pūrau of his nights when he was little, the pūrau of his afternoons when he was bored. The pūrau that took in his dreams when he was a teen, those dreams full of bodies. The pūrau that had watched over births and funerals and kept so many secrets. This time the shadows were twisting this way and that, in rhythm with a chant that the 'ū'upa's keening cut into sometimes, a green pigeon's song: ooh, ooh, ooh. Those fears from when he was little rose up again out of nowhere. White. Black. Lonely. His father and his mother hadn't ever let him be scared of that mournful keening. Forty years, it had taken him forty years for the keening to come back and the cold sweat running down his neck and streaking his back too.

He'd been watching the guests for a good two hours now. Not moving, settled on the roof of the east wing. They'd already downed five magnums. Loud voices, high-pitched laughing, vulgar laughing, some laughs wilder than others. No cocktails tonight, definitely not any sweets yet. The place was supposed to be under strict surveillance.

But at the front gate they hadn't even asked him for ID. They'd just figured he was a hired worker, and that suited him just fine. He'd been there every day for two weeks now. He always came at seven in the morning and left at three.

But tonight, he hadn't come back down. Around four, in the middle of a little thicket of eucalyptus a ways down from the villa, he'd hidden his device under old 'aito branches that he'd gathered a few days earlier. Then he waited until seven in the evening before crawling up the gutter and settling on the roof. He knew the host and his guests never got back until ten at night, after a fancy meal and after sipping all sorts of grand crus at the home of the oldest one in the group. Tonight, that fellow was supposed to join the rest here at the villa. Auguste decided that was a good omen. Two birds, maybe more, with one stone. He'd been lying flat for three hours now, dressed in black. Ever since he'd discovered his mission, waiting and staying calm had become second nature to him. Blending in too. Being invisible was an accomplishment. He was a father, a husband. Normal, unnoticed, still respectable. Going invisible was an important part of him surviving now, just like having his scooter. That was why he was going to become an "exclusive" pastor. He'd already started giving sermons to a tiny parish in Pirae, one nobody knew about, far from the current church and its thinking. He found that it suited him rather well. Then he'd found a job. A well-paid one, better than when he'd been a mason. As a bouncer. He'd become a bouncer. After the Georges murder, the owners of all Papeete's nightclubs had formed an association and decided that the police weren't good enough. So they'd hired plenty of people not just to keep the clubbers safe but them too. Faceless, anonymous, but still imposing. He was a perfect fit. The day of his interview, someone thought they recognized him as one of the old "heavies" from the famous elite squads that had been formed during the darkest years, when the money had been easy. He let them. He knew that was his in. They had him start that night.

It wouldn't be long before the midnight bloodbath; the host was setting champagne buckets around the huge Jacuzzi and flipping on the jets and bubbles and the pool lights. Then there were other shadows around the pūrau branches. Shadows of young girls. Shadows of themselves. They were twirling and spinning on a small dance floor up high so that the guests could ogle their thighs and crotches and more besides, those girls knew that if they wanted to come down to the champagne buckets they only had to wear nothing under their microskirts and dance lasciviously. The guests were never the same. Nor were the dancers, and later on people would say that getting up onstage had been a big deal. You'd had to catch the eye of S., a nightclub promoter, catch her fancy. In just a few years of doing her thing, S. had become the high priestess of steamy nights in Papeete . . . Two security guards were at the bottom of the stairs. Two others at the top. One way back keeping an eye out through the window for whenever the cops made their rounds, and another one standing behind the long couch in the corner. Electronic music was pounding in the background while Auguste peered past the white spotlights, getting worried while he waited for Richie, the Chinese bartender with a super trendy haircut and a tight-fitting polo to bring up the Tagada strawberries. Even with the perfume, the sweat, the smell of cocktails and liquor, he could smell those candies. Sour, chemical, bittersweet. The fake Tagada strawberries. Twice as big as real ones, which could be bought in Tenaho. They were filled with drugs, sedatives, they were a magic wand for the rich men. Those candy strawberries got them past the castle walls of good manners and inhibitions. Slipped them right in. They could go and do illegal things and never get in trouble. They were way past all the taboos, the moral no-nos. It had been orgies at first, but getting consent and letting people in slowly, carefully had been such a hassle . . . And now, upstairs, they had pure, total control, they were almost like animals. For free. It was so sleazy to pay a fifteen-year-old girl for a blow job. They wanted better. They deserved better. Taking their anal virginity, for example, right there, with their "friends," deflowering the country girl with the neck of a magnum of Bollinger champagne while the latest girlfriend went up and had the girl pleasure her with her tongue . . . Using their genitals to defile, to dirty these girls scared of being sent away to more respectable clubs, those girls who tried their best to go along, hot chicks with ultra-rich sugar daddies, pearl magnates, investors.

Every time Richie came over, his plate held up and perfectly flat, the women were sent to him. Sometimes they were supposed to go sit by the host. The bowls of Tagada strawberries were set down beside the pails that the staff kept full. They had big smiles, they were sure they'd passed some sort of test, and they happily swallowed the strawberry placed right in their mouth or slipped into their cocktail glass . . . And that was when things changed. When death got into their still-young souls. When the powder slipped in, like the drops of a water clock, and the slow poison of guilt, shame, remorse spread through them . . . When life became nothing but giving up, giving in, going crazy, going suicidal, sometimes even going through with it. The drug erased everything they saw, everything they'd remember, wiped their thoughts clean, but it didn't wipe away the bruises from choking, the hurt, the cuts on their skin. The rich guys had won. They'd ground those girls who were already outcasts even further down, those girls and sometimes boys from the poorer parts of Papeete's outskirts. These men were slimier than the old rich Chinese owners, the new kings of Tahiti's nights. They never looked one bit vulgar. They strutted through the haut-commissaire's house, circled around whichever government was in place, calling themselves the lifeblood of the land. Sometimes they even got distinctions.

He could feel the cold sweat on his back. Big fat droplets running slowly down his spine. Almost tickling. And it wasn't time yet. For the first time, he felt afraid. That he might not pull it off. He didn't feel ashamed. On the contrary. Those who died would be worth the effort. They'd pay with their lives. And they'd even be paying for this justice system that was too slow, too bogged down, too deaf, too blind to what these real criminals were doing. Tomorrow morning, once the news was on TV and the radio, the young women who'd been raped would be secretly thanking him. Upstairs, on those nights, he kept his cool. More than once he'd wanted to step in. Pull out his long knife and slit their throats right then and there, but the voice told him to wait. Always that voice. Always his mother. Some had to be sacrificed to a god who was jealous and cruel. Divine justice would be handed down from up on high. The fate of all humanity was in his hands, and afterward he'd execute himself. He liked his mission but, well . . . Working at a nightclub, watching and keeping his mouth shut while those rich folks sank into bestiality forced him to remember Rosa. Those girls who he'd always hoped would leave before they'd even shown up, these girls all ended up reminding him of his own, gone all too soon, and of himself too. His faults, his absence, his violence, his shortcomings: how he couldn't declare his love because that made him less of a man. But he couldn't dwell on that. He couldn't let himself be weak. He had to focus on the mission and nothing but the mission. Around half past eleven, the men came out of the house. Auguste squinted, on the lookout for those Tagada strawberries, eager to see them make their appearance, gleaming on an offered-up plate . . . But there weren't any Tagada strawberries, not for the moment. Suddenly he felt wary. He couldn't stand the thought of some unexpected detail getting in the way of his mission. But he'd heard the owner telling Richie just last night that he'd be coming at eleven . . . Without these strawberries there wouldn't be any depraved orgies happening. Those men didn't just turn into mindless animals on their own. There'd be a boring old normal orgy. The women wouldn't really be defenseless, just tipsy and willing. And that wouldn't work for him. Not like that. He felt a stabbing pain like a toothache on the right side of his head.

Like a long thin drill bit right beside him, within him. It was painful
and then there was also this creepy hooting . . . ooh, ooh, ooh. Blasted
bird just deciding to open its beak and fuck everything up. To make
him feel as scared as a seven-year-old boy who had to go grab burlap
from the Chinese man's, ten kilometers away from the house. For
the copra, he had to run and not stop, not look up from the long
coral-and-māmū-clay road . . . Running while there was a gruesome
"oohoohooh" in the background, imagining the ancestral Matahi's
eyes, imagining that he'd get caught in the dark night, once the sun
at the other end of the sea had taken all its red rays with it. Out of
breath, trying to flee. That was what he'd always done, in fact, but for
no good reason. But here he had madness on his side, violence that he
was right to carry out, a purpose: to right wrongs.

Then he saw the girls come down from the terrace and stum-
ble and coo and giggle as they headed for the neon-green pool.
There were six of them. Three were dressed decently: a gaudy bikini,
shipped from Brazil probably. Two others had thongs on, while the
last one had drunk so many flutes of champagne that she hadn't even
undressed. The shrill laughs didn't bother him and Auguste thought
he could make out Tahitian words, even phrases. Then he realized
they didn't want the men to understand what they were saying. This
late at night, Auguste was sure, they were just thinking, "Let's hook
up and have fun." Tears started welling up but he caught himself
immediately because according to his plan, if things were going to
take a turn for the worse, he'd decided that he wouldn't be sparing
these girls. For this cause, for the whole mission, he owed it to himself to hold it together. Not to feel anything other than an absolute
need for punishment. And he'd already reminded himself: the stakes
of his mission were the world itself.

One of the girls pushed a button on a side table. A bossa nova
tune started filling the place. And right then the bar owner, his boss,
appeared. Wearing ugly, ragged shorts, his fat gut came in before

the rest of him. He was bald all over, there was no question that he was a Périgord man. Behind him was the businessman, the heir of a huge local family. He was short and everyone knew about his love for booze, parties, and very young girls. The oldest one in the group was nearly eighty. He'd gone under the knife plenty of times already, and his skin was so taut it almost shone in the half darkness. His nose had been shortened, lifted, tucked, and he made his way forward with difficulty, but it was clear that the prospect of a fountain of youth had him humming along with that smart-sounding bossa nova song that had already played a thousand times over all around the world. Then came the half-Asian man and another businessman. The last one had gotten himself into just about everything. Fine lingerie, hotels, even recycling: before long he'd be a right-hand man to the government. And what was there to say about the Half-Asian, 'Āfa Tinitō, whose mother had gotten pregnant by the boss, a rapist who owned farms, Auguste thought. What a shitty liar, he wasn't a victim of the system, he was actually the most arrogant of them all. The most self-important one. Auguste decided he would kill him last. Because he hated him personally. Because he was a bastard but he still acted like he had the power of life and death over those of his "kind," those who were born to his mother's race.

At this hour the night had gotten awfully chilly. High above, the residence was already seventeen degrees Celsius. Auguste had his devices. Had on a black turtleneck sweater. A knit cap on his head as well as cheap canvas pants, black as well, an almost-perfect uniform for his mission. Combat boots would have been ideal, like in the movies, but considering they cost twenty thousand Pacific francs, Auguste had had to go with dark sneakers. He ran through the scene to come in his head: the actions he'd carry out, the order in which he'd execute each one, maybe a small speech, in case . . . But until the girls swallowed those strawberries, it would all have to remain hypothetical, perhaps fantastical.

At forty past eleven, they were still having drinks in the massive Jacuzzi. Some were giggling and others were pecking and kissing one another with glasses in hands. The music was even schmaltzier, and the water was warm. Then the atmosphere changed; Auguste could tell it was sudden. It became almost unbearable. The men seemed unsettled. Not so sure of themselves. The host climbed out of the tub and picked up his phone. After a few seconds, everyone could hear his throaty voice asking someone at the other end of the line, clearly Richie, what he was doing. The young man didn't get to explain; the host hung up on him and then went and settled back in with his guests. "Just a few more minutes . . . unbelievable, they're paid a fortune and they can't be bothered to show up on time . . ." That was enough for the guests to start going on about kids these days and how lazy they were, getting the evening going again.

He worked out every day and he was used to strict diets, but Auguste's thighs were aching. He'd stayed put for too long and the sloping roof forced him to keep his feet in the gutters. What was the Chinese man with the Tagada strawberries waiting for anyway? One day he'd have to answer for his actions too. You can't get away with doing evil by saying you have to earn a living. Being a collaborator is almost worse.

And then deliverance finally came. A buzz at the security gate forced the host to get out, the bathrobe tied in a hurry around his belly. A few minutes later, he returned to the group, all ecstatic now, oohing and aahing over the package he was carrying. Instead of a tray they'd sent a basket full of bottles and clear boxes that held a good twenty strawberries.

Auguste was relieved but he was still wary. It was almost ominous. Something seemed off. Was it him, his brain that was wired for madness now? Or was it the voice? He'd find out in a few minutes. He shut his eyes to recall a detail. Something that shouldn't have been there. That shouldn't have come. The Chinese man. He'd been late.

Usually he was eager, too eager. That wasn't like him . . . and the detail came into clearer focus. But the host had shut the front gate again, hadn't he? So why was there this gap? This opening? All the while, one of the girls, probably bothered by the music that was too old for her, plugged her phone into the console. Eminem and Rihanna launched into "Love the Way You Lie," which was enough to get the girls amped up. Auguste watched them stand and dance, all energy again. Lighthearted. Young girls who'd have given everything to live the life that Rihanna did. Black, just like them. Maybe they felt that much closer to the star for that, for her skin color?

> *Just gonna stand there and watch me burn . . .*
> *Well that's alright, because I love the way you lie*
> *I love the way you lie . . .*

Later on, Auguste would think back on that. He'd replay the scene. The girls standing in the Jacuzzi, the pervs turned on by the water dripping down their bodies, their thighs, their sexy hips. He the father, Auguste the assassin, feeling downright ill seeing that. As they held up their glasses and sang into them like microphones, the half-Chinese man and the investor who'd opened the small boxes brought them to their mouths to slip a candy in between their lips. The sky was black. In the distance were the lights of the other island. No 'ū'upa singing sadly. Just his heart pounding and the music getting deafening and the detail. Always there. He hadn't looked away even once. The half-open security gate. The detail felt like it was getting bigger and bigger like those shadows that only he could make out past the high wall. And another detail, a tiny red light, like a cell phone, a walkie-talkie that came on at moments. No, this was his mission alone. Nobody else's. Rihanna kept on singing, the girls kept on dancing, but more unsteadily. At this point they were laughing to keep their composure because their legs were getting wobbly. Their arms heavy. Their heads were already spinning. Everything was already starting to freeze, like hot metal setting. This was his mission and his mother's. Nobody had any right to get in the way. Someone was moving behind the security gate, he could tell. So he didn't have a choice anymore. His back muscles were tense, his calves were aching, but he stayed nimble as he made his way down the gutter, went around the building, and headed for the Jacuzzi, his knife in his right hand. He grabbed the host who had his back to him, cut his throat open. It was all unreal. The blood, the red, the bellowing. The girls' dumb gazes, their brains deadened by the drug. The men's stupor. How nobody there was moving. The host's massive body slumped onto the Jacuzzi's rim. Auguste caught the old man who couldn't get up quickly enough, slit his throat. He just barely had time to grip the rich heir as well as the other businessman. Hasty knife thrusts. The half-Chinese man had just enough time to get away as he knocked over three of the girls. And Auguste could already see four men in uniforms headed toward him. "Police, stop, don't move!" All he had to do was get his leg over the barrier and he'd landed four meters down. There was a heap of dead branches under a tarp he'd put there on purpose, that was his cushion. He groped around, found his scooter a dozen meters to the left. Up above the police were aiming their flashlights and their guns on the guy who was fleeing. He could hear a few gunshots. A bullet hit his shoulder. A small blaze that didn't matter. He was Matahi, the man unbent by bullets. He was the heroic, proud, haughty, demonic ancestor. In an act of sheer madness, before starting off, he turned around and raised his eyes to Maui. Half a second, a jagged moment . . . The son as powerful as the father, same body, same dark gaze. Maui raced to the end of the immense garden. The fleeing man sped down the dirt path to the island's ring road, his headlight switched off.

He only slept a few hours. He was fitful, feverish. Voices jolted him awake. Suddenly he was scared of the cops. Then, after a few seconds, realized that the voices were coming from the radio. To the west, the roadblocks had caught fire, all the stations had sent their reporters there. They were worried that the people who'd done that might be headed for the city . . . Groggily, he recalled his nightmare little by little. A fucking nightmare where he'd seen his wife fornicating with the guy who'd put up those roadblocks, who'd somehow, without any big organizations behind him, brought the massive work site on the west coast to a stop. One of those people on the yes side of the referendum. What was he doing in his dream? Then the murderer remembered having passed that way, a few hours earlier. The man was the one who'd let him slip past while he was fleeing. Just by chance. His brain was full of images now getting mixed up with his own fears. A nightmare is just our fears showing themselves again. It didn't take long for his irrational thoughts to win out. Auguste didn't like dreaming. More that he didn't like recalling his dreams because he knew it was his mother coming and telling him things. She was the one who'd told him about everything that was happening, especially in his family. Pauro being queer. The murders and François's attack . . . she'd told him everything.

He stared for a few moments at the water spots on the yellowing ceiling, it was like he expected to find directions for what he should do in those off-brown specks. His responsibilities. But a pain in his shoulder kept him from moving. Then he remembered. The villa up in Punaauia. His boss, the others, the girls, the Tagada strawberries. The mission cut short by the cops. They'd stolen his success. But how did they know? Why did they come that night?

Fever, hunger, exhaustion, the ceiling—it was all too much for his stomach. He couldn't get up, he just sat at the end of the bed and threw up. Hard, almost without any stop. After a few minutes, emptied out, stunned, he felt better. The bed was vile, stained with blood, the ground was rotting under his vomit, his bile . . . Small. He felt small, very small, awkward, alone. That was when Pina came in to change the sheets, maybe to help him. But he wasn't a man anymore. Definitely not a warrior. He'd become an animal. He had no more mission for the moment. No more judgment, no more punishment. He thought he could make out breasts beneath the child's T-shirt. They were just pink dots. He felt like she was a woman, he wanted to see a woman there . . . She was just a child, far smaller than he was. It was at that moment that she decided that she would be dead very, very soon. While her body, too small for such assaults, broke under his harsh blows, which just kept coming. While her head thought that she was as guilty as this creature because a wild animal could be tamed, like those cats in the mountains. She cried out as loud as she could while she felt her father's hands tearing at her shorts. But soon she was crushed. She could hear the sound of the river, not far off. Tenaho, its river. Its water lapping at the banks and sometimes, in fury, suddenly carrying away the shacks' filth. If only it could carry them all away. She could make out Moïra's crying. She held her breath so she could die more quickly. Could hurt less. Then everything slipped into darkness. She was slipped into darkness.

They managed to blockade the territorial road with totaled cars, rusted out-of-service Case tractors from who-knew-where. They'd even managed to roll the huge stones meant for backfill for the hotel nearby into the middle of the road. There were already hundreds of cars backed up right where it dipped down from the hills. Week-night party animals, probably. Or workers coming home late. It was almost midnight. By the white light of the new streetlights that had just been put in, it was almost possible to see the heavy weight of no going back. A few wisps of smoke from a makeshift fire rose up as if to escape all this. It was like one of those unreal films where everything, even the music, stops. Where you wait for the camera to start moving again, to pan across, to show you a panorama. The better to see things. To escape this feeling of suffocation. In all their hearts there was the feeling that they were clutching their futures in their hands. That the sacrifice would pay off, even if nobody was totally willing to acknowledge that fate wouldn't be written down, not even in blood. Those living further up in the area that was a no-go zone for years now had come down to help the protestors. Like any other uprising, there were all sorts to be found there. Hard-nosed men and women. Driven by dreams, fueled by fury. Unemployed people. Drug dealers who wanted to let rip at these stupid policemen who refused to mind their own business. Ideologists. Politicians and union supporters trickling in later. Lost souls. Grown-ups. Children. Their faces sometimes showing. But most wearing makeshift ski masks.

A country about to explode, an uprising in the making focuses your attention, in a matter of minutes it paints a real picture of a whole society. On one side poverty rejoicing, exorcising its demons. On the other, comfort, habit, individuals suddenly becoming scared and, in a fit of pride, struggling to prove who the masters are.

Horns were already filling the night. It took so little, it would have taken so little for everything to blow up. A drunk driver climbed out of a huge American pickup, headed for the blockade. He was told that only ambulances and motorbikes could go through either way. There were heated words, then a few minutes later he made his way with his tail between his legs into the stopped traffic. Ten minutes after the roadblocks were up and "secured," a riot police car filled with municipal officers and two national police vans pulled up. At that moment Maui's unmarked car stopped, stuck on the west side of the blockade. He'd been speeding at 130 kph, pushing the Dacia that he'd been given that night to the limit. He started cussing out his bosses who had decided that "economy" meant "cheap" and felt deeply ashamed at the thought of the murderer, his own father, speeding along almost peacefully on his souped-up old white Vespa. He'd have given anything right that minute to be sitting on his old R1200GS Aventure, the only expensive present that he'd accepted from his stepfather, Martial Thomas. Dripping with sweat, shaking, terrified, horrified by the sight of the corpses up by the residence, he was in such a hurry that he couldn't get through to the police chief who was "on the line." He finally bellowed into the radio that they needed reinforcements up there. The dispatcher said that everyone had been sent to the hotel, barely two kilometers away, to deal with a blockade situation that could explode at any moment.

On this side, the traffic wasn't too bad. Not many cars wanted to make their way into town, it wasn't that time yet. In two or three hours though, workers would start heading in. There were so many ways to warn them before then: on TV, on radio, on social media. In the distance he could make out a hubbub, the orange and blue and red lights of a police siren, movements, back-and-forths . . . He turned off the engine. Ran his hand through his hair. How would he deal with this? Why hadn't he been expecting this? He'd been so hot on Auguste's heels that he hadn't even kept an ear out for those rumors about a blockade, he'd just left all that to his colleagues who handled general matters. He hadn't paid much attention to whatever Hannah and the others had been whispering. Whether or not France accepted defeat, the United Nations would step in at some point. Maui was all for negotiations. Things needed to be sorted out. That was what international law was for. They just had to wait, even if every media outlet, here and abroad, seemed to be hell-bent on keeping freedom from coming. This was the big night. They just had to keep faith that it would happen. Everything Maui cared about was right there in the life they led with their father. Almost a god. A faraway, heavy one. He was everything at once: feared, adored. Hated, never mind all his good reasons for being cruel. Uneducated, but still far smarter than anyone had figured. A golden touch. That steely look. Full of madness. Love. Wisdom. As handsome and strong as those warriors of yore were said to be. Male. Ill-suited to this world, but if there could only be one, it would be this one. He genuinely believed that he'd gotten a clear sense of Auguste the father, had plumbed the farthest depths of his soul. And as these half brothers told him about their origins, of Raiatea the Sacred Island, it drove him slightly crazy. He'd pieced together these scraps at last, these scraps of a past that his mother had taken care to sow far and wide. He'd put it all together at last, with his own self included. For weeks, Maui had gone to the nightclub where Auguste had been working. Of course he'd never actually gotten upstairs. Sometimes he saw him on the ground floor and he got flustered. Because of those similarities that anybody who bothered to look would notice . . . He met Richie. Got to be friends him. It hadn't been hard; Maui was such a good-looking guy in the Chinese man's eyes, and he had clearly fallen in love straightaway. And had ended up telling him out and out about those Tagada strawberries. About the powder, about all the money involved. Making the connection between Auguste who wanted revenge and these fat pigs wasn't hard at all. Maui told his supervisor about it and the wheels started turning. S. the party promoter and Richie were brought in as witnesses. If they wanted to stay out of this mess, they had to cooperate. Which they did and . . . they'd prepared perfectly. Or so they'd all thought. Even Maui hadn't suspected a thing. Which was what had screwed it all up. He'd figured Auguste would follow the group of happy fellows to the villa. They'd have caught him easily enough there. But Auguste had come back from the dead, he was stronger than death, and he'd slipped out of fate's clutches, toyed with fate himself.

He had to be stopped, and Maui had to do it himself. All the same, deep down, a small voice started to whisper that the rich bastards absolutely deserved to die that way, and Maui had never felt so much like a cop. Decided he had to think of himself as a cop because so many other things were suddenly starting to dance a death dance and his soul was about to join in too.

Things that he'd never been taught to notice at the police academy. There were too many, all of a sudden. Like blood. This blood crying out for more blood. This part of himself born of a monster. How could he actually look it in the face and not be affected?

Tired. In a matter of seconds, his adrenaline levels had dropped. He felt so much pain. Drained of all energy, his heart started pounding faster then slower. He felt like he was gasping for air, had to get out of the car. He leaned against the door, squatted down, set his hands on his thighs and started yelling. It was a nightmarish scene. All around him, people stopped gesticulating. Like a thick fog suddenly coming down on a mountain peak, silence fell over this side of the road. Some twenty pairs of eyes turned his way. He could feel it. There was nothing for him to do. He'd have given anything to take back the assignment he'd asked for and opt for a Parisian banlieue rather than this Tahitian hell.

It was Junior who saw him first. Junior who, among the group, had had the most trouble accepting the young cop. Mainly because he was a cop, but also because humanity wasn't his sort of thing. He eventually came to see that Maui was a brother-in-arms. They were born the same year, just a few months apart. They were two sides of the same coin. Maui was heads, well acquainted with feasts, luxury, love, and security. And Junior was tails, having been thrown into this world with no thought as to what might come of it. They were polar opposites, but bound to each other. Apart from their cleft chins, their bowed legs, their muscles, their dark eyes, all these similarities that ate at Junior, he recognized that soul. Wild and yet still generous. A soul that had seen the worst of humanity and yet still dreamed on.

They weren't thirty yet, and they'd gotten past almost every hurdle, but they'd gotten stuck for a long while on the last hurdle: abandonment. But not enough that bitterness turned into poison. Just enough that they were still connected, dreaming up ideas, staying standing, still believing.

How long did they stay there, beside each other, against the car? Sometimes quiet. Sometimes pacing around. Hannah joined them. Had she been shaken the most? Nobody could say. She made her way straight to the roundabout a dozen meters off. She didn't know anything anymore, she didn't remember anything anymore. Didn't think about anything anymore, although that was simply impossible for her.

The two brothers saw the first gleams of dawn through the clouds to the east. They could have left sooner, John and the others would have let them through, Junior was one of the people behind the blockade . . . later on they'd regret it, to their death. But who knew why they needed to hang on to one another so much, hold on to some small bit of normalcy, stave off the end, needed to sit on the harsh asphalt with all its hard gravel. So much sudden information. They needed time to take it all in, to digest it all. Brothers-in-arms and then by blood. Descendants of rebels. Rejecting the new order and . . . sons of a murderer. Maui thought about the sequence of events again. First there had been Georges, then Alain and Yves, a journalist. And then the businessmen who were sleazy, horrible, and clearly pedophiles. It's not possible to mete out justice all alone, Maui thought out loud. Junior remembered that he'd left E., that manic social worker, for dead, then set a fancy shop on fire. When he felt ready to confess this to his "new" brother, he shot back that this was above his pay grade and tried to change the subject.

Then they stood up. Called out to Hannah, who was behind the Dacia now. Junior went to help the two giants who needed to move the heavy stone blocking the road. The siren he turned on made it clear to the other drivers stuck in the jam that the emergency was a real one.

Executions

HE THOUGHT THAT SOMEDAY, if he had the time and the guts, he'd go to the city hall and complain about the potholes that only got deeper with every rainy season. It was a stretch to call Tenaho a neighborhood, but at least fifty families lived there. With at least four grown-ups each, presumably. No small detail when it came time to vote and yet nothing had changed. For twenty-five years now they'd voted for the same mayor who'd listened thoughtfully to their complaints in the weeks leading up to the elections and who'd just as thoughtfully forgotten about them the moment he was reelected. He drove around carefully and stopped just before the first bridge off the road that circled the island's coast. There were five of them. This bridge had never been the sturdiest one, but at this point the wood really was rotting. So he made his way slowly, keeping in mind that his Twingo had been banged up by too many craters already. The dashboard clock read 5:57. Day was starting, but streetlights still lit up the narrow path. The sad look of those houses still in darkness had him remembering all the unemployed folks there who didn't see any point to getting up before daybreak. At the second bridge, he took just as much care to slow down all the way and as he made his way forward he had the sinking feeling that he was headed toward something horrible that couldn't be put into words. Both the fear

of seeing his father again and François's words were why, at least
for a little bit in the night, he hadn't gone back to Tenaho yet. That
was why he'd wanted to sleep in the main room of François's place.
Better to lie down, his eyes watching the fan's blades, the music from
the old dance club on the ground floor not even a bother. Of course
he'd rather have been at the blockade with Hannah and the others,
he'd even gone over to help earlier that night. But it was what it was.
Pauro thought about Pina. For the two weeks since his father had
kicked him out, that was all he'd done. Think about her. Think about
the promise he'd made her at the worst moments of their life, when
everything was falling apart, when he'd said to her: "We have to go,
Pina, we have to get out of here." But she'd always said: "You have
someone, you know where you'd go, I don't." Two weeks torn between
François slowly getting better but still weak and the referendum, the
battle. In the meantime, he'd found out that he'd passed the baccalaureate, with merit, but he was already done with school. It felt
like it had been a good decade since his coming out, as quiet as he'd
been about it, and his political awakening beside his sister Hannah,
whom he really did feel dedicated to. He knew he was taking a huge
risk and he didn't really have what it took to face his father, but he
couldn't bring himself to abandon his little sister. They had to escape.
François had everything ready, he'd asked for his parents' house in
Yvelines just west of Paris, he'd started talking to various universities
nearby about job prospects and whether or not his lover could study
there. He said that they needed to change their life. But Pauro didn't
know if he was ready for that yet. As long as he still hadn't seen his
sister, as long as she wasn't safe, he couldn't leave. Fleeing just wasn't
an option. Sometimes Pauro wondered if François really understood
the facts, the feelings that bound him to the other members of his
family and especially Pina. He even had a suspicion that François
was a bit jealous. And would be so long as he wasn't part of the clan
in Tenaho, far more so than from any snobby high society.

He'd reached the fourth bridge when his thoughts came back to reality. The sleepless night had him so worn out that he didn't realize that he wasn't even twenty meters away from the shack, which was why he kept creeping onward toward the bottom of the valley so he could turn off and then go on down with the engine off. His windows were rolled down, and he stuck out his head to take in the morning dew. The humus, a mixture of māpē leaves and fruit and wet earth and ferns, practically slapped him. He'd nearly forgotten those smells, after so much time in a town full of the smells of barbecue sauce, Chinese food, and exhaust fumes. He was surprised to find himself thinking that they could have kept on living there a long while, even if Auguste had died and even if the mayor had evicted them since it had been declared a "risk area" after a landslide had killed the grandfather living in a house higher up in his sleep. Pauro liked the valley because he'd never known anything else. Because there had to be worse places, because, of course, a man always loves what he knows best.

He parked, a few meters ahead of their shack. He and Junior had repainted the whole thing just before Hannah's return, but there was no painting over how poor they were. Could it have changed one bit after just two weeks away, the young man wondered.

Ten minutes after six, the cocks started crowing. The river's babble could be heard. Swift. Metallic. Almost threatening. It must have rained so much the last few days.

Two minutes before six, Ma was looking at the screen of her vini, hoping to find the picture of an envelope holding a message for her. Ever since she'd gotten a cell phone, she'd finally felt like she was part of the world. John had taught her how to send texts, how to reply to his own. She finally felt connected. It was so silly, come to think of it: feeling like she was being reborn simply because she finally could do the same things everyone else did. Someone had given her the opportunity. Had given her a taste of those pleasures she'd always imagined were grand. This someone who'd also filled her with need, left her feeling abandoned like some old rag. Pathetic. Her eyes were still all swelled up as she silently thanked Candice for the sunglasses she'd given her that morning, just before leaving the house. It had been three days since she'd escaped Tenaho. The Caribbean woman had picked her up, so that she'd have someone with her as she made her escape. In tears, of course. And in blood too. Humiliated by Auguste, who'd gotten it into his head to spy on her every day, standing at the entrance to the perfume shop where she worked. Of course the owner was worried it would scare away customers, and she'd begged Ma to find another job. She'd been prepared for him as she came back to Tenaho. Taken just a few belongings, run out despite the punches, specifically because of the punches. Taken shelter. Called John. Even though that meant abandoning her children for a while. In order to save her skin. Everything played out as expected when she arrived in the afternoon. Auguste, full of contradictions, had hollered at her for losing her job. Ma shot back that she'd gotten herself a few hours at a cleaning agency and she could start the next day. "Oh, is that how bad you need to get out of the house, is that it? Are you in a hurry to go and be a slut?" Ma's responses, Ma's silences, Ma's "yes, okay, you're right," and even Ma's "no, don't say that" made no difference. She was a punching bag, a sack of sand, a doll to be thrown, to be stomped on. Nothing about this was odd, apart maybe from Auguste turning up the volume on his old stereo to cover the noise. Thankfully, none of the children were there. She knew that at this time of day Pina always took Moïra to the bottom of the valley for their afternoon walk, with a stop at the children's basin. The others were grown-ups who'd long since left, who wouldn't be getting back until after sundown.

Auguste saw she wasn't screaming anymore and stopped to make sure she wasn't dead . . . not her body, at least. Out of breath, he

changed his clothes and then went out. It had to be half past three.
Ma didn't want her daughters to see her. She could already feel the
bruises forming, especially under her eyes. From her hair down to
her thighs, along her ribs that were a bit more cracked now and her
swelled-up arms already starting to turn blue and black—everything
felt heavy. Like lead. The silence ate at her. After a few minutes she
dragged herself into the bedroom, grabbed a few clothes, her papers.
She splashed some water on her face, pulled on a hoodie. These
clothes were too big but that was a good thing. She knew from experience that tight clothes just squeezed her wounds and made her hurt
worse. She left, went a few meters further down, and waited for Ah
San the Chinese man's roulotte to come back this way after going
around Tenaho looking for kids who wanted ice cream and candy. It
pulled up and nearly ran her over because her jaw hurt too much for
her to open her mouth. Ah San knew them all, even Auguste. He'd
seen all their children grow up. He told her that she could sit in the
back, between the crates of candy. He didn't ask any questions, he just
took her downtown and dropped her off by the firehouse.

This morning, the bruises weren't gone, but they were hurting less.
Ma was hardy and that might have been one of the few things she
was sure of. She'd been waiting twenty minutes now and other travelers were standing around the stop. The bus was a few minutes late.
Nothing odd there. And the place she was supposed to go to wasn't
opening for another two hours anyway.

She could even let this one coming go by and wait for the next
one, and take the time to stand there, think. Think about how her
plan had gone awry. Yes, she'd found a way to escape, an association
that took care of battered women and children, and a nice lawyer
who'd talked her through how she'd separate from Auguste, but her
dream of fleeing with John, of finding him, had been a mess. After
she'd gotten out of Ah San's vehicle, she'd gone to the studio that
John had been renting for some time. It was "their" place, sort of. She

knew that her lover was a very busy man. And with this referendum she'd mostly only seen him on TV. In French and in Tahitian, he had a knack for talking circles around reporters, when he talked he was so easy, so charming, that was what had made her fall in love with him. He talked so powerfully about the "cause" . . . He was so radiant and, even though it was hard, at the start of their relationship, for Ma to believe that it could work, she'd decided, that day, to give them a chance. Who knew why she still believed, at forty-seven years old, in miracles, second chances, happiness pure and simple? After making her way painfully up the two stories, she knocked at the studio door. At that point, the sun was pounding on the front of the building. She was dripping under her hoodie and soon her head would look like a wave had hit it. She thought the pain was playing tricks on her, but no. After a whole minute, as she heard a shower running, as she recognized her lover's voice saying, "If it's the union official, tell him to wait," she had to face up to the facts.

The mirage. The truth. Naked under a towel. The curvy woman who sometimes appeared on TV. Beautiful. Looking satisfied, happy. A delight that radiated all over, especially from her Colgate-perfect smile. "Can I help you? Are you hoping to speak to John?" "No," she stammered painfully. "Sorry, I got the wrong door," and with a super-human effort headed down the stairs. Grubby Ma, humiliated twice over by two different men in a single day. What a pro she was. And not one bit beautiful. Less than nothing. As night fell, after going all over town, she finally called Candice. Sobbing harder than she ever had before. She had lost seven kilos in just three days. She ignored John's calls and messages. The nurse cleaned up every wound of hers, one by one, except for her wounded heart. She accepted the Caribbean woman's helping hand and repeated, after her, the prayers she hadn't prayed in a long time. In her bed, she reread the psalms that Auguste had made a point of reciting with his eyes shut for the entire family before bedtime. Here, they sounded different. It bothered her how much truer they sounded now because they seemed to talk to her, her fears, her sorrows. She buried herself in the New Testament, the Gospels. Then something happened. That night, the last one she'd spend at the Caribbean woman's, she realized that she had a mission of her own too. Not a big one, sure, not a big one at all, just an obligation, really. She was a mother, wasn't she? Because she was lucky enough to be a mother, she owed it to herself to get the kids out of there.

She tapped another button on her vini but she wasn't really looking. Five minutes after six, yes, the bus ought to be here already. Ma let herself think on how much the path ahead was going to hurt. There was no just wiping away thirty years of her life with a sponge. Nobody ever comes back from the land of the dead just like that. If Auguste had made it back, it was the better to show them the two choices they had. Just two. Live with him, accept suffering and death. Or be done with him and choose life. And there, as she waited for the bus, her life was going to begin with a visit to the shelter for single-parent families. She couldn't do anything else for her older kids, she knew they were strong. She might not have been there for them much, she might have been a whore, always forgetting about what she ought to have been doing, but all that was over now. Had been over once she'd held the book in her hands that night at Candice's. Everything had become clear then. Straightforward. From her sins to her redemption. From her cowardice to today. Everything had been revealed to her. She'd changed, but there was no explaining why. She felt, that was all. She knew, that was better. The child she loved least, wanted least, the child she'd abandoned would be their guide. It was past all her hopes and all her reasons that the one who'd suffered more than anyone, more than all of them put together, was going to become the face of a new order. Pina. It sounded so nice, even across oceans. Ma didn't know the first thing about how the world worked. Barely understood the stakes of the self-determination referendum. She didn't care about it. Life just had to change. Just needed to be better. For them, but also for the Tenaho kids. There was no reason for them not to get out of there. There was no reason to accept the same old fates, the same old hassles. Later on, she would understand that this revelation was what let her to heal, in no time, all her wounds, all her hurts. She smiled. She wasn't all that happy. She was simply, well, freed . . . it was nine minutes after six . . .

At that same moment, the Dacia came to a sudden stop. The light had just changed to red. The sirens were blaring, the driver wasn't so sure the group of schoolkids crossing the street would look both ways. It was like the small group suddenly decided to snub the cops: they slowed down in the crosswalk. They could hear curses and laughter. That was what caught Ma's attention in the bus shelter. She saw Hannah at the back, and then Junior. Their hard, steely faces made it clear that all wasn't well. That at least one of her children was in danger. Pina. She didn't even think about Auguste. Once she was finally able to stand up, she saw them headed toward the racecourse on the way to Tenaho. She didn't care about oncoming cars, tires squealing, the honks and yells. She ran like she never had. She was wide awake. Totally over her breakup with John, her body all better now.

"That's a negative, captain. I lost him just last night. Remember I sounded the alarm, asked for reinforcements . . . As you know, with the blockade, we lost his trail . . . Yes, last night's team and I forwarded his description to the station . . . No, right now I'm headed to the informants . . . Yes, I'll give you the full story at the debrief . . . Yes, I was there, I saw it all. Yes, it's terrible . . ."

Maui was this close to sending his boss packing. He'd been trying all night to get hold of him and now, in the middle of this whole mess, he was finally getting the news. Worse still, he'd just been told the fallout from the Punaauia villa. Three dead. One seriously wounded. Seven completely shell-shocked people who couldn't give

them a single useful detail, and on top of that, a roadblock set up by
total idiots. Their investigation was being slowed to a crawl. And to
top it all off, the cops hadn't bothered to notify the police who had
jurisdiction over this area. In short, a shitstorm. There'd be all sorts of
finger-pointing from the haut-commissariat if not from the minister
of the interior himself.

"You didn't tell him that you found him," Junior said.

The Dacia got caught in a mud-filled pothole. They could feel the
gravel scraping the underside. They'd reach the first bridge soon.

"No, I didn't. That's later."

Junior turned around to check on Hannah, whose silence was
starting to scare him. No reaction. She had on her sunglasses, those
Ray-Bans she loved so much, even though it was getting dark out. The
phrase "fucking bullshit" had become a mantra. Junior had hung on to
that the whole way down. Fucking. Bull. Shit. Maybe because there
was nothing else to say. Maybe because they had to accept that this had
been nothing more than that and, if an explanation had to be found
for all of this, it would be the experts who did that, not him. Junior
thought through the last few months again. Starting with the dates of
the murders that Maui had listed, he tried to make sense of Auguste's
doings, only to decide that those reasons were wrong. Auguste Junior
had been out most of the time, had bouts of drinking, been getting
high, and gotten into all the political stuff—he couldn't have spent
four days at the shack at most. There was no point guessing; apart
from the rules Auguste had laid down after getting all pious, religious, almost nothing had changed. It wasn't really the father who'd
changed. It was them. The mother and the children. They'd needed to
shake off all the filth and same-old-same-old so bad, they'd needed
some right to dream. To change their land, to change their life. No, the
father hadn't changed, he'd been true to himself. Full of fury, driven by
that death he'd escaped. While they'd gotten sucked into a whirlwind
of dreams with no room for normal life. For others. For the littlest

ones. A sense of family wasn't one of Junior's qualities. Far from it, but all of a sudden his mind was filled with the thought of his two little sisters. Moïra, the pretty baby who was so quiet. And Pina with her huge heart, her grown-up fears. Two pairs of huge, dark eyes staring at him. A few stolen smiles here and there. A few fleeting pleasures at the price of a red snow cone that he'd offered them when he had a bit of money left over after beers. Fuck! How had they come to this? Putting up a fight for other people when they couldn't even look after their own? They were supposed to be strong adults, but they'd left the girls alone with the monster. The thought made his blood run cold.

"Are you sure it's him, at least? Do you have any proof?"

Hannah's voice had never sounded so cold. Faraway. Maui said that he'd seen him and that today they could prove it with a few DNA tests.

"Yes, but do you realize? What's going to happen next?"

Junior turned to his sister.

"What, do you think we're going to end up in jail? If it's anyone, it won't be us. It'll be him."

"I know, but you don't understand . . ."

"I don't understand what? What's to understand is that you're ashamed. Are you scared to say that you're the daughter of a criminal? You don't want that to get in the way of what you're doing? Of whatever plans you've got? For fuck's sake. You're scared of what's going to happen now? Don't you give a flying fuck about your family? Your little sisters? Of course not, you've never cared! Just look at your guy, your farāni, you sent him back home because you didn't want that pasty-faced wimp getting in your way! Mea ha'amā! You should be ashamed."

"Shut up!"

Junior was about to turn around again and give her a piece of his mind when Maui started yelling, "Junior, that's enough! Stop! There's no need . . ."

The third bridge. The car stalled, Maui looked so angry with himself. Junior looked away, to the river. It'd been ages since he'd dived in. Eons since he'd lost sight of his friends. All of them had gotten hitched and fat with a dozen kids running around now. And he was still alone. There was no hand to stroke him, no mouth to kiss him, to whisper sweet nothings or even scold him for his stupid ideas, his mistakes, his laziness. Nothing. On the other bank, he saw Firi's house. With a new coat of paint, this time so orange it hurt. He'd often made fun of his head. Called him "one of those sheeple" because of his hair, because he'd joined the independence party after everyone else did. More than the river between their two houses, politics had pulled them apart. But that "sheep" wasn't a stupid guy. Nor was he, for that matter . . .

The old barrier that only had one good hinge left fell away with a push. Pauro was in a daze. Not two minutes ago he'd shut the door of his Twingo carefully, done his best to walk quietly when he heard his sister yelling. A shriek that made his blood curdle. Then he understood. And it all happened so fast. From the little room to the bedroom, he wasn't sure how, or why, but he knew what he was going to see. Pina's cry was nothing like how she hollered when Auguste was giving her one of his traditional "corrections." The radio kept on blabbing about the latest on the roadblock. But he could make out the moans, the groaning. The young man's heart was in his mouth.

"Lady, why are you running? Hop on!"

Ma was at the first bridge. She'd never run so far, or so fast. She was out of breath, her mouth was dry, her ribs felt like they could snap, but Ma just stared, befuddled by young Roméo. How old was he? Twelve, thirteen at the most? He was short and seemed to be struggling to stay balanced on the souped-up motorcycle.

"You know how to drive?"

"Yes, ma'am. I saw you running past the store. Are you Pina's mother?"

"Yes, yes . . . she's my girl."

"Pina and I sit next to each other in class. I live over by Firi's. Please, ma'am, get on so I can take you."

Yes, that was her girl. For the first time in her life, she'd said it out loud, that she had no doubt about. The trip was a helter-skelter one. The jolts and bumps with every gear shift nearly threw her off but she held tight. Better that, better the engine backfiring and almost making her deaf than running, maybe falling, maybe not making it at all, or maybe just a moment too late.

"Pa, what are you doing?"

Suddenly he saw that his voice was showing his feelings. He was shaking. Scared.

"Pa . . . ? What the hell?"

As the sobs rose up, hate and dread had him shivering. For half a second he wished he hadn't seen a thing. But only for half a second. What his eyes took in was unthinkable. A father bent over like a monster over a child's body.

"Pinaaaaaaaa . . . Noooo!!!!"

In a second, he saw everything. In two, he was on his feet, pulling up the vile pants around his ankles. Then they were at each other's throats. Pauro might not have been as big, being so slim, but he still barreled his whole body into this hand-to-hand struggle. For every blow he took, he landed two. He used his legs, sometimes kicked into the air. Auguste was a born killer. Even when he was hurt, he had enough fury to kill again. Pauro was bleeding and he only had to be distracted for a second to be pinned on his back. The father started choking him. Right then, the young man turned his head and saw his sister.

Her eyes were empty. There wasn't a single tear dripping from them. She looked like a ghost. Her body was stripped bare. Her skin, from her belly down to her knees, was so pale. A suffering body, a sacrificial body. Pauro's eyes were begging her: "Get up, hit him, try to save us . . ." and then just "Pina, get up . . ." He was choking now. Auguste had eased his hold the better to slap him. A punch to his left eye. He raised his fist again. And that was when Junior kicked at the upraised arm. Pauro finally wriggled loose. Then it became a free-for-all. A frenzy. Junior was no longer the faraway big brother who the kids were scared and in awe of. Junior was a hero like in the movies. Maui tried to get in between, but not for long. "Get away, Maui, lmeave us alone or you'll get me killed . . ." Moïra was bellowing in Hannah's arms, shaking, livid, upset. "Shhh, baby, quiet now . . ." The young woman was hollering too, "That's enough, Junior. Stop it now. I said stop!" But nobody paid her any mind. Her heart was pounding as she realized that it was all over now. Nothing and nobody would stop her big brother now. Finally there was someone stronger than Auguste. More dogged. All that could be heard was punch after punch. They could almost be felt, even outside, they were so raw, so brutal. Harsh. Violent. Auguste's body, thrown like a rag doll, broke holes in the plywood. Auguste lay with his back on the bed, his head slumped back. Maui had managed to drag Pauro out of the bedroom to slap him awake. The younger boy was unconscious. When he came back to, he looked around for his sister. In the middle of the uproar, nobody'd seen her slip out. At that moment they heard Ma's sobbing. So shrill it hurt. Almost cavernous. An "Oh! 'Auuuēēē . . ." reached up almost from her guts. She was in the kitchen on the beaten-earth floor. Her face was so tense it hurt. With Roméo who was now crying beside her, she'd dragged over a chair and was getting her hands around the body of the child, trying to lift her up. Roméo, with his clumsy fingers, was trying to untie the thick knot of the rope.

A small body sways. Spins, rather, this way and that.
Calmly, a calm far too calm. A calm that means
that was the last gasp, too late now.
A small body dangling from a rope tied
good and tight to an old ceiling. It ought
to have collapsed but hasn't, that shirker.
That long frizzy hair's loose and free for once.
The only keening is a river not far off.
A body that's a tender sacrifice on the altar of squalor.
The neck's going purple, the face deathly pale.
There's that small smile on those dead lips.
She knows now that life rises out of ruin,
finds redemption further on, later on.
A little girl for whom too many things fell apart.
Her body's stopped turning now.
She'll never be ten, she's decided. She was strong.
She was empty.

Settling Accounts

THE SUN WAS HIGH in the sky now. Eight in the morning, a perfect blue. The head warden had given her a heads-up the night before, "Your pretrial custody is over, Madame Laurette." Laurette, what a ridiculous name. How long had it been since anyone had called her that? Thirty years? Before leaving, she'd joked a bit with Marae, the warden. Everybody in there was nice to her. She was a hefty 158 kilograms and nobody was going to tangle with someone her size.

"What do you mean, over?"

"Don't ask me. Didn't you talk to your probation officer?" Ma wasn't about to say no, wasn't about to risk everything falling apart somehow. "Oh yes, yes, actually I did." It was only the next morning, at half past seven, that her officer finally laid out the facts. Someone had confessed to murdering Auguste. Some Monsieur Teanuanua Terii a Taumihau. Of course she hadn't understood the words right there and then. Of course she'd only felt tears welling up. Teanuanua. Her brother-in-law . . . But why?

The prison door squeaked. That shadow of a woman who barely had any hold on anything real made her way out of Nuutania jail. She had no idea whether anyone was waiting for her, if any of her children had even been told . . . She started walking faster, almost scared that she'd be pulled back in. Ten meters off, she saw Hannah by an SUV.

"Mommy."

Two syllables. The prettiest word ever heard on this earth.

Right then all she wanted was to be a mother. A mother who gave in and broke down in her daughter's arms.

She barely got out the words. "I'm so sorry, sweetie. For what happened." Everything had to be said now. And then she sat down on a big stone on the roadside. Families were starting to show up for visiting hours.

"Give me a cigarette please, sweetie."

"Ma, have you taken up smoking again?"

"Just to kill time . . ." She took a long drag and spat out a thin line of blue smoke. After a few seconds, her eyes stuck on the pebbles by her feet, she came out with it: "The knife was me. I was the one who cut his throat. Me, not your brothers. When the boys got your little sister down, when Maui started doing CPR, I grabbed the knife. That was why I didn't go through the main room when I came in. I went in through the patio. I wanted to grab the knife in any case. And that was when I saw Pina."

"If it had been me . . . I wouldn't have done any different."

Ma nodded. "So what's this about Teanuanua?"

"Did you know he had cancer?"

"Yes, Poe told me before everything happened."

"That was his gift to Pina, he said. His lawyer got him a hospital stay instead of prison because it's terminal. He didn't want it, but that's where Teanuanua is. He has an ankle bracelet. Ma, he's going to die. It could be a matter of days. He's on morphine. Sometimes he comes out of his coma but honestly everyone would rather that he's asleep."

"What about the cops? The judge? Do they really believe what you guys said?"

"Maui says that what with the riots, the police misconduct, it's almost a civil war, so the courts have too much on their hands. And it works out for Auguste's old bosses. The nightclub was shut down. That was a crackdown on drug trafficking and all the small fry. There won't be any more candy with drugs in it anytime soon . . . And Auguste committed rape . . . That's a whole mess they don't have time to go into right now. Even though they threw us into solitary right away. Honestly, that was just them playing it safe. Maui and I were just eyewitnesses . . . Maui got the short end of the stick, I think. I'm pretty sure he's going to have to quit."

"Aïe. I do like that half brother of yours . . ."

Ma had uttered those words almost sarcastically, clearly thinking about that final image of Auguste.

"Yes, everyone seems to be fond of him."

"What about the other stuff?"

"It's slow progress. The UN is sending a team of election observers."

"I saw you on TV. You were good, you should keep doing this, Hannah. We have to get back to our lives. Clean slate. You can do politics. You're a good talker and you look good on TV. You do me proud."

"We've agreed to a truce, in any case. While we're waiting for the observers to come, some of us have left the construction site. And gone back home . . ."

Her heart twinged at the mental image of John smiling. Hannah knew she had to tell Ma.

"Ma . . ."

"Yes?"

"This nice car here? It's John's. He says it's for you, Ma."

"Huh?"

"John. He feels bad. He really wants to make it up to you. You think you'll give him a second chance?"

Sometimes life really can be that simple, if you just try. If you're given the chance. But if their life, as members of this clan in Tenaho, was anything, the one thing it wasn't was simple.

"We'll see, sweetie. There's a lot to deal with."

He'd spent a good while preparing his little speech that he'd give with his resignation. When Maui walked into the police headquarters, he wasn't one bit surprised. His boss was having a terrible day. Bags under his eyes. Dripping sweat because of "this fucking AC that still hasn't been fixed," a cigarette dangling from his mouth even though there were a good thirty notices pinned up about the smoking ban for the Papeete city police. Maui did like him, deep down, this moron who never got off his butt but still had the brains when he absolutely needed them. He even had some admiration for this guy who'd spent his best years in the Paris police's research and investigation department, focused on organized crime, Mesrine ... On November 2, 1979, he'd turned twenty at the Porte de Clignancourt. He'd been there when they'd gunned him down, and at every birthday since he'd never missed the opportunity to raise a glass to the memory of the Big One, keeping that memory of a straight-up execution fresh in his mind.

Police Chief Guenguant, "Breton and proud of it," had come with a bad reputation. A stint at the directorate of territorial security, and plenty of rumors that he'd taken all sorts of bribes, like a vintage Rolex, and been friendly with a few "terrorists" or double agents. He'd eventually gotten out of all that and been hired at the Paris police's research and intervention brigade. After four years in retirement, he'd ended up there, racking up a nice "isolation allowance."

"It's clear, Monsieur Thomas, that in this whole mess, you haven't been ... impartial."

"No, chief, and actually that's why I'm handing in my resignation."

The leather executive chair with a high headrest swiveled around. Like a little boy, the chief seemed to be rocking back and forth on the seat. His head looked up to the ceiling.

"Bullshit, it's all just nonsense."

"Sorry?"

"You heard me. Bullshit, nonsense. Or maybe the other way around."

Maui thought back to the investigating judge. He'd been summoned two days earlier and he'd said that although the situation was still ongoing and they still didn't have much proof, his instincts hadn't been wrong: the young inspector was at best "guilty of negligence" and at worst "complicit." He'd added that if "properly legal procedures" weren't followed, he'd be insisting firmly on an internal investigation. Which was why Maui had decided to resign. If he had to suffer consequences, no matter how small, he didn't want a stain on his record. He'd rather be sentenced as a civilian.

"Do you really think we'd just let ourselves lose an inspector? Workforce reductions, civil unrest—do those words mean anything to you?"

Maui stammered, but the chief cut him off.

"I'm talking here. As I said, bullshit and nonsense. I've made proper use of this thing that destroys documents for the first time. And that's plenty. It's more reassuring that way. Out of sight, out of mind."

Guenguant exhaled one last bit of smoke from his cigarette before stubbing out the butt in an overflowing ashtray. It reeked.

Maui decided to broach the prospect of an internal investigation.

The old chief scowled. He actually seemed to snicker.

"I . . ." He dragged out the vowel. "I will be the one deciding what does or does not warrant an internal investigation. For now, I'm asking you to leave my office. I think you'll need a few days, maybe a week at most. But I expect to see you back on the beat and back in your damn office before long."

The young man, stunned, was silent for a few seconds. The old chief added:

"Sometimes we cops decide to bend a few rules here and there. There are cases where it's completely illegal, especially when it's a matter of abusing a position . . . When it's to pad your own pockets, you've got a lot to risk there . . . but there are times, maybe once or twice in a very long career, when a cop, a good one, understands that justice comes in many sizes and shapes. When the mother of a family with young children, when she's pushed to the limit, just a hypothetical example, I'm speaking purely hypothetically, when she has no choice but to snuff out the sickness that's made their lives hell. So when you can clean up a mess like that you do. And I did. No regrets." Guenguant paused and then, with a smile, went on: "Kiddo, your very detailed and attentive little report matches up on every single point to the eyewitness account of that old fellow, the one who confessed on behalf of this mother. Do you really think I bought that? And besides, if the body was found in the middle of a city while riots were happening, with all the blood drained out, and starting to swell up, do you seriously think anyone would believe that it really was a fast, clean job, and that a guy with terminal cancer pulled it off? Of course not. Nobody would buy that. Especially not an investigating judge. So there you have it. I think you've got the makings, Monsieur Thomas. The makings of a real cop. You're a fighter but you get that justice comes in all shapes and sizes. Locking up a mother with kids who've had a bad start would only make them delinquents of the worst sort. Sometimes you have to make a very careful choice, for the future. Which you did. And I appreciate it. Now, scram!"

Epilogue

"YOU HAVE TO GO back to the events of 2016, the year before the presidential elections. France was worn out and had to deal with the threat of the National Front. There wasn't a single survey or columnist that didn't see the far right winning. The situation in the banlieues had become a flash point for all the citizens the way it did before every single election, even the farmers deep in Vaucluse who'd never seen hide or hair of those 'casseurs.' The unemployment numbers weren't going down, of course. The deficit was nearing 5 percent . . . and that became the only thing anyone talked about. Impending defaults. Local governments would be hit first, especially the departments that were all red tape and no action . . . some Tahitian politicians, most of them staunch defenders of autonomy and a permanent connection to France, found themselves tangled up in all sort of political imbroglios. Others were viewed with suspicion and the image of local politics, which was already in bad shape at this point, only worsened. New faces came to the fore. Men and women without any charisma, technocrats, who were sticklers for French regulations. The bomb had been a godsend. But the bomb didn't exist anymore. So France no longer owed Polynesia anything, if it ever had . . . In light of this, the French authorities were subordinated to a government that half-heartedly insisted that 'financial and human resources' follow suit (in terms of education, health, towns, safety . . . and soon immigration too).

"A tug-of-war between France and a growing group of 'citizens' made up of union workers, separatists, and people who didn't fit under any category but all of whom were worried about what was looking more and more like a jettisoning, was sinking the administration, the economy, and even the morale of society itself. Three years earlier, in May 2013, Polynesia had been relisted on the UN list of territories to be decolonized. The place had been a thorn in France's side, so this relisting amounted to a blessing in disguise. But rather than follow the resolution asking 'the French government to escalate its conversation with French Polynesia in order to facilitate and accelerate the creation of an equitable and efficient process of self-determination,' no process was undertaken, no agreement, and ditto for New Caledonia. Nothing equitable about that . . .

"One morning in January 2016, a decree from the president of the Republic came to the haut-commissariat (equivalent to a prefecture). A self-determination referendum would take place six months later. Despite the C-24 bureau's protests, and those of three permanent members of the Security Council, the Pacific Small Island Developing States, and also those of a large part of the local population, the stakes seemed too 'remote' and too 'unreal' to register in the media, let alone the French and European public opinion already consumed by their own challenges. And yet . . .

"At the advice of a little-known 'specialist in overseas matters' certain that Polynesia wouldn't wind up in the pockets of independent countries, the president of the Republic decided to go for broke. According to his plan, the results of the surprise referendum would allow the state to beef up its presence in Polynesia. By refusing emancipation, the voters would end up clearing the way for him to 'establish' a sort of 'region' for the long term.

"Then the unthinkable happened. For all the international conventions and resolutions, the electorate wasn't taken into full consideration, and the majority of the population, 50.3 percent, voted yes. Yes to self-determination. Yes to freedom. It was clear that the majority had chosen independence and full sovereignty. Never, up to this point, had the prospects of free association with an independent state and/or integration with that same state been raised. Long years of legal wrangling lay ahead of this archipelago at the end of the world.

"In the wake of those results, the gears starting turning. The no side would have had the French government's blessing to begin 'negotiations' with China. The five million square meters of ocean contained within the limits of Polynesia brimmed with rare-earth minerals and other gems that could have made China and other developing countries pioneers in nanotechnology. The Asian countries could have brought in money and infrastructure, while France would deal with international conventions as well as the environmental associations that would have inevitably protested, all of which would have helped extricate the Hexagon from dire financial straits . . ."

Her reading was interrupted by a phone call. It was Pauro. He was running late but he'd be able to make it to the meeting with the lawyer on the rue La Boétie. She thought back to the young reporter who'd interviewed her, almost gawking, staring at her scarf . . . He had to have known. Courtesy had to be the only reason he hadn't asked about it.

". . . In the first year alone, France would have gotten at least between two and five billion euros. Better yet, several officials at the time were certain that France's debts could be wiped out completely. In such circumstances, according to a few of them, it amounted to an offer that no president, no government could refuse. The same went for the Republic itself, even if such a line seemed ridiculous. And yet none of them had taken into account the possibility of a sufficiently sizable 'group of citizens' that would eventually become the leading political party. Even now, we still don't know the source of the leak, we still don't know how the top-secret agreements between France and the Chinese mining company's representatives ended up in the hands of the yes party's members. It's not unlikely that the United States played a role there. A long-standing rumor has it that they were informed by a former secret agent, a police chief just about to retire. In any case, it was the 'Polynesian episode' or the 'Tahitian nightmare' that led to the downfall of the former president of the Republic. And last but not least, it has to be remembered that Polynesia was literally paralyzed by a full year of upheaval. All the major construction sites were blockaded, the city was destroyed after the state interceded to 'nullify' the results of the referendum, citing numerous irregularities.

"The moratorium that the UN Security Council voted on a few months after these sad events still has not been lifted. Polynesia managed to pull off the incredible feat of being neither independent nor French. The legal and political battle has been playing out for twenty years now. An international omertà seems to hang over these islands at the end of the world. But not for much longer, hopes the Free and Victorious association, which organized the conference that was held two days ago in the packed auditorium of the UNESCO headquarters. Among the speakers was this small powerhouse of a woman who . . ."

She decided to stop reading and folded up the newspaper; she never could stand reading about herself. She had been there to talk about a country stuck in a horrific no-man's-land. She was there to talk about her books, to describe or sum up her meetings. To talk about the foundation that she'd created with her little sister and which helped children who were suffering. Sometimes she went so far as to talk about her trajectory ... but never about what she'd endured. The most she'd ever shared was when she'd let slip one day: "I've hit rock bottom, like so many others, but someone held a hand out to me. So I'd like to do the same for anyone who might need some help ..."

She wouldn't call the paper. She had no interest in fighting the same fight all over again and yelling that she didn't want people talking about "that" ...

Coming out of her daze, she realized the buzzer was ringing and she got up slowly. In the entryway, she noticed an old photo of the Île de la Cité. She thought, momentarily, of how nice it would be to go, when she had a bit of time, to light a candle at Notre-Dame. A candle for all those in her life who had died, every one of them. Rosa, Teanuanua, Aunt Poe, Michel, and even Auguste. Yes, even him.

On the pont Mirabeau. The instructions had been crystal clear. At the exact center of the bridge, face the Eiffel Tower and the Île aux Cygnes. As the canal boat *Bel Ami* reaches the end of its course and heads back to the pont Alexandre III, turn over the urn in its wake. Not before, not too long after. It was eleven at night. Bitterly cold. She couldn't understand Michel's choice of this bridge, which he'd confirmed was perfectly ugly. "You really do have to wonder what old Apollinaire saw in this place." Those were his words. On every one of their walks. "Look! Isn't that just a completely godforsaken place? There's only Arabs crossing it ... Not even the least hint of Guillaume Musso!" She'd never really understood why he was so determined to be so, well, petty. And as for the *Bel Ami*, could Maupassant have possibly imagined any of this after his own death? While he was alive, Michel had never had the man's name on his Famous French Writers List that waxed and waned with his mood. The night before, she'd noticed a nice canal boat called *l'Insolite*.

"The Freak," that would have suited him better than a boat with a name that meant "good friend." But no, of course he had to impose yet another one of his particular quirks on them, when he'd always hated tours, throngs of tourists, and, above all, these little cruises that middle-class French folks bought themselves when, just once in their lives, they had the money for it. Michel had left his not-so-few belongings to them. A rather fancy apartment that he'd never lived in, by the Porte Dauphine. Shares in the publishing house that he'd built and kept going. Money, plenty of it, but for the foundation, and last of all, this urn an undertaker had poured his ashes into. And the manuscript. Unfinished. Never begun, in fact. He'd left it with the lawyer: a few typescript pages that talked about Hannah, his eternal love. For years he'd begged her to write their story, as he hadn't felt like he had any right to do so himself. Those few pages had, of course, reopened one by one the wounds that she'd spent twenty years covering with the balm of political and humanitarian action.

A year earlier, he'd finally told her that he had cancer. No matter how much she'd pleaded, he'd insisted: "No. We can always talk on Skype. Uganda is a long way away . . ." Of course she wasn't in Africa. Maybe in New York or London or Fiji or on the Marshall Islands . . . She didn't remember. And after several months through various screens, he seemed to be growing thinner by the minute. Just skin and bones, practically bald . . . it was all happening so fast. "Are you absolutely sure you don't want me to come?" was answered by a change of topic.

"Oh, Pina, you haven't gained weight, have you?"

"I'm pregnant, Michel . . ."

"Well, that's great news! Although aren't you a bit old for—" A dry coughing fit cut him off sharply.

He managed to coax a laugh out of her despite the lump in her throat and the welter of memories, images, words, feelings that rose up in turn. So much had happened, and then it'd all been put on ice.

Even her future, especially her future. After six months she was on the road to recovery, but along with the pain of what she remembered she still had the purplish, thick mark around her neck. The rope hadn't choked her, it had literally cut her throat. Hence the scarf. Always a scarf, or a turtleneck sweater, or a ribbon, or one of so many other pieces of clothing or accessories that would do the job.

A year after Auguste's death, she was still in residential care. She saw Ma turn into a mama bear. Watched Hannah's rise to power as she also found a fiancé. Maui had become a lieutenant. Junior was working in Poe and Teanuanua's fields. Among them all, he seemed to have been the most shaken. His silences were terrifying. And the country's economic situation was worsening. It was decided that she would go and live with Pauro and François for a little bit. She'd ended up staying there fifteen years. Between Yvelines and Michel's place in the fifteenth arrondissement. An unlikely friendship where he'd helped her discover a love of reading, so many unusual authors, protest movements, battles that he didn't necessarily have a personal stake in. But at the heart of everything he read was an enormous, genuine hunger for justice. Wishful thinking, of course, but Michel had made her see how the dream of a revolution was what the elite abhorred above all and yet she could claim it. Under the pont Mirabeau, people were singing schmaltzy old songs. "La Vie en Rose" with an accordion . . . Roméo set another coat on her shoulders. All these years, he'd protected her. As he'd promised he would, even across thousands of kilometers. In the wake of the canal boat, she turned over the urn. And then she understood. *Bel ami*, indeed.

Translator's Acknowledgments

Pina has been a stunning addition to the still-nascent canon of Mā'ohi literature, and translating it has meant immersing myself not only in this canon, but also in all the nuances of Tahiti itself, and forging a voice in English that feels true to Titaua Peu's rough-hewn, oral, humane prose.

It is thanks to the recommendation of my extraordinarily well-read colleague David Ferrière and the unstinting enthusiasm of Lucile Bambridge of Au vent des îles, Violaine Faucon of Trames, and above all Alison Gore of Restless Books—a dream editor for this book—that *Pina* has a new life in English.

I am indebted also to Anaïs Maurer for having all the answers and then some; to Ted Palenski for reengineering the pronunciation guide for American readers; to Jordan Koluch for an eagle eye and making this book a spotless read in English; and to Julia Frengs, Bruno Saura, and Kareva Mateata-Allain for their support in a thousand intangible ways. And I will always be grateful to the French Voices Award jury who saw promise in this book and awarded it the 2019 Grand Prize.

And of course this translation would not even exist without Titaua Peu herself, a force of nature I admire so deeply. May this new *Pina* be a balm and a ray of hope for, in her words, all the Pinas of the world.

TITAUA PEU is a Tahitian author known for her politically charged, realistic portrayal of the effects of colonialism on contemporary Polynesia. Peu's unsparing first novel, *Mutismes*, was published in 2003, sparking immediate scandal and making her the youngest-ever published Tahitian author at age twenty-eight. *Pina* was awarded the 2017 Eugène Dabit Prize, a first for Polynesian literature. She currently lives in Tahiti where she serves as the general manager of the municipality of Paea.

JEFFREY ZUCKERMAN is a translator of French, including books by the artists Jean-Michel Basquiat and the Dardenne brothers, the queer writers Jean Genet and Hervé Guibert, and the Mauritian novelists Ananda Devi, Shenaz Patel, and Carl de Souza. A graduate of Yale University, he has been a finalist for the TA First Translation Prize and the French-American Foundation Translation Prize, and he was awarded the French Voices Grand Prize for his translation of *Pina*. In 2020 he was named a Chevalier in the Ordre des Arts et des Lettres by the French government. He currently lives in New York City.

RAJIV MOHABIR is the author of *Cutlish* (Four Way Books 2021), *The Cowherd's Son* (2017, winner of the 2015 Kundiman Prize), and *The Taxidermist's Cut* (2016, winner of the Four Way Books Intro to Poetry Prize and finalist for the Lambda Literary Award for Gay Poetry in 2017), and translator of *I Even Regret Night: Holi Songs of Demerara* (1916) (2019), which received a PEN/Heim Translation

Fund Grant Award and the Harold Morton Landon Translation Award from the Academy of American Poets. Currently he is an assistant professor of poetry in the MFA program at Emerson College. His debut memoir, *Antiman: A Hybrid Memoir*, won the Restless Books Prize for New Immigrant Writing and was a finalist for the 2022 PEN Open Book Award.

RESTLESS BOOKS is an independent, nonprofit publisher devoted to championing essential voices from around the world whose stories speak to us across linguistic and cultural borders. We seek extraordinary international literature for adults and young readers that feeds our restlessness: our hunger for new perspectives, passion for other cultures and languages, and eagerness to explore beyond the confines of the familiar.

Through cultural programming, we aim to celebrate immigrant writing and bring literature to underserved communities. We believe that immigrant stories are a vital component of our cultural consciousness; they help to ensure awareness of our communities, build empathy for our neighbors, and strengthen our democracy.

www.restlessbooks.org